SHARON VIRTS

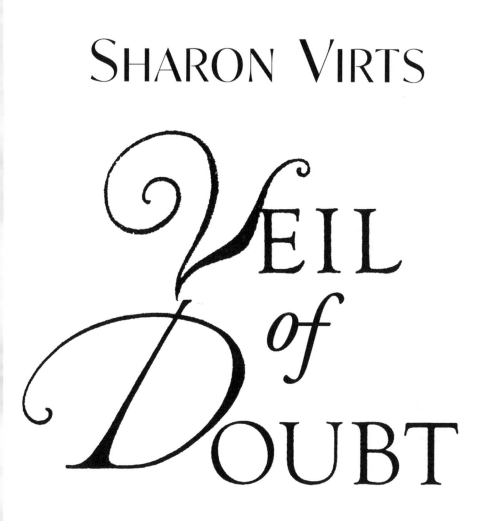

VEIL of DOUBT

GIRL FRIDAY BOOKS

GFB GIRL FRIDAY BOOKS

Published by Girl Friday Books™, Seattle
www.girlfridaybooks.com

Produced by Girl Friday Productions

Cover design: David Fassett
Production editorial: Bethany Fred
Project management: Sara Spees Addicott

Image credits: Shutterstock/NeoStocks

ISBN (hardcover): 978-1-959411-44-4
ISBN (paperback): 978-1-959411-25-3
ISBN (audiobook): 978-1-959411-43-7
ISBN (ebook): 978-1-959411-33-8

Library of Congress Control Number 2023904981

For my husband, Scott

THE YEAR 1872

Leesburg, Virginia

A mighty wrong had fallen upon the household and swept away the last of its treasures as ruthlessly as chaff before a whirlwind.
—*Loudoun Mirror*, March 1872

PROLOGUE

"Please step down from the window," he urged as he entered the sterile room, its walls pale and eerily bare. A woman in a gossamer nightgown stood on the sill, steadying her balance with the tips of her fingers, the long toes of her bare feet jutting over the edge as she contemplated the ground below.

"I think I shall go headfirst," she said as she leaned farther out the opening. "To make certain, you know."

"Alice, please," he said, frantic. "Step down so we can talk about whatever is bothering you."

"Bothering me?" she snapped, nearly losing her balance as she turned toward him, a strand of umber hair loosening and falling into her face. "You promised, Powell. Promised to protect me. Instead, you had me locked away in this . . . this asylum!"

"Father thought it was best," Powell said as he made his way toward her as if approaching a frightened kitten.

"Father hates me!" Alice cried. Her eyes glistened as water pooled in their corners. "He can't even look at me." Her voice broke. "I'm ruined."

"You're not ruined. And Father doesn't hate you."

"I've shamed him, Powell," she whispered, the tears now rolling over her cheeks. "You know he disowns anyone who brings the family shame."

Powell drew a sharp breath, the truth of her words striking like a kick to the gut. "What happened wasn't your fault," he said, forcing a reassuring smile. "You have no reason to be ashamed."

"What I have is no reason to live."

"You have me. Surely that is reason enough." He offered another encouraging smile and extended his arm toward her. "Now, please. Give me your hand and let's step down from there."

"All right," she said as Powell continued his measured approach toward her. "I'll step down." The corners of her mouth curled into a sad grimace before she turned from him, bent her knees, and jumped.

"No!" Powell lunged toward her, both arms outstretched, grabbing at the gown as she fell, his hands fleetingly catching a bit of hemline in the sweltering afternoon air. He anticipated the thud of her body hitting the ground more than fifty feet below. Hearing only the beat of his own heart, he looked down. There was nothing but scorched brown grass beneath. He leaned his head out the window, looking first left, then right. *But I saw her fall.* Hope welled in his chest, and he shouted her name: "Alice!"

"Poe," he heard her call behind him. "I'm here."

He turned and scanned the room's barren walls.

"Alice?"

"It's all right, Poe. Look at me," said the voice from somewhere above him.

He lifted his head, bringing his gaze to the wrought-iron gas lamp and the lifeless body suspended from it. It was Alice, her face contorted, eyes bulging from their sockets, her neck awkwardly bent.

"No!" he cried, blocking his sight of the horror that swayed above him with his hands.

"Powell." Another voice and a tug at his arm. *If I don't look, it can't be real.*

"Why, Lord? Why?" he sobbed, squeezing his eyes tight as the tears welled. *I should have fought for her . . . challenged Father's demand!*

"Wake up, darling." The soothing voice of his wife interrupted the images in his head as the dreadful room faded into the darkness. "It's all right," she said as he felt the stroke of her hand on his forehead. "It's just a dream."

SPRING 1872

There came an appeal from almost every Christian heart, seconded by a mighty voice from an unseen world, pleading on behalf of a score of new made graves.

—*Loudoun Mirror,* March 1872

CHAPTER 1

SUNDAY, MARCH 24, 1872

Sky-splitting thunder cracked like canisters firing from twelve-pound cannons as drenching rain cascaded in blinding sheets onto two physicians picking their way through muddied Virginia clay to the front stoop of a modest home on Loudoun Street. When they stepped onto the porch, a young woman with tawny skin and warm, tired-looking eyes, glassy and red, opened the door.

"She's upstairs," said the maid, Delphi Lozenburg, as she threw open the door and invited them inside.

The house was stale with sickness—the sour smell of vomit and lye intermingled with the sweetness of damp ash from a dwindling fire. Wind gusts howled overhead and rumbled down the chimney, sparking embers to glow and crackle. Delphi took their coats and hats and brought them up the narrow stairs that led to the child's room.

Not twelve hours ago, when Dr. Randolph "Randy" Moore had walked into the small room at the top of the stairs, little Maud Lloyd had been sitting up against the headboard, playing with a new bisque doll that, she had explained, was her birthday present. Her blue eyes had been alert, and she'd told him that both her tummy and her dolly were feeling much better. Though she was pale and weakened from nearly three days of purging, he'd been confident that she would recover. The porcelain doll now lay near the foot of the bed, its fair hair disheveled and its wide eyes cast vacantly at the ceiling. Like the doll, Maud's flaxen hair was tangled, and her eyes were half open, staring upward. He was having trouble believing this to be the same child. Her skin was pallid, the lids of her eyes dark and sunk deep in their sockets. She gasped for air between parted, pasty lips, just like her older sister, Annie, who had died the month before. Dread washed over him.

Next to the bed in a rocking chair sat the mother, Emily Lloyd, her arms crossed over her chest, rocking back and forth, looking like a small child herself. Her eyes, set wide under a high forehead etched with worry lines, were pale, a bleached green like the color of lichen in moonlight. She was a slight woman with refined features and honey-brown hair parted in the center and pulled back into a tight bun. She, too, stared vacantly, her ghostly gaze fixed on nothing.

"Mrs. Lloyd," Moore said gently. Emily startled to attention with a rush of words at the sight of him.

"Oh, praise be to God! Praise the Lord you are here!" she said, jumping from the chair to her feet. "You must do something. Please don't let her die! You can't let her die." Tears poured from her eyes, and her whole body seemed to be trembling with desperation and fear.

Moore took Emily's shaking hands in his and watched as his colleague Dr. William Cross took a seat on the child's bed. When Delphi had summoned Moore during the supper hour, his father-in-law, Mayor Robert Bentley, had insisted Moore bring Dr. Cross along for a second opinion. Moore had pushed back, but the mayor was resolute.

"You must tell me what has happened since my visit this morning," Moore said.

"I don't know precisely," Emily said. "She was feeling better when you left. I went downstairs and prepared the powders with lime water and milk like you said. She took that just fine. Sometime after that, she became ill again. She was crying so with pain. I put a hot compress on her belly, but she kept getting sicker and sicker. I gave her more of the medicine, but she couldn't keep it down. Then she began to shake and convulse. I tried to hold her, and then suddenly it all just stopped. She wasn't moving, the lifeblood left her little body . . . just like Annie. Please, don't let her die like Annie!"

"Do you know what time she became ill again?" he asked.

"I don't," she said. "I don't remember when exactly. Maybe Delphi knows. I can't remember one hour from the next these past few days." She moved her eyes to her daughter lying listlessly in the bed.

"Are you, too, feeling ill?" Moore asked, and placed the back of his hand on her forehead and cheek, checking for fever.

"I can't bury another child, Dr. Moore. I just can't."

"Worry won't help either you or the child," Moore said, the backs of his fingers lingering on her cheek before he moved his hand to her shoulder. Her collarbone protruded under the fabric, and he wondered how long it had been since she'd eaten a proper meal. Forcing a reassuring smile, he walked Emily back to the chair. "Let me take a look at her and see what we can do."

Dr. William Cross was in the midst of his exam, forcing Maud's lids open with his thumbs, studying her lifeless eyes. As Moore neared, he recognized the look of approaching death. His breath caught in his throat, and his heart felt as if it were being ripped from his chest.

Moore opened his bag and riffled through his instruments, fumbling his stethoscope and sending it flying to the floor. Drawing a long breath to calm his nerves, he retrieved it and settled on the bed next to the little girl. With an aural tube in each ear, he placed the chest piece on the child's breast and listened. Her heartbeat was rapid and erratic, her breathing shallow and labored.

Dr. Cross, who sat at the girl's opposite side, looked up. "I have a few questions for the maid," he said and stood from the bedside.

Moore nodded and closed his eyes, listening to the fitful beating of the child's heart. *Please, Lord, not little Maud.* For the life of him, Moore could not fathom what could have gone so wrong. *Could she have accidentally eaten something she shouldn't have?* He opened his eyes and moved the chest piece to her abdomen and tried to listen over the roar in his mind. *No, my initial diagnosis is the only explanation.* As he finished his exam, Moore returned his instruments to the case and glanced at Emily in the rocking chair. She sat preternaturally still, the only movement the wringing of her hands in her lap, her eyes fixed somewhere beyond the window. Dr. Cross caught his attention and motioned to him from the doorway. Moore glanced at the child again.

With his heart breaking, he rose from the bed and stepped into the hall with the other doctor.

"I haven't changed my impression, William," Moore said out of earshot of Delphi and Emily. "It's congestion of the stomach."

Dr. Cross peered over his spectacles at his colleague. "And you said she was improved this morning?"

"She was. Sitting up in bed. Playing. I thought she was on her way to recovery."

"And did you prescribe anything further?"

"I told the mother to continue with lime water and milk, and I had my assistant send over more bismuth salts and told her to continue with that routine until tomorrow."

Dr. Cross raised his brows.

"The child has been afflicted with stomach ailments off and on now for a number of months," Moore explained. "And since the bout of cholera that took her sister, it's been worse."

"I understand the need for aggressive treatment," Cross said, "but I am not convinced this is stomach congestion."

Moore pulled in his chin, unable to mask his irritation. "This is the first time you've seen her, and your exam was cursory at best. The only other thing it could be is cholera, but that wouldn't explain her improvement this morning."

"Her symptoms are consistent with a reaction to poison."

Moore felt a rush flood his veins. "What are you suggesting?"

"I believe the child is suffering from an unnatural condition, most likely induced by a chemical toxin. White arsenic. Possibly antimony."

Moore scoffed and rolled his eyes. "Your suggestion is preposterous."

"I've seen enough in my day to recognize an unnatural condition!" Cross snapped. "There's no other explanation for the child's recovery and subsequent rapid demise. A postmortem will tell us for certain."

Incredulous, Moore looked over Cross's shoulder into the room to ensure that neither woman was listening. "She'll have to die for that to happen," he said in a low voice, "and as her physician, I have an obliga-tion to do everything in my power to save her."

"Surely you realize there is nothing that will save this child's life," Cross said. "At this point, the only thing you can do is to make her as comfortable as possible. You can try Huxham's with a grain of cerium. And a warm bath with a bit of opium to ease any suffering. My guess is that she'll be gone within the hour." Cross glanced at Emily and frowned.

"You think the mother is responsible, don't you?" Moore said, following Cross's eyes.

"It's not my place to judge. But the town will not sit quietly and allow her to bury another child without an inquiry."

"I am telling you the child is suffering from severe stomach congestion." Moore was insistent.

"Look," Dr. Cross said, "I am more than happy to let the mayor know that you and I are in disagreement about the source of the child's malady. Best to leave it to him and the sheriff to decide what to do next."

"I know Emily Lloyd," Moore said. "She's a caring mother and would never harm her child."

"In my opinion, Randy, something has harmed this child. Something or someone."

CHAPTER 2

MONDAY, MARCH 25, 1872

"Jesus, JW!" said Matthew Harrison as the spring storm rushed in ahead of a dark-haired man struggling to keep the knob from flying out of his hand. Matt spread his stubby fingers over his desk to keep the papers from taking flight as the dank air spun into the hall. "Shut that door before half my casework ends up over on Powell's desk."

"That's where it will end up anyway," Powell called from his office across the hall. Of medium height and build, Powell Harrison was not one to stand out in a crowd. But in a courtroom, his colleagues and the judges took notice. Born into a family of attorneys, Powell had followed in the footsteps of his great-grandfather, grandfather, and father, and the law was his life. After graduating at the top of his class at the University of Virginia, he set out on his own to establish a practice far from his hometown and the shadow of his father. Except for the war years, Powell had run a thriving law practice in the city of Staunton and would have been happy to remain there had his father not died and it became clear that his eldest brother, Matthew, was unable to manage the Harrison law office alone. After a year of his family's pleading, Powell had left his lucrative practice in Augusta County and returned to the town and the firm that he had managed for so long to avoid.

"That's what seniority buys, Powell," Matt boasted as the visitor fought the pressing wind and closed the door. "The luxury of having a junior partner."

Powell rolled his eyes and shook his head. Matt seemed to conveniently forget the terms of their equal partnership when it suited him.

Nicknamed the Lion of Leesburg for his ferocious arguments in the courtroom and his fearlessness in taking on both the Virginia legislature and the Confederate generals who had declared martial law on his town during the war, Matt had practiced law with their father for as long as Powell could remember. Fifteen years Powell's senior, Matt was the tallest of Burr Harrison's four sons, and over the years his frame had widened and his waist thickened from the overindulgence that had come with success. The brown hair of his youth had silvered, and his hairline had receded to reveal more of a deeply creviced brow that hung heavily over the drooping lids of his blue-green eyes. But Matt's formidable exterior was deceiving. His cold and stern manner had softened since their father's passing and been replaced by a warmth and sense of humor that Powell was certain would have disappointed their father.

"Gentlemen, you aren't going to believe this!" James William "JW" Foster said, tossing his hat on the settee in the hall and entering Powell's office.

"After the morning I had in court today, nothing would surprise me about the goings-on of this town," Powell said, smiling at the wet, windblown attorney.

JW threw himself into the cane-bottomed chair that fronted Powell's desk, water dripping from his overcoat onto the rug. The nephew of an esteemed attorney and war hero, JW was handsome, his face angular with a strong jaw and cleft chin. His brown eyes were narrow-set on either side of a nose that could have been sculpted for a Greek statue. At six feet, JW was about Matt's height and taller than Powell by a few inches. Much like the Harrison brothers, JW was a natural in the courtroom, and both juries and judges gravitated to his affable personality.

"Were you in court defending that woman accused of stealing silver from Sam Orrison's tavern?"

"Connie Lozenburg," Powell clarified. "Entire indictment based on hearsay and speculation."

"Pro bono, right?" JW asked. Powell nodded. "And did you win?"

"My motion was granted and the case dismissed," Powell said. "Of course, the state can file again should they produce any actual evidence."

"Kilgour certainly knows better than to cross you twice," JW said with a half laugh. Powell and the state prosecutor's lively courtroom clashes were well-known throughout the town. "I doubt your sparring with Mort Kilgour will top the fiasco at the Lloyd place today."

"Please don't tell me that the widow's last child died," Powell said.

"Sadly, yes," JW confirmed.

Powell's heart fell in his chest. His daughter and the Lloyd girl played together at Sunday school. "There ought to be an inquiry this time," he said with a grimace.

JW nodded. "There was. But that's only part of the news."

"What news?" Matt asked, having found his way from his office to Powell's doorway.

"From what I hear, Mayor Bentley summoned a coroner's inquest last night before the child had yet to die," JW explained. "Not an hour later, Bernie Atwell showed up at the Lloyd place with Sam Orrison, the child's guardian, to convince the mother to allow Bentley to do a postmortem." Bernie Atwell had been the town's sheriff since the war.

"Was the child alive when they arrived?" Powell asked.

"According to my source, she had passed just minutes before. The widow, being hysterical with grief, denied Atwell's request. I mean, think about it. Her daughter's body isn't yet cold." JW shifted in the chair and leaned forward. "Then this morning, as the little girl is still lying on her deathbed and they're awaiting the undertaker, the sheriff comes barging in with Bentley, Randy Moore, ol' Doc Cross, and some other man—a witness of sorts, I heard—telling her how much trouble she'll be in if she doesn't consent to a postmortem. And after she is coerced to agree, Bentley directs the doctors to cut the child open right in front of her!" JW threw his frame back in the chair.

"Dear God!" Powell said under his breath. His left thumb bent under his palm to rub the inside of his wedding ring as he envisioned the child's mutilated body under bloody hands. Flashbacks from the war—the aftermath of Gettysburg—crowded into the scene in his head: roadside amputations, field surgeries, mangled limbs discarded in the mud. Powell swallowed hard to force the ghosts back to where he kept them buried.

"Jesus!" Matt exclaimed. "In the presence of the mother? What the hell was Bentley thinking?"

"And it gets worse. After the doctors leave, Bentley carts in a jury he's summoned, and they conduct an inquest, right there in Mrs. Lloyd's parlor." Powell's eyes widened. "A dozen men crowded in that little parlor with a dead girl in her bed, and they proceed to interrogate a grieving mother."

"Did they charge her?" Matt asked.

"No, not yet," JW said. "I don't know the specifics of what the jury recommended, if anything. But I did go by the sheriff's office to confirm that there had been an inquest convened. Beyond affirming that Drs. Moore and Cross initiated it, Atwell wasn't talking."

"So why are you telling us this?" Matt asked, twirling the tip of his mustache with a finger, leaning against the doorframe.

"I plan to represent her," JW said. "Her late husband, Charles, served in the 8th Virginia under my uncle's command. And I want the Harrison brothers as co-counsel."

"And we're sorry to disappoint you," Matt said, "but no. Not our type of litigation."

For once, Powell couldn't agree more with his brother. "Charlie Lloyd was hardly the kind of man that your uncle would feel any indebtedness toward," Powell said. "The man was intemperate and bad-tempered and, as I recall, ran a saloon that doubled as a brothel."

"In addition to all of those compelling reasons, the Harrisons are not getting involved in an infanticide case," Matt followed up.

"Emily Lloyd did not have anything at all to do with her child's death." JW was defiant.

"Come on, JW," Matt said. "You must admit that it's more than a coincidence that not long after her husband died, the rest of her family ends up over in Union Cemetery."

"Mothers don't kill their babies," JW said, "and Emily Lloyd didn't poison hers. And might I remind you gentlemen of the presumption of innocence? She's a decent woman and is entitled to fair representation. Representation that the law firm of Hunton and Foster intends to provide."

"I think your uncle might have something to say about this," said Matt under his breath, frowning.

"If she's innocent, as you say, the autopsy will exonerate her," Powell reasoned. "You won't need co-counsel in that instance."

"You don't trust Mayor Bentley any more than I do," JW said.

"Powell doesn't trust anyone," Matt said.

"Considering the pressure Bentley is under from the taxpayers, he won't back off, regardless of the autopsy results," JW said. "It's an election year, and you know how he looks upon the small people, especially the Negroes and indigent widows—those he called in his last campaign 'the millstones around the neck of the community.'"

"'And oppress not the widow, nor the fatherless, the stranger, nor the poor,'" Powell said, quoting, as he often did, from scripture.

"Tell that to the mayor. And then there's Kilgour." JW rolled his eyes. "We all know that he'll do anything to be reelected this fall. The only thing he cares about is winning over the court of public opinion." JW brought his gaze to Powell, pleading. "This is your kind of case, Powell—and you know it."

"We all know how my brother loves a good charity cause," Matt said. "But a mother who may have deliberately poisoned her children? I am not about to face the wrath of my wife to defend a baby killer."

Matt had a point. Matt's wife, Hattie, would have Matt's head if he took an infanticide case. And Powell's wife, Janet, would most certainly have Powell's.

"Have you considered the attention a trial like this will draw?" Powell said in hopes of discouraging JW. "It will be front-page news across the country."

"Exactly!" JW said.

Powell threw JW a pointed look. JW's motivation was clear. A successful defense would put the Leesburg office of Hunton and Foster on the map. And damage the reputation of the losing side.

"The newspapers and Janet are only two of a hundred good reasons I am not taking this on," Powell said.

"I beg to differ," JW argued. "The visibility is the exact reason you should want this case. Just think of the reputation you'll earn when we win."

Powell shook his head. "What you mean is *if* we win."

"With your experience at trial, how can we lose?"

Powell scoffed. "And Janet?"

"She loves you. She'll get over it." JW winked. "Eventually."

"I don't think so," Powell said, admiring his friend's persistence.

"Just come with me tomorrow morning while I interview the widow," JW pleaded. "Not as counsel, but as a consultant." Powell looked from JW to Matt and back to JW. "I could really use the help." JW's eyes locked on Powell's.

Powell blew a reluctant sigh and nodded. "Only on consult."

"Yes!" JW exclaimed and leapt from the chair.

"Jesus, Powell!" Matt cried. "We've got a full caseload already."

"It's only an interview to assist a colleague," Powell said.

Matt shook his head. "Let me cancel my conference tomorrow, then."

"You're coming, too?" JW asked.

"Only to keep you from twisting Powell's arm any further!"

◆ ◆ ◆

"Papa's home!" Powell called, bursting through the front door of the yellow-painted house with his satchel in one hand and a handful of daffodils in the other. He set his satchel on the bench by the door, tossing his hat beside it, and removed his rain-soaked overcoat.

"Papa!" A dark-haired girl in a white smock with a pink bow pinned at the top of her head came running from the back hall. Kneeling to the floor, Powell scooped the three-year-old into his open arms.

"How's my Nannie today?" he asked as he lifted the child onto his hip. Powell kissed her on the side of her face, deliberately moving his mustache over her cheek.

"That tickles!" She giggled.

"Tickles, eh?" he said with an easy laugh as he wiggled his fingers on her belly, and she squealed in delight. Powell put her down and took her hand into his.

"Are those for me?" she asked, a pointed finger aimed at the flowers.

"For you to share with Mummy."

Powell walked with her down the hall, looking in the parlor, study, and dining room as they headed toward the kitchen.

"Where's your mother and baby sister?"

"Lalla is still on her nap," said Janet Harrison, emerging from a doorway at the back of the hall. She had the same dark hair as her daughter, pulled back into a bun at the nape of her neck. Her cheeks were high and flushed, and her eyes were such a deep blue that they appeared violet, reminding Powell of the flowers that bloomed on the hillsides at Morrisworth, the farm where he had grown up.

"There's Mummy!" Smiling, Powell wrapped both arms around his wife's waist and kissed her.

"You seem to be in a good mood, Mr. Harrison." She placed her palms on his chest and turned her head toward the flowers he held behind her. "Who are those for?"

"For my angel," he said, releasing her. As he presented Janet with the yellow bouquet, he bent his head toward Nannie, who was clutching her mother's skirt. "And my little princess."

"And whose lawn did you pick them from?" Janet asked with a brow raised.

Powell placed a hand on his chest. "Your husband is an officer of the court and would never abscond with flowers from a neighbor's yard. No, dear. I can attest that these flowers were purchased legally from a nice lady who, in spite of all the rain, was selling them near the courthouse. Did you forget today was court day?"

Janet brought the daffodils to her nose and smiled. "I did not forget. In fact, I heard you had a good day."

Powell knitted his brows. "You did?"

Janet gave him another scrutinizing look and a half laugh before shaking her head. "Powell Harrison. Did you forget that you sent another one of your charity cases over here this afternoon?"

Powell had, indeed, forgotten that he had promised Connie Lozenburg, the woman he had defended in court that morning, part-time employment helping his wife around the house.

"Sorry, Jan. I should have mentioned it."

"I've learned to expect it," she said as she linked her arm through his. "I'm not complaining, mind you. I could use help with the children, especially in the evenings while Rebecca is preparing supper. So I asked Connie to start with us tomorrow evening."

With a nod of acknowledgment, he cupped his hand over hers and walked with her down the hall to the kitchen. Wearing a rusty-red cotton dress and a white apron, their maid, Rebecca, was standing at the stove stirring a steaming pot. Powell pulled a chair from a small table in the corner. Nannie climbed into his lap as a gray tabby slunk into the room. Purring, it ribboned itself around Powell's leg.

"Mr. Whiskers!" Nannie exclaimed, giggling as she reached down, trying to catch the tip of his tail in her fingers.

"I worry, Powell," Janet said, pulling a cut-crystal vase from a cabinet. "People are talking about all of these indigents you keep defending."

"Let them talk," he said, repositioning Nannie on his lap to keep her from falling to the floor. He shooed the cat away with a foot. "You should have seen them today, Jannie. Shaking their heads. The scornful looks. The hate in their whispers. None of them give a cent about the truth. All they want is to dish out vengeance." He huffed under his breath.

Janet eyed him with a raised brow as she ladled water into the vase. "Vengeance for what?"

"For all they lost during the war, I guess. When they aren't blaming the Yankees, they're blaming the Negroes and the poor." He looked over at the woman in the faded red dress. Busy with her work, their maid Rebecca seemed to be paying no attention to their conversation.

Janet shook her head. "While I share your sympathies, I do not want them to start blaming us. Even your sister has brought up your sympathies for these people as an issue."

"Let me guess. Anne Marie?"

Janet nodded. "She said it reflects poorly on the family."

Powell rolled his eyes. "Who elected Anne Marie mayor of the family? And if not me, then who? Who will stand up for what's right?"

"Isn't that up to the prosecutor? The judge? To find the truth?"

"If only it were that simple. And with Mort Kilgour as the commonwealth's attorney for the county, how can anyone trust justice to be fair?"

"Well, it doesn't have to always be you. It's high time someone else took on these cases. Why not Mr. Foster? Lord knows there is little else that could stain that rogue's reputation." She walked over and placed the vase of daffodils in the center of the table. "How's that?"

"Beautiful, just like my wife." Powell smiled at her as she took the chair across from him, hoping that their discussion would not shift to yet another argument about his friendship with JW. Despite a ten-year difference in age, the two had become fast friends when Powell returned to Leesburg. Janet, on the other hand, could not understand how a principled man like Powell could take a liking to someone who spent Sundays sleeping off hangovers instead of attending church services with his widowed mother. JW's tryst with the maid of honor at Powell and Janet's wedding had only furthered her disdain for the young bachelor.

Powell fell silent as Nannie attempted to unfasten a button on his vest. The wind whistled outside and rushed down the chimney, causing the fire in the stove to roar.

"You know, darling," Janet said, interrupting the stillness that had settled between them. "Maybe you should consider electioneering for the commonwealth's attorney's office. Restore the people's confidence in the justice system. And it would certainly put an end to all this fighting with Mr. Kilgour."

Powell laughed. "If you think I'm fighting with Mort Kilgour now, just imagine if he thought I wanted his job!"

"I'm serious, Powell. You seem to be the only attorney in this town who cares about finding the truth."

"That's just it. Too many in this town don't care one iota about the truth, especially when it doesn't support what they want to believe." Powell shook his head. "I don't think so, Jan. And then there's Matthew to consider. He relies on me so."

"That's true. But Matthew was the county's commonwealth's attorney once, just like your father and grandfather. Your brother, of all people, would encourage you in such a pursuit."

"Your supper's almost ready," Rebecca announced as she spooned vegetables from a pot into a serving bowl.

Powell took Nannie into his arms and rose from the chair.

"Oh, by the way," Janet said, "I heard the little Lloyd girl died. Some are saying it might have been cholera that took her. The whole town is talking about it." She stood and picked up the vase of daffodils from the table. "Something needs to be done, Powell."

"Not to worry, darling. The sheriff and mayor are looking into it," he said as he headed for the dining room, holding his daughter.

"Well, it's about time. Because my intuition tells me that cholera had nothing to do with it," said Janet, carrying the vase and following behind. "Nothing to do with it at all."

CHAPTER 3

TUESDAY, MARCH 26, 1872

Lara pushed aside the lace curtain with the back of her hand and watched the three men below traverse the mud-spattered street to the house. Although it was nearly ten in the morning, sheets of heavy rain and steely gray clouds darkened the skies as if it were dusk.

"Emily has visitors," she said. "By the looks of them, I'd say they're lawyers."

"It didn't take them long," Lilith said. Lara glanced at the form-fitting dress Lilith wore and frowned. While Lara disapproved of the tightness of the dress and the low cut of the bodice, there was little she could do about it.

Lara shook her head and turned her attention back to the street. "Poor Emily is going to need them after yesterday."

"Poor Emily," Lilith said with a grunt. "She brings it on herself!"

"Hush!" Lara scolded, keeping her attention on the men outside. "None of what has happened is Emily's fault."

"It is, indeed, her fault. She should have never allowed the sheriff in the house. Dr. Moore told them the girl had been ill. She should have sent them to go see him and slammed the door in their faces."

"While I agree that there was no reason for an inquiry, Dr. Moore was with them yesterday morning, lest you forget." She could hear Lilith's scoff behind her. "No use fretting over it now. What's done is done."

Gusting wind whipped a sheet of rain across the backs of the attorneys as they huddled on the stoop. "That tall, dark-haired one on the right is quite the looker," Lilith said.

Lara shot Lilith a scathing glance. "The last thing Emily needs is you seducing one of her lawyers."

"Oh, I don't think she'd mind."

"I'm serious, Lilith," Lara warned. "We don't need the trouble."

"Speak for yourself, sister," Lilith said. "I wouldn't mind his kind of trouble at all."

With one brow raised higher than the other, Lara turned to Lilith. "You will behave yourself. Am I making myself clear?"

Lilith glanced down at the floor and shuffled her feet, mumbling under her breath.

Hearing the door below open, Lara turned back to the window. She watched as a woman in a jade-striped dress appeared in the doorway, pushing her way past the housemaid to greet the men.

"Interfering slut!" Lilith said.

"Why is it that you don't like Maggie Greene?"

"She's always sticking her beak into everybody's business and dropping off her sewing for Emily because she's supposedly too busy. She uses Emily. And I don't trust her motives."

"You need to mind yourself," Lara warned. "Mrs. Greene has a relationship with the shorter fella in the middle."

Lara pushed the curtain back farther. Together they watched the three men disappear into the shadows of Emily's side of the double house. Lara let the curtain fall back over the window's glass.

"So what's so special about the one in the middle?" Lilith asked.

"From what Mrs. Greene says, he's never lost a case."

Lilith rolled her eyes. "Mrs. Greene."

"Do not let your notions about Mrs. Greene sour Emily's opinion of her." Lara raised an eyebrow in Lilith's direction. "We need her at present."

A murmur of men's voices rumbling through the walls from the floor below interrupted their exchange. They quieted, trying to make out the words.

"Is he the one Mrs. Greene told Emily she was once sweet on?" Lilith said, her voice low.

Lara nodded. "According to Emily, the two had been in courtship."

"Why didn't they marry?"

Lara shrugged her shoulders.

"Who is he?"

"Harrison," Lara whispered. "Powell Harrison."

◆ ◆ ◆

Powell pulled his collar up to keep the wet away from his ears as Maggie Greene invited the three attorneys inside. The house was actually half of a house—a twin to the one next door—with a long wall and a stairway to the second floor on the left, and a parlor on the right. The foyer and hall were painted Pompeian red with the underlying plaster cracked and delaminating in places. On the left wall hung a crucifix surrounded by framed family portraits.

"Mrs. Greene," Powell said with a nod. When Powell had first met Maggie Greene, she was Maggie Newton, a bold, brash strawberry blonde with mesmerizing eyes. He had been in his last year of law school, and she was barely sixteen. But that was twenty years ago. Before his father refused to allow them to marry. Before the war.

"Mr. Harrison," she said, holding his gaze before redirecting her attention to Matt and JW. "Mr. Harrison. Mr. Foster. Thank y'all for coming."

Matt shot Powell a cautionary glance as he removed his hat. Powell acknowledged his brother and nodded back.

Crowded into the cramped foyer, the men shook the rain from their coats and handed them to Delphi, who took them to hang.

"Mrs. Lloyd is upstairs resting," Maggie said, inviting them to the chairs in the parlor. "How horrible it's been for her."

"Is the child's body still here?" Powell asked, glancing around as he took a seat.

"Upstairs as well," Maggie said. "Undertaker was to come yesterday, but with all the commotion . . ."

"I doubt he'll arrive until the rain subsides," JW said. "Could make for messy business moving a body with the mud and all."

"Delphi," Maggie said to the housemaid, who had returned from hanging the coats. "Might you see if Mrs. Lloyd is feeling up to speaking with these gentlemen?"

"Sure enough. I'll go fetch her for you." Delphi turned and left the room.

"How well do you know Mrs. Lloyd?" Powell asked.

"As neighbors, we're friendly. And we're both seamstresses. Sometimes I help her if work piles up. Sometimes she helps me."

"Mrs. Greene," JW interrupted, "would you tell the gentlemen what you told me yesterday about this weekend and what happened?"

"Certainly." Maggie looked at Powell. "I had heard from Delphi that little Maud had taken ill again. Delphi works for me, too, sometimes," she explained. "When I saw Maud on Saturday morning, I brought her some ginger cakes I had made, but she was too ill to eat them. I helped Emily bathe her, hoping that would make her feel better. When I stopped by on Sunday, she was much improved, playing in the bed with her doll. Dr. Moore had just left. I assumed she was on the mend. But then yesterday—" She hesitated, overcome with emotion.

"Just tell Powell and Matt what you told me," JW coaxed.

Taking a heavy breath to calm herself, Maggie continued. "When I arrived, they wouldn't let me in the parlor. There were a dozen of them, maybe more. Sheriff Atwell was standing like a sentry inside the door, letting no one in or out. They had Emily in there for the longest time. Delphi and I waited until they finished speaking to her. When she came out, they shut the door and stayed in there. That's when Emily told me everything that had happened. I told her she needed a lawyer, and that's when I came to see you, JW."

Maggie moved her gaze beyond Powell's shoulder to the hallway. Delphi was leading Emily Lloyd into the parlor, holding her by the arm. Powell recognized the woman from Sunday services, but as she typically sat behind his family in the rear of the church and nearly always wore a veil, he had never before noticed the uncanny color of her eyes. The gentlemen stood as Delphi helped Emily into the chair nearest the door.

"Mrs. Lloyd, I am James William Foster. Mrs. Greene asked me to come. And I brought along two of my colleagues, Mr. Powell Harrison and Mr. Matthew Harrison."

"I know you," Emily said to Powell, her voice soft. "And you as well." She nodded at Matt. "I see you both at church."

"And I think I can speak for Mr. Foster and my brother here and tell you how sorry we are for all that you have been through," Powell said with sympathy in his voice.

"You have no idea what I have been through," Emily said, her reddened eyes narrowing, her voice suddenly low and angry.

"My apologies," Powell said. "You are right that we couldn't possibly—"

"They come barging in here Sunday night," Emily cried, leaning forward, "my baby not yet cold, demanding I allow them to desecrate her! And then yesterday morning before I even have a chance to prepare her, they trick me by sending Dr. Moore like he's . . . some kind of a ruse so I'll allow it. I agree because Dr. Moore—he—I trusted him! Then the sheriff, the mayor, Dr. Cross, and some other men come traipsing up the stairs, saying that since I agreed, I had to let them cut up my baby." She bit her bottom lip, fighting tears. Maggie got up from her chair and went to Emily, sitting on the armrest to take her hand. Emily jerked away, extending her finger, pointing at Powell and glaring at him. "And do you know what they did? The butchers! They lift my daughter's nightdress, and that swine of a mayor hands Dr. Cross a knife with a big shiny blade like one used to carve a roast. I screamed at them. Screamed and screamed, I did, and tried to stop them, but the sheriff and another man held my arms, restraining me from tearing their eyes out." Emily was shouting and crying all at the same time, tears streaming down her face.

Powell stood and handed her his handkerchief. "Do you need a minute, ma'am?"

Sniffling back sobs, she shook her head. "Then Dr. Moore steps in. He puts his hand over Dr. Cross's that held the knife and tells him that he will perform the procedure. He brings out a smaller knife—a scalpel, I think he called it. Dr. Moore tells me that it will be all right.

That he will take care." Emily spit on the floor, her anger returning. "Dr. Moore starts to cut into her, then stops and tells the sheriff to take me out of the room. I refused to go, but the sheriff and this other man forced me, dragging me down the stairs. They brought me in here and wouldn't let me leave.

"Next thing I know, this deputy, the one with the yellow hair, comes down the stairs with pieces of my daughter wrapped in a white rag with her blood soaking through. He stops at the doorway here"— she waved her hand in the direction of the foyer—"and has a discussion with the sheriff as her blood drips on the floor. Then he leaves, carting half her insides out the front door!" Pursing her lips tightly, Emily quieted and began to rock back and forth in the chair.

An awkward hush fell over the room as Emily rocked, dabbing the corners of her eyes with Powell's handkerchief. Powell visualized the scene, the chaos and screaming, imagining the blood-dripping gauze being carried through the streets of town. The thought made him sick to his stomach. He glanced over at JW and cleared his throat.

"I know how difficult this is, ma'am," JW said at Powell's prompting, "but it's important that you tell us everything else that happened yesterday."

Emily released a long sigh. "Dr. Moore and Dr. Cross, when they finished with Maudie, they left. Mayor Bentley and the sheriff stayed, and this big man with black hair wearing a black suit arrived with more men, and he was in charge. Mr. Killington . . . Killrod—"

"Mr. Kilgour?" Powell suggested.

"Yes, that was his name. Mr. Kilgour." She drew a short, nervous breath. "They had me sit where you are sitting now, and all these men, they stood all around me. He asked me when Maud got sick, what she had eaten, what she drank. What medicine I gave her. Things like that."

"'He' being Mr. Kilgour?"

"Yes, Mr. Kilgour. He had so many questions. I told him that I had followed Dr. Moore's instructions exactly. Exactly! And when I gave her the powders on Sunday, she got worse. Dr. Moore assured me that morning she would be all right. And she just got sicker and sicker!"

"Did you tell Mr. Kilgour this?" Powell asked.

"Yes. But he kept asking the same questions over and over again in different ways. I was tired and angry and worried and then I couldn't remember anymore. I had one of my spells where I forget where I am. I do that sometimes, you know." She wrung her hands and rocked, her gaze drifting to the floor.

"Absentmindedness?" Powell asked.

"Yes, something like it. I couldn't keep track of all his questions. I sort of drifted off."

"It's understandable," JW said. "You've been through a lot."

"Besides Mrs. Greene and Delphi, did anyone else come by over the weekend?" Powell asked.

Emily nodded. "Dr. Moore was here on Thursday night when Maudie first got sick, and then again on Friday and Saturday, and twice on Sunday. And on Sunday the second time, Dr. Cross came with him." Powell made a mental note. William Cross, Bernie Atwell, and Bobby Bentley. All close friends.

"Any callers besides the doctors while Maud was ill?"

Emily thought for a minute, her demeanor calming. "Mollie Ryan. She lives down the street with her mother, who's widowed, like most of us on this end of town. On Saturday, Mollie dropped off some candies that Maud likes. Maudie says they look like the roses on the wall in her room." Emily smiled briefly. "And Colonel Nixon from across the street. He checks in regularly."

"Anyone deliver anything? Medicine, food, milk?" Powell asked.

"Yes. The young man from Dr. Moore's apothecary—Jason, I believe, is his name—he dropped off more bismuth powders for Maud. And my brother-in-law delivered milk." She thought for a moment more. "Oh, and there was Mr. Orrison."

"Sam Orrison?" Powell asked.

"Yes. He came by on Saturday and said that as Maud's guardian he had responsibility for her well-being." She scoffed. "He never came by to check on her before then. And Sunday night he shows up with the sheriff, wanting to cut my baby's body before her soul has a chance to leave it. Heathens, they are. He and the sheriff!"

Powell looked at Delphi, who was standing in the doorway. "Delphi, did Mr. Kilgour ask you any questions?"

"They asked me much the same questions that they asked Miss Emily," Delphi said. "I told them I didn't know nothin'."

Maggie turned. "Delphi, you need to tell them what you told me."

"They asked me if we had rats. I told them that we have some rats and we have mice. Heaps of mice. And then they wanted to know if I had kept little Maud's vomit. I told them *no*! Why would I keep a bucket of vomit? Told 'em I tossed it out in the yard. Seemed like a bunch of silly questions, if you ask me."

Maggie raised a brow. "All of it, Delphi."

Delphi lowered her eyes to the floor and drew a long breath. "They asked me if I saw Miss Emily give rat poison to Maudie. And I told them that Miss Emily would never do such a thing!"

"The man should be struck down by God Almighty for insinuating that I would harm my own child!" Emily cried, hanks of skirt in her fists.

Powell looked at JW, who nodded, then back at Emily.

"Mrs. Lloyd, as awkward as it may seem," Powell said, "I have to ask the same question. Did you administer poison to Maud?"

"Are you out of your right mind? Why, in heaven's name, would I do anything, *anything*, to hurt my baby girl?"

"Did Mr. Kilgour ask you this, too?" Powell insisted.

"Yes, he did," she said. "And I answered him the same way I answered you."

"So you denied his charge?" Powell asked.

Emily looked confused. "I asked him to give me one good reason why I would do such a thing."

Powell nodded. "But did you outright tell him that you did not administer any poisons to your daughter?"

"I don't know," she answered. "I thought I was clear enough."

"Mrs. Lloyd," said Matt. "What about the others? Did Mr. Kilgour ask you about the other children?"

"Yes," she said, moving her eyes to Matt on the far side of the room. "He asked me about Annie."

"And the boys? Did he ask you about your boys who died last summer?"

"Henry and George?"

"Yes, Henry and George. Did Mr. Kilgour ask if you had poisoned them?"

"Yes, he asked me about them, too."

"And your aunt who passed away, and your husband a few

years ago. Did the men who were here ask you if you had poisoned them?"

Emily's gaze fell to the carpet. Slowly, she moved her head from side to side.

Matt pressed her. "Are you saying that Mr. Kilgour didn't ask you about your aunt and your husband? Or that he did?"

Emily shook her head as if attempting to rid herself of a thought. She lifted her eyes to Matt. "I told them in plain terms that I would never do such a thing!" Her voice was low and sharp as she spoke.

"Of course you wouldn't," Maggie said as she patted Emily's forearm.

"I think that's enough for now," JW said, rising from his chair. "Do you mind if we have a quick look at Maud before we leave?"

Staring at Matt, Emily shook her head and folded her hands in her lap. "Look all you want."

"Delphi," Maggie said and stood. "Why don't you sit here with Mrs. Lloyd while I put on a kettle for tea."

Delphi nodded and took the chair beside Emily. Maggie left for the kitchen, and JW, Matt, and Powell started toward the front hall. Emily's eyes remained locked on Matt as he walked past her.

"I'm heading back to the office," Matt said. "You and JW can handle this." He glanced in the parlor at Emily, who sat with her back to them. With a shake of his head, he put on his coat and left.

◆ ◆ ◆

The room at the top of the stairs was dimly lit, papered in emerald-green trellises and cherry-pink roses. Delicate lace curtains hung over the windows that faced the backyard. JW was standing beside a satinwood bed covered by a multicolored quilt of greens, pinks, and creams. On top of the coverlet lay a little blonde girl in an ivory cotton nightdress, her eyes closed, her lips parted, and her skin pallid. But for the dark impressions around her eyes, she looked like she could be sleeping. She seemed so small in the bed and as innocent as Powell's three-year-old son, Bo, had, lying on his own deathbed the summer before. The chubby fingers of his hands folded over his chest as he lay ever so still in the feather ticking.

"What do you want to do, Powell?" JW asked, disrupting the memory.

"I want to confirm where she was cut," Powell said as he joined JW at the bedside.

Powell reached over her body and with both hands lifted the nightdress. Above her navel was a vertical incision about four inches in length over a depression in her abdomen. The incision was uneven and had been stitched closed with black thread. JW turned his face away.

Powell lowered the dress. Had they done the same to Bo, he wouldn't have been able to restrain himself. He shuddered and moved his gaze to the window. Rain was pouring from the sky, and a mix of mud and floodwater was pooling in the yard below. A stream stained red with Virginia clay cut through the winter grass. *"For as the rain cometh down and watereth the earth, so shall My word be that goeth forth and shall accomplish that which I please,"* Powell recited in his head, trying to make sense of it. *What does taking the lives of four children in eight months accomplish?* he asked himself, watching the muddied water push its way to the side yard and the street. *How is that pleasing to a God of goodness?*

Thunder rumbled in the distance as the rain intensified. "'For as the heavens are higher than the earth, so are my ways higher than your ways,'" Powell muttered, doing his best to push his disdain and misgivings aside.

"What?" JW asked.

Powell turned to face him. "Isaiah 55:9. Trying to wrap my head around the Lord's design."

"Whatever His design, that child didn't deserve this," JW said.

"I won't allow myself to believe that God had a hand in it," Powell said.

"The work of Satan?"

"Through the deeds of evil men. Or by the hands of a sick woman."

"What are you implying?"

"All her children dead? In less than a year? What are the odds, Jay?"

"Coincidence," JW insisted.

"Even God isn't that merciless."

"I don't know, Powell. We've both seen more than our fair share."

Powell clenched his jaw. "You need to prepare yourself for the autopsy analysis to confirm what is obvious."

"And that is?"

Powell couldn't bring himself to say aloud what his gut was telling him. "An insanity plea will be your best option. It's the only way you can win this."

◆ ◆ ◆

"Papa's home!" Powell called as he flung open the front door and dashed in from the rain. "Nannie," he hollered and removed his hat and coat and hung them on the rack by the door. "Nannie!" The house was still except for the gray tabby in the parlor, stretching from his slumber. Powell walked to the banister and called up the stairs. "Janet?"

"She's up on the third floor in the nursery," said a husky voice from down the hall.

"Jack?" Powell walked down the hallway to the study. Behind Powell's desk sat his father-in-law, Dr. Jack Fauntleroy, his white hair as wild as ever. "Didn't expect you for supper tonight," Powell said as he entered the room. "Is everything all right?"

"Jan sent for me," Jack said, peering above his wire-framed spectacles. "Nannie was complaining that her stomach hurt, and having heard that the Lloyd girl maybe had cholera, Jan was worried."

Powell felt a wave of apprehension rush through his chest. "Should she worry?"

"I don't think so. Looks like it's just a tummy ache. Gave her some milk and a little lime water. Jan's just now putting her down for a rest. But out of an abundance of caution, Janet did insist that we send Lalla over to my place."

Powell nodded and took a chair across from him, and Jack resumed his reading. Crossing one leg over the other and reclining in the chair, Powell rubbed his ring with his thumb as he reviewed the day's events in his head. Maggie Greene. The interview with Emily Lloyd. The dead girl in her bed.

"You said you gave lime water and milk to Nannie. Did you administer bismuth?"

Jack looked up from the book. "Why would I? She wasn't suffering from diarrhea, just a stomachache. And besides, I would never prescribe bismuth for a child."

Powell uncrossed his leg and straightened in the chair. "Why not?"

"A child that young wouldn't tolerate it well. Why are you asking?"

"I'm curious."

"And a fibber. You're involved in the inquiry into the Lloyd child's death, aren't you?"

"I didn't say that."

Jack closed the book and leaned forward. "Listen, Powell. I don't want to second-guess a colleague. If Randy Moore prescribed bismuth for a child, it wouldn't be without good reason."

"Hypothetically speaking, what might be some of those reasons?"

"If there was substantial fluid loss or if all other treatments had failed. Perhaps he felt he had no other choice to save the child's life."

"When you say that young children don't tolerate it, what do you mean?"

"Bismuth is a metal. Heavy as lead. A grown man can process it through the liver and kidneys well enough, but a child's system cannot easily do so."

Powell brought his eyes to his father-in-law. "Could it kill a child?"

Jack shrugged his shoulders. "I suppose anything is possible. I've never witnessed it, but it doesn't mean it hasn't happened. I'd have to examine the body to see if there were any signs of toxicity."

"What signs?"

"There'd be a dark-blue tinge where the gums meet the teeth. And the tongue would look as if black hair were growing on it."

"I didn't think to open her mouth," Powell said to himself, but loud enough for his father-in-law to hear.

Jack raised a brow. "So you are involved. Are you and your brother representing the Lloyd widow?"

Powell shook his head. "JW Foster is her attorney. He asked us to consult, that's all."

"If I were you, I'd advise you and Mr. Foster to be careful about insinuating that Randy Moore had anything to do with the child's demise."

"Unlike you, I'm not his colleague."

"My concern is the reaction you might receive from his father-in-law."

"I'm not concerned about Mayor Bentley's reaction either," Powell said, his mind racing. Perhaps his instincts had been wrong, and the death of Emily's daughter was explainable after all. "The undertaker was arriving at the Lloyd house as we were leaving today. Would you mind taking a ride with me over to his place?"

Jack clicked his tongue against his teeth. "Janet will not be happy if we're late for supper."

"We'll be back before she realizes that we left."

◆ ◆ ◆

The undertaker's parlor was little more than a shed behind the cabinetmaker's shop. Having interrupted the mortician's supper, they were given the key to the building with instructions to lock up when they were finished. Jars of chemicals and various instruments lay on a wooden bench next to the child's body, draped with a quilt. An odor of mold and pickles pinched Powell's nostrils as the rain drummed monotonously on the tin above their heads. He crossed his arms and watched Jack raise the coverlet. Little Maud looked the same as she had that morning, her eyes closed as if she were sleeping. Jack lifted the child's upper lip with a finger. Powell moved the lantern closer. A thin dark line edged her gum.

"Is that what I think it is?" Powell asked as Jack's finger followed the line around her teeth.

"It appears so." Jack pulled down on her chin, forcing the mouth to open. With the same finger, he dislodged the tongue from the upper palate. Powell leaned in for a closer look.

"Anything?" Powell asked.

"Nothing unusual that I can make out," Jack said, and he closed the child's mouth.

"So what does that mean? Was she poisoned by the bismuth or not?"

"I have seen blue in the gums of patients with a variety of ailments. But in my experience, an overabundance of bismuth in a person causes both the bluing of the gums *and* the blackening of the tongue. As I told you earlier, even if she did suffer a toxic dose, it would be a stretch to attribute her death to bismuth. It would take some time for the effects to cause death."

"But it's not impossible to die from too much of the stuff, right? Especially in a child."

"Not impossible, but, in my opinion, not likely."

"Does the tongue remain blackened postmortem?"

Jack thought for a moment. "I don't rightly know. As I said, I've never known anyone to outright die of bismuth poisoning."

"My cousin might know. He's a physician in Richmond. Dr. Graham Ellzey. You met him at Janet's and my wedding."

"I remember him well. An expert in chemistry, as I recall."

"That and postmortem analysis. I'll send him a telegraph in the morning."

"I thought this wasn't your case."

"I'm just consulting. And I'm curious."

"You know what they say about curiosity."

"Not to worry," Powell said with a grimace. "No cat is getting killed. I'm just helping a colleague explore alternate theories should the analysis not be favorable."

"And you suspect that it won't be."

"You know, sir, I've learned to trust my instincts and the truth." As Powell opened the shed's door, he glanced at the shrouded body before looking back at his father-in-law. "And so far, neither has failed me."

CHAPTER 4

At his first knock on the slick varnished wood, the door jerked and opened slightly.

"Dr. Moore," Emily said, a startle in her voice as she peered through the opening. She wore a black skirt with a matching blouse buttoned high under her chin. Her hair was pulled from her face, and he saw the weariness around her eyes.

"I've been worried about you," Moore said, removing his hat. Emily stared at him blankly.

"How could you!" The calm in her face was instantly replaced with anger.

"Might I come in and explain?" Dr. Moore pushed his way into the house. Emily turned away from him as he closed the door behind him. He grasped her arm, forcing her to face him.

"I wanted to come by before now, but with the inquest and the funeral and all that has transpired, I was unsure how my presence here, after, you know—"

"I trusted you and you betrayed me!" Emily shouted.

"I am sorry. Truly I am."

She pushed him away. "You lied to me. Told me she would get

better. Then you leave just before she dies. And when you do show up, you bring those barbarians into my home—into Maud's bedroom—to desecrate her! Why?"

"Had I not performed the postmortem, Dr. Cross would have. And he would not have taken the same care with Maud."

"You allowed them to use you as an instrument for their wickedness." Emily was crying now.

Moore put a hand on her shoulder. "Please, Mrs. Lloyd. You must understand that I had no choice in the matter. And that I am implicated just as much as you."

Emily turned to look at him, her brow narrowed over tear-filled eyes. "It isn't you who they are accusing!"

"Indeed they are. My diagnosis is being challenged and my skills as a physician questioned. The talk is that either I am incompetent or that I am complicit."

"Complicit in what?"

"That I am protecting you."

"It is not me who needs protection," she said. "It was Maud."

Moore remained silent for a moment, searching for the right words.

"You know that I would have done anything, given anything, to have made her well. I did everything I could. I tried." He felt his own tears welling as he fought to keep the emotion from his voice. "And I failed."

At his admission, Emily fell against him. Moore took her in his arms, holding her as she wept.

"It's all so unfair," she sobbed. "I don't understand why God has forsaken me so."

"He hasn't forsaken you. 'Trust in the Lord with all thine heart; and lean not unto thine own understanding.'" Lifting her face with a finger, he looked at her. "You mustn't lose your faith, Emily."

"'Let not mercy and truth forsake thee,'" she said, following his lead and reciting from Proverbs. "I shall bind them about my neck and write them upon my heart." She pulled a handkerchief from a pocket in her skirt and dabbed her eyes. "You are right. All I have left now is the Lord." Her eyes met his. "And my friendship with you."

"You will always have my friendship," he said with an assuring smile.

Sniffling, she stepped away from him and straightened her skirts as she gathered her composure.

"Would you like a cup of coffee?" she asked, turning toward the hall. "I have a pot on in the back."

"That would be nice, thank you."

He followed her to the kitchen. Emily poured them each a cup and offered him a chair at the table. An awkward silence gathered between the two.

"Are you sleeping?" Moore asked, finally.

"Fitfully some nights. But I manage as best I can with the new medication you gave me."

"You're taking both of the compounds, yes? Are the nightmares subsiding?"

"Somewhat, but they never completely leave me."

"Emily." Moore drew a long breath, struggling to find words. "Are you certain that the only compounds you administered to Maud were the ones that I gave you for her? That you didn't accidentally give her your medicines by mistake?"

Emily shook her head. "It's not possible. I keep my medications in my room, whereas I kept Maud's in the kitchen."

"And there are no other compounds in the house—no poisons of any kind—that she could have consumed?"

"Anything like that I would burn, just like you told me." Tears welled in Emily's eyes and her voice broke. "I loved her with all my heart, Randy."

"As did I," Moore said.

Emily wiped her eyes and forced a smile. "Might you stay for supper? A neighbor dropped off an apple pie today, your favorite."

"I must get going. I've told you how cross my wife becomes when I'm late."

"I certainly wouldn't want to add to your stress at home."

Moore could see her disappointment as she glanced away.

"Very well, then," he said and reluctantly stood from the table. "I had best be on my way."

She rose and walked with him down the hall past a litany of framed portraits to the front door. "Are you certain you can't stay? I could use the company tonight."

Moore caught her gaze, her eyes beseeching. He touched his hand to her cheek. "Another time," he said as he opened the front door. Grabbing his hat from the hook on the wall, he stepped outside, and Emily closed the door behind him.

• • •

From the window, she spotted Moore on the stoop. Her heart leapt with excitement. Rushing to the bombe chest in the entrance hall, she grabbed a few items from the drawer. She applied carmine stain to her lips and cheeks and unfastened the top button on her blouse before splashing violet water on her throat. She checked her appearance in the mirror. With a quick nod of approval, she raced back to the door and glanced out the window again. Moore's hat was on his head, and he had turned to leave.

You are not getting away that quickly, Dr. Moore, Lilith thought, and she swung the door open.

"Randy," she said.

Moore turned to face her.

"You can't leave yet." Lilith stepped toward him and watched as his gaze drifted to her bosom.

Moore moved his eyes to hers. "I really need to get home."

"You and I both know that what you need isn't at home."

Moore shook his head. "I can't—"

Lilith reached out and took his hand. "Yes, you can." She stepped close so he might smell the fragrance of her perfume.

"I can't keep doing this."

"Then why do you keep coming here?"

"I am weak, that is why."

"You love how I make you feel. That is why." She knew she was right. And attending to Emily and her sick children had become his perfect excuse.

"I should go."

Tugging on his arm, she leaned to his ear. "Stay," she whispered, her breath on his neck. "Come inside. I promise it won't take long."

As their eyes met, Lilith sensed his yearning. She pulled him through the doorway. Once inside, Moore took her into his arms and ran his hands down her back to her hips, pulling her to him. Lilith looped her arms around his neck and drew him closer, feeling his growing desire through the fabric of her skirts. Her lips unfurled in a smile as she lifted her face to his.

"This has to be the last time," he said as he put his mouth over hers and kicked the door shut.

CHAPTER 5

SUNDAY, MARCH 31, 1872

"Now, Anne Marie, don't you start," Powell said, in a half-hearted attempt to thwart the badgering from his older sister, who was seated across from him.

Every Sunday, following morning services, the Harrison siblings gathered for the midday dinner at one of their homes. This week, it was Matt's turn to host. Anne Marie and the rest of the Harrison family were scattered in rockers and wicker chairs across the expansive porch of the brick home as their children played in the yard below. Anne Marie was the oldest of the eight Harrison siblings, followed by Matthew, their late brother Edward, and William. Powell was the youngest of the brothers. Powell's sisters—all but Anne Marie—were younger than him.

"I am not starting anything, Poe," Anne Marie said.

The muscles of Powell's jaw tightened. His siblings had compared him to the sullen Edgar Allan Poe for as long as he could remember. While Powell was introverted and often lost in his thoughts, he was hardly morose, and the comparison irked him.

"I simply stated that it is in perfect alignment with the character of someone like Mr. Foster to represent that crazy woman," Anne Marie continued, her mouth drawn as tight as the graying chignon at the top of her head. "The man is a scoundrel!"

"Oh, sister! Mr. Foster is hardly a scoundrel," cried Bettie, the second youngest of Powell's sisters. "Scandalous, yes. Scoundrel, no."

Although neither JW nor Bettie would admit that there was anything beyond friendship between them, Powell had his doubts. He'd caught JW on more than one occasion admiring Bettie's dark wavy locks, her alabaster complexion, and her moon-eyes of forget-me-not blue. And like Anne Marie, Bettie was impetuous and nearly impossible, which partially explained, he thought, why she and her sisters had yet to marry. Another reason might be that no suitor could live up to the standard set by their late father.

"And I wouldn't go so far as to call Mrs. Lloyd crazy," Bettie continued with a dismissive flit of her hand. "She's just a bit odd in her ways, that's all."

"A *bit* odd?" Anne Marie said, turning her head abruptly to the chairs at the far side of the porch where Bettie was sitting. "Everything about that woman is odd!"

"I think Mrs. Lloyd feels awkward around people," offered Corrie, the youngest of the Harrison women. Like Powell, Corrie resembled their mother more than their father, both in personality and appearance, with umber hair, gray eyes, and a heavy brow. Corrie and their late sister, Alice, were the docile members of the sisterhood, and Powell adored them both.

"Awkward?" Anne Marie questioned, clearly annoyed that no one was agreeing with her.

"I don't know if 'awkward' is exactly the right word." Corrie thought for a moment. "Withdrawn, maybe." She shrugged her shoulders. "Like me. I think she's just shy."

"Oh, sister, that woman is nothing like you," Anne Marie said, shaking her head. "You've seen her at church, mumbling to herself half the time. Just look into those eyes and you can tell there's something not right. The devil himself is in that stare of hers."

Powell, too, had been struck by that stare during his interview of Emily Lloyd. Something in her gaze and her antics chafed at him. It wasn't satanic, but something else.

"Oh, for heaven's sake, Anne Marie," Matthew was saying as Powell ruminated. "Mrs. Lloyd is hardly the devil. Though I will grant you that she is a little strange."

"See, Bettie." Anne Marie threw her sister a satisfied smile. "Matthew agrees with me."

Bettie rolled her eyes. "He did not agree. He is only humoring you to shut you up."

"Matt, did she remind you of Alice?" Powell asked, interrupting the brewing spat as he made the connection.

"Our Alice?" Matt asked.

"The way Mrs. Lloyd stared at the floor. And how she rocked herself in the chair. The moodiness. The erratic behavior."

"Now that you mention it, yes, there is a similarity," Matt said.

"And when she snapped at you—that's just the thing Alice would do when her mind returned from wherever it had been."

"Powell Harrison!" Anne Marie said. "Certainly you are not comparing our sister to that mad Lloyd woman."

"Alice *was* mad," Powell said.

"Through no fault of her own," Anne Marie retorted.

"And what if Mrs. Lloyd, through no fault of her own, is also mad?" Powell said. "We all know that Alice and her friend weren't the only ones to suffer at the hands of rogue soldiers. What if what happened to Alice also happened to Mrs. Lloyd?"

Anne Marie shifted in her chair as an awkwardness blanketed the porch. The Harrisons rarely spoke of the event that had led to their sister's breakdown. Or of their father's despotic decision to send her to the lunatic asylum in Staunton.

After a long moment, Corrie broke the silence. "If something similar did happen to Mrs. Lloyd, why kill her children? Wouldn't she kill herself like Alice did?"

"I don't know," Powell said. "But it's a question that I intend to put to Dr. Stribling at the asylum."

"Oh no, you don't!" said Janet, who had been sitting quietly next to Powell on the wicker settee. "Insane or not, you are not defending anyone who murdered her own babies! It's unconscionable!"

"I agree with Janet," said Matthew's wife, Harriette, who was sitting in a rocker opposite the settee. "The whispers and finger-pointing . . ."

"I don't care what others say," Janet said, turning to Powell. "I care about our children. What do I tell my daughter when she asks why Papa isn't at supper? That you're off defending a woman who murdered her Sunday school playmate? And you'll be totally absent from the family. We all know how you and Matthew become when you've got a big trial, disappearing for weeks on end. I can only imagine your obsession with your work on a case with this much notoriety."

Powell moved his arm from the back of the settee to her shoulder and leaned toward her. "I'm not going off anywhere."

"And what about your head, Powell? Can the same be said for where your mind goes?" Her face reddened, and she looked away. Another long silence befell the porch.

"Janet's right," Harriette said at last and turned to her husband. "She and Powell don't need this. And *our* family doesn't need it either. You two need to steer clear of this case and this woman."

"For the love of Pete!" Matt said with a roll of his eyes. "We are not involved."

"Then pray tell, why is my husband sending telegrams off to Richmond and Staunton, asking all these questions on Mrs. Lloyd's behalf?" Janet asked, turning her head to Powell again.

"As I've said, we are simply helping Mr. Foster explore possible theories in the instance that Mrs. Lloyd should need a defense." Powell gave her shoulder a reassuring squeeze. "That's all there is to it, Jan."

"Mr. Foster," Anne Marie huffed under her breath with another shake of her head. "Pa would not approve. And he certainly would not take kindly to you gentlemen *consulting* in the defense of a murderess either."

Powell had hated having to answer to his father when he was alive, and he hated answering to his memory even more. Despite the known consequences of arguing with Anne Marie, he was unable to hold his tongue.

"Might I remind you that, per our father and the law of both the commonwealth and of God Almighty Himself, Mrs. Lloyd is entitled to a presumption of innocence?"

"What law of God presumes her innocent?" Anne Marie asked with indignance.

"John 7:51," Powell replied. "'Doth our law judge any man before it hear him and know what he doeth?'"

A look of satisfaction spread over Anne Marie's face. "That simply means Mrs. Lloyd has a right to tell her side of the story. God doesn't deem her innocent just because she says she is, crazy or not."

"And what about when God chastised those who had made false allegations against Job?" Corrie offered.

"Whose side are you on, sister?" Anne Marie snapped with a cutting glance in Corrie's direction. "And Job *was* innocent."

"I'm on no one's side," Corrie said, a flush erupting on her cheeks. "I just don't believe we should rush to judgment until the truth comes out."

"'Ye shall know the truth, and the truth shall make you free,'" Matt quoted with a chuckle.

Powell shot Matt a look. "And that is all that I am doing," he said, turning his attention back to his sister. "Assisting a colleague in seeking the truth."

CHAPTER 6

It had been gloomy and overcast all day, the dampness of spring seemingly penetrating the walls as Lara sat alone by the fireplace in the parlor, reading the Book of Romans and praying for Lilith.

"'Because the carnal mind is enmity against God,'" she read aloud, and drew a sigh. Lara didn't know exactly where Lilith was or what she did when she wasn't present. While she didn't approve of Lilith's risqué behavior, there was little she could do about it other than pray. Lara had long ago accepted that it was better to let her sister have her way than to deal with her rebellion. One day Lilith would have to answer to God for her actions. All Lara could do was hope that the Lord would somehow have mercy on her sister and save her soul from an eternity of damnation.

A chill settled over the room. Lara glanced up from her reading and saw that the fire had dwindled. Setting the Bible aside, she rose from the rocker to put another log in the fireplace. As she stoked the coals, she noticed how dark the room had become. Dusk's shadows were gathering outside the window as night fell. Lara generally preferred darkness to the illusion of a sunny day, but tonight she felt an ominous unease.

Then she heard it. A wagon with rattling chains on the street. It halted, and all was quiet for a moment. Then boots were thudding on the cobblestones. Closer and closer. A loud knocking. *Is that my door? What has Lilith done!* The knock sounded again. *They're at Emily's door.* She rushed to the window, lifting the lace curtain at its edge.

The jailer's wagon was on the street with a deputy at the reins, and two men were on the front porch, Sheriff Atwell and another deputy. *They've come for her!* She moved from the window and grabbed her shawl, wrapped it around her shoulders, and headed for the door to stop them. Her heart was in her throat when she took the knob in her hand. Another loud knock sounded.

"Mrs. Lloyd. It's Sheriff Atwell. I've got a warrant here, and I need you to open the door."

Lara froze. Should she intervene? And what would she say to the authorities? What could she do? *No! We don't need to get involved. We can always step in, should it come to that.*

Drawing a long breath, she closed her eyes. She heard the door open and Emily's small voice. "How can I help you, Sheriff?"

◆ ◆ ◆

Settled in his favorite armchair at home after spending most of the cold, damp day with Janet's parents, Powell was reading by the fire when JW burst into the sitting room. Startled at the intrusion, Powell looked up from the book and marked his page.

"I knocked and no one answered, so I let myself in," JW explained before Powell had a chance to ask. "Emily Lloyd was taken into custody."

"What?"

"Yep. Sheriff Atwell showed up at my place just after supper and told me that the inquest jury had been reconvened and had issued a warrant for Mrs. Lloyd's arrest. When I got to the jail, Charles Lee was there with Mort Kilgour and the magistrate. The chemical analysis came back. You were right. They found arsenic."

"This is one instance where I wish I had been wrong. You say that Charles Lee was there?" Charles Lee was another prominent Leesburg attorney well-known for assisting in the prosecution of criminal cases.

JW nodded.

"Makes sense," Powell said. "A case this big, Kilgour is going to need the help. And Lee is much better with juries than Kilgour."

"Lee is no match for you. You're the best there is when it comes to charming jurymen." JW brought his eyes to Powell's. "I'm going to need you, Powell."

"I need a drink to have this conversation again," Powell said, setting his book on the side table.

"Make that two," JW said as Powell walked to the Parsons table behind the sofa and removed the top from the decanter. He poured bourbon into two snifters and handed one to JW before returning to his seat.

"Where's the missus?" JW asked, taking the chair on the other side of the fire.

"Lucky for you, she went to bed early."

"She's still mad at me?"

"What do you think?" Powell said with a half laugh and took a sip from the glass. "You know, if you're worried about Charles Lee, you might want to think about reaching out to John Orr. He's a seasoned barrister and has charmed a few juries into seeing things in a different light. And he's got an incredible library as well. He'd be a good choice for second chair."

"Orr?" JW said, shaking his head. "Not a fan."

Powell pulled in his chin with a questioning look.

"Yes, he's nearly as good with juries as you are, but he's arrogant," JW said. "Thinks he knows more than he does."

"That's a bit of pot-and-kettle name-calling coming from you, my friend."

JW laughed and threw back a mouthful of the whiskey.

"Who did the autopsy analysis?" Powell asked.

"A Professor Tonry from some institute over in Baltimore."

Powell furrowed his brow. "Tonry? Name sounds familiar."

"You know him?"

"I think he was the chemist brought in to rescue the prosecution's case in the Wharton trial."

Earlier that year, Baltimore widow Ellen Wharton had been

accused of murder in the poisoning death of her financial adviser and a business investor in a highly publicized trial that became a battle of forensic experts. Because of doubt cast on the chemical analysis, Mrs. Wharton had been acquitted. If Powell's memory served him, a professor named Tonry was one of the chemists who testified at that trial.

"It makes no sense to me. Why wouldn't Kilgour send the postmortem specimens to one of the experts in Richmond?"

"Probably because my cousin is among those experts in Richmond," Powell reminded him.

JW leaned close and lowered his voice. "Do you think they're trying to set Mrs. Lloyd up?"

"What would be Bentley's motive?"

"Did you know that her uncle was one of the town's most outspoken abolitionists? Gave the mayor a heap of trouble before the war."

"Even Bobby Bentley wouldn't hold a grudge that long. And against the man's niece?"

"She's a widow and, in Bentley's eyes, a drain on the town's purse."

"But Mrs. Lloyd is not indigent."

"He could use the opportunity to get at you."

Powell blanched. "To get at me for what?"

"You know his zeal for prosecuting the coloreds. Every time you beat Kilgour and him on one of those cases, you make them look bad to the voters."

"You give me too much credit. And while I don't trust either the mayor or Mort Kilgour as far as I can spit, they aren't so corrupt that they'd prosecute a widow as a vendetta against me. And besides, this is your case, not mine."

With a defeated sigh, JW leaned back in his chair.

"You're going to need chemistry experts to examine that analysis," Powell said. "If you recall the Wharton trial, the prosecution's case came undone once experts began to pick apart the forensics. I'll send a telegram to my cousin in Richmond tomorrow morning if you'd like."

"Please do. I'm going to need a battery of experts, from the looks of it."

Powell took another drink and set the glass on his knee, his eyes studying its contents as he thought.

"JW," Powell said, bringing his gaze up from his glass, "you have to consider the possibility that Bentley got it right. That Mrs. Lloyd is, indeed, responsible for the child's death."

"To your previous question, what would be *her* motive?"

"I'm not certain she needs one if she's delusional."

"Does she seem crazy to you?"

"I'm no more qualified to make that determination than you are. All I know is that if the autopsy results are accurate, which they most likely are, because Tonry won't make the same mistakes that were made in the Wharton analysis, there are only two ways that the child was poisoned—by accident or on purpose. And if it was a deliberate act, only someone with a compromised mind would harm a child."

"And we have an obligation to exhaust other possibilities first."

"Indeed you do. And when you find that I'm right, that she is responsible, the only plausible defense will be an insanity plea."

"Then all the more reason for you to defend her."

"I've told you—"

"No one has the experience you do arguing insanity cases," JW said, cutting him off. "How many times did you defend the asylum down there in Staunton to keep those lunatics locked up? And how many petitions did you file for those who'd recovered to be released? Dozens?"

Powell shrugged his shoulders. "More than I can remember."

"If she's insane, all the more reason why I need you. And why Mrs. Lloyd needs you."

Powell stared again into the glass resting on his knee. "I promised Janet I would not get involved."

"What about your obligation to God?" JW said. "You're always saying it's your moral duty to defend those in need."

"Mrs. Lloyd has no want for charity."

"Powell, she's defenseless—just as defenseless as those Negroes you're always representing. And she's alone. She has no man to take up her cause. She needs us. She needs you."

"There are other attorneys who have successfully put on an insanity defense. You should reconsider approaching Orr."

"What if Emily Lloyd were one of your sisters? What if she were

Alice? Would you want John Orr before the jury arguing for her life . . . or Powell Harrison?"

"My sister Alice harmed no one but herself!" Powell said testily.

"My apologies. My intent was not to speak ill of your sister. But you and I both know that if Emily Lloyd did kill those children, she's insane and cannot be held responsible. Why would she be any less worthy of a defense than your sister or mine?"

Powell drew a long sigh. "I need to think about it."

"You don't have a lot of time. The arraignment is Monday morning."

Powell moved his gaze to JW's pleading eyes. "If I do agree to do this, I'd need to be lead counsel."

"Agreed."

"Before I make any decision, I'll want to interview Mrs. Lloyd again."

A broad smile broke across JW's face. "I'll meet you at the jail tomorrow."

CHAPTER 7

SUNDAY, APRIL 21, 1872

"She's in the first one on the right." The sheriff's deputy waved his hand in the direction of the door behind him. "Y'all need me to let you in the cell?"

"That would be most helpful, Freddie," Powell said with a polite smile.

Freddie Roberts pushed back from the desk and stood from the chair. He was shorter than Powell with a mass of blond curls, round blue eyes, and a childlike face. One might mistake him for a boy if it weren't for the silver star pinned to his lapel indicating that he was a sheriff's deputy. With a ring of keys in his hand and a revolver in a holster on his hip, Freddie escorted Powell and JW into a narrow corridor that led to the cellblock. The corridor was dimly lit, its brick walls covered in black soot from the lanterns that hung along the way and the old iron stoves that burned at each end of the passage.

Emily Lloyd was standing at the window of her cell with her back to them, wearing a black dress, staring at a row of sheds across the jail yard that had been used to detain runaway slaves years before. They now sat vacant, dilapidated, and decaying under a tangle of vines.

"Mrs. Lloyd," Freddie said, keys jangling. "Your lawyers are here to see you."

Emily startled, turning abruptly, her face drawn and tired. Dark circles under red puffy eyes told Powell that she had cried most of the night.

"Mr. Foster. Mr. Harrison," she said, her voice breaking as she rushed toward them. "Please, you have to help me. Please."

"Stand back, Mrs. Lloyd," Freddie warned as the cylinders turned, releasing the lock. Emily stopped where she stood. "Just step aside while I let these gentlemen in." Emily brought her hands in front of her, wringing them together as she waited.

"Grab yourselves a chair there, and I'll close you gentlemen in with the lady," Freddie said as he held the barred door from fully opening.

JW picked up one of the ladderback chairs that were sitting along the corridor wall. Powell picked up a second chair and followed JW into the cell.

Freddie closed the iron door behind them and, with a rattle of keys, locked the attorneys in the cell with Emily. "I'll leave the door to the block open, and y'all can just holler for me when you're through."

"Mr. Harrison, I—"

Powell raised his palm to interrupt her, and nodded in Freddie's direction.

Emily waited until the deputy had passed through the outer door, then lowered her voice to a near whisper. "Mr. Harrison, I don't understand what is happening." Her eyes darted nervously toward the corridor. "Maud is dead, my last child, my only reason for living. I don't know that I even want to go on, and I don't care what happens to me, but I have not done any of what they said. None of it! I love my babies. I would never hurt them. Never!" Tears welled in the corners of her eyes.

"Mrs. Lloyd, let's sit, shall we?" Powell extended an arm toward the chair that he had brought in from the hall, and Emily sat.

"How are they treating you?" JW asked, taking a seat.

Emily's eyes darted around the cell. "Why, I don't know. How are they supposed to treat a lady in prison? It's cold in here at present, isn't it?" She shuddered as she crossed her arms. "And I shouldn't be here!"

"I understand," JW said, "and I will do everything in my power to convince the judge to release you tomorrow. But we must ask you some questions."

"Questions! Questions! All you men have is questions and more questions!"

"I can understand your frustration, but it's important that we get to the truth," JW said.

"I didn't kill my baby."

"Our problem is," Powell said, "that the sheriff says the analysis from the autopsy shows that your daughter consumed arsenic, and that is what most likely caused her death."

"There must be some mistake. Dr. Moore said it was congestion of the stomach. How could she have died from arsenic?"

Powell softened his tone. "The inquest jury believes that it was you who administered the arsenic."

"On my word, Mr. Harrison, I did not poison my child." There was desperation in her voice.

"Could she have consumed it by accident?" Powell asked. "Might Maud have mistaken arsenic for sugar or candy? Or might you have confused it with medicine and administered it unknowingly?"

"No. It's not possible."

"Have you ever purchased arsenic?" JW asked. "Tainted bait with it to kill rodents?"

"No. I would be too afraid to use something like that around the children."

"What about someone else?" Powell suggested. "Maybe someone who came to visit brought poison into the house?"

Emily shook her head.

"What about Miss Lozenburg?" JW asked.

Emily straightened in the chair, narrowing her eyes at JW. "Delphi? Hurt Maud? Heavens no!"

Powell took in another long breath as he carefully formed the wording of his next question. "So here is our dilemma. If there was no poison in the house that Maud could have mistakenly eaten and if there was no visitor who could have harmed her, then how do we explain the presence of arsenic in her stomach?"

Emily looked at him, her eyes staring at him blankly, her eyelids fluttering.

"Mrs. Lloyd . . . ," Powell said, unsure if she had understood him.

"It would not be someone who wished *Maud* harm, but someone who wished *me* harm," she said, her eyes widening. "Yes, yes, that has to be it. Someone who would benefit from hurting the mother by hurting her child!"

"Who?" Powell asked. "Who might that be?"

Emily moved her gaze to the floor, searching the cobblestones with her eyes. She jerked her head up and looked directly at Powell. "Billy Ray Lloyd! Charlie's brother!"

"Your brother-in-law?"

Emily sprung to her feet. "He is a hateful man, he is!" She rubbed her hands over the front of her skirt and began pacing in front of them. "He brought milk the day before Maud got sick." She turned abruptly toward them. "My God, Mr. Harrison, Billy Ray Lloyd killed Maudie!"

She brought her hand to her mouth to keep the sobs at bay.

Powell and JW stood. Powell put a hand on her back to comfort her. "It's all right, Mrs. Lloyd," he said. "Just try to stay calm."

Emily closed her eyes momentarily and nodded.

"Now, let's sit back down," Powell said.

With her hand still at her mouth, she drew a long breath of air through her nostrils before nodding again. The two attorneys helped her to her chair and waited until she regained her composure.

"This Mr. Lloyd," Powell said after Emily had calmed. "I assume his given name is William?"

Emily nodded.

"He delivers milk to you?"

"No. Not regularly. His wife makes him bring some to us every now and again."

"And Maud drank this milk?" Powell asked.

Emily nodded again.

"Did you drink the milk?"

Emily furrowed her brow in thought and shook her head. "No . . . I think only Maud had the milk." She brought her hand to her mouth again. "I gave it to her all weekend with lime water and bismuth as Dr. Moore prescribed." Her eyes searched their faces as tears welled again. "Oh my God! I gave it to her! I poisoned her!" The tears gave way and she broke down in sobs again. Both Powell and JW went to her side.

"It isn't your fault, Mrs. Lloyd," JW said as he offered her his handkerchief, pulling his chair next to hers and taking a seat. "And if Mr. Lloyd did taint the milk, he'll be brought to justice."

"How will you do that?" she asked between sobs as she took the cloth.

"We'll speak with him and get to the bottom of it," JW said, placing his hand on her shoulder.

"We need to discuss tomorrow's proceedings," Powell said after a long moment. Emily sniffled and looked up at him.

"In the morning, you'll be brought before the judge for your initial pleading. Once the court is called into session, Mr. Kilgour will read aloud the complaint. Although the charges against you are serious, they are only allegations at this point. No matter how upsetting, you must not say anything while the charges are being read. Only when the judge asks you 'how do you plead' will you speak. Your answer will be 'not guilty.' If the judge asks you a question directly, you must listen very carefully and answer only what was asked and nothing more. And it is of utmost importance that you answer him honestly. You will do that, yes?"

Emily acknowledged Powell's instructions with a nod.

"And should Mr. Kilgour ask you a question, you are not to answer. Mr. Foster will answer his questions, not you. Do you understand?"

"Yes."

JW offered an encouraging smile. "Not to worry, Mrs. Lloyd. We'll see you through this."

Blinking back tears, Emily nodded again.

The bells of the courthouse clock interrupted the stillness in the cellblock, their chiming clamoring through barred windows and resounding over stone and brick. After the fourth chime, the bells silenced. Powell pulled his watch from his vest and confirmed the time.

"We must leave now," Powell said and turned toward the door that led to the corridor.

"Deputy Roberts," he called. "We're done here."

He looked back at Emily as the jailer arrived at the cell door. "We will see you on the morrow."

◆ ◆ ◆

"You know, she's not a bad-looking woman," JW said as the two stepped onto the street into the crisp April air.

"Oh, for God's sakes, Jay," Powell said with a scowl.

"I mean, look at her. Her face is handsome enough, and she still has a figure even after all those children. If she held herself with a little more confidence—she might be attractive."

Powell shot JW a disapproving look. They walked together in silence toward the center of town.

The town of Leesburg was laid out in a grid with the main thoroughfare, King Street, running north and south, and its two other major streets, Market and Loudoun, running east and west. The jail sat on the corner of Church and Market Streets to the east of the town's center, behind the courthouse and across from the old Episcopal church. Powell lived on the opposite end of Market on a side street not far from Dr. Moore's home, while JW lived on north King Street with his mother in a beautiful brick manor next door to Matthew's stately townhome. The lawyers lived in the more affluent neighborhoods of town, with carriage houses and stables at the back of their lots. Mrs. Lloyd's home, on the other hand, sat at the edge of the town's Black community on the far west end of Loudoun Street, where, after the war, many of Leesburg's poor had taken up residence.

"I'm surprised your wife let you out on a Sunday," JW said as they reached the intersection of King and Market.

"My sisters joined us for dinner and are keeping her entertained."

"They overnighting with you?"

"Not this time," Powell said, waiting for a coach pulled by twin bays to turn at the intersection before crossing the street. "Anne Marie wants to get back before nightfall."

JW nodded west in the direction of Powell's house. "You heading home?"

"I think I might walk over to the Lloyd place. If the door is unlatched, I want to take a closer look at that kitchen of hers to investigate any potential 'accident' theories."

"Mind if I tag along?"

Powell smiled. "Not at all."

The pair headed south on the main street of town, then turned west to the double house on Loudoun Street. As they stepped onto

Emily Lloyd's front porch, Powell's eyes were caught by a woman wearing a white skirt in the yard of the house three doors down.

JW turned the knob of Emily's front door. "We need to talk with Mrs. Lloyd about locking her doors," he said, diverting Powell's attention from the house down the street where Maggie Greene lived alone.

"I suppose locking up was the last thing on her mind when the deputies showed up last night," Powell said. He looked at the second front door, the one on the left. "Who lives on this side of the house?"

"A pair of spinsters."

"Do the spinsters have names?"

"I don't know them, but I can find out."

"You need to know everything about her neighbors, JW. Especially ones living in such close proximity." Powell gave JW a sharp look. While JW was skilled at charming judges and juries, attention to detail wasn't his strength.

"Understood," JW said as he pushed the door open. Powell followed him into the house.

Although the afternoon sun was low and bright in the sky, the house was dark. When the front door opened, sunshine flooded the foyer, corridor, and stairs, illuminating portraits of children on the walls. In the center of the grouping was a large, framed silver gelatin print of an attractive woman and two little girls. The girls were dressed identically in muslin dresses trimmed in dark ribbons with lacy bloomers showing under the hemlines of their skirts. Bows tied at the top of their heads held curly blonde locks from their cherubic faces. As Powell scrutinized the photograph, it took him a minute to recognize the woman. The well-groomed woman in the portrait barely resembled the Emily Lloyd he knew. In the photograph, her hair was piled in a loose coiffure at her crown with curled ringlets resting on the shoulders of her dark, high-collared dress. A cameo on a velvet ribbon was tied around her neck. Her catlike eyes were staring over the heads of her daughters, who were looking directly forward. Powell studied the portrait while JW opened the curtains in the parlor.

"Pretty little girls, they were," Powell said as JW joined him in the hall.

"The boys were handsome as well," JW said.

Powell's eyes followed JW's to the opposite wall. It was a portrait of two boys, the younger seated in a willow chair wearing a checked ensemble of a tunic over a matching velvet skirt. His hair was poker-straight and blond with bangs cut just above his brow. A lace collar spread over his shoulders. And his eyes—they were the same as his mother's. The older son was dark in complexion, his hair wavy and cropped above his ears. Holding a stick and iron ring in his left hand, he stood proud in a short woolen coat, matching knickerbockers, and leather boots. Powell guessed their ages at seven and nine, thereabouts.

"Do you see any of the entire family?" JW asked.

Powell scanned the photographs on the walls as he walked down the corridor. At the end of the long hall near the turn toward the kitchen, he spotted a small tin portrait of a man with a grin reclining in an overstuffed upholstered chair with two boys standing on either side and a baby girl on his knee. An expressionless woman in a plain dress stood behind them. Powell recognized the man's receding hair-line, bushy sideburns, and long, distinctive nose. The man was Charles Lloyd. There were no smiles on the children's faces. They were young in this portrait, and their clothing clearly not as fine as their attire in the later portraits.

"Here's one," Powell said, nodding his head in the direction of the framed tin on the wall.

"Ah," JW said, joining Powell and stepping to get a closer look. "Where's little Maud?"

"Probably not yet born," Powell surmised, his eyes fixed on the somber tableau, bothered by something in the children's expressions. "Come on, Jay. Let's take a look at the kitchen."

"What are we looking for?"

"Poison, medications, anything that might have caused the child's death. Whatever we find, we'll send it off to Richmond for analysis."

The pair continued down the corridor into the kitchen. For such a small house, the kitchen was larger than Powell expected, accommodating a long oak table and six chairs. A new Michigan stove, adorned with an angel cast in nickel on its door, stood against the shared wall of the double house. Powell opened a cupboard. Jars of canned peaches and beans were lined on the shelf. No sign of medications. He closed the door and scanned the room. There was nothing on the table or on the open shelves other than neatly stacked china and glassware.

He noticed a crack between the baseboard and floor under the window and walked over to investigate. In the corner to the left-hand side, there was a small hole on the interior wall. And mouse droppings.

"She's definitely got mice," Powell said.

"Yeah," JW replied, lifting the tablecloth and peering at the floor below. "Evidence of rodents here, too."

"Rats?" Powell asked, moving to the window and pushing the lace curtain aside to look outside.

"And how would I know if it belonged to a rat or a mouse?"

"One's bigger than the other."

"Really, Powell. I know that much."

"That goes for their droppings, too," Powell said, his expression unmoved, eyes scanning the greening backyard.

"You are assuming, my friend, that I have some frame of reference."

Powell turned from the window to look at JW. "You can't tell me that you spent nearly three years in Yankee prison camps and never saw a rat."

"Well, you got me there!" JW laughed. "More vermin than you can imagine! And not all of them with four legs and tails!" He bent lower, examining the floor. "Looks like mice to me. Best way to check for rats is the yard. They tunnel in, you know."

"You seem to be an expert after all," Powell teased. "Why don't you check the backyard while I have a look around upstairs."

JW opened the door leading outside as Powell headed down the hall to the stairs. Once on the second floor, Powell made his way to the bedroom that faced the street.

Pushing open the door, he entered Emily's chamber. The furnishings were sparse. A medallion-patterned quilt of cream, brown, and red overlaid the bed, and the walls were covered in yellowed damask paper of similar colors. A nickel lamp sat on a table beside a rocking chair. A carved wooden crucifix hung on the wall behind. As Powell opened the drawers of a chest, he was surprised by how few items they contained. Had he not known otherwise, he'd have thought the room was the guest chamber. A door on the far right side of the room caught his eye. He was impressed that a house this small, especially a twin, would have such a luxury. He opened the closet door. A number of cotton dresses hung on the rack with boots and slippers paired on the floor beneath them. Behind the clothing he noticed a panel papered in the same damask as the walls. He pushed the garments to the side and saw that it was a frameless door about four feet high and two feet wide. Powell bent to his knees to have a closer look. It was, indeed, a secret door. He pushed on it, but it wouldn't release. Secret rooms were built during the war as hiding places for runaways and for young women and children to take refuge during raids. Running his hand along the panel's edge, he located a keyhole near the top. He stood, looking around for the key, and put his hand to the shelf above. Nothing. With a knuckle, he rapped on the door. From the hollowness of the sound, he was sure there was a space on the other side. Powell walked back into the bedroom and checked the chest of drawers and the little drawer of the table for a key. Again, he found nothing. With no way to unlock the panel, he arranged the dresses as they were, closed the closet door, and made a mental note to ask Mrs. Lloyd about it. Finding nothing else of interest in her chamber or in the other two bedrooms, Powell headed downstairs to meet JW in the yard.

"Over here," JW called from the fence line adjacent to the neighboring property at the back of the lot. "Looks like a couple of dead chickens." In a pile of compost were the decaying bodies of feathered birds.

"Mrs. Lloyd didn't raise chickens." Powell eyed the chicken coop in the neighbor's yard. "Must have belonged to the neighbors."

"Seems like a waste of meat."

"Perhaps they were diseased or something."

"Why toss them onto the Lloyd lot?" JW questioned.

Powell shrugged his shoulders.

Finding little else, they headed toward the street. From the shadows of the narrow passage along the side of the house, Maggie Greene, wearing a white dress with a straw hat tied under her chin, emerged in front of them.

"What on earth are the two of you doing here on the Sabbath?" she said.

"Mrs. Greene," JW greeted, tipping his hat.

Powell tipped his hat as well and nodded.

"You know they showed up here yesterday at nightfall and just took her away," Maggie said with anger in her eyes. "Poor thing hadn't had supper yet. And they had given her nothing of substance other than a little tea when I stopped by this morning to visit her." She shook her head at JW. "It's not right."

"Powell and I are going to do everything in our power to get her out of jail until the trial," JW said.

Maggie looked at Powell. "You need to tell the judge that jail is no place for a woman. She'll die in that wretched hole!"

"I'll do my best," Powell said, and for an instant, he let himself notice the deep green of her eyes under the brim of the hat.

"Perhaps you can help us," JW said.

"Anything," Maggie said with a shiver and crossed her arms even tighter. The sun had dipped behind the roof of the neighboring house, and a cold shade had fallen over the yard.

"Why don't we go inside before you catch a chill," JW said, motioning toward the back door of the Lloyd house. "There's a couple things I'd like to ask you."

"Why don't we go to my house. There's fire in the stove, and I can put on a pot of coffee."

"Works for me," JW said, with a hand at the small of her back.

As Maggie and JW started toward the street, Powell glanced at the sun sinking near the horizon. *Five o'clock or thereabouts,* he thought and pulled his watch from his vest to check. *Four forty-five.*

JW turned as Powell put the watch back in his pocket. "Are you coming?"

His sisters wouldn't head back to the farm until five thirty at the earliest. He had time.

"Just a quick coffee, and then I need to get home."

"Well, come on, then," JW said, turning toward the street. Powell followed them through the narrow passage to the stone house three doors down.

◆ ◆ ◆

"Do you know if Mrs. Lloyd has any family?" Powell asked as Maggie poured coffee for the three of them.

"She was orphaned, you know," Maggie said as she filled Powell's mug. "And the aunt who raised her passed away a few years back."

"Do you know William Lloyd, Mrs. Lloyd's brother-in-law?" Powell asked, cupping the mug and resting his hands on the table.

"Billy Ray? I've seen him around town sometimes and over at Emily's. Wild eyes and an ugly scar. A good-for-nothing, like Charlie Lloyd. Mean. Beats his wife."

"Did Charles Lloyd beat Emily?" Powell asked.

Maggie lifted the mug to her mouth and blew across the rim before taking a drink. "I heard that he would strike her when he didn't get his way. And he beat the boys. Especially the older son."

"And the girls?"

"I can't imagine he would have struck Annie, as she was just an infant. Charlie died before Maud was born. But I know how brutes like Charlie Lloyd treat their daughters. Eventually they tire of molesting their wives and move on to the girls."

Powell glanced at the floor, knowing Maggie spoke from experience. "Did Charlie abuse Emily in that manner?"

"You mean, did he take liberties against her will?" Maggie asked.

Powell nodded.

"Whenever the pig felt like it. He'd come home full of liquor, grab her by the hair, and drag her up the stairs. And smack her around if she refused him."

"Emily told you this?" Powell asked in disbelief.

"Emily never spoke of it, but I heard it from Delphi. And there was the backyard incident a number of years ago. Before you moved back. JW knows about it."

Powell looked at JW.

"I don't recall the specifics," JW said.

"I wasn't witness to it, but her friend Mollie Ryan was," Maggie continued. "She said that Charlie had Emily pinned to the ground behind their house. Emily was kicking and screaming bloody murder, trying to get away from him. Had her by the throat, he did, and nearly choked the lifeblood from her. And I hear all of this happened in front of the two boys."

Powell shook his head at the thought of Emily's young sons witnessing the assault of their mother at the hands of their father.

"Did anyone inform the sheriff?" Powell asked.

"Her neighbor Colonel Nixon made a complaint. Sheriff Atwell made an investigation, but there was nothing he could do. Charlie was her husband. It was his right, they said."

"There's nothing right about it," Powell said.

"This William Lloyd, what's his relationship with Emily?" JW interjected.

"He blames Emily for Charlie's death. And the death of their mother."

"Their mother?" Powell asked. This was a rumor that hadn't made its way around town.

"Anne Lloyd, I think her name was. It was Thanksgiving. The whole family—Billy Ray, his wife and kids, and the mother—had been over to Emily and Charlie's for dinner. The old woman died a couple days later. Charlie said it was Emily's cooking that killed her. Not sure if he meant it as a joke or not, but a few weeks later when Charlie got sick, Billy Ray accused Emily of poisoning them both."

"Is there any merit to the claim?" Powell asked.

"Of course not," Maggie said with a spark of annoyance. "The woman was in poor health. A drunkard as well. And as for Charlie— I'm betting the Good Lord decided it was time to send him to meet his fate. And you can bet it ain't in heaven."

Resisting the urge to correct her poor speech, Powell remembered all the hours during their courtship he had spent teaching her etiquette and proper English. *Why?* he asked himself, wondering whether he had done it more for himself than for her.

"What about her neighbors?" Powell asked.

"There's Colonel Nixon across the street. Mr. Slack and his wife on the right. The Ryans in the house on the left. But Emily doesn't socialize with them. She keeps to herself mostly."

"She lives in a twin," Powell said. "Who lives on the other side of the house?"

"A pair of sisters rent it, but they're hardly ever there."

"Do you know them?"

"I've never been introduced," Maggie replied, fiddling with her hair. "Emily talks about the older one. Lara, I believe, is her name. I don't recall the name of the younger one."

"You've lived on the same street all this time and have never met them?" Powell asked.

She shrugged her shoulders. "They're never at home, and when they are, they don't seem to venture out."

"Surname of these sisters?"

Maggie shook her head. "You'll have to ask Emily."

"What about enemies?" JW asked.

"Emily?" Maggie said. "Not what I would call enemies. She doesn't care much for Sam Orrison."

She crossed her legs and sat back, resting her hands in her lap.

Powell studied her. "Orrison was the guardian of her children, correct?"

"Yes," Maggie replied. "And executor of Charlie's estate. When he bought Charlie's tavern, Emily questioned the transaction, convinced he'd sold it to himself at a bargain. I know they had words."

"Did Emily take any action against Mr. Orrison?" Powell asked.

"She threatened to sue him. And before things got real ugly, Sam found religion and paid her more."

"Everything that she was asking?"

"I wouldn't know. But whatever their terms, it certainly left a sour taste in Sam's mouth. The mayor's, too. He called Emily out when she filed for Charlie's pension. Said she had no need. Only greed, were his words."

A clock on a shelf began to chime. Powell looked up. It was six o'clock. Janet would be furious.

"Late for supper?" Maggie asked, following his gaze to the clock.

"As a matter of fact, yes. I really must go." He pushed himself from the table and stood.

JW and Maggie stood with him.

"I should be heading out as well," JW said. "I've offered to walk a young lady to the seven-o'clock service this evening and would not wish to disappoint her."

"What is this I'm hearing?" Maggie said with an exaggerated look. "JW Foster is attending church services?"

"That is not what I said," JW replied with a sly grin. "I said that I was walking her *to* church. That does not mean that I'm going *in* the church."

"Oh, for heaven's sake, sir! I think the lady will expect you to attend the service with her if you are escorting her there."

"We'll see about that," JW said. "But I wouldn't hold my breath!"

"I've learned not to," Maggie said with a laugh.

She walked with JW and Powell to the foyer. Powell took his hat from the rack and turned to her as she opened the door.

"Thank you for the coffee, Mrs. Greene," Powell said, his eyes catching hers.

"I'm happy to do whatever I can to help," she said. "And for Emily's sake, I pray that you will do the same."

◆ ◆ ◆

Powell rushed through backstreets to get home before his sisters left for Morrisworth, unable to take his mind off the case. *No one in their right mind would poison a little girl to settle a score.*

As he dashed into the alley that cut to the main street, angry voices flew from the shadows up ahead. Nearing the backyard of the Orrison house, the voices were louder. He looked over the fence and to the house. Through the window, he saw a woman with one hand on her hip and the other pointing, shouting at a red-faced man. The man roared back, his expression contorted and filled with rage. The woman waved her index finger at him. Seizing her wrist, the man twisted her arm. She fell to her knees with a cry and tried to pull away. The man raised an opened hand and brought it violently across her face. The woman cried out again.

Adrenaline flooded Powell, and he bolted toward the house. He hopped the fence and raced across the yard, not stopping to pick up his hat as it fell from his head. The man struck the woman again. She was on her knees on the kitchen floor with her free arm shielding her face from the blows of his fist when Powell pounded on the door. The door flew open, and Sam Orrison, reeking of whiskey, glowered at Powell.

"What the hell do you want!"

"Do not strike her again!" Powell demanded, stepping forward.

"What I do with my woman in my own house is none of your business."

"As an officer of the court, it is every bit my business. It's a crime in this state to take your fists to your wife."

"Then I'll just cut me a switch," Orrison said as he grabbed the waistband of his trousers and adjusted them higher on his hips, his eyes challenging.

Of no mind to explain that Virginia had also banned the doctrine permitting husbands to whip their wives with sticks no greater than the circumference of a man's thumb, Powell glowered back. "By God, if you hit her again, I'll have Sheriff Atwell arrest you."

"And charge me with what? Chastising my wife?"

"That and attempted murder. With a good attorney, maybe you'll get the charges dropped to aggravated assault. Either way, it's trouble you don't want."

"Good luck with that, Counsellor. Bentley will see to it that it all goes away."

"Perhaps, but not until you spend a night in jail."

Orrison glared.

"Mrs. Orrison," Powell called, his eyes meeting her husband's glower. "Go on up to your chamber, if you please, and lock your door. Your husband will have sobered up by morning."

From the corner of his eye, Powell watched her leave the room. "Give it a rest, Sam."

"Get off my porch."

Powell held the man's stare for a long moment before straightening his shoulders and stepping back. With a lift of his chin and one final piercing look, he turned and stepped from the porch. Orrison remained in the doorway, watching as Powell crossed the lawn to retrieve his hat.

As he left through the gate, Powell looked back. Orrison had closed the door and was in the kitchen, leaning against the table on straightened arms, his head hung low between his shoulders, his eyes cast to the floor.

A movement from the upper floor caught Powell's attention. It was Mrs. Orrison, watching Powell from an upstairs window. Nodding in her direction, he placed his hat on his head and continued on his way home. Any possibility of getting there in time for supper had long since passed.

"What I do with my woman in my own house is none of your business."

Powell's thoughts moved to the day long ago when he had first seen welts on Maggie's arms and a bruise on her cheek. Bile had erupted in him then as it had tonight. *And at the hands of her own father!* Where was God? And what about justice? Wasn't that Kilgour's job? Kilgour, who didn't care about truth. Or protecting the weak.

He rubbed his hand over his brow as he reached the town's main street. *Emily Lloyd.* He couldn't shake her from his head. Abused by her husband. Her daughter's body not yet cold when it was desecrated in front of her. *Nobody has ever stood up for that woman.*

If there had been any lingering uncertainty in his mind about whether he should take the case, it was now gone. The only doubt was what plea he would make at Emily Lloyd's arraignment in the morning: not guilty or not guilty by reason of insanity.

◆ ◆ ◆

"You gave me your word that you were only consulting," Janet said, standing in the center of the parlor, her arms crossed over her chest and face reddening.

"I know, darling, and I'm sorry to break my promise, but I have no choice," Powell said, reaching for her.

Janet shrugged from his touch. "You indeed have a choice. You simply decline Mr. Foster's request."

"JW does not have the experience to mount an insanity defense."

"His lack of experience isn't your problem," she argued.

"But it is," Powell said as his eyes pleaded. "The burden of proof shifts to the defense in an insanity case. Law schools don't teach that well. The jury knows up front that the defendant committed the crime. And it is the defense's job not only to prove that the defendant is insane but to convince the jury that an insane person can't be guilty of the crime. It's counterintuitive—that a person responsible for committing a heinous act is, in fact, legally not responsible. JW will need to convince the jury that Emily deserves more sympathy than the child and absolve the jurymen of any burden on their conscience for ruling that way. It takes experience, building rapport with the jurymen, earning their trust. That's the job of a lead attorney, not a consultant. As a consultant, I can only advise so much."

Janet shook her head. "It's too distracting, Powell. It will consume all your time and your attention."

"I promise I will not allow it to disrupt our family."

Her mouth tightened. She gave him a hard look. "Do not make promises you cannot keep."

"I understand your concern, Janet. I do. But Mrs. Lloyd will not have a fair trial unless I step in as lead counsel."

"That's what you always say—that so-and-so won't get a fair trial." She shook her head again. "You are not the only attorney in the county."

"I'm the only attorney in the county with experience successfully defending an insanity plea." Janet narrowed her eyes and glared at him before turning to the window.

Powell stepped behind her and placed a hand on her shoulder. "Jan, they will hang her if she's found guilty."

"And what about how your distraction will affect our lives?" she said, spinning to face him. "And the lives of our girls?"

"I promise that I will not allow it to interfere."

She glared at him, her brow stitched. "Like last summer?"

Her words struck like the blow of a fist. He dropped his gaze to the floor. "I will never forgive myself." A painful silence fell between them, amplifying with each monotonous tick of the room's grandfather clock. After a long minute, Powell lifted his head and looked at her. Janet was staring out the window again, her lips tight over her teeth. "A woman's life is at stake. I cannot have that on my conscience, too."

"You cannot represent this woman," Janet said.

"Janet—"

"You are not being fair to me."

Powell felt his body tense as his composure snapped. "It's you who is unfair," he shouted, the vein on his temple twitching.

She glowered at him, her nostrils flaring as she drew a noisy breath before pushing past him to the doorway. Powell watched her leave the room and listened as she stomped up the stairs. With the echoing slam of her chamber door, he turned, running his fingers through his hair before walking to the window. He stood before the paned glass and stared out into the night. Darkness had blanketed the street, with only the amber glow of the gaslight on the corner piercing the pitch-blackness. Leaning on straight arms against the sill, Powell forced his breathing to slow, lowered his head, and closed his eyes.

It had been hot that Sunday last July, and the exterior doors had been opened to allow what little air stirred outside to waft into the house. After church services, Janet and the girls had gone to Morrisworth for the afternoon, while Powell had returned home with their three-year-old son, Bo, who hadn't been feeling well. Janet had suggested they all return home together, but Powell had been insistent she go with his sisters. He had a big trial starting that coming week and could use the time to work on his opening statement, he had explained. He remembered the skeptical look on his wife's face before she acquiesced. "Keep a close eye on him," she had said.

Since the servants didn't work on the Sabbath, Powell and Bo had the house to themselves. Upon their arrival home, Powell put the child down for a nap before setting to work in his study. Engrossed in writing his argument, hours had passed before he looked at his watch and left his desk to check on his son.

Powell choked back a sob as he relived the moment. His panic when he saw the child's empty crib. His desperation as he searched the house, calling his son's name. His fear when he saw the opened springhouse door. His horror when he discovered his son's body floating face down alongside his favorite toy, the wooden sailboat Powell had given him a few weeks before.

Powell drew a long, deep breath to quell the guilt that knotted his gut and the grief that serrated his heart. He still didn't know who'd left the high latch of the springhouse door unfastened. Or how the child had climbed over the railing of his crib and walked past the study without his notice. None of those details mattered. God had failed him. And he knew who was to blame.

Opening his eyes, he lifted his head and stared back into the darkness. Regardless of what Janet believed, he knew that he would never—could never—allow himself to be so distracted again. There was nothing he could do to bring Bo back. But he could keep other lives from being snuffed out too soon. From being wrongly sacrificed in the name of justice.

Powell did not believe in the death penalty. Judges and juries were too steeped in their own biases to make those kinds of judgments. It was up to him and honest men like him to defend the innocent and those too weak to defend themselves.

CHAPTER 8

MONDAY, APRIL 22, 1872

Powell pressed through the crowd in the courtyard to the doors of the courthouse. It was unusual for him to be late. After the argument with Janet, he had tossed and turned most of the night and had overslept as a result. The clock tower bells were chiming the ten-o'clock hour when Powell entered the courtroom. JW was already seated at the defense table, and Mort Kilgour and Charles Lee were across the aisle. Men and women were gathered in the center corridor, making it difficult for him to pass. As he reached the gate at the front of the gallery, a hand grabbed his arm. Powell turned to find Dr. Thomas Edwards, his sister-in-law's father.

"Powell," Edwards said with a look of surprise. "Are you defending the Lloyd widow?"

"As of last night, yes."

Edwards narrowed his eyes. "Then we need to talk."

"I can't right now. The judge will be announced at any moment."

"You need to hear what I have to say." Edwards glanced in the direction of Kilgour. "I don't want you to be caught off guard." There was concern on Edwards's face.

"What is it?"

With the courtroom crowd at his back, Edwards leaned close to Powell and lowered his voice. "I was called before the inquest jury on Saturday to validate the medical treatment the Lloyd child received. A simple professional courtesy." He glanced quickly at Kilgour before looking back at Powell. "At the end of my testimony, Mort asked if my pharmacy ever sold Mrs. Lloyd arsenic. I told him not to my knowledge. He asked if I recorded arsenic sales, and I said that of course I did, as it was required by law to do so. He then asked if I would consult those records and confirm my testimony that no arsenic had been sold to Mrs. Lloyd. I agreed but said it would have to wait until this morning, as I do not labor on the Sabbath. So this morning when I arrived at the store, Atwell and Bentley had already come and gone. They had asked my clerk to show them the ledger." Edwards licked his bottom lip as he leaned closer. "Powell, Mrs. Lloyd purchased arsenic from my pharmacy on February 8. Just days before the older daughter became ill and died."

Powell's thumb found the inside of his ring, his hands tingling. Edwards's revelation validated both his instincts: that Emily had had a hand in her children's deaths and that JW's investigative work was sloppy.

The rumbling murmur of the crowd in the gallery quieted as their attention moved to the front of the room. Powell and Edwards followed their gaze to the defendant box. Sheriff Atwell had entered the room with Emily Lloyd, who was heavily veiled and dressed entirely in black. The sheriff escorted Emily to the dock and helped her step onto the platform and into the chair before closing her in. Powell looked back at Edwards and extended his hand.

"Thanks, Thomas. We'll talk more after court."

Nodding, Edwards shook Powell's hand and then took a seat in the front row behind the prosecution's table. Powell joined JW at the defense table.

"Where have you been?" JW asked as relief spread over his face.

"We have a development," Powell said. Unbuckling his satchel, Powell took out his notes and moved the case to the floor. He looked at JW with a seriousness that creased his brow. "She bought arsenic."

JW's eyes darted in confusion. "Emily? When?"

Powell gave a quick nod. "In February, just before the other daughter perished."

"Jesus!" JW swore under his breath.

"You should have caught this before Kilgour did."

"I didn't think—"

"You have to be thinking all the time."

"I know. You're right. It won't happen again."

"All rise," announced the bailiff as the door of the judge's chamber swung open.

"At least now we know how to plead," Powell said under his breath as the two stood.

"The court of the county of Loudoun is now in session, the Honorable Judge William Wallace presiding!" the bailiff proclaimed as Judge Wallace entered and took his seat behind the cherry dais.

As the onlookers settled back into their seats, Judge Wallace looked over the courtroom. "Seems we have a crowd today."

"Yes, Your Honor," said the bailiff.

"What's on our docket this morning?" Wallace asked.

"The people of the Commonwealth of Virginia against Emily Elizabeth Lloyd."

"Very well, then," the judge said as he turned his focus from the bailiff to the prosecution table. "Mr. Kilgour?"

Mort Kilgour and Charles Lee stood from their seats. "Good morning, Your Honor. Mortimer Kilgour as attorney for the commonwealth and Charles Lee as assistant prosecutor."

Powell and JW stood. "Your Honor, Powell Harrison as counsel for the defense, along with James William Foster as co-counsel," Powell announced.

A loud rumble rippled over the gallery at Powell's declaration. He felt dozens of pairs of eyes bore into his back.

"And the charges?" Judge Wallace asked as Kilgour handed the bailiff a set of papers.

Kilgour cleared his throat as he read from the complaint in his hand. "Your Honor, the commonwealth charges that on March 21, 1872, in the town of Leesburg, the defendant, Emily Elizabeth Lloyd, murdered her three-year-old child, Maud Lloyd, by administering white arsenic that thereby caused her death on March 24, 1872."

At the announcement, gasps could be heard throughout the courtroom. Kilgour continued. "The first count sets forth that Mrs. Lloyd administered poison by mouth to Maud Emily Lloyd, thereby causing her death. Count two sets forth that Mrs. Lloyd administered poison to Maud Lloyd by injection." More gasps waved over the courtroom. "In the third count, the people charge that the defendant administered the poison in solution with water or some other substance."

Powell shifted his gaze to Emily in the defendant's box, her head bowed, staring at her hands in her lap.

"In the fourth count, the people charge that six weeks prior, on or about February 14, 1872, the defendant, Emily Elizabeth Lloyd, administered white arsenic to her five-year-old child, Annie Elizabeth Lloyd, and thereby caused her death on February 16."

Judge Wallace looked up at Kilgour as the prosecutor turned to the next page in his hand. "Count five sets forth that on July 22 of the previous year, 1871, the defendant, Emily Elizabeth Lloyd, administered poison to her eight-year-old son, Henry William Lloyd, thereby causing his death on July 26, 1871."

The rumblings of the townspeople in the gallery grew louder. Judge Wallace raised the gavel and furrowed his brow. "Order!" He rapped the gavel on the bench. "I will have quiet in my courtroom!"

Kilgour cleared his throat. "In the sixth count, the commonwealth charges that on the same day, July 22, 1871, the defendant administered poison to her ten-year-old son, Charles George Lloyd, thereby causing his death on July 24, 1871." Powell noticed Emily's shoulders shaking as she softly wept.

"Count seven sets forth that on or about April 9, 1869, Emily Lloyd administered poison to Mrs. Elizabeth Hammerly, thereby causing her death on April 11, 1869."

Gasps of disbelief erupted from the crowd as Judge Wallace hammered the gavel on the bench again. "Order! Order!" He struck the gavel on the desktop harder still. "I will have order or I will clear this courtroom!"

The crowd calmed to low mumbles.

"On the eighth count, the people set forth that on or about December 26, 1868, Emily Elizabeth Lloyd administered poison to her husband, Charles Henry Lloyd of this county, thereby causing his death on December 28, 1868." Kilgour looked up from the document.

"Your Honor, attached to the charges is the analysis from Professor William P. Tonry of the Maryland Institute indicating the presence of fifteen grains of arsenic in the stomach of Maud Lloyd." Powell looked at JW. It was the first time they were learning the amount of arsenic found in Maud's stomach. Fifteen grains was nearly a half teaspoon and enough arsenic to kill a horse.

"Additionally," Kilgour continued, "you will find the sworn statements of Dr. Randolph Moore, Dr. Thomas Edwards, and Dr. William Cross. Dr. Cross, who examined Maud Lloyd hours before her death, provided testimony that the child presented symptoms indicative of poisoning. Dr. Randolph Moore testified that the child had become ill on Thursday, March 21, and by Sunday, March 24, was markedly improved. Dr. Thomas Edwards reviewed Dr. Moore's notes and testified that the course of treatment provided by Dr. Moore was consistent with standard medical practice and should have otherwise resulted in the child's recovery.

"Moreover, upon further investigation, it has come to the commonwealth's attention that Mrs. Lloyd purchased thirty grains of white arsenic from Dr. Edwards's pharmacy on February 8, 1872, just one week before the death of her daughter Annie. This evidence contradicts the testimony of Mrs. Lloyd before the grand jury on March 25, when she claimed that she had not made such purchases."

The gallery exploded again in disbelief. Judge Wallace pounded the mallet on the desk to silence them.

"Mrs. Lloyd," Judge Wallace said as the crowd quieted. "Do you understand the charges against you?" Emily nodded with her head down. "Mrs. Lloyd?"

"Your Honor," Powell interrupted. "Her counsel has explained the charges, and she understands them."

"And does she understand the full range of punishment for these offenses?"

"She does, Your Honor."

Judge Wallace turned back to Emily, who had lifted her head and now seemed to be paying attention.

"Mrs. Lloyd, how do you plead to the charges set forth against you?"

Emily stood from her chair and placed her hands on the bar to steady herself. "Not guilty," she said loudly with a conviction in her voice that surprised both Powell and JW.

"Your Honor, on the matter of bail, the defense would like to motion the court to release the defendant on bond until the initial hearing and subsequent trial," Powell said.

"Your Honor," Kilgour interrupted. "Bail has already been denied by the magistrate."

"The magistrate deferred to the court to decide the matter today," Powell argued.

"Mrs. Lloyd has murdered six people!" Kilgour said, his face reddening. "It would be irresponsible to allow her to be released on bond."

Powell persisted. "The evidence against Mrs. Lloyd is circumstantial at best. She is a devout Christian, an active member of the St. James Episcopal parish, and a contributing member of our community, working as a seamstress. Her pastor, Reverend Isaac White, and her neighbor, Colonel Lewis Nixon, have provided sworn statements attesting to her character, which I am providing to the court." JW handed the affidavit to the bailiff to give to the judge. "Further, Your Honor, the defense requests that the indictment hearing be delayed until the defense has conducted a full evaluation of the defendant's state of mind."

"Is the defense considering an insanity plea?" Judge Wallace asked as he took the statements from the bailiff.

"We are, Your Honor."

"All the more reason that the court should deny her bail," Kilgour said, interrupting the judge's review of the documents Powell had presented. "The people need assurance that they are safe in their community."

Judge Wallace returned his attention to the affidavits and then riffled through the complaint a second time. Powell watched his face for a sign of his decision as moments passed. The justice lifted his head and looked at Lewis Nixon, a graying man with a receding hairline dressed in a stark black suit who was sitting in the second row.

"Colonel Nixon," Wallace said. "Do I have your personal assurance that Mrs. Lloyd will not leave the confines of her home should I release her into your custody?"

The colonel stood. "Yes, Your Honor," he said with a nod.

The judge shifted his gaze to Kilgour and then Powell.

"I will take the matter of bail under advisement and will issue my ruling on Thursday morning. This should give Mrs. Lloyd ample time to make arrangements for her household should I decide to remand her into custody until trial. Meanwhile, Mr. Harrison, get your evaluation underway."

The townspeople were not pleased with the judge's decision, and their dissatisfaction could be heard throughout the courtroom. The judge pounded his gavel again to bring them to order.

"Mrs. Lloyd, you are hereby released under the guardianship of Colonel Nixon until I make my decision. You are not to leave the confines of your residence for any purpose other than to return to this court at ten o'clock on Thursday morning. Understood?"

Emily nodded from the dock. "Yes, sir."

Judge Wallace slammed his gavel on the wood again, bringing the hearing to an end.

Chaos erupted in the courtroom, with men shouting from the back and women lamenting in loud whispers. Colonel Nixon pushed his way down the aisle and stepped through the gate that separated the gallery from the court. Although Emily's expression was obscured by her veil, Powell could feel her glare. She stood as Colonel Nixon approached, her back straight and shoulders pinned, eyes locked on Powell. Powell watched her as the colonel opened the bar that enclosed the box and assisted her from the dock's platform onto the floor.

"We need to talk with her," JW said.

At the rear of the courtroom, the sheriff's deputy, Freddie, motioned for Colonel Nixon and Emily to avoid the mob at the front of the building. Emily stood still, holding her stare at Powell for one final moment before turning her head and disappearing through the side entrance on the colonel's arm. As the door slammed shut, Powell ran his thumb over his wedding ring. "That we do."

• • •

Freddie was holding open the door to the first cell as Powell and JW emerged from the small corridor into the cellblock. Bent over at the foot of the bed, Emily was gathering her few belongings as Colonel Nixon waited. A change of clothing, a nightgown, shawl, hairbrush, and a Bible were lying on the cot.

"Gentlemen, if you'll excuse us," Powell said. Emily lifted her head from the small chest. She had removed the veil that had shrouded her swollen red eyes. "We need a word with our client."

Colonel Nixon nodded in Powell's direction. "I'll be in the office," he said to Emily and walked past the two attorneys, following Freddie out of the block.

Powell instinctively knew that it was best to use a soft touch with Emily. He rehearsed the words in his head until the door at the other end of the corridor latched.

"Mrs. Lloyd," he said. "Mr. Foster and I have some ques—"

"How dare you!" Emily said, fire in her eyes. "I am neither crazy nor insane! You had no authority to suggest such a thing!"

Powell was taken aback. "In matters such as these, it's best to keep our options open. Especially considering the circumstances."

"Circumstances? What circumstances?"

"We specifically asked if you had arsenic in your house, and you said that you didn't," JW said. "And now we find out that you did have it in your house!"

"That is not what you asked!" she hissed. "You asked if I had bought arsenic, and I told you I had not, but I never said that it hadn't been in the house before."

JW huffed out loud. "If you didn't buy it, then how did it get in your house?"

"I don't rightly know. Maybe Delphi or someone else brought it in. But I got rid of it, so it didn't matter." Indignation sparked in her tone.

JW was incredulous, and it was written all over his face. "What do you mean it didn't matter? Of course it matt—"

"Mrs. Lloyd," Powell interjected, knowing that JW's approach was going nowhere. "We are not here to accuse you or to judge you. We are here to defend you." He spoke slowly, his voice low and his tone even. "You said that you didn't purchase arsenic from Dr. Edwards, but there was arsenic in your house and you got rid of it?"

Emily nodded her head again. "I was afraid one of the girls might get into it."

"How did you dispose of it?" Powell asked.

"I burned it."

"And when did you do this?"

Emily looked confused.

"Do you remember when you burned the arsenic?" Powell asked.

"When I saw it on the table in the kitchen. I thought, why is this here? I mean, one of the girls might mistake it for sugar or something, so right away, I took it into the parlor and set it alight in the fireplace."

JW shifted in his stance, his frustration growing.

"Did you use any of it to kill the rats?" Powell asked, lowering an opened hand in JW's direction, signaling him to calm down.

"I did not."

"Then why did you purchase it if you had no intention of using it?" JW asked, ignoring Powell's instruction.

Emily clenched a fistful of her dress's skirt and shot JW a look. "I don't remember purchasing it."

"You don't remember?" JW asked, his agitation apparent.

"I don't. As I said, perhaps Delphi purchased it and put it under my name. I know that she was tired of the rats. All I know is that when I saw it in the kitchen, I got rid of it."

"So there was no poison in the house when Annie got sick?" Powell asked.

Emily shook her head. "No, sir. I burned all of it."

"And what about when Maud became ill? Was there any arsenic in your home then?"

"No, as I said."

"You are certain?" Powell asked again.

"Not that I had anything to do with. But who knows what that scoundrel Billy Lloyd brought to my doorstep!"

"We understand your concern about Mr. Lloyd, and Mr. Foster and I will look into his conduct. But, Mrs. Lloyd, we cannot be blindsided like this again. You understand the importance of telling us the truth?"

Emily nodded.

"Good," he said, gently placing a hand on her forearm. "Try not to worry."

"Mr. Harrison," she said, looking Powell in the eye. "I am not insane."

Powell offered a kind smile. "I understand, ma'am. But we will need for you to talk with a psychiatrist. As I said, so we keep all our options open."

Emily held Powell's gaze for an awkward moment before shifting her focus from Powell to the corridor beyond the iron bars of the cell.

"Very well, then," she said as she composed herself. "Please tell Colonel Nixon that I am ready to go home now."

CHAPTER 9

"We cannot allow the judge to put Emily *back* in that awful jail!" Lara said as Lilith watched her pace across the kitchen floor in a frenzy. "It was so austere and musty and cold."

"The jail didn't seem that bad," Lilith said, smoking a roll of tobacco as she warmed herself in a chair near the stove. "The guard, what was his name . . ." She thought for a moment, blowing smoke in a long stream from the side of her mouth. "Freddie, that was it. Pretty blue eyes and cute blond curls." She closed her eyes momentarily. "Mmm, mmm, mmm," she said dreamingly. "Wouldn't I like to entwine my fingers into those ringlets and pull him right down—"

"Lilith!"

Lilith shrugged her shoulders. "You know, it wouldn't have hurt Emily to have invited him into her cell. I bet he'd have kept her warm." She could feel Lara's glare.

"Why is it that all you think about is men?"

"Because I like men. Perhaps Emily should try liking them more."

"She's not that kind of woman."

"Truth be told, she likes them all right. Likes having one in her bed, too. It's just that she won't admit it. She thinks it's unchristian or immoral or some such nonsense."

"First Corinthians 6:18. 'Flee from sexual immorality.' Copulation with a man outside of marriage is immoral."

Lilith scoffed. "Emily didn't seem to think it moral inside of marriage either."

"Perhaps if you hadn't constantly indulged her husband in his depraved indiscretions, he wouldn't have been so perverted with her!"

"She didn't get anything from Charlie that she didn't deserve. And for your information, I enjoyed Charlie's affection. But then you put an end to that."

"What did you expect me to do?" Lara released a frustrated sigh. "Can we not talk about this and focus on Emily's current predicament instead? I need to find a way to keep her out of jail."

"Fine. But frankly, if you think about it, jail really isn't all that bad. Someone else will do all the cooking for her. There's no house to clean. No sewing to do. No pesky neighbors. And there are all those men." Lara gave her another disapproving look. "All right. We'll leave the men out of it." She drew on the tobacco again. "For now," Lilith said under her breath.

Rolling her eyes, Lara resumed her pacing. "Emily couldn't harm anyone, let alone her children. The attorneys need to do their job and convince that judge to allow her to stay home until the trial!"

"You know, I thought I liked that dark-haired one—Mr. Foster. But after watching him today, I like the other one better."

"And no lewd conduct around the attorneys."

"You haven't let me near them!"

"You need to steer clear of them. Especially Harrison. Do you understand, Lilith?"

Lilith nodded, drawing on the tobacco and releasing smoke into the air. A sudden seriousness washed over her face. "Are you worried about this evaluation Harrison mentioned in court?"

"Nothing to concern ourselves with. You and I both know that there is nothing wrong with Emily's mind."

"What if she remembers?"

Lara stopped midpace and gave Lilith a stern look. "She was too young."

There was a knock at the front door. Lilith got up from the chair and tossed the tobacco into the stove, following Lara to the hall. Lara walked into the parlor and looked out the window. "Dr. Moore is on the stoop."

"Well, that didn't take long."

"Don't tell me you called him here."

"Indeed I did! I sent Delphi for him. Told her to tell him that Emily wasn't feeling well. It's our signal, you know. And since she'll probably be in jail for a while, I figured I'd lure him over one last time."

"I told you to stay away from him! He's a married man. And how do you think your affair with him makes Emily feel?"

"Emily doesn't know a thing about it," Lilith said, unbuttoning the top buttons on her blouse. "Since he had that first bite of forbidden fruit, well, let's just say that Dr. Moore has become quite fond of the taste."

"Lilith!"

"Oh, stop being such an old prude!" Lilith said as she primped. "You're not my mother."

"Mother would have never approved of such behavior."

"And do you think she would have approved of yours?" Lilith threw Lara a sharp look before turning her attention back to the mirror. Checking her image one last time, she pulled a few strands of hair around her face and rubbed her lips together before turning toward the door. "Now go on, sister. Get out your Bible and pray with Emily or something. I have a doctor to attend to."

CHAPTER 10

"I see that you survived the evening," Matt said, standing in the frame of the doorway to Powell's office.

Powell lifted his head from his work. "Why wouldn't I?"

Matt chuckled. "Considering how Janet reacted to your involvement in the Lloyd case, I'm surprised you still have your head after yesterday's arraignment hearing."

Powell laid the pen down on the desk. "My head is firmly attached to my shoulders, thank you. Although my wife may never speak to me again."

"I should be so lucky," Matt said with a half laugh. "If only Hattie refused to speak to me. All that woman does is talk!"

Powell didn't find it funny. Past silent treatments from Janet had gone on for weeks. After Sunday night's fight, she might not speak to him for months.

Matt remained in the doorway, cup of coffee in hand, eyeing him.

"Well, go on, then," Powell said. "I might as well hear it from you, too."

"You'll get no grief from me. I learned a long time ago that once my little brother makes up his mind, there's no changing it. What's best now is to figure out how we win this thing."

A wave of relief fell over Powell, and he smiled. "Then pull up a seat."

"I hear that Wallace wanted a couple of days to decide on bail," Matt said as he took the chair in front of Powell's desk.

"He's to rule on Thursday morning, although he all but confirmed that he'll remand her until trial."

Matt nodded. "As he should. And he'll want this over quickly. I expect he'll set the grand jury hearing next month when the county court convenes again."

"I'll insist that we need until the August court, considering it's an eight-count charge. Then after the indictment hearing, I plan to petition to move the trial to the circuit court in October."

Matt whistled between his teeth. "Are you thinking Wallace isn't up to a case of this magnitude?"

"I'm thinking that he doesn't want the pressure of this case for the same reasons you and I didn't want it. And I think the circuit court is our best opportunity to get Mrs. Lloyd a fair trial."

"And let's not forget that your win record is better in the circuit court than county court."

"Because the judges on the circuit are more decisive when it comes to evidentiary motions."

"And more experienced in hearing insanity defenses," Matt said with a shake of his head. "Every now and then, I am reminded of what a good attorney you are."

"What choice do I have if I am to keep up with you and Pa?"

Matt laughed again. "You know, Pa would have put a boot up my backside for taking a case like this without his approval."

"Good thing for me that you aren't Pa!" Powell laughed. "Speaking of Pa, I want to run something by you."

"If it's fatherly advice, I'm only good at the brotherly kind these days."

"That will work just as well," Powell said, and pulled a long breath. "I'm thinking about campaigning for commonwealth's attorney." He brought his thumb to his wedding ring and turned it on his finger. While Powell wouldn't openly admit it, he still looked up to his older brother and relied on his counsel.

Matt sat back in the chair, a mixture of disbelief and shock on his face. "And you only thought you had trouble with Kilgour."

"Janet's idea."

"Fulfilling your wife's ambition will certainly get you back in her good graces."

"It's not her ambition that's driving my decision but more my duty to do what's right. The people need a commonwealth's attorney without an agenda."

Matt rubbed a hand over his chin. "You'd make a damned good one, that's for certain. But campaigning for office is a commitment. With the pressures of a case this size, plus a young family at home that you already don't spend enough time with, I don't know, Powell. Maybe you should wait."

"Wait for what? I'll be forty in December. And I'm not certain the people of this county can tolerate another four years of Mort Kilgour's kind of justice."

"Well, it's the people of this county that put him in that position."

"Not all the people of this county, Matt. Just white men who share his views."

"You do have a point there." Matt sat back in the chair. "If you decide to make a run for the commonwealth's attorney's office, then you have my support. Hell, I'll even help you campaign."

"Thanks, Matt. I appreciate it." Powell sat back in his chair.

"Not to change the subject," Matt said, "but did you telegraph that doctor friend of yours down at the madhouse?"

"This morning."

"How long do you think it will take before he can do the evaluation?"

"Couple of weeks is my guess. I also want to investigate other theories on the chance that the doctors don't find her insane."

"Like accidental poisoning?"

"Or intentional."

Matt furrowed his brow. "By whom?"

"The widow suggested that her late husband's brother may have tainted milk that he delivered to her home the day before the little girl became ill."

"That makes no sense. What motive would he have for poisoning a little girl?"

"Mrs. Lloyd seems to think he would harm the child to settle a vendetta with her."

"She is mad!"

"She may be, but with the children and the widow out of the way, William Lloyd would be next in line to inherit his brother's estate."

"That's motive. But to kill a child?"

"I've witnessed enough senseless killing in the war to know better than to dismiss the possibility."

"Could be over a man," Matt suggested. "With all those widows on that street, maybe one of them wanted to punish Mrs. Lloyd out of spite."

"And I plan to canvass the neighborhood to investigate just such a motive."

"Take JW with you. A good-looking, eligible bachelor might come in handy."

"Great minds think alike," Powell said with a laugh.

"Speaking of like minds," Matt said, clearing his throat. "I got to thinking yesterday afternoon about how much time it takes to prepare for a case of this magnitude. And you know, my caseload . . . I can barely keep up as it is now. I don't want to leave you shorthanded. And now that you're campaigning for the—"

"What have you done?"

"It was last minute, I assure you. John Orr stopped by yesterday, and the two of us had a couple of drinks and got to talking, and, well, I thought it would be a good idea for him to consult." Matt brought his eyes to Powell's. "Hope you don't mind."

Of course I mind! Powell didn't like consulting attorneys who had all the opinions but none of the affiliated risk. Although he respected John Orr, Powell didn't like being second-guessed. But he needed Matt's support. "I suppose we could use help with the case-law research. As I recall, John is good at that sort of thing."

Matt nodded. "Built himself a nice little library over there. And he clerked for Pa. He's smart like you. And he's familiar with poisoning cases. His firm consulted on one up north a few years back."

"No question that Orr's a good attorney."

Matt looked over at Powell again. "Are you sure you're all right with it?"

"Just as long as he knows who's lead counsel."

"I'm certain you'll remind him," Matt said with a chuckle.

Powell smiled back, hoping he wouldn't come to regret his words.

◆　◆　◆

"Papa's home," Powell shouted as he flung the door open.

Nannie, who was sitting on the parlor rug with her younger sister, sprang from the floor.

The two were playing with a child's Staffordshire tea set, its blue floral cups and saucers spread over a blanket at their mother's feet. Janet looked up from the pinafore she was sewing as Nannie ran to her father with Lalla toddling behind. Powell tossed his satchel on the bench and scooped his daughters up in his arms. Janet glanced at him briefly before turning back to her needlework.

"Looks like you two are having a party," Powell said as he walked around the room with the girls.

"Me and my friends are, but Lalla isn't playing nice. She keeps spilling the tea over everyone," Nannie said with a pout.

"I'm sure Lalla doesn't mean to. You must remember that she is still little," Powell said. "How many guests do we have today?"

"Well, there's Nancy and Polly and Nellie. So that's three."

"Hello, Nancy, Polly, and Nellie," he said with a nod toward the settings on the blanket.

He set the girls down. "Best not to keep your imaginary friends waiting."

"They are not 'maginary, Papa," Nannie said defiantly, crossing her chubby arms. "Can't you see them?"

"Of course he can," Janet said. "And very nice friends they are." She raised a brow in Powell's direction.

Powell leaned to Janet and kissed her cheek. "Hello, darling."

Janet ignored him. He took the chair next to her, watching as his girls settled on the blanket and resumed their tea party.

Minutes passed until he broke the silence. "I've decided to launch a campaign for the commonwealth's attorney's office."

Janet's hand froze midstitch at his announcement.

"I've been thinking about what you said," Powell continued. "It's the only way justice will be served in this town. If not me, then who, right?"

Though Janet didn't answer him, she seemed to weigh his words for a long moment before pushing the needle through the fabric again.

A cold silence settled in between them, interrupted only by the sounds of the girls' play. Powell absently watched as Nannie poured pretend tea from the small blue pot into cups while Lalla banged a silver spoon against a saucer.

"I am so sorry, darling," Powell said at long last. "I should have never let my emotions get away from me. Will you forgive me?"

Minutes more passed as Powell awaited her answer.

"I had Rebecca set a place for you in the dining room," she said finally, her eyes steady on her stitching. "The girls and I will take our supper in my room this evening."

Powell bowed his head, not knowing what to say. After another long moment, he lifted his frame from the chair.

◆ ◆ ◆

Janet said not a word for the rest of the evening, taking their daughters upstairs with her, leaving Powell to eat alone. He withdrew to his study and poured himself a brandy before setting to work. He took Dr. Frank Stribling's correspondence from the desk drawer and pulled the letter from the envelope. Unfolding it on the desk, he opened his journal and picked up a pen, writing *Lloyd Interview* across the top. With the pen still in his hand, he moved his attention to the letter and read it again.

My Dear Friend Powell,

I must say that I was most enthused to receive your letter. A bright spot in an otherwise dismal day. My apologies if I sound dismayed, but with continued overcrowding and so many incurable patients, my ability to cure those with hope is nearly impossible, rendering my spirits ever more depressed. But enough about my problems here at Western State. On to helping with yours.

In your correspondence, you had inquired as to what might cause a woman to murder her children. The obvious, of course, and as you suggested, is insanity. I would make

*inquiries regarding any falls or injuries she might have suf-
fered; any familial record of insanity; inhospitable or abusive
treatment from a spouse, son, father, or other male; excessive
loss and grief, especially when she was a child. And, of course,
issues with menstruation, although I would advise you to
refrain from asking her questions on this topic. Best to let a
physician enter into that fray!*

*A diseased mind capable of murdering multiple children
over a period of several years is, in all probability, incurable.
As such, we have no capacity here at the asylum for incurable
patients should the mother be found not guilty by reason of
insanity. My advice is to restrain her so that she is not a harm
to herself or others. Antimony, bromides, and acetate of morphine or morphine sulfate would all be acceptable medicines.
As for treatments, options are few, but mercurial bowel purges,
regular warm baths, and tonics certainly would not hurt. But
there is no cure for such chronic dementia. The best we can do
is protect the patient from herself and her actions during the
periods of mania when the disease takes control of the mind.*

*I will gladly send Dr. Allen Berkley to you to conduct an
evaluation and to offer testimony at the proceeding when the
time comes. Have Mr. Foster send us a communication over
the wire when he's ready.*

*Give my best to Mrs. Harrison and the girls. And don't be
a stranger. Staunton misses you, as do I.*

Your Obedient Servant,
Frank

Powell startled when Nannie's tabby jumped onto the desk.
Purring, it nudged Powell's wrist with its nose.

"What is it you want, Whiskers?"

The cat lowered its head and rubbed its face against Powell's hand.

"I've no time for you tonight," he said, stroking its head before
shooing it away. The cat moved to the opposite side of the desk and
settled near the edge, paws tucked under its breast, watching Powell
with attentive eyes.

"What should I ask her?" Powell addressed the cat. "Definitely about her marriage to that sot." He made a note. "And about her childhood." He made another note before looking at the gray tabby again. "Do you think she had one of you growing up?"

Purring loudly, the feline closed its slit-lids over its eyes, seemingly losing interest.

"A lot of help you are!" Powell shook his head and continued to scribble his list of questions for Emily. He was tapping his pen on the desk, strategizing his approach, when his thoughts drifted to his sister Alice. Stribling had said Alice was unable to live with the shame of what had happened. She was so traumatized she could not rid her mind of the memory. A fever would spike without warning, Stribling said, sending her into a delirious state. Yet, throughout, even when Alice was not in her right mind, she was always aware of her actions. Felt guilt and remorse for the things she said and did. This didn't seem to hold true with Emily Lloyd. Ms. Lloyd claimed no knowledge of poisoning the children. She expressed no remorse, displayed no guilt.

That's a question for Frank, he thought and picked up the letter. *"The best we can do is protect the patient from herself and her actions during the periods of mania when the disease takes control of the mind."*

He looked at the purring cat. Both Maggie and Delphi had been with Mrs. Lloyd during periods of time when she was supposedly administering the poison, yet neither of them had witnessed any mania or abnormal behavior.

"Why?" he asked the sleeping tabby. "How is it no one took notice?" He looked down at his notes and then back to the cat, not liking the answer that was forming in his mind.

CHAPTER 11

WEDNESDAY, APRIL 24, 1872

"My childhood?"

Emily's brows furrowed at Powell's question. When he arrived at the Lloyd house, she had been packing a case, expecting the judge to remand her the next morning. She had removed her children's portraits from the wall and laid them next to the case to take with her to jail.

"There's not much to tell. I have lived here nearly all my life. Grew up in this very house with my aunt and uncle."

"I had heard that you were orphaned," Powell said, glancing at the clock between two lamps on the mantel. The clock was old and its face yellowed, and, not wound since Emily's incarceration, its crooked hands were frozen on the numbers one and ten. Trinkets were scattered over the mantel and side table, and quilt squares sat in a basket on the floor by her feet.

"My mother died in childbirth," Emily replied. "And my father and stepmother died in a fire. Somehow I escaped without so much as a scratch. My aunt said they found me wandering around in the snow afterward."

"How horrible!" Powell said, reminded of his sister Alice. "That must have been a terrifying experience for you."

"As I was not yet four years of age at the time, I have no memory of the event. Nor of my father, nor of living in Clark."

"So you came to Leesburg to live with your aunt and uncle?"

"Aunt Liza and my mother were sisters, so she and Uncle Frank took me in."

"What about siblings? Any sisters or brothers?"

"The only person who might be considered a sibling would be my cousin Mary. She is Aunt Liza and Uncle Frank's daughter. She's about ten years older than me but treated me like a little sister until she married and moved to Chicago with her husband."

"I'd like to speak with her." Powell pulled his notepad from his pocket. "What's her surname now?"

"Reynolds. Mrs. Mary Reynolds." Emily lifted her head and watched as Powell wrote the name in his book.

"Her husband's first name?"

"William? Or maybe Walter? Then again, it could be Robert." Emily sighed. "I have a terrible memory for such things."

"Do you have an address for her?"

"Last I wrote to her was when she was in Chicago. A few years back, she moved to Canada. Somewhere near Toronto, I think. With the war and all, I lost contact with her."

"I'll see if I can find her for you, assuming you'd like to be in touch with her."

"That would be very nice."

Powell made a note and shifted in his chair. "About this fire, do you know when it happened?"

"It would have been the winter of '40 or '41, I reckon."

"Do you know how the fire started?"

Emily shook her head.

"What was your father's occupation?"

She shook her head again.

"Do you remember him at all?"

"As I said, I have no recollection of the man or of the fire." Emily's gaze drifted to the floor as if she were searching for something. "Who knows what demons lay buried in the ashes." Powell cocked his head as she brought her eyes back to his. "Aunt Liza used to say that forgotten memories are sleeping demons we need not wake." She smiled. "It was a long time ago, Mr. Harrison, and I was very young."

Powell nodded and made another note. "Do you mind if I ask a few questions about your marriage?"

"Not at all."

"How did you meet Mr. Lloyd?"

"Charlie?" She smiled again. "He was driving a coach when I met him. Had big dreams back then, Charlie did. We married in '59. George arrived a year later. And not long after, Henry. Then came the war, and Charlie was gone. When he returned, he wasn't the same man. But I can understand when you experience things, when you've seen things. Horrible things can change a person."

"Did you see something, experience something, that might have caused a change in you? During the war, maybe?"

Emily narrowed her eyes and scrutinized his face to understand his meaning.

"Those things of which you speak can change a woman as well," Powell said. "I'm sure you know that I have three sisters, because you see them at church." He was going out on a limb here, but he knew of no other way to get to what he wanted to know. "I had a fourth sister, Alice, whom I was very close to. You remind me of her sometimes. She would be about your age now if she were still with us."

"I'm sorry for you, Mr. Harrison."

"During the war, something terrible happened to Alice. The incident threw her into a state of deep melancholy. Something so terrible that she was unable to live with its burden."

"What happened?"

"It was through no fault of her own. Alice had been taking care of a sick friend whose husband, like most able-bodied men, was off fighting the Yankees. One afternoon, a rogue band of Federal cavalry arrived at the farm where the two young women were staying alone. For hours, these men terrorized my sister and her friend. My sister's friend died from the assault. And while Alice's body recovered, her mind was never the same again."

Emily brought her fingers to her lips, her eyes staring down to a point between the chair and the floor.

"That's a horrible story, Mr. Harrison. What a monstrous thing. Your poor sister."

"Indeed, it is all very tragic, yet occurred all too often, I'm afraid." Powell shifted in his chair. "Did you witness something similar during the war?"

"Not at all. I found the Yankees to be polite when they occupied the town. It was mostly the Rebels who would visit my door, robbing our supplies and stores. But nothing like what you described."

"You mentioned that your husband was a changed man after the war. Was he abusive toward you?"

"Like all men, I suppose, he would on occasion discipline the boys with the lash. And then there were times when he would come home from the tavern and lose his patience with them."

"I was asking about you, Mrs. Lloyd. Did Mr. Lloyd lose his patience with you?"

Emily moved her gaze to her hands resting in her lap. "Sometimes."

Powell leaned toward her and lowered his voice. "I was told about an incident in your backyard a few years back. When Colonel Nixon called the sheriff. Were there other occasions when your husband assaulted you—or took liberties without your consent?"

"I am quite uncomfortable with these questions. And what on earth does any of this have to do with finding out who hurt my little girl?"

"Mrs. Lloyd, you have been accused of not only causing the deaths of your children but also the death of your husband. If he were abusive toward you, the prosecution will surely claim that abuse as motive. I am simply trying to understand the circumstances. And to get to know you better so that I might provide the best defense possible."

"Nothing that happened between me and my husband had anything to do with the deaths of my children. I can assure you that I had nothing to do with any of it." Emily shifted uncomfortably in the chair.

"And that's what we are trying to prove," Powell said. Getting nowhere, he decided to change the subject. The doctors from Western State would have ample opportunity to delve deeper into her relationship with her husband and what, if anything, had happened to her while her husband was gone. "Have you suffered any falls? Any injury to your head where you lost consciousness?"

"No, none that I remember. I wasn't much for being out of doors or climbing trees." She laughed. "But I do get confused and sometimes become a bit disoriented. I'll find myself in a room and, for the life of me, can't remember how I got there. And I am so forgetful." She clicked her tongue and shook her head.

"Have you always had bouts of forgetfulness? Or is it something that has developed more recently?"

"I think I've always been this way. Uncle Frank used to tell folks that I had my head in the clouds. Always talking to my imaginary friends in my make-believe world, he'd say." She laughed at the memory. "But that was when I was a little girl. You have daughters, Mr. Harrison. You know how vivid young imaginations can be."

"I do indeed," Powell said with a laugh. "Just last evening, my Nannie and her little sister had tea with three imaginary guests in our parlor. And our poor cat. Sometimes she puts a bib on him and forces him to join her for tea as well."

Emily smiled. "Annie and Maudie would have similar parties. I couldn't possibly remember the names of all the dignitaries who attended their teas. I do remember one time Annie told me that Queen Victoria and Prince Albert were joining them. And she was quite insistent that I needed to bake a wedding cake for the occasion."

"You don't say," Powell said with a British accent, stiffening his lips. They laughed together.

"I miss them, you know," Emily said, the laughter in her voice fading. "And I ask myself: Why? Why did the Lord take my babies?"

"In his Gospel," Powell said, recalling a lesson that his pastor in Staunton shared when Alice died, "John the Apostle tells a story of Jesus healing an impotent man on the Sabbath."

"John 5," Emily said. "The cripple by the pool of Bethesda."

"You know it?"

"I do," Emily acknowledged. "But Jesus cured that man. He didn't cure my babies."

"Jesus did, in fact, heal the man. But there were hundreds, perhaps thousands, of others, lame and blind, lying around the pool. Jesus stepped over them all, leaving them to suffer while only saving the one. John tells us later in the chapter that Jesus acts only at the direction of the Father. 'For the Father loveth the Son, and showeth Him all things that Himself doeth: and He will show Him greater works than these.' God had not yet disclosed all of His works to Jesus. Just as He does not disclose all of His works or share all His thoughts with us."

"You're quoting Isaiah now," she said.

"Yes," Powell said, impressed with her knowledge of scripture. "And together with John 5, it tells us that we aren't meant to understand."

"It doesn't make it any easier, Mr. Harrison." She brought her eyes to her hands that lay folded in her lap.

"Having lost a child of my own, I understand your doubt and pain more than you know," Powell said, glancing down at his notes.

Emily brought her gaze to Powell. "I remember your boy."

She reached over and placed a hand on his sleeve.

He looked up from the journal, his eyes catching hers.

"There is no pain worse," Emily said, her voice filled with compassion.

Powell felt the familiar lump of sorrow rising in his throat. He swallowed hard, forcing it down.

Emily smiled empathetically before removing her hand.

"When I don't understand God's ways," she said, most certainly seeing the anguish on his face, "I cling to God's worth. Every night, I fall to my knees and ask Him to guide me through my suffering."

"I haven't spoken to God since Bo's death," Powell said, moving his gaze from hers.

"'He healeth the broken in heart, and bindeth up their wounds.'" She smiled at him. "We must hold fast to our faith, Mr. Harrison. And trust that the Lord is good even when our worlds are falling apart."

Powell inhaled a long, silent stream of air deep into his lungs, and released it slowly. He had not admitted his abstinence from prayer—his rift with God, as he coined it—to a soul, not even to Janet, yet here he was confessing to Emily Lloyd, a near stranger. What had gotten into him? He glanced at his notes again and cleared his throat.

"When I was here with Mr. Foster the other day, I noticed a small door at the back of the closet in your chamber," he said, moving the discussion back to his questions.

"It's an access to the chimney flue and was locked off by my uncle. He was afraid one of us girls might fall to our deaths thinking it was a secret hiding place to play in."

"Do you use the door now?"

"I've never had a reason to access the chimney. The door is locked, and I have no idea where the key might be."

Powell flipped the page to his final topic. "One last question, Mrs. Lloyd. I notice that this house is a twin. Who rents the other half from you?"

"I don't own the other side. But there are two sisters who live there. Lara and Lilith are their names."

"How well do you know them?"

"I'm friendly with Lara. She's kind to me. And a God-fearing woman. The other one, Lilith, she is an immoral woman, she is. And a filthy mouth, that one has. I don't care for her at all."

"They are unmarried, yes?"

Emily nodded.

"And their surname?" Powell asked, brows raised.

Emily gave him a blank stare. "I don't rightly know. I've only known them by their first names, and if they have told me, I most certainly forgot. As I mentioned, I am terrible with names."

Powell thought it odd that she didn't know the full names of neighbors living in such proximity, especially with young children in her household. "Perhaps you could ask about their surnames the next time you visit with Lara?"

"I'm not certain I will talk with her anytime soon."

"Why is that? Are they avoiding you because of the arrest?"

"Not at all. They came to visit when I returned home from that awful jail."

"I shall call on them when I finish here, then."

"I'm not certain that they are home at present, as I haven't seen or heard from them since Monday."

"Did they say when they would return?"

"They don't tell me where they go or when they will return. It's odd, frankly—sometimes here and then suddenly gone. But that's just how they are, I suppose. Carefree, coming and going as they please."

"How long have they lived next door?"

Emily paused for a moment. "They have been there as long as I can remember."

．．．

When Emily closed the door behind him, Powell lingered on the stoop. Not three feet to the left was the entrance to the other side of the double house. With a knuckle, he rapped on the door. There was no noise, no movement. After a minute, he knocked again and waited. He leaned to look in the window that fronted the parlor. A yellowed lace curtain obscured the view into the room. Giving up, he turned toward the street and headed toward the wheelwright's house next door to the right.

With thinning hair and a thickening midsection, Pendleton Slack looked to be a decade or so older than Powell. He greeted Powell warmly and invited him into the parlor. The man was friendly enough and seemingly more than eager to answer Powell's questions.

"The widow has always been quiet," Slack said as he settled into the chair across from Powell in the parlor of the modest home. "Not aloof, mind you, always pleasant. She doted on those children, she did. For the life of me, I found it hard to listen to rumors that she could be responsible. But then all my chickens died."

"I noticed there were carcasses of fowl in Mrs. Lloyd's trash heap. They were yours?"

"I threw them there to keep my hogs from eating them. Didn't want to risk losing them, too."

Powell looked confused. "I'm sorry, but I don't understand the connection between the dead chickens, your hogs, and Mrs. Lloyd."

"The little girl's vomit. The housemaid said she dumped it in the trash heap, and my chickens, well, I didn't have them penned before all this happened. They got into the rubbish over at the Lloyd place, and not a day later, they all died. Don't you find that strange?"

Powell looked at him blankly.

"I didn't know what to make of it at first either," Slack continued, "but then I heard that little Maud died, and people fancied that Mrs. Lloyd poisoned her, and, well, then I got a little suspicious."

"So your chickens ate from Mrs. Lloyd's trash and then all suddenly died."

"That's what I said."

"And you are certain about the timing."

Slack nodded. "I remember the day because it was Palm Sunday."

Powell made a note in his journal. "Does Mrs. Lloyd have many visitors?" Powell asked.

"Yes, indeed. Folks are always dropping off their mending and picking it up."

"What I mean is, are there people who come by to visit her or the children on a regular basis?"

"There's a couple of women in the neighborhood that she's friendly with. Mrs. Greene, and that Miss Ryan from down the street used to go by quite often before her mother got sick. There are others, but they aren't pretty enough for me to take notice and remember their names. My wife could tell you, though. And, of course, there's Randy Moore."

"Dr. Moore had tended the children quite often, then?" Powell asked.

"Oh, I'd say he's been tending to more than just the children."

Powell raised his brows. "What do you mean, exactly?"

Slack leaned forward in his chair, looking over his shoulder as if someone might be eavesdropping from the hallway.

"If I had a nickel for every time I've seen the doctor's carriage parked in front of that house until the wee hours of the morning, I'd be a rich man. Even after the woman spent the weekend in jail, he comes a knocking, if you know what I mean. Not that it's any of my business. Good-looking woman like the widow might make an aging man feel young again. And with a nagging wife like the doctor's, well, I can't say that I blame him." Slack chuckled. "Of course, there is a strong possibility that you might find yourself over there in Union Cemetery, messing with a woman like that." Slack chuckled again.

"Dr. Moore was at Mrs. Lloyd's last night?"

"Monday night. Came by 'round about suppertime. It was long after dark when I heard his carriage pull out."

"You're suggesting that Dr. Moore and Emily Lloyd are engaged in an amorous relationship?"

"Call it what you will, but it seems like more than just doctorin' to me." Slack snickered. "Does make you wonder, though. If the doctor wasn't dipping his wick into the widow, would the husband and children still be alive?" He shook his head at the thought.

"Have you mentioned this to anyone else?"

"You're the first who asked me about it. My wife is the one who brought it to my attention. Of course, she never thought much of Emily Lloyd in the first place. Says she's possessed by the devil, got Lucifer in her eyes."

Powell recalled his sister Anne Marie saying the same thing about Mrs. Lloyd.

"And you?" Powell asked. "Do you share your wife's opinion of Mrs. Lloyd?"

"Hell no. The woman's got no control over the color of her eyes. And my wife, she's the jealous type, you know. Doesn't like it when I'm out in my yard and Mrs. Lloyd comes to the fence and strikes up a conversation with me. Threatened one time to cut my tallywacker off should I so much as consider sticking it into anyone other than her."

Powell nodded his head, his expression void of any reaction. "Might I speak to your wife?"

"Sorry, Counsellor, but you'll have to wait. Cathy's across the river in Frederick for a few weeks. Her sister is with child and due any day now."

Powell made another note on the pad. "What about the women who live on the other side of Mrs. Lloyd?"

"Mysterious."

Powell raised a brow. "Mysterious how?"

"Never see them in the daylight hours. They come and go at night, the one does anyway. They ain't there too often, as far as I can tell. Keep to themselves and don't cause no trouble. Like I said, mysterious."

◆ ◆ ◆

After leaving the Slack residence, Powell stood for a moment looking at the neighboring house with its double front doors. *Randy Moore in an intimate relationship with Emily Lloyd? A doctor taking liberties with his patient?* Powell found it difficult to believe. Not to mention how such a rumor would undermine the credibility of an insanity defense. And if true, an illicit affair would provide motive of a different kind. *But motive for whom?*

With a hard last look at the two doors, he turned toward King Street to Moore and Metzger Drugstore and the offices of Dr. Randolph Moore.

◆ ◆ ◆

A little brass bell at the top of the door jingled when Powell entered the pharmacy. Randy Moore was standing at the far end of a wooden counter that extended nearly the width of the store and divided it in half. A measuring scale, pestle, and a discarded marble gravestone used as a mortar for grinding medicines sat on top of the counter, while apothecary jars and crocks lined shelves on the wall behind. At the wall's center was an opening, screened by a curtain, that Powell assumed led to the doctor's office and an examination room at the rear of the building. Moore looked up and greeted Powell. After an exchange of pleasantries, Powell delved into the purpose of his visit.

"From what I've been told, little Maud was a sickly child. As was her sister, Annie," Powell said with a look requesting confirmation.

"Both children suffered from chronic digestive ailments," Moore said. "They were ill quite often."

"Do you know the cause of these ailments?"

"Both girls were colicky as infants, their constitutions weak since birth."

"And did you often treat them with bismuth?"

"Occasionally, and sometimes with a little opium to ease the pain from cramping."

Powell nodded, pulling his diary from his pocket, and made a note. "How much and how often did you prescribe bismuth and opium?"

"Off the top of my head, I couldn't tell you. It would be in my notes."

"I'd like to see those notes. And your records for the entire Lloyd family, if you wouldn't mind."

The bell jingled as a woman entered the store.

"Just a moment," Moore said and called for his clerk. "Jason!"

A young man in his early twenties appeared from the back of the store. Moore held the curtain to the side for the clerk as he passed through and disappeared behind it to retrieve his files. Powell watched as the clerk fulfilled the woman's request, observing silently while the two chatted. Jason removed two jars from the shelf, opening each one and weighing the powders on the scales before moving them to the marble stone and grinding them with a pestle. When he finished, he scooped the silver-blue powdered compound into a glass bottle, corked it, and handed it to the woman.

"Just put it on my account, please," the woman said before leaving. The clerk pulled a large clothbound book from under the counter and recorded the transaction.

"Jason Roberts is your name, am I right?" Powell asked.

Jason smiled and nodded. "That's right, Mr. Harrison. I'm Grey Roberts's son. My father was with you in Gettysburg. You remember him?"

"Of course." Grey Roberts and Powell's childhood friend Danny Greene—Maggie's husband—had both served under JW's uncle during the war. Like Danny, Grey had been wounded at Gettysburg, and the two had shared the same wagon on that long, miserable trek home when Danny died. Powell remembered the afternoon as if it had happened yesterday. Danny in his arms in the pouring rain, blood seeping through the bandages onto Powell's uniform as Powell made his solemn promise and Danny slipped away.

"Your pa's a good man." Powell raised his chin and moved his eyes toward the large cloth book. "Do you record every compound you sell in that log?"

"Just when a customer buys on credit."

"The state requires sales of certain chemicals, like arsenic, to be recorded. Where do you record those transactions?" Powell asked.

"We keep a separate register for those," Jason replied. "It's right here." He pulled a smaller ledger from under the counter. "We organize the account book by name. The register is by date."

Powell nodded again. "Thanks, Jason. And give your father my regards."

"Sure 'nough, Mr. Harrison." As Jason disappeared behind the curtain, Moore returned with a file of papers.

"Here we are," Moore said, handing the file to Powell. "I don't have my notes on Maud Lloyd at present, as Mr. Kilgour has them. But these are my notes for Annie."

Powell opened the file and glanced at the illegible writing on the pages. "Might I borrow this and have my father-in-law translate? While I have represented many physicians in my practice, I have yet to master the ability to read a doctor's handwriting."

Moore laughed. "Of course. Anything to help Mrs. Lloyd."

"And where is her file?" Powell asked, flipping the folder over in his hand. "And the files for the rest of the family?"

"I am uncomfortable making my notes on Mrs. Lloyd available without her permission. As for the rest of the family, those records are in boxes somewhere. It will take me some time to pull them from the storeroom."

"I'll have Mrs. Lloyd sign an authorization when I see her next." Powell smiled, making another note in his diary. "Speaking of Mrs. Lloyd, were you at her home Monday evening?"

"Yes, as a matter of fact. Delphi sent for me. Said that Mrs. Lloyd was a bundle of nerves with the arrest and all and needed something to calm her."

"And you made a call to her home."

"I did."

"About how long were you there?"

"An hour or so."

"Seems like a long time to drop off a prescription."

Moore narrowed his eyes at Powell. "The woman was distraught and needed a friendly ear. Once I was comfortable that her hysteria had subsided, I left."

"Does Mrs. Lloyd often suffer from hysteria?"

"I would imagine no more than any other woman faced with these allegations and charges against her."

"Have you treated her for any other diseases of the mind—melancholy, mania?"

Moore lowered his head and his voice. "Look, Powell. I know what you're angling for. And frankly, claiming insanity ordinarily might make sense considering how damning the evidence against her is, but I attended that family, and despite rumors to the contrary, every one of their deaths resulted from natural events. Charles Lloyd had a weak heart. Mrs. Hammerly was in poor health and succumbed to a flu. The boys, by a sheer freak accident, mistaking the poisonous pokeweed for huckleberries on a berry-picking outing." Moore grimaced and shook his head. "Suffered for days until they both succumbed to the toxoid. And sweet little Annie died from cholera. As you well know, there was a bout of it going around this past winter. Horribly unfortunate and tragic, but all natural causes."

A heavy wagon thundered down the street outside, jarring the bottles and crocks on the shelves in a noisy clamor.

"And you are confident in your opinion?" Powell said as the cart passed and the rattling settled.

"I'm certain."

"And what about Mrs. Lloyd?" Powell asked. "You didn't answer my question. Does she suffer any mental condition?"

"I probably know Emily better than anyone. And I can assure you that she is not a lunatic. Yes, she's forgetful from time to time. Completely explainable by the trauma she has suffered in her life, first at the hands of an abusive father, then an abusive husband. Add the grief of losing all of her children. So, of course, she has a wont to forget and is plagued by the sleeplessness that nightmares can bring. But, in my opinion, no more than is normal given her circumstances. No more than normal for any of us who lived through the horrors of war."

"You say her father was abusive? Abusive how?"

"I don't know the specifics other than what her uncle, Frank Hammerly, mentioned. That the child had bruises in places that couldn't be explained. Frank and Liza had offered to take Emily, but the father wouldn't hear of it. That's all I know. Of course, Emily has no recollection of him or the tragic fire that took his life, and I suppose it's best that she doesn't."

Moore paused, looking out the window and the street beyond as he fought the emotion creeping into his voice. He looked back at Powell. "Emily Lloyd is a gentle woman with a kind heart. There is no state of mind that would cause her to intentionally poison Maud, let alone the rest of her children."

"Then how do you explain the presence of arsenic in the postmortem results?"

"Perhaps it was an accident. Arsenic can be confused with sugar. And Emily is forgetful. She could have forgotten when it was that she burned it, just like she forgot that she purchased it. Or perhaps the results are inaccurate due to a mistake on the part of this chemist in Baltimore. Frankly, I have no idea why. That would be your job to determine."

How do you know about her burning of the arsenic? Powell made a mental note.

"And I have every intention of looking into the validity of the autopsy and the analysis," Powell said. "Which brings me to my next question. During the hearing Monday, Mr. Kilgour stated that it was you who conducted the postmortem."

Moore squared his shoulders as he nodded. "I did."

"After you removed the little girl's stomach, you stitched the incision closed, yes?"

"Of course I did. It was the decent thing to do."

"And carefully, I might add, from my inspection of the child's body that afternoon."

Moore stared at Powell, a blank expression on his face.

"My question, Dr. Moore, is where was the stomach while you were carefully stitching the incision?"

"It was brought back here to my store."

"How?"

"I'm not certain I understand—"

"How was the specimen transported? And who brought it?"

"Freddie, the sheriff's deputy, brought it over from the Lloyd house. I sealed it in the jar, and Freddie took the jar and its contents by train to Baltimore."

"Did you place the specimen in the jar here at your pharmacy?"

"No," Moore said carefully. "At the Lloyd house."

With a glance at his journal, Powell wrote *Freddie* on the top of the page, reminding himself to stop by the jail on his way home to get the deputy's statement. If memory served him, Emily said the organs had been taken from her house wrapped in a blood-soaked rag. The bell jingled again, and another patron walked into the store. Moore called through the curtain again for Jason.

"As an apothecary, you sell arsenic here, correct?" Powell asked.

Moore nodded.

"Do you mind if I have a look at the log used to document those sales?"

"Not at all," Moore said and pulled the smaller journal from under the counter. He handed it to Powell. "You'll find all the controlled chemicals recorded by date of receipt with the initials of the purchaser."

Powell opened the book and scanned the purchases, paying close attention to the dates. There were no recorded arsenic sales to Emily before the deaths of any of her children earlier that year or in the summer of 1871. Powell turned the pages to April 1869. No sales of arsenic to Emily then either. Flipping the pages back, he searched for December 1868. There was a gap in the dates. Powell examined the ledger closely. It appeared that a page had been cut away at the stitching.

"There's a page missing," Powell said, looking from the book to Moore.

"Surely you are mistaken," Moore said.

Powell showed him the cut at the seam.

"That's odd," Moore said, his brow furrowed.

"Why would someone have removed a page?"

With a bewildered look, Moore shook his head. "I have no earthly idea."

Powell thumbed through the log. "It's not here." He looked up at Moore. "This is the time period that Charles Lloyd died."

"I don't recall off the top of my head."

"It is. Mr. Lloyd passed away around Christmas of 1868." Powell riffled through the book again.

"You know, now that I think about it, I remember an inquiry by the state about our sales a few years back. Perhaps the clerk sent them the page in response."

Powell looked at Jason, who was on a stool reaching for a jar on the top shelf.

"Jason's only been with me for six months now," Moore said. "I've had a number of clerks over the past several years. I'm not exactly certain who was here when the state made its inquiry."

Powell cocked his head and raised a brow. He made another mental note to reach out to his friends in Richmond to validate Moore's story. "Would you check your records, when you have a chance, of who was working for you then?"

"I'd be happy to," Moore said.

Jason stepped off the stool, jar in hand, and placed it on the counter. Powell watched Jason open the container and measure powder onto the scale. As Powell closed the ledger and handed it back, his glance caught the marble slab. A slight residue of silvery pale-blue powder from the previous order was still on the stone.

"May I see your account book?" Powell asked, keeping an eye on the clerk as he removed the powder from the scale and poured it onto the stone.

Moore pulled the account book from under the counter and handed it to Powell. He opened the book to the *L* tab while glancing at Jason, who had opened another jar and was measuring its contents onto the scale. Locating Emily Lloyd's account, Powell ran an index finger down the debits, noting the number of orders for bismuth, potassium bromide, and chloral. There were no specific debits for arsenic, but there were multiple transactions for "compounds" without further descriptions. He glanced again at the clerk, who had dumped the second powder onto the marble slab and was grinding the two chemicals with the pestle. Powell made a few more notes before closing the ledger.

"You've been Mrs. Lloyd's physician for a while now, yes?" Powell asked, handing the book back to Moore.

"Since the war."

"You mentioned earlier that Mrs. Lloyd's husband was abusive. Did she tell you this?"

"No, Liza Hammerly, Emily's aunt, told me that Emily had a tough go of it with Charles when he returned."

"As her physician, did you see any evidence of abuse?"

"No physical evidence." Moore hesitated. "But emotionally, I know that she suffered."

"Did she share with you the details of her suffering?"

"She never spoke of it directly, but I knew. How could I not know? And after her husband died, her outlook improved almost immediately. Cause and effect."

Powell scratched a few words on the paper before glancing again at the clerk. "Has Mrs. Lloyd mentioned anyone who had a grudge against her? Anyone who might wish her harm?" he asked, watching as Jason packaged the compound in a jar and handed it to the woman.

"Have you spoken with Sam Orrison?" Moore said, following Powell's gaze to his clerk.

Powell returned his attention to Moore. "He was the guardian of her children."

"There are ill feelings between him and Emily, and Sam Orrison isn't the kind of man to have as an enemy."

"Any idea what might have caused these ill feelings?"

Moore shrugged his shoulders.

"I heard something about a property dispute," Powell offered.

"I think there is more to it than that."

"Such as?"

"Couldn't say."

Couldn't or won't? Powell made another note and closed his journal. He had all he needed at the moment.

◆ ◆ ◆

The oil in the lamp was low and needed replenishing, but Powell was too absorbed in his work to notice. Janet had joined him for supper but had hardly spoken to him and had long since retired to her chamber for the night. His daughters were tucked in their beds on the third floor, with Rebecca sleeping across the hall from the nursery. The gray tabby had followed him into the study and assumed its spot on the edge of the desk, eyes closed and purring loudly over the scratches of Powell's pen. Finishing a correspondence to Mary Reynolds in Toronto, he laid the pen down and cradled his head in his hands, watching the cat as it dozed.

"So many avenues to pursue, Whiskers," Powell said. "So many theories to consider."

Despite the many paths to explore, his instincts told him where they all would lead. Mrs. Lloyd was insane and had murdered her family, even though she had no memory of having harmed her children—no knowledge of what she had done or why. In a sense, therefore, she was innocent of their deaths. Yet, by law, criminally insane.

All he needed to execute this theory was to have Dr. Berkley verify his instincts, find the cause of her hysteria, and convince a jury of twelve men that it wasn't Emily Lloyd's fault.

It isn't that simple, is it, Poe?

He hated when that nagging voice of doubt crept in, obscuring a perfectly good argument and a straightforward defense strategy.

A tragic fire. An abusive spouse.

"Insanity is the only logical explanation," he told the cat.

But is it?

He glanced away from the cat, moving his eyes over the study's walls.

Whether she was insane or not, Powell's doubts that the mother had deliberately poisoned the child had started in this very room the night Nannie had the tummy ache. And resumed at the Slack residence. They had grown louder during Moore's interview at the pharmacy. And again when Powell stopped by the jail on his way home and Freddie confirmed that the autopsy specimen was carried from the house in a rag. Worse, Freddie said that when he reached Moore's store, he laid it on the counter until Dr. Moore arrived and placed it in a jar.

So what, Poe? It's an insanity defense.

"Or is it?" he asked the cat. He tapped the pen on the desk. "What if the specimen was contaminated by arsenic on the counter? It would explain the fifteen grains." The tabby squeezed its eyes tighter.

But would Moore be that careless?

"Randolph Moore," he said aloud, shaking his head. The way Moore had kept referring to Mrs. Lloyd by her given name. The emotion in his voice when he spoke of her suffering. "Doesn't that strike you as odd?" Powell asked the cat.

His instincts told him that Dr. Moore was, indeed, having an inappropriate relationship with the widow, a woman whose mind Moore most certainly knew, despite his dismissal of the idea, was . . . diseased.

A diseased mind.

He riffled through his notes again. *Chloral.* He was familiar with the drug. Used to treat insomnia. *Potassium bromide.* He hadn't encountered it since a case in Staunton and was uncertain which particular disease of the mind it was prescribed to treat.

"What other explanation could there be than she is insane?" he asked aloud, looking at the cat. "And why would Moore deny her mind was compromised?"

Because he's protecting himself.

Powell threw his shoulders against the back of the chair. The tabby opened its eyes.

"Could it really be that simple?" he said aloud and rubbed a hand over his chin. Was Mr. Slack on to something? Could Randy Moore be complicit in helping Emily get rid of her husband and her children so that the two could be together? And what if Emily was unaware of Moore's actions? Perhaps the good doctor had acted alone. Arsenic was tasteless and odorless. He could have easily tainted her family's medicines with it. With her family out of his way, the doctor could have her all to himself. But this theory made no sense. Randy had children of his own. And if he were to poison anyone, Powell imagined that his wife, Virginia, would be the first on Dr. Moore's list.

He tossed the pen down on the desk, chastising himself for the thought that Moore might kill the children, but he had to consider the possibility. Kilgour certainly would in his arguments should he get wind of the rumors.

Look at the bismuth, Poe.

There it was again, that nagging voice. Powell recalled watching young Jason combine the chemicals on the unclean stone.

"What if the residue had been arsenic when the bismuth was ground?" he asked aloud and leaned forward in the chair. "That would mean Maud's death was an accident." He picked up the pen to make a note, but stopped, his mind racing. It wouldn't explain the deaths of the older children, unless, as Moore said, they were all unfortunate natural tragedies. But what was the likelihood of that? Four children dead in eight months? No mother was that unlucky.

Insanity is the only plea that makes sense.

Isn't that what he'd told JW? He reminded himself of his obligation to consider all plausible theories. Just in case his doubts were confirmed. As he mulled his thoughts over in his head, Powell had an idea. A brilliant idea that might just shut up that nagging voice.

SUMMER 1872

Side-by-side lay the father and the two little boys—the green grass spreading like a mantle of velvet over their peaceful graves—while at their feet, the fresh turned earth of two little mounds spoke more plainly than words could utter.
—Loudoun Mirror, May 1872

CHAPTER 12

"Shall we get started?" Matt asked the three attorneys sitting around the table in the Harrisons' law office. Matt, as always, was seated at the table's head with Powell to his right.

JW and John Orr sat opposite Powell to Matt's left. "Powell, why don't you brief us on where we are."

Powell glanced at JW before moving his gaze to Orr. John Orr was about Matt's age, but lanky, with sallow skin and sunken eyes behind wire-framed spectacles. His face was clean-shaven and his gaze scrutinizing, giving a professorial look to his overall impression. Unlike the other attorneys in the room, Orr didn't wear a jacket or a vest, but instead donned a burgundy woolen cardigan over his linen shirt.

"As you gentlemen are aware," Powell began, "last month, Judge Wallace remanded Mrs. Lloyd to the custody of the sheriff until trial."

"And as I understand," Orr interjected, "Wallace is set to convene the grand jury to hear the charges and make their indictment at the August court with the trial commencing the following week."

"That's correct," Powell said, pushing aside his annoyance at the interruption. "At the indictment hearing, we'll petition to move the trial to the circuit court."

"Circuit court?" Orr asked. "The circuit court won't meet again until when? The following quarter?"

"October," Powell said, his patience strained. "It allows time for the emotions of the town—and potential jurors—to calm. And gives us more time." He opened a book that was sitting in front of him and fixed his gaze on Orr. With an aloof shrug of his shoulders, Orr lifted his chin and peered down his nose at the book.

"As you know, we are pursuing an insanity defense and are required to meet the burden of proof established by the M'Naghten rule." Powell looked down at the book and read aloud. "'Every man is to be presumed to be sane, and . . . that to establish a defense on the ground of insanity, it must be clearly proved that, at the time of the committing of the act, the party accused was laboring under such a defect of reason, from disease of mind, and not to know the nature and quality of the act he was doing; or if he did know it, that he did not know what he was doing was wrong.'" Powell closed the book and looked across the table at his colleagues. "Basically, we need to show that Mrs. Lloyd was either unaware of her actions at the time she poisoned her family *or* that she doesn't know right from wrong. It would be ideal if we could demonstrate both, but for her to be deemed legally insane, we only need to prove one of the criteria, which, in my opinion, is the former."

"That she didn't know what she was doing?" Matt said.

Powell nodded.

"Kilgour will rely on the Thorn case in his argument," Orr said.

"Mrs. Lloyd has made no confessions," Powell replied. "She has no knowledge of purchasing poison or of administering it, and expresses all the outrage and anguish one would expect from a grieving mother."

"I'm not familiar with the Thorn case," JW said.

"It was a precedent-setting insanity case in Virginia that was heard about twenty years ago," Powell explained. "A servant girl named Mary Thorn used arsenic to poison the family she was indentured to. Her attorneys argued that her mind was diseased at the time of the murders and therefore she was not guilty by reason of insanity. But Miss Thorn expressed remorse and had confessed to the crimes, indicating that she was aware of her actions and thus not meeting the criteria of the M'Naghten rule. The jury found her sane and guilty."

"And sentenced her to hang," Orr said. "Your big challenge in this case is that the murders took place over a period of time. And that the victims were so young. In my opinion, it's easier for a jury to accept an insanity plea for a crime of passion than one that seemingly involves premeditation. Take the case of Margaret Howard in Cincinnati. She found her husband in bed with his paramour and in the heat of the moment stabbed his lover to death. She pleaded temporary insanity and was found not guilty."

Powell nodded, reluctantly impressed by Orr's knowledge of the case.

"Which is exactly why Kilgour will focus his arguments on premeditation and intent," Matt said.

"Agreed," Powell said. "His first order of business will be to establish motive and provide an expert to say that she's as sane as me or you, which won't be hard. He'll have Randy Moore testify, her neighbors and friends testify, all agreeing that she has never demonstrated any behavior of hysteria or insanity. Once he thinks he's established that her mind is not diseased, he'll try to convince the jury that each member of the family died from arsenic at the hand of Mrs. Lloyd. That will be a more difficult task and require physical evidence that, other than in Maud's death, he currently doesn't have. So he'll build his argument on circumstantial evidence. Mrs. Lloyd's purchase of arsenic at Edwards's store is one example." Powell glanced at JW to confirm that his protégé had learned a lesson. JW nodded in acknowledgment. "And he'll be searching for others.

"The theory behind our defense is that Mrs. Lloyd lacks the intent required to perform a criminal act because she is neither aware of, nor in control of, her actions, even as she understands that the act is wrong. While the forensics usually don't matter in an insanity plea, with so many victims, it's going to be difficult to explain her compulsion to kill in such a systematic way. Her lack of any knowledge of her actions will help our argument, but I'm going to need to cite a case of a similar circumstance where the insanity plea was confirmed by a jury. And I'm hoping you can find such a case, John."

"There was a case in California last year—San Francisco, maybe— of a woman charged with murder who was acquitted on appeal," Orr suggested. "Her claim was that when she killed her lover, her mind was temporarily diseased as a result of repressed menses. Perhaps this could be a logical explanation for the death of Mrs. Lloyd's family."

"We'll pursue that cause with the doctors," Powell said, "but I'd rest easier if the case involved multiple victims rather than a single crime of passion."

Orr nodded and made a note. "I'll see what I can find."

"What about that woman in New York?" Matt asked. "Vander something-or-another."

"The Elizabeth Van Valkenburgh trial," Powell said.

"That's it. Poisoned both her husbands for their intemperance," Matt said. "Said she killed them because they drank too much. God help me if Hattie got something like that in her head." He had a good laugh, despite Powell's frown.

"Not a good case for us," Orr said. "They hanged her."

"We just need one case that is similar enough," Powell said. "And after we get an evaluation from Dr. Berkley, we'll have Dr. Stribling corroborate the findings. Meanwhile, we need to make inquiries into any calamity in Mrs. Lloyd's background that caused her dementia and use it to build sympathy with the jurors. We need to find family members who will testify to strife in her early life. When we cross-examine the neighbors that Kilgour produces, we'll evoke the stories of the abuse she suffered at the hands of her husband."

"Careful not to accuse the victims," Orr cautioned. "Kilgour will roast you with the jury if you do."

"No need to worry about that, John," Matt said. "Powell knows how to handle juries—and Mort Kilgour."

"And then there will be our cross-examination of Randy Moore," Powell said, with an appreciative glance at his brother. "We'll use Moore's records against the prosecution by pointing out that Moore had no suspicions of foul play when he treated each victim and deemed the causes of death to be natural. When I was at Moore's pharmacy, I got a look at some of the purchases on Mrs. Lloyd's account. It seems Dr. Moore was prescribing her medications consistent with mental disease. We can use that also to undermine Kilgour's argument. And there's the fact that Moore lied to me about details of the autopsy. My guess is it is to cover up his lack of adhering to protocol for such procedures. In any event, I intend to use it to cast doubt on the integrity of the postmortem analysis."

"Aren't the forensics irrelevant?" JW asked. "Why not focus our efforts on proving her insanity?"

"The more doubt in a juror's mind, the better," Orr said. "Powell's got it right. Muddy the waters as much as possible."

"What about that cousin in Canada?" Matt asked. "Has she replied to your correspondence?"

"I've heard nothing. I sent a telegram to the Toronto police asking for their assistance in locating her, but have not had a reply from them either."

"The Canadians have their hands full with those Irish Fenian rascals," Orr said. "Trying to ransom Canada to Britain for Irish independence." He shook his head. "I doubt you'll get much assistance from them."

"How important is it to find her?" JW asked.

"She's the only person who can give testimony to Emily's childhood. Dr. Stribling insists that insanity most often correlates with some tragedy that occurred when the person was young. There was the fire. Could that be it, or was there something more?"

"What about alternate suspects?" Orr asked. "If someone else might be responsible, that will help a jury find a defendant not guilty, whether they're insane or not."

"We need to explore all other possible theories and potential suspects as part of that strategy," said Powell. "Kilgour, no doubt, is looking for more physical evidence. I suppose y'all know that they plan to exhume the graves of the boys and the other daughter tomorrow."

"How do they expect to autopsy a rotted corpse?" Matt said.

"You'd be surprised at how sensitive the Marsh test is in detecting arsenic," Orr said. "There was a case in the north where a husband was suspected of poisoning his wife. Long after he had her buried, the family was successful in petitioning the court to open the grave to conduct an autopsy. And sure enough, there were plenty of innards left to do an analysis and determine whether or not there was foul play."

"And was there?" JW asked.

"Like this case, enough arsenic to kill a horse," Orr said. "The husband was tried and sent to the gallows." He looked across the table at Powell. "You're going to have your hands full with this one, Powell. If they find arsenic in the bodies of the other children, I'd seek a change in venue. Maybe have the case transferred to Augusta County, where the judges like you. With that lunatic asylum there in Staunton, the court has more experience with insanity pleas. Plus, Mrs. Lloyd is an unknown in that community."

Maggie Greene and Powell's sister Corrie appeared in the office doorway.

"Pardon our interruption," Corrie said, removing the bonnet from her head. "But you told us to come straight here. 'No stops, no exceptions,' I believe were your words."

"Did you get it?" Powell asked, standing from his chair. Corrie nodded.

"What in blazes are you up to, brother?" Matt asked.

"Just investigating a theory," Powell said. "Ladies, please follow me."

Matt, JW, and Orr exchanged looks as Powell left the conference room.

"Did you have any issues?" he asked the women as they followed him down the hall.

"It went just as you explained," Maggie said. "It was the clerk that waited on us. Dr. Moore didn't pay me any mind, but he did question Corrie."

"What was his issue?" Powell asked as he rounded the corner to his office.

"He was surprised that I didn't purchase the compound from Edwards's pharmacy since we're family," Corrie said. "I told him that Dr. Edwards was out of inventory."

Powell nodded. "Did the clerk document the transactions in the logbook?"

"Just as you said."

"Perfect," Powell said. "And, Corrie, you watched him fulfill both orders, yes?"

"I did, and you were right. After he finished Maggie's transaction, he fulfilled my order and didn't clean the stone well at all. Just a quick swipe of the brush."

Powell smiled. "I'll take your statements on what you did this morning and exactly what you witnessed. All right?"

"Of course," Maggie said. "Anything to help."

Powell brought a jar from his credenza to his desk and removed the lid.

"Corrie, place your bag in here, please," Powell instructed. "I'll have a courier deliver it to Richmond." Corrie placed the brown bag inside the vessel.

"What about mine?" Maggie asked.

"Just set it on the credenza for the moment. I'll keep it here as evidence to corroborate your testimony, if the need should arise." Powell lowered the handles of the jar's lid, sealing in the contents. "And, ladies, please, not a word to anyone about what transpired today or about the content of your statements. The last thing we need is for Mr. Kilgour or the mayor to get wind of our little experiment."

"When I took the coach this morning, I had to tell Anne Marie that I was meeting you today. What should I tell her when she asks me about it tonight?"

"Tell her you've sworn to secrecy in your affidavit. And let that be the end of it."

Corrie eyed him with a raised brow, shook her head, and laughed. "That may work for you and Matt, but it's doubtful I'll get away with it. But don't worry, I'll think of something."

"How about after you swear out your statements, I take you both over to the inn for the midday meal? That way, you won't have to think of anything other than the truth. That your beloved brother treated you to dinner."

"What a delightful plan!" Maggie said.

Corrie glanced to the hall and the room where the other attorneys were still embroiled in discussion. "Are you sure you can break away?"

"It's the least I can do to repay you both for the favor."

◆ ◆ ◆

A cardinal was busy building a nest in the bush under Powell's office window, his red feathers flashing among the green leaves as he wove a twig into the labyrinth of sticks and straw. While he watched the bird, Powell's thoughts drifted to Maggie—strands of crimson in her blonde hair, glints of emerald in her eyes—her intoxicating smell had distracted him during the entirety of their luncheon hours before. Lavender and musk and a swirl of memories he was unable to shake: their long walks along the Tuscarora when they were young, sharing his life ambitions, her body so close to his. Abruptly, the warm feelings in his chest stopped as he remembered that afternoon when he'd brought her the grim news. Powell had arrived in full uniform at the doorstep of the stone house. When she had opened the door, the look on her face—the knowing. Her tears had started before he'd opened his mouth. She collapsed in his arms, and all he could say was "I'm so sorry." He held her through the night as she talked and cried. How easy it would have been for them to fall into bed, to reach for that comfort. But he would never have taken advantage of her while she was so vulnerable, so filled with grief. That night as she lay in his arms, Maggie had begged Powell to tell her how her husband had died. He told her that Captain Daniel Greene had died on Cemetery Ridge as part of General Garnett's first wave in the Gettysburg campaign. That he was killed in action and didn't suffer. *But that isn't the whole story, is it, Poe?*

His mind went back to that awful day in early July of 1863. Powell had been told that Danny was on foot and in front, leading his men, when the Yankees fired their big guns—grapeshot everywhere, riddled bodies dropping to the ground. Powell found him in a wagon with other wounded officers, his arm a mangled mess and his body weakened by the loss of blood. The horror and grief of that summer washed over Powell again as he pictured the scene of the dying men who had been loaded into wagons, limbs missing, gaping wounds of gnarled flesh, their bodies and faces covered in blood and mud, with God nowhere to be found.

It rained cats and dogs for days as they worked their way through the Pennsylvania countryside in the seventeen-mile wagon train toward Virginia. Powell rode up front alongside General Imboden and the rest of the command. Danny's wagon was about a half mile behind them. Grey Roberts, Moore's clerk's father, and JW's uncle, General Eppa Hunton, were injured, too, and in the same wagon. General Dick Garnett was dead. So were many of Powell's friends—General "Lo"

Armistead, Colonel James Hodges, Major Jack Owens, Colonel Ned Edmonds—nearly all the officers in General Pickett's brigade were killed or wounded. *So much loss. And for what?*

Powell closed his eyes. It was on the second day of the return—the axle on the wagon that carried Captain Daniel Greene broke in the mud, and Powell needed to come quick, a muddy-faced private had said. By the time Powell reached his friend, all the officers had been moved to the side of the road to shelter under an old oak. Danny was alive, but barely. The arm that, in hindsight, should have been amputated, had festered and fever had set in. Powell took his friend and held him, begging him to be strong and to fight. Danny laughed, or tried to anyway, and told him that he was sorry to be a disappointment.

"Fightin' ain't in the cards for me today," he said.

Powell opened his eyes and drew a sharp breath, remembering the gut-wrenching pain Danny's words had brought. Danny had made him make that promise and then looked at Powell with his crystal blues and winked, telling him not to worry so. It was then that Danny moved his gaze into the canopy of the tree. Powell could still hear his words:

"It's the most beautiful thing I have ever seen," Danny said.

"What?" Powell asked.

"The sun. It's so bright."

Powell looked up, and the rain was still pouring, the sky overcast and gray. There wasn't a ray of sunshine to be found that day.

"Take care of her," Danny had said.

"I see that you had dinner with Mrs. Greene," a voice boomed from behind Powell, interrupting the memory.

Powell startled and turned from the window. His brother Matt was standing in the doorway, a peculiar look on his face.

"And with our sister," Powell said.

"You need to be mindful, brother."

"Mindful of what?"

"'As a dog returneth to his vomit, so a fool returneth to his folly.'"

"Proverbs 26:11," Powell said.

"You get my point."

"It was only dinner."

Matt eyed him. "Let's not forget that you were a fool in love with her once. Careful not to let her make a fool of you again."

CHAPTER 13

A small crowd of the curious had gathered in the cemetery as the blossoms of the lilacs that fronted the neighboring crypt gently waved in the warm breeze. Onlookers watched in anxious silence as the laborers dug into the grave with their spades. JW, Orr, and Powell stood at the footstone, while at the headstone, Mort Kilgour, Sheriff Atwell, and Bobby Bentley kept a close eye on the gravediggers. Drs. Randy Moore, William Cross, and Jack Fauntleroy stood to the right, waiting. A gasp broke the silence when a hollow thud echoed from the pit.

"Sounds like they've reached the vault," JW said.

"That was fast," Orr said.

"He hasn't been in the ground that long," JW said, leaning forward to get a closer look.

Powell glanced at the name carved on the tombstone and the date. *Henry William Lloyd, July 26, 1871.* Powell's son, Bo, had been buried three weeks before the Lloyd boy died that same summer. Powell moved his eyes in the direction of the Harrison family plot about thirty yards away, where his young son lay in his grave. *How do You justify taking the lives of those so innocent?* Forcing back a mix of anger and grief, he returned his attention to the digging in front of him.

Once the laborers reached the top of the vault, the real work began as they unearthed around its edges to remove the lid. After a bit of effort, the heavy lid was removed, and the coffin gently lifted. Powell drew a sharp breath, forcing himself to watch. The three doctors hovered over the coffin. Powell willed his feet to step closer. Among the swaddles of creamy silk of the casket's interior lay the skeleton frame of a child fast crumbling to pieces. Powell closed his eyes for a moment, trying not to imagine the jumble of bones as his son. *"He healeth the broken in heart, and bindeth up their wounds,"* he thought, recalling the psalm that Mrs. Lloyd had quoted, as he glanced at his father-in-law across the open grave.

"Put the little sleeper back to rest," Kilgour said. "No point in disinterring the other boy—or the father."

"We'll have better luck with the girls," Bentley said, his face reddened with more than just the midday heat.

"Girls?" JW questioned, drawing the attention of the crowd. "You already conducted an autopsy on the youngest one."

"We only analyzed the stomach," Kilgour said. "I want analysis of the liver and entrails as well."

The gathering of observers stirred at the exchange between the attorneys. Powell pushed his grief aside and moved a hand onto JW's forearm.

"There may be potential jurors among the onlookers," Powell whispered. "Let's not give them a reason to think we have cause for concern."

"I think Kilgour might be on to you regarding Moore's bungling of the first autopsy specimen," Orr said under his breath.

Powell nodded in silent agreement.

The lid was replaced, and the coffin lowered back into the ground, before the laborers moved their work to Maud's grave. In less than half an hour of shoveling, the workers raised Maud Lloyd's coffin from the ground. When the lid was lifted away, the putrid smell was so foul, it nearly knocked over those closest to the grave. Powell pulled his handkerchief from his pocket and covered his nose and mouth.

"Jesus!" Bentley swore as he, too, reached into his pocket. "Don't you have something for that?"

"I brought some lime," Cross said, reaching into a case on the ground.

Despite the smell, Powell stepped close to look inside the coffin. There lay the little girl in a crisp white dress, her golden curls pulled from her face with a white ribbon. A golden chain around her neck sparkled in the sunshine. But for the stench, she looked as if she were merely asleep.

The laborers had tied bandanas around their faces to protect them from the foul odor. A bed headboard covered with a white sheet was brought to the graveside. The workers lifted the child's body from the coffin and placed it on the headboard. Dr. Cross sprinkled lime dust over the corpse as Moore approached, knife in hand.

"Just a minute," Powell interrupted. "Defense is opposed to Dr. Moore's conducting the postmortem."

The crowd stirred as Bentley's face reddened again.

"What's the basis for your objection?" Kilgour asked.

"Defense contends that Dr. Moore has a conflict of interest."

Bentley scoffed. "You must be joking! A conflict of interest?"

"Dr. Moore was the child's physician," Powell said. "Evidence of an unnatural cause of death would relieve the doctor of any claim of malpractice, would it not?"

"Are you suggesting that my son-in-law may have deliberately compromised the previous autopsy result?" Bentley asked.

"It's a theory," Powell retorted.

"You and your goddamned theories!" Bentley said, coughing, his face reddening more.

Powell could see outrage on Kilgour's face, too, as Bentley continued coughing and grasped his chest with his right hand.

"Are you all right, Mayor?" Kilgour asked as Bentley continued to hack.

"I'm fine," Bentley said, struggling to catch his breath.

"As you wish, Counsellor," Kilgour said, turning his attention from the mayor to Powell. "We'll submit to your objection. Dr. Cross will perform the procedure with Dr. Moore and Dr. Fauntleroy as witnesses."

"And the custodian of the samples?" Powell asked.

"I'm the custodian," Bentley said, still red-faced and his voice hoarse. "I plan to take the specimens on this afternoon's train to

Baltimore myself." He held his chest and struggled through another coughing fit.

Powell nodded and stepped back to stand with JW and Orr.

"Clever," Orr said with a nod and a subtle smile. "Interrupting Kilgour and provoking the mayor in the process. It's a smart move. Brilliant, actually."

Powell watched closely as William Cross cut into the dead child's abdomen with a knife. As gases released, the smell of death exploded from the body. Cross sprinkled more of the blush-colored powder from the jar. Pulling a handkerchief from his pocket, the aging doctor wiped his brow and held it to his nose before excising the liver from the body. Randy Moore pulled a thick glass jar from a bag and held it in an outstretched arm.

"Mr. Kilgour," Powell called from the footstone. "Would you please ask Dr. Fauntleroy to inspect the containers to ensure that they are clean before placing the specimens inside?"

"Jesus H. Christ!" Bentley bristled and coughed again.

Kilgour narrowed his brow, giving Powell a black look before yielding to the request. Jack Fauntleroy took the jar from Moore and looked inside. Upon finishing his inspection, Jack nodded to Powell and handed the container back to Moore.

"Satisfied, Mr. Harrison?" Kilgour asked, his eyes still on Powell.

"As long as Dr. Fauntleroy is satisfied, so is the defense," Powell said.

Dr. Cross cut more parts from Maud's abdomen and placed them in separate containers, while Moore labeled each one and sealed the lids with wax. When the doctors finished the procedure, the laborers picked up the corners of the sheet and moved the body to the coffin.

After lowering Maud's coffin back into the ground, they turned their shovels to Annie's grave. Within thirty minutes of digging, the vault was unearthed, the coffin lifted, and the lid removed. She, too, was dressed in white with a delicate chain of gold around her neck. Her blonde hair was tied with a bow on the top of her head, much like her image in the photograph that hung in Mrs. Lloyd's foyer. Other than the moss that covered her face in a green shadow, her remains were surprisingly well preserved. *This should please Bentley,* Powell thought. Within seconds, the smell of death, much stronger than before, permeated the air, causing a number of the observers around the grave site to gag and retch. Dr. Cross once again dusted the corpse with powder before the body was moved to the headboard.

Powell caught his father-in-law's attention and gave him a nod. With a handkerchief over his nose and mouth, Jack approached the child's body. Using his index finger, he lifted the child's upper lip and examined the gum.

"Is there something in particular you are looking for, Doctor?" Kilgour asked.

"Nothing in particular." Jack stepped away, looked over at Powell, and nodded. Powell folded his arms over his chest.

More jars were brought for Jack Fauntleroy to inspect. Dr. Cross reached to the ground and picked up the knife used to cut into Maud's body. Powell leaned toward JW and Orr.

"Are you gentlemen witnessing this?" Powell said in a low voice.

"What do you want to do?" Orr said.

"Nothing," Powell said.

"Shouldn't we object?" JW asked.

"No," Powell replied. "Just take note."

JW removed his journal from his pocket while Orr and Powell watched Cross cut into the corpse. Powell lifted his chin to catch Jack's attention, hoping that his father-in-law had noticed Cross's error. Jack followed Powell's eyes to Cross and offered another confirming nod. *Good*, Powell thought. A physician's testimony would go further with a jury than attempting to impugn Dr. Cross at trial. Not that it would matter much in an insanity case. But Powell's instincts told him that it might.

◆ ◆ ◆

The table was set with their best china and the silver that had belonged to Janet's grandmother. The candelabra and its tapered candles burned brightly at the center of the table. Janet rarely drank wine, let alone served it with supper, yet a bottle of claret had been opened and poured into leaded crystal goblets.

"I heard you had a rough day," Janet said as she came through the servants' door into the dining room.

Powell stared at her. This was the first time she had willingly spoken to him since the fight.

"Papa mentioned it when he stopped by to pick up the girls," she explained.

"The girls?"

"I thought you and I could use a night alone after today."

"What did your father say?"

"He told me what happened at the cemetery. How the two of you watched them pull those babies out of the ground. And how much it had bothered him. Especially when they brought up the little boy." She dropped her gaze to the floor before looking up at him. "I can't imagine how it must have upset you." She stepped toward him with an outstretched hand. "I'm sorry, darling. For what I implied during our row. And my behavior since. I've been so selfish. I should learn to be more supportive of you and your decisions."

Powell reached for her and took her into his arms, refusing to submit again to the grief and guilt he had felt at the grave site. "I've missed you," he said and kissed her.

"And I, you," she said as she pulled from him. "But I am worried. I'm worried about you and what this case is going to do to you. And to us."

"There's no reason to worry."

Before he could assist her with her chair, Janet seated herself to the left of Powell's usual spot at the table's head. He pulled out his seat and joined her at the table.

"Digging up a child that was buried within weeks of Bo. And what happened to those little girls. Being not much older than Nannie and Lalla. It's all too close to home, Powell." A worried expression darkened her face as she spoke. "And then there are the peculiarities of this Lloyd woman. It's too similar to what you and the family went through with Alice."

Alice wasn't what was troubling Powell. It was the images of Henry Lloyd's skeletal remains that he couldn't shake from his mind.

"This is not my first insanity defense since Alice." He reached for her hand, taking it into his.

"But this is not like the others, and you know it." Her eyes caught his. "And it's the first time you've defended a woman accused of killing her children. Mrs. Lloyd didn't simply lash out in a moment of hysteria and kill her husband. She is a woman so damaged, so deranged, that she took the lives of her entire family over many months without so much as a second thought. And I worry that your sympathy for her is personal. That it is your sister Alice you see, and not Mrs. Lloyd."

"When I said that Mrs. Lloyd reminded me of Alice, I didn't mean it in a literal way. It is simply some of her habits and mannerisms that the two share. That many who suffer a diseased mind share. That's the extent of it, I assure you."

"I have an ominous feeling about this, Powell. I really wish you would let it go. Let someone else defend her."

"There *is* no one else. That's what I tried to explain to you. No one that can take on Kilgour, Bentley, Charles Lee, and the warped sense of justice we have in this town—in this state. And while JW is skilled at developing and delivering solid arguments in the courtroom, his research and attention to detail is lacking. Plus, he's inexperienced with insanity cases. And Matt's entirely too busy. Who else is there?"

"What about John Orr? Pa said that he's working with you. Let him take over."

"John Orr is too confident. And confidence causes you to overlook the small things that will unwind an insanity defense. Insanity cases are different. They're difficult. They require making the jury see the defendant as a victim. John Orr has not the rapport with Mrs. Lloyd nor the empathy for her to pull on the jury's heartstrings. I'm sorry, Jan, but I have to see this thing through. It's what I've been called to do."

Janet lowered her head and nodded. "I understand." She looked up at him. "And even though I disagree with your decision, once made, it becomes our decision. Just as you, as her attorney, are committed to do all in your power to defend Mrs. Lloyd, as your wife, I shall do all in my power to support you. Whatever my own feelings on the matter."

A rush of emotion filled Powell's chest, and he reached for her hand. "You don't know what this means to me, darling."

"It is my duty," she said, her violet eyes warm and unwavering. "And my love for you."

As his eyes met hers, Rebecca pushed through the swinging door from the kitchen. She set a platter of sliced meat and a bowl of vegetables on the table.

"So how can I help?" Janet asked as she released Powell's hand and sat back in the chair, allowing Rebecca to serve.

Powell thought for a moment while Rebecca spooned peas and onions onto his plate. "That's plenty, Becca," he said. "Thank you."

Rebecca nodded and served Janet before leaving the room.

Powell took Janet's hand and bowed his head. "Bless us and these Thy gifts which we receive from Thy bountiful goodness through Christ our Lord. Amen."

"Amen," Janet said, releasing his hand as she pulled a napkin to her lap.

"Did you know Mary Reynolds?" Powell asked as he picked up his fork and knife and sliced the ham. "Her maiden name was Hammerly. Mary Hammerly."

Janet shook her head. "I don't believe so. Who is she?"

"She is Mrs. Lloyd's cousin. According to Mrs. Lloyd, she left Leesburg before the war and is in Canada now. So far, I have been unable to reach her, and no one I have interviewed on Loudoun Street has maintained contact with her. I need to ask her a few questions about Mrs. Lloyd's childhood."

"You're trying to find out if there was any sort of behavior in Mrs. Lloyd's past that would have predicted her insanity?"

Powell nodded. "Any trauma or strange behavior. If there was any family history of mental disease. She grew up in the same household as Mrs. Lloyd and is the only living relative the woman has."

"I can ask around if you would like."

"It would be of great help," he said as he reached for his wineglass. "And while you're at it"—he paused, gazing into the hock as the thought occurred—"ask if anyone is friendly with those sisters that live in the other half of that double."

CHAPTER 14

"Why?" Emily howled, tears welling in her eyes. "I don't understand why they continue to desecrate them so."

"I know it's upsetting. But it's done now, and your girls are resting in peace with the Lord," Lara said as Emily paced back and forth over the cold stone floor.

Emily jerked her head toward the bars, where she saw Lara in the shadows. "It wasn't just Maud and Annie they dug up. Freddie tells me it was Henry, too. My baby boy!"

"He wouldn't have been a boy for long," Lara said. "Sooner than later, he would have become a man. And we both know what that would have meant. It's just as well that he'll forever remain a little boy."

"Well, it doesn't make it right that the Lord took him from me, nor does it give that awful mayor the right to disturb him while he sleeps! Did I tell you that Freddie said my Henry was nothing more than dust and bones? Dust and bones, Lara!" Emily clenched handfuls of her skirts as she paced and wept.

"Emily. You must calm yourself. You'll not find any sleep at all to-night if you continue like this. Henry is with Jesus now. As are the others. And you know how Jesus loves children. Find comfort in that. Remember the song we used to sing to the children when I'd visit and they were frightened? Shall we sing together now?"

Emily nodded and hummed a few notes before joining Lara in singing the words.

"Jesus loves me, this I know, for the Bible tells me so. Little ones to Him belong. They are weak, but He is strong..."

"I hate him, Lara!" Emily shouted abruptly.

"Emily Samson!" Lara said sternly. "Saying such a thing about the Lord is blasphemy."

"Not our Lord. That mayor! I hate him! Hate him for what he did to my babies today. Hate him for putting me here!"

"I hate him, too, Emily. And though it is a sin to hate, in this case, I do believe the Lord will forgive us both. I've heard there's been all sorts of nefarious conduct on his part, including how unkind he is to his son-in-law."

"Dr. Moore? Where did you hear that?"

"It matters not. What matters is that you are not alone in your feelings about Mayor Bentley."

"Who else besides us shares this view? Because, to me, it seems he has the entire town fooled."

"Your attorney doesn't appear to care much for him. I know that Lilith despises him."

"Lilith?" Emily shuddered at mention of her name. "What motive could she possibly have for hating the mayor?"

"Let's just say that she has her reasons."

"The man is evil, Lara. Pure evil."

"The Lord knows evil and will hold Mayor Bentley accountable for his transgressions. He'll have his due soon enough."

Emily looked through the bars and into the shadows, unable to read the expression on Lara's face through the darkness. "What are you saying?"

Lara sighed. "It's getting late, my dear, and I must go."

Emily nodded reluctantly. "Oh, I forgot to mention. Mr. Harrison wants to meet with you and Lilith."

"I cannot fathom why he would want to speak with us."

"He's interviewing everyone in the neighborhood."

"Well, that just won't be possible. Lilith and I are taking leave for a while."

"You won't go too far away, will you?"

"Of course not! I will come to you if you need me."

"Thank you, Lara. For being such a friend. For everything."

"I will be here for you. Just like always. And do not worry any more about Mr. Kilgour or Mayor Bentley. Men like that get what they have coming. Sooner or later, chickens come home to roost."

CHAPTER 15

WEDNESDAY, MAY 22, 1872

It was a gorgeous morning, with horse-drawn carriages on the street and loaded wagons heading into town from the western villages. Standing on the stoop of Emily Lloyd's double house, Powell rapped on her next-door neighbors' door a second time. He leaned to look in the curtained window.

"There's been no sign of anyone there for weeks now," hollered a voice from across the road.

Powell turned to see Colonel Lewis Nixon on his front porch.

"I had heard from Mrs. Lloyd that they were leaving this morning and was hopeful I might catch them beforehand." Powell stepped off the porch and made his way across the street.

"As I said, haven't seen them in weeks."

"Do you know them?"

"My wife and I have only been here a few years now," Colonel Nixon said, a galvanized watering can in his hand. "Sold what was left of the farm after the war and decided to spend our last years in the comfort of town. As for the recluses, I couldn't recognize them any more than I could Adam's house cat. Occasionally I will see one of them watching the street from the window. Night owls, they are, with a lamp burning well into the evening."

Powell stood on the bottom step of the porch as the colonel poured water from the can onto potted geraniums in boxes on the window-sill. "What about Mary Hammerly? Emily's cousin that grew up in the same house with her. She's married now and has moved to Canada. Did you ever meet her?"

Colonel Nixon shook his head. "As I said, Counsellor, my wife and I haven't been here that long. I never met the lady."

Powell sighed.

"There's another matter I need to ask you about," Powell said, joining the colonel on the porch. "It's sensitive, so I ask you for the utmost discretion."

"I'll answer as honestly as I can. Any conversation between us will remain private."

"It concerns Dr. Moore. Have you noticed anything unusual about his visits while attending to the Lloyd family?"

Nixon shifted his stance, and his eyes darted.

"I'm not one to judge another man," Nixon said as he set the can down. "But I do worry about Mrs. Lloyd. She's a fragile person and has been through more than her fair share, you know."

Powell nodded, noting the change in Nixon's expression.

"Before her husband passed away," Nixon continued, "I noticed that Dr. Moore's carriage would often be on the street adjacent to the house just after supper. Now, her husband, Mr. Lloyd, worked evenings at his tavern, often not arriving home until long after midnight.

"At first I thought nothing of it. With so many children in the house, it wouldn't be unusual for one of them to be ill with any number of ailments. But one day I was walking home and caught Mrs. Lloyd out front as I passed. Dr. Moore's carriage had been there for a number of hours the evening before, so I inquired about the children's well-being. Mr. Harrison, I must say, she gave me one of the blankest stares I have ever experienced. She proceeded to tell me that all of her children were in perfect health. I explained that I had seen Dr. Moore come to call and I assumed someone to be ill. She looked right through me with those eyes of hers and told me that I must be mistaken. That it had been ages since Dr. Moore had tended the children or anyone in the house, for that matter. So either Mrs. Lloyd didn't want me to know that Dr. Moore was at her home for fear I might mention it to her husband, or Dr. Moore was making a house call to one of the women next door. Mrs. Lloyd has said that the one has a reputation for promiscuity, so perhaps that's the explanation. Or perhaps Mrs. Lloyd was attempting to deflect. In either instance, it's really none of my business."

Powell forced an uncomfortable smile. *This will soon become everyone's business,* said the voice inside his head. He thanked the colonel and cast his eyes to the house across the street. *It goes to motive, Poe. And you know it!* The voice in his head was booming. He needed to interview this Lilith. He moved his gaze to the stone house three doors down. If anyone knew, Maggie Greene would.

He pulled his watch from his waistcoat. Eight thirty. *It'll have to wait.* He was to meet JW at the clerk's office at nine.

◆ ◆ ◆

When he entered the office of George Fox, the clerk of the court, JW was sitting at a small table with a pile of documents in front of him.

"Until her death in 1869, both sides of the house were owned by Emily's aunt, Elizabeth Hammerly," JW said as Powell slid into an oak chair beside him. "In her will, Mrs. Hammerly deeded the twin where the Lloyd family resided to Emily. The other side of the house was inherited by a Mary Reynolds."

"She would be Emily's cousin, whom I've been looking for. Is there an address for her?"

"Nothing in here," JW said as he thumbed through the file. He looked at Powell. "No response to your letters or telegrams?"

"None."

"So the house was never part of Charles Lloyd's estate," JW said, skimming through the papers.

"That's right. Since the aunt died after Charles Lloyd's death, the half where the Lloyd family lived went to Mrs. Lloyd directly. And the children would not be entitled to any aspect of it until Emily died."

"Had they survived her."

"True."

"Are you thinking that the aunt bequeathing the twin to Emily provided Emily motive to kill her?"

"It doesn't matter what I think. But you can bet Kilgour will find a way to make it motive." Powell thought for a moment. "Ask the clerk to pull Charles Lloyd's will. And any records the court has of probate or chancery filings on his estate. Let's find out how much Lloyd's brother stands to inherit if Emily is convicted."

JW stood from the table and called for George Fox.

"Have George pull the property records for Orrison's tavern, too," Powell said. "And any suits filed against Sam Orrison."

"Orrison?" JW asked with a puzzled look on his face.

"Yes," Powell said. "I want to see if Orrison was enriching himself as Lloyd's executor and guardian of his children."

"I heard you had a run-in with him."

"Which is why you'll be the one to interview him."

"Powell Harrison isn't afraid of a confrontation with a bully, is he?" JW said with a wink.

"You get more with honey than vinegar, my friend. And there is no reason to put a sour taste in the man's mouth."

◆ ◆ ◆

"It's a sensitive matter involving the Lloyd case," Powell said as Maggie Greene joined him in the parlor carrying a porcelain mug in each hand. "One that I need to be assured you'll keep between the two of us."

"How long have we known each other, Mr. Harrison?" she said, handing him the coffee and settling onto the settee beside him. "You have always had my confidence. Without question."

"I'm on uneven footing here, as I'm not one to put much credence in gossip. But if the information I have is more than rumor, it's important that I know the truth. Yet to pursue the possibility, well, it's something that isn't to be done lightly, as it would destroy not only the gentleman's reputation but most certainly his family. I simply cannot act if I'm not sure."

Maggie stared at him, her brows knitted together. "What are you talking about?"

"It's concerning Dr. Randolph Moore."

"What about him?"

Powell drew a long breath. "Is he . . . involved with Mrs. Lloyd?"

"Involved?" She tilted her head and looked at him as if to read his mind.

Powell gave her a knowing look, willing her to follow his thinking. "You know."

Her eyes widened. "Why on earth would you pursue something like that?"

"Several neighbors have reported seeing Dr. Moore's carriage in front of her house for long periods of time and well into the evening hours. Now, perhaps it's all explained by him tending to her children or the women next door, but during my interview with him, I became suspicious that the rumors might have merit. The two of you are friends. Surely Mrs. Lloyd might share with you if she had feelings for him."

Maggie tightened her mouth and shook her head. "She's not said a word about anything like that. I do know he has taken supper with her occasionally. And that she's quite fond of him. But nothing inappropriate that I know of. Emily doesn't share her life with me in that way. She's a private person and a bit of a religious zealot. Even if she were having an amorous relationship with Dr. Moore, she would never discuss it openly. Not with me or anyone. It would be a sin, and she wouldn't want anyone to think her a hypocrite, if you know what I mean."

"I thought you'd have been more surprised, Maggie."

"The women in the neighborhood talk about her. They've mentioned Dr. Moore before. They've also nattered on about Emily being involved with some other man, a huckster from someplace in the Midwest that comes through the area every few months selling his wares. I did ask her about him, and she was quick to tell me that the fellow was visiting her neighbor. The one she doesn't think much of."

"Does this huckster have a name?"

"I'm certain he does, but I don't know what it is." She gave an easy laugh. "I've even heard it suggested that she had Sam Orrison in her bed. How outrageous is that?" She shook her head. "I've told you how she despises the man."

"Could these men be visiting Lilith, that woman who lives in the other half of the twin?"

Maggie shrugged her shoulders. "Maybe."

"Is there anyone else they talk about?"

"Well, there's you."

Powell blanched. "That I'm romantically involved with *Mrs. Lloyd*?"

"Heavens no." She brought her eyes to his. "Mind you, there are those who have that to say about your representing her. But the gossip to which I'm referring, sir, are the positively horrifying rumors about you and me."

"You and me?" Powell cocked his head.

"Your visits here seem to cause a sensation on the street."

"You can't be serious."

"Apparently our teas are seen as quite the salacious affair." With a gleam in her eye, she brought the cup to her lips and sipped the coffee.

Powell shook his head with a laugh. "If occasionally having tea with the widow of my childhood friend to ensure her well-being is salacious, then I suppose I am guilty as charged."

"I am quick to tell them that you are a happily married man and that if Janet Fauntleroy has no concern, neither should they. That seems to quell some of their excitement."

Powell felt as if his stomach had dropped to the floor.

Maggie narrowed her eyes, reading the expression on his face. "Jan—Mrs. Harrison—doesn't know?" Powell didn't have to answer. "Powell Harrison! This is a small town. People talk. Surely Janet has heard."

"Not that she's indicated."

"Why wouldn't you say something to her? It's not like there's anything scandalous going on."

A sudden uneasiness fell between them. Powell knew that Maggie was right. Nothing had gone on between them, but not telling Janet about his visits seemed to indicate that there might be.

"Perhaps I should mention it to her," he said finally.

"What you discuss with your wife is your business and none of mine."

From her tone, Powell wasn't certain she believed her words. And he wasn't sure he believed them either.

"And that goes for Emily and Randy Moore. None of my business."

"Not entirely, Maggie—Mrs. Greene—"

"Oh, come, Powell! We are old friends. I think 'Maggie' will do." Her eyes caught Powell's.

Powell glanced away. "If those two are engaged in an intimate relationship, it could impact her defense."

"How so?"

"Trust me when I say that it could be important to know, one way or the other."

Maggie thought for a moment. "Do you want me to ask her?"

"If you could, it would be most helpful."

"Then I'll drop by the jail and pay her a visit."

"I would greatly appreciate it."

Noticing the darkening sky beyond the window, Powell placed his mug on the serving table and stood. "Thank you for your hospitality, but I should be on my way home."

Maggie set her mug down and stood with him. "I'm happy for the company and happy to help," she said, walking with him to the hall. At the front door, she put her hand on his forearm. Powell turned toward her.

"Why haven't you told Mrs. Harrison?" She brought her eyes to his. "We are such old friends, you and I! Why not tell your wife?"

"It's nothing. I'm just a heel for forgetting to mention it to her." He took her hand, fighting against the surge of warmth in his chest at the touch of her skin. "Good night, Mrs. Greene. And thanks again."

CHAPTER 16

"How did your interview with Sam Orrison go?" Powell said as the carriage clipped along on the high grade of the road to William Lloyd's dairy farm in Philomont.

"It went nowhere," JW replied from his perch on the bench across from Powell.

Powell raised his brows.

"He refused to answer a single question."

"On what basis?"

"Other than it was none of my goddamned business?"

Powell scoffed under his breath. "It went that well?"

"And then some." JW laughed. "Hopefully we'll have better luck with Mr. Lloyd today."

Powell was skeptical that they would get any helpful information from Emily's brother-in-law. He redirected his attention to the scenery beyond the carriage window. Queen Anne's lace and the faded blue flowers of wild chicory dotted the dusty roadside as yellow-green waves of winter wheat rippled in the fields beyond. He moved his thumb to his ring, turning it on his finger. *Philomont.*

The carriage slowed, then turned onto a narrow lane lined with scrawny locust trees and the tangled vines of honeysuckle and briars of blackberry. Powell spotted the charred remains of a barn amid overgrowth.

"Another casualty of Merritt's burning," JW said as the carriage approached the ruins. "Those raids starved nearly half the county that winter. Not even the damned Unionists were spared."

"Neither was my sister," Powell said, his voice low.

Powell held his stare on the blackened boards rising from the crumbling foundation as they passed. During the last year of the war, Union brass had had enough of the guerilla attacks from the cavalry unit in which JW had served before his capture. General Grant had ordered General Wesley Merritt to burn every barn and mill in the county; destroy all crops, grain, and hay; and seize all livestock belonging to the county's residents. The intent was to eliminate all sources of sustenance and winter supplies for the Confederates. But more than grain and barns were devastated.

It was early December 1864. Union soldiers had arrived at the small farm where Alice was staying with her friend Eliza. The captain in command assured the women no harm would come to them. Soldiers ransacked the home, took silver and all the winter stores, burned the barn, seized Alice's horse along with the farm's livestock. When the soldiers left, Alice and Eliza probably thought the ordeal was over. Until later that evening, when three soldiers returned to the farmhouse, filled with liquor and foul intentions.

Remembering the jagged scar on Alice's shoulder where one of the men had bitten her, Powell closed his eyes. He hadn't seen the bruises on her face or marks on her wrists that Matt had seen. Those had healed by the time his leave was granted and he arrived at Morrisworth.

According to Matt, the rogues had bound the women and beat them mercilessly before assaulting them. By morning, Eliza was dead, and Alice was barely conscious. The men set the structure on fire and left, Eliza's body and Alice still in the farmhouse. Matt didn't know how Alice managed to escape the blaze. Half clothed with her hands still bound, she walked over a mile in the winter cold to the safety of a neighboring farm. Within days, Matt's telegram with news of the attack reached Powell at his post in Richmond, but it would be Christmas before he was permitted to travel home. When he arrived at Morrisworth, Alice wouldn't look at him. She barely spoke.

And neither would his father, still angered by Powell's refusal to practice in the Harrison firm and shamed by Powell's continued friendship with Maggie. Powell had cursed God that day. Cursed Him for forsaking his sister. Cursed Him for his father's rejection.

Powell searched for the identity of the men responsible for the attack and spent the week he was home interviewing residents of Philomont and the surrounding farms. Apart from vague recollections of their general physique, Powell learned nothing that distinguished the attackers from any other soldier in the Union army. And he cursed God again.

"It happened out here, didn't it?" Powell heard JW ask. He turned his attention from the window and his sorrow to his friend on the opposite seat.

"Yes," he said, his expression pained.

JW nodded and sat silent as the carriage rocked over ruts in the road.

As they rounded a bend in the lane, a two-story farmhouse surrounded by a number of wooden sheds came into view. Powell recognized the farm from his interviews to find Alice's rapists eight years before. Paint on the house was now peeling, and the sheds leaned in awkward directions under their rusted rooves. Brown cows were grazing behind the house, and a large new barn stood at the pasture's edge. Chickens and guinea fowl scratched in the dirt lawn, skittering out of the way as the coach approached. When their carriage halted at the front of the house, a withered woman poked her head from the doorway of the chicken coop. Powell opened the door and stepped out onto the dusty ground with JW following behind.

"Can I help y'all?" the woman asked, emerging from the building, an egg-filled basket in her hand.

"Mrs. Lloyd?" Powell asked, her face vaguely familiar.

She nodded warily.

"We'd like to speak to your husband. Is he at home?"

"What y'all want?" said a gravelly voice from the porch.

Powell turned to find a large man in a dirty undershirt and

indigo-dyed jean-cloth trousers held up by red-brown suspenders. His dark hair was uncombed, and as he moved from the shaded porch into the sunlight of the yard, Powell noticed a heavy scar under his left eye extending in a long crescent down his cheek to the angle of his jaw.

"Mr. Lloyd," Powell said with his hand extended. "Powell Harrison and my colleague James William Foster."

Hesitantly, Lloyd took Powell's hand.

"Billy Lloyd," he said and nodded in JW's direction.

"Some nice-looking cows you got back there," JW said. "Durham Shorthorns?"

"Nah," Lloyd said, glancing at the field. "Shorthorns don't produce long enough. Them there are Jerseys. Only ones I breed these days." He looked back at Powell and gave him the once-over. "Now, y'all ain't here to buy no dairy, so what'd y'all come out here for?"

"We represent your sister-in-law, Emily Lloyd, and have a few questions that we'd like to ask you."

"Y'all're lawyers?"

Powell nodded. "Yes, we are Mrs. Lloyd's attorneys. Might we step inside and have a word?"

"Y'all can ask me whatever it is y'all want to ask right here."

Powell glanced at JW. "Very well, then," Powell said. "We have a few questions about your late brother's estate. Do you know how much Mrs. Lloyd and the children received at the death of your brother?"

"Other than that tavern, Charlie didn't have much. Least not that I knew of. And from what I hear, Sam Orrison sold the tavern to himself for a song."

"Mr. Orrison was the executor of your brother's estate, yes?" JW asked.

Lloyd nodded.

"So you didn't benefit from your brother's death?" Powell said.

Lloyd gave Powell a menacing look. "What benefit would I have?"

"Just want to make sure I fully understand the situation," Powell said. "What about your mother's estate? I understand that she passed away not long before your brother. How was her estate settled?"

"Mama lived here with us. What little she had was split between me and Charlie. Course, Charlie never saw any of it. Only person that saw Charlie's half was that devil-eyed bitch."

"That 'devil-eyed bitch' being Mrs. Lloyd," JW said.

"Only one I know," Lloyd confirmed with a spit.

"Am I to assume that the rumors are true, then?" Powell asked. "That you blame Mrs. Lloyd for the death of your mother and your brother?"

"Don't it bother you, Counsellor? We eat over there with 'em, and my mother ends up dead. Then not a couple weeks later, Charlie up and dies. And then all them little kids." Lloyd rubbed a hand over his chin. "She's a cold-blooded killer, that one. Emily Samson may have y'all fooled, but she sure as hell ain't fooling me."

"Mrs. Lloyd tells us that you brought milk to her and her family," Powell said. "If you felt that way about her, why take her milk?"

"My wife made me take it for the girls. And I was in town anyway, so I dropped some off every now and then."

"How often did you take milk to the Lloyd residence?"

"Like I said, every now and then."

"Once a month?"

"Maybe."

"In February?"

"Dunno, maybe."

"Was Annie still alive when you delivered the milk in February?"

"She could have been. I don't remember."

"Was it a few days before she died? Like with Maud?"

"What are you trying to—wait." Lloyd's face reddened and his eyes hardened. "What are you accusing me of?"

"I'm not accusing you of anything. I'm simply asking about the timing of your milk deliveries to Mrs. Lloyd's house, to confirm if those deliveries coincided with the deaths of her daughters."

Lloyd stepped toward Powell. "You tryin' to say that I put poison in the milk to kill my own kin?"

"I'm not accusing you, Mr. Lloyd. I'm simply asking questions."

"And why would I do something like that?" Lloyd stepped closer.

"With the children out of the way and Mrs. Lloyd incarcerated for their murders, you would be the next legitimate heir to their estate." Powell held his stance, his eyes fixed on Lloyd.

"Why, you dirty—You *are* accusing me of murdering my nieces!"

Lloyd was fuming. "Get off my property. Get the hell out of here before I do something you'll regret."

"These are questions that we must ask in order to find the truth," Powell said. "Either you answer them now or you'll be compelled to answer before a judge and jury later."

"Y'all come to my home and threaten me?" Lloyd's anger rushed over his face as he took another menacing step toward Powell. "How 'bout I come to your home and threaten you?"

JW moved forward, placing himself between Powell and Lloyd.

"No one is threatening you, Mr. Lloyd," JW said, his hands raised in submission. "We just want to know the timing of when you delivered the milk."

"You want to know when I delivered milk? I tell you I don't remember when I delivered milk. And if you dare accuse me, Mr. Goddamn Lawyer Harrison, you'll be sorry you ever crossed paths with Billy Ray Lloyd."

• • •

JW pounded on the door of the other half of Emily's house as Powell pulled his collar tight around his neck. Dusk was falling, and the weather had turned disagreeable, drizzle pooling on their coats and gathering into small streams that ran down their shoulders and sleeves. Rain dripped from the roof onto Powell's hat as he leaned to peer in the window of Emily's neighbors' parlor.

"No light that I can see." Stepping back from the drip line, he squinted through the raindrops, looking up. "And no smoke from the chimney. It seems no one is here."

"Well, I'm not leaving until we've had a look inside for clues as to who these elusive women are," JW said, with another loud rap. "There's a dead bolt on this door. Why don't we go around back and see if that door is as secure?"

Powell raised a brow. "What are you suggesting?"

"Come with me. And don't ask questions if you don't want answers."

They walked through the side yard, water from the saturated ground sloshing above the soles of their shoes. Stepping onto the back porch, JW tried the door. "Locked but no dead bolt," he said, and pulled a metal ruler from his coat pocket.

"What are you doing?"

"Captain Foster came prepared," JW announced. He shoved the ruler between the edge of the mortise lock and the jamb. With a little jiggling, the mechanism released, and the door opened.

"This is breaking and entering," Powell protested.

"Don't worry," JW said, striding into the house. "I know a good lawyer."

The house was dark and damp. It took a moment for their eyes to adjust to the dim light filtering through the heavy curtains.

"Hopefully they're not lying in wait with a shotgun to greet us," Powell whispered.

"Hello?" JW called out. "Hello? We're attorneys representing your neighbor Mrs. Lloyd and wish to ask you a few questions. Hello?"

"There's no one home. Let's have a look around," Powell suggested as he reached for a lantern on a shelf and lit it.

They wandered through the kitchen and down the hall to the front parlor and stairs.

"It doesn't appear that anyone's been here for months." Powell dragged a finger over the top of a chest that sat in the hall. "And the furnishings seem decrepit."

The furnishings were old. And sparse. A braided rug in the foyer. No rug at all in the parlor. Just a worn settee, a rocking chair, and a small serving table. A large, ornate cross hung in the center of the wall.

"Shall we try our luck upstairs?" JW asked, taking the lantern from Powell and leading the way.

The house mirrored Emily's home, with three rooms on the second floor, one at the front of the house and two facing the rear. When JW reached the top of the landing, there was a thud.

Powell's heart jumped as something moved along the corridor floor.

"Rats," said JW with a knock on the first door. "Hello?"

Hearing no response, JW opened the door. Extending the lamp through the doorway, he squinted. "It's empty." He closed the door, and Powell followed him down the hall to the second chamber. JW's knock and announcement were met with silence again.

When he opened the door, Powell could see that this one had been occupied. There was clothing strewn over an unmade bed and on a chair by the window.

"Someone left in a hurry," JW said as he walked toward the bed.

"Or she's simply untidy," Powell suggested.

A dressing table caught Powell's attention. It, too, was disorderly, with perfume bottles and various tubs of creams and beauty powders scattered across the surface. He picked up a silver-plated brush.

"Looks like the lady is fair," he said, noting the light-brown hair entwined in its bristles.

"Well, hello, darling!" JW said, holding a cylindrical white object with rounded ends between his thumb and index finger.

Powell looked over at JW. "What is it?"

"It's an old maid's friend."

"A what?" Powell asked, his brow pinched.

"A dildo, my friend. And there, on the night table, are a couple of French ticklers for when the lady has company."

Powell glanced at the knobbed rubber rings on the table in silent curiosity. "Emily said that the one called Lilith is a woman without morals."

"She certainly seems to be without inhibition. Even I'd be taken aback if one of my lady friends had these on her night table."

"I don't want to know. Do you see anything that identifies her? A letter or anything?"

JW dropped the dildo on the bed where he had found it and looked around. "Nothing."

Other than clothing and cosmetics, they found no clues that identified the room's occupant. They left the room and headed to the chamber that fronted the street.

This bedroom was decorated in the same sparse style as the parlor. A small bed with a metal headboard was neatly made and covered with a yellowed quilt. The only items on the night table were a Bible and a glass kerosene lamp. A rocking chair was positioned by the window. And a carved wooden cross hung on the wall. Powell thumbed through the pages of the Bible, looking for any inscriptions. Finding none, he placed it back on the stand and walked to a chest of drawers in the far corner of the room. He opened the drawers. Inside were only a few pieces of clothing, most of which had been fashioned much earlier in the century. They were larger than the clothes in what Powell presumed to be Lilith's room. On top of the dresser was a framed photograph of a bearded man with three girls—two older, perhaps six and ten, and the youngest, a toddler.

JW opened a door on the wall abutting Emily's side of the house.

"This is a big closet."

"Hold on," Powell said and stood the silver frame back on the chest. He crossed the room and took the lantern from JW, stepping into the closet. The pungent odor of mothballs filled his nostrils as he pushed aside the clothing hanging at the back. There it was. Not disguised by wallpaper, but a short, painted door with a handle. He lifted it and the door opened. Behind was a foot or so of space running parallel between the two sides of the house. There was no floor, only floor joists. To the left, Powell could make out the chimney at the far end. In front of him was the back side of another door that most certainly adjoined Emily's closet.

"What is it?" JW asked.

"I'm not quite certain. Mrs. Lloyd said it was an access space to the shared kitchen chimney. Beyond the gap, there's a door that opens into Mrs. Lloyd's closet on the other side."

"Could they access Mrs. Lloyd's home from here?"

"Possibly. It doesn't look like there's a keyhole on this side. But the door is locked on Emily's side, and she doesn't have the key." Powell stepped onto a floor joist and pushed against Emily's door, trying to force it open. The door wouldn't budge.

"Won't open?" JW asked as Powell came back through the doorway.

Powell shook his head and shut the little door.

CHAPTER 17

A crack of thunder caused Moore to flinch. Pelting waves of rain whipped across the tin roof and sideways against the batten boards of the house. A decade ago, during a similar storm on the battlefields of Williamsburg, there had been no batten boards sheltering him, no protection from assault and the unrelenting battering. No rain could have washed away the carnage of that night. There was no thunder loud enough to wake the dead strewn across the sodden fields in that inky blackness. The storm had poured further agony on the wounded and dying and more misery on doctors like himself, who remained behind after the battle to ease their suffering.

"It never fades," said Bentley. "Ten years ago for you, sixty for me. No matter how much time goes by, it never fades away."

Moore lifted his eyes to his father-in-law at the opposite end of a long mahogany table.

"Autumn of '14, and I remember it like it was yesterday," Bentley continued. "Camped to the south of Baltimore, we were. A nor'easter just like this one. Drenching cold rain. Lightning. Sky so loud you couldn't tell if it was thunder or one of them damned rockets exploding.

I don't know which was worse—the beating the Brits gave those poor souls at Fort McHenry or the pounding that bitch of a storm gave us up there on Hampstead Hill."

"Papa!" scolded Virginia, Moore's wife. "We don't curse or speak of war in front of the children!"

Moore followed her eyes around the table to the three children, who were paying little attention to the adults as they devoured the potato cakes and gravy on their plates.

"Hogwash," Bentley responded loudly, the volume of his voice compensating for his hearing loss. "War is the price we pay for liberty, Virgie. No need to protect them from that. And I'm not saying anything the older ones didn't witness in that last damned war. Goddamned Yankees!"

"Stop with the cursing, Papa," Virginia said, the disapproval in her voice mounting. "And, Randy, stop encouraging him!" Her eyes fired at her husband like a warning shot.

I haven't said a thing! Moore thought.

Before she became Virginia Moore, the woman sitting to Moore's right had been Virginia Bentley—a strong-willed debutante with a pretty face and bright eyes who had melted his heart. But twenty years, seven children, a long war, and loss had hardened her temperament and the gentleness of her youth. Her hair, once deep chestnut with spicy glints of cinnamon and paprika, had faded to the cold gray of rusted metal flecked with pepper and salt. The bright and curious eyes he had so adored were now filled with skepticism and judgment. Her bewitching smile had long since turned unhappy. And somehow, he was to blame. The bride who had taken his breath away was now the wife who had him holding it in trepidation and despair.

"Why it always poured from the heavens during the worst battles, I'll never understand," the old man said, ignoring his daughter's glare. "Just adds to a soldier's burden."

"Perhaps it's God's hand, Bobby," Moore said. "His way of washing it clean."

"From the earth, yes. But never from our minds," said Bentley. His distant look landed between the sideboard and the clock above Virginia's head as if the memory were a painting on the wall.

"Dr. Moore?" interrupted a voice from behind him. Moore turned to find Silas, the family butler, wearing a crisp white jacket and a somber face.

"Deputy Roberts is here to see you, sir," Silas said as another clash of thunder shook the house.

Silas's interruption had provoked his wife further. "Don't tell me that woman is calling for you again."

"Let me find out what the trouble might be," Moore said.

"This is the third time this week," Virginia barked.

Moore excused himself from the table to find Freddie dripping in the hall, his coat soaked as glistening droplets of water clung to the ends of his blond curls.

"Dr. Moore, we need you over at the jail."

"Mrs. Lloyd?"

Freddie nodded. "She's in a state of hysteria. Started this morning. Wouldn't take breakfast and has been pacing all day. Talking to herself, hollerin' and a crying. Sheriff says you need to give her something to calm her down."

"I will need to go to my store," Moore said.

"I'll drop you by there on our way."

• • •

Moore heard the wails when he entered the sheriff's office.

"By God, I hope you brought something to shut her up," Sheriff Atwell said.

"How long has she been in distress?" Moore asked, medical bag in hand and worry etched on his brow.

"All day. And getting worse by the hour."

Sheriff Atwell led Dr. Moore into the cellblock. Tearful cries intensified as they neared Emily's cell.

"I must get to him! He will not rest unless I go to him. My poor Georgie! Sweet Georgie!"

Emily was lying on the bed, her hands tied to the headboard's metal bars with baling string, and her feet bound together with rope. Her wrists were bleeding where the twine had cut her skin. Her forehead was bruised and swollen, and there was dried blood on the side of her face.

"Randy," she cried, her eyes darting over his face when she saw him. "I need to get to him. You must take me to him. Please." She arched her back and pulled against the bindings.

"What have you done to her?" Moore exclaimed as Atwell unlocked the cell door.

"Had no choice, Doc," Atwell said, yanking the door open. "She was trying to get out and was banging her head against the cell door so hard we thought she might knock herself unconscious."

Moore rushed to Emily's bedside.

"I need to go to him!" she shouted, thrashing on the bed.

"Emily, please, you need to calm yourself," Moore said, and placed his hand on her cheek while examining the contusions on her forehead. She turned her face from his touch.

"You tell them to cut me loose! I need to get to Georgie!" She pulled against the ropes again, blood oozing from her wrists.

Moore brought his eyes to Emily's. They were wide, wild, and filled with desperation.

"I need you two over here," Moore said to Atwell and Freddie as Emily screamed again. He opened his bag and pulled out a syringe. "You'll need to keep her still."

Atwell grabbed Emily's shoulders and pushed her body firmly into the mattress.

"Untie her right arm, Freddie, and hold it steady," Moore said. "I need to find her vein."

Freddie pulled a knife from his pocket and cut the rope that constrained her. When her right arm was freed, Emily struck at Moore. Freddie grabbed her wrist and forced her arm to extend as Moore prepared the injection. Moore moved his fingers gently over her skin in the crook of her arm, searching for a vein.

"Let me go!" she shouted as she struggled against them.

"Got one," Moore said. "Now hold her tight." He patted the vein with two fingers to encourage it to rise. "Steady now." He pushed the needle into her flesh and pressed the plunger that released the tranquilizer into her body. Emily screamed at the puncture, arching her back and kicking her bound feet. Within a minute, her body relaxed.

"There's my girl," Moore said under his breath as Emily quieted.

He brushed the hair from her face and touched the bruises lightly with his fingertips. He turned to the sheriff. "Let's get these ropes off."

The sheriff nodded to Freddie, who cut the other arm loose.

"Mrs. Lloyd," Moore said, taking her bloody wrists and holding them in his hands while Freddie released the binding at her feet.

With heavy lids, Emily's eyes met Moore's.

"What's all this fuss about George?" Moore asked, rubbing his thumbs over the base of her palms above the cuts.

"Today is July 24. The day he died," she said, slurring the words. "I have to get to the cemetery. Put flowers on the grave. So he can rest another year."

"I see." Moore offered a sympathetic smile. "Why don't you let me clean up these abrasions and put a little arnica on those bruises, and then, after I've got you all patched up, I'll stop by the cemetery and pay George a visit. And perhaps, if the sheriff agrees, maybe tomorrow, he'll take you over there so you can put flowers on all the children's graves." Moore glanced at Sheriff Atwell, who was leaning against the cell wall. Atwell thought for a moment and nodded. "How's that sound, Mrs. Lloyd?"

Emily smiled as she dozed off.

"She gonna be all right?" Freddie asked.

"She'll sleep through the night, then starting tomorrow, I will want you to administer some powders to her with her meals and at bedtime. I'll drop them off first thing in the morning."

"Sure thing, Doc," Freddie said.

"You really want me to take her to the cemetery?" Atwell asked as Moore applied a salve to Emily's wrists.

"A visit to the cemetery will do her better than any medicine. And I'll bring a bouquet of gladiola from my garden for the occasion."

CHAPTER 18

SATURDAY, JULY 27, 1872

Powell was getting dressed for the day when he heard screams. With no socks on his feet and shirttails flying, he raced down the stairs to the source of the cries. The front door was wide open, and Janet was standing on the porch. She was holding a lid in one hand with the other palm against her cheek. "Oh, dear God! Oh, dear God!" she wailed over and over.

Powell rushed to her, taking her into his arms. She buried her face in his chest and held him tightly. "What is it, darling? What's wrong?" he asked.

"In the can," she bawled. "In the can."

To the left of the door stood a tin milk can. Powell leaned to look inside. A lump of gray and black fur was floating in the white cream. Releasing his wife, he reached into the can and pulled the furry lump out of the milk as he tried to comprehend what his eyes were seeing. The lifeless dripping head of an animal rolled backward, its eyes half closed and its mouth open.

Whiskers!

Powell felt the air leave his lungs. "No, no, no," he cried as he cradled the cat in his arm. Milk and cream dripped from the fur over his shirtsleeve and onto his pant leg. He pressed his hand to its breast, hoping for some sign of life. From the coolness of the animal, he knew it was too late. Stroking the cat's head like he always did, he wiped the congealed cream from its face and closed its eyes as tears pricked his own.

Rebecca came running down the hall from the kitchen, a dish towel still in her hand. "Miss Janet, are you all right?"

"It's Whiskers," Janet said between sobs.

"Hand me that towel, Becca," Powell said, extending his free arm.

"What happened?" Rebecca asked, giving the towel to Powell. Milk continued to drip from the fur onto the porch as he gently wrapped Mr. Whiskers in the cloth. With the bundled cat cradled in his arms, Powell took the lid from Janet with his free hand and put it back on the can.

"Come, Jannie, Becca. Let's go inside," he said and led the women into the house.

"What happened to Nannie's cat, ma'am?" Rebecca asked as Powell closed the door behind them.

"I came downstairs and saw something on the porch through the side light. So I went out to see what it was, and—" Janet brought her fingertips to her lips and closed her eyes. "What are we going to tell Nannie?"

"We'll figure something out," Powell said and turned to Rebecca. "Would you take Whiskers out to the shed? I think there's a crate in there we can put him in. After we tell the girls, I'll dig a grave out back for him, and we'll give him a proper burial."

"Sure enough," Rebecca said, taking the cat from him.

Powell waited for Rebecca to leave before turning to his wife.

"Did you see who left it?" he asked.

Janet shook her head.

◆ ◆ ◆

"Probably just a hungry cat crawled in the can and drowned itself," said Sheriff Atwell, lifting the lid from the can as he and Powell stood on the front porch.

"It's my daughter's cat," Powell said, his temper sparking at Atwell's obtuseness.

"Still, it could have crawled in of its own accord," Atwell theorized.

"And how did the lid get back on if it wasn't a deliberate act?"

"Are you sure it's your cat? I mean, there are a lot of feral tabbies around the milk barns. It could have been one of them, and your man didn't notice the cat in the can when he loaded up his wagon this morning."

"Yes, it's our cat. And our milkman doesn't deliver milk by the can. I told you when I called you over who was responsible."

"So you say," Atwell said, replacing the lid on the can.

"The man threatened me and my family, Bernie. Mr. Foster was witness to the exchange."

"I don't question that Billy Ray Lloyd threatened you," Atwell said. "The trouble is that if he did, indeed, drown your cat, he hasn't committed a crime."

"He destroyed my property," Powell said, his anger mounting.

"The property you're referring to is the cat?" Atwell asked.

"Yes, the cat."

"You know the law better than I, Counsellor. There's no value applied to a cat. What would I charge him with? Felonious murder of a feline?" Sheriff Atwell glanced at the can and rubbed his goatee. "Look, Powell, there is nothing I can do about a drowned cat in a milk can. If I had to guess, Billy Ray will either deny the act outright or say that he brought you the milk to show his appreciation for your assistance in defending his brother's widow."

Atwell was right, and Powell knew it. There was no broken law that Lloyd could be charged with, however cruel the act. He released a defeated sigh and extended his hand.

"I'm sorry to have wasted your time, Bernie. I appreciate you stopping by."

Atwell took Powell's hand and looked at him sympathetically. "Billy Ray Lloyd has always been a bully. And you know as well as I that a bully has a coward's heart. So I wouldn't worry too much about him doing any direct harm to you or your family." Atwell stepped off the porch. "If it makes you feel any better, I'll let Lloyd know that I'll be keeping an eye on him when he's in town."

"I appreciate it, Sheriff," Powell said.

"Not a problem." As the sheriff started down the street, he turned back to Powell. "And if I were you, I wouldn't be getting your daughters any more cats until after this trial is over."

CHAPTER 19

After arriving by train from Staunton earlier in the week, Dr. Allen Berkley spent three days analyzing Emily Lloyd and had at last completed his evaluation. The psychiatrist from Western State Lunatic Asylum had joined Powell, JW, and John Orr in the conference room of the Harrisons' law office to discuss his findings. Like the asylum's director, Dr. Stribling, Berkley was of a quiet nature, cautious in his opinions and mild in his manners. Powell was not surprised at all that Frank Stribling had selected a deputy in such likeness to himself.

"As I mentioned at dinner this afternoon," Dr. Berkley said, lifting his index fingers from his steepled hands, "most of those who are criminally insane are happy to admit their transgressions. The act of confessing helps relieve their anxiety. Yet Mrs. Lloyd adamantly denies any wrongdoing. She denies any responsibility at all. She genuinely believes that someone else is responsible and that her incarceration is all a terrible mistake. Now, could she be denying her role because it's all too horrible?" He waved his index fingers again. "Possibly. To admit accountability would most certainly throw her into an irrecoverable state of melancholy. But she believes that she is innocent. And I must say, she is quite convincing."

"Do you believe that she is telling the truth? That she did not administer the poison to her children?" Orr asked.

"I must say that I do," Dr. Berkley said.

"So she is not insane?" JW asked.

"Clinically speaking, no," Dr. Berkley said. "Not as I can discern anyway."

JW pushed his frame back from the table, his shoulders falling against the back of his chair.

"Perhaps you can explain insanity for us, Doctor," Powell said, noticing JW's frustration.

Dr. Berkley folded his hands on the desk and leaned forward. "Insanity can be divided into three clinical categories—mania, melancholia, and dementia—and each of these can present in acute or chronic forms. Whether or not these divisions embrace all forms of the disease included under the general term 'insanity' is uncertain. Personally, I have witnessed variants at the asylum. But by and large, these are the most common forms."

"So which form would cause a mother to kill her own children?" Orr asked.

"Hypothetically speaking, of course," Dr. Berkley said, "if Mrs. Lloyd had committed the deeds of which she is accused, she would most likely suffer from acute mania or periodic insanity, which is a combination of mania and melancholia together." Orr raised his brows.

"Let's start with the former," Dr. Berkley suggested before Orr could ask his question. "Acute mania is the most violent and the most dangerous form of insanity. Its accession is generally sudden, often violent, and its symptoms generally unequivocal. It's usually attended by increased heat of the head, facial flushing, frequent pulse, furred tongue, constipated bowels, sleeplessness, loud talking, rapid change in feelings and mood, and, most notably, delusions. As for periodic insanity, it's far worse than acute mania. In my opinion, there is no form of insanity that is more troublesome or more difficult to cure."

"What is it, exactly?" JW asked, lifting his back from the chair, a hint of encouragement in his eyes.

"Periodic insanity assumes intervals of violent mania and deep melancholia. It begins with extreme expressions of the acute mania that I described, followed by a period of deep depression, overall wretchedness, and a tendency for suicide. These transitions occur at recurring intervals—annually, semiannually, or more frequently. The violence of one form of the disease may generally be predicted by the severity of the preceding form. In some cases, the mind seems to be nearly rational for long periods of time; in others, the delusions remain long after the excitement subsides. The extremes can last for months. Sometimes the transition is very sudden, and the patient is either greatly excited or greatly depressed. But they most always occur sequentially and always in the most intense forms."

"And you don't believe Mrs. Lloyd suffers from either?" Powell asked. "Acute mania or periodic insanity?"

Dr. Berkley hesitated, lifting both index fingers of his folded hands as he formed his answer carefully. "Let me explain it this way. If she is, indeed, responsible for the crimes with which she's charged, Mrs. Lloyd is the most organized insane patient that I have ever evaluated. She doesn't present the characteristic signs of acute mania or periodic insanity. Yet there could be no other explanation if she did, in fact, poison her family."

"So is she or is she not insane?" JW asked.

"Mr. Foster," Dr. Berkley said, "if you need an evaluation deeming Mrs. Lloyd insane in order to keep her from the gallows, I can certainly provide you with such a report. Based on her background and the abuse she has suffered, any doctor would corroborate such a finding. She has memory issues and suffers from blackouts, nightmares, and insomnia. These are typical responses of the mind to trauma and stress. Females also have secondary issues caused by their reproductive systems that can bring on temporary bouts of hysteria. But I must say, she does not present the typical kind of acute mania, melancholia, or dementia that would explain her alleged crimes. And that supports the theory that she might very well be wrongly accused."

The door to the conference room opened, and Matt poked his head through the doorway.

"Apologies for interrupting," Matt said, "but I thought y'all would want to know right away."

"What is it?" Powell asked.

"It's Mayor Bentley," Matt said, stepping in the room with the knob still in his hand. "His daughter found him in their backyard about an hour ago. The whole town is buzzing with the news." His complexion was ashen.

"He's dead," Matt said. "Bobby Bentley is dead."

◆ ◆ ◆

On Saturday morning, the townspeople gathered at St. James' Episcopal Church to pay their respects and say their goodbyes to Mayor Robert Bentley. Hundreds of mourners had tried to push their way into the chapel, with those arriving late standing at opened windows in the churchyard to hear the service. When the eulogy concluded, Janet held tightly to Powell's arm as they stood from their seats, watching the pallbearers carry the coffin past them toward the carved double doors. Matt, his wife Harriette, and the rest of the Harrison clan stood alongside them, waiting for their pew to empty into the aisle. The Harrisons followed the others out of the church and made their way to the grave site on the north end of the town. People now lined the streets as the funeral procession passed, waiting to fall in line behind the mourners walking to the cemetery. The outpouring reminded Powell how popular Bobby Bentley was in the community. Powell also noticed glances and stares in his direction as he and the Harrison family walked to the cemetery. He was aware of rumors that Bobby Bentley's heart attack had been brought on by the pressures of the Lloyd case and Powell's role in it.

"Served in the Virginia 57th in the second British war alongside General Armistead Mason and General George Rust at Baltimore," Matt said, nodding toward the uniformed militiamen standing in salute by the opened grave. "Legends, those men were."

"It was a different time," Powell said. "A time when the country was truly united."

"Not so sure about that," Matt said. "I think we've always been divided over one thing or another. That's what democracy breeds. The freedom to express a different opinion. It's what makes us Americans."

"And what nearly destroyed us," Powell said as the internment service began.

Seated by the grave was Bentley's immediate family: Randy Moore and his wife, Virginia, along with their children; the mayor's son,

Robert, and his family; and members of the Bentley clan that Powell hadn't seen in years. Moving his eyes over the crowd, he spotted JW with his mother on his arm standing just behind the militiamen. John Orr, too, was in attendance, along with Judge Wallace, Sheriff Atwell, Mort Kilgour, and every lawyer in the county. The Harrisons stood in silence, listening to the vicar's words. As the service concluded and the coffin was lowered into the ground, they fell in line with the others to toss a handful of earth into the grave.

When he reached the grave site, Powell picked up a fistful of soil and looked down at the coffin. There were scatterings of red clay and stones strewn over its lid.

"By God's Grace, may you rest in peace," he said under his breath and dropped the earth into the pit. He turned from the opening in the ground to Bentley's family sitting alongside the grave. Randy Moore was on the end with his wife, Virginia, heavily veiled beside him.

"Mrs. Moore," Powell said. "I am so very sorry for your loss."

"Are you, Mr. Harrison?" Virginia snapped in a voice loud enough that those in earshot could hear.

"Virginia," Moore said in a hushed voice, leaning toward her.

"Yes, ma'am," Powell said. "I know the despair of losing a father. My heart is heavy for you and your family."

"He'd still be with us if it weren't for Mrs. Lloyd and all the stress that case caused him," she said, anger rising in her voice. "You, Mr. Harrison. It is you I hold responsible. You!"

Powell stood before her, frozen.

"Come, Powell," Janet said with a gentle tug on his arm. "Let us leave Mrs. Moore to her grief."

He followed Janet's lead as she pulled him past the rows of chairs filled with Bentleys and Moores. He scanned the men and women in the procession behind them as he walked past their stares.

"Pay her no mind, Powell," Janet said as they left the cemetery and headed toward the church, where their carriage was waiting. "She's just a bitter woman looking to deflect her anger. How could you possibly have had anything to do with her father's death? He had a heart attack, for goodness' sake."

"I suppose she could be referring to my argument with him over how the autopsies were conducted. It's not exactly as if Mayor Bentley and I got along."

"Arguing your position is hardly a crime, nor can you be faulted because, after all his intemperance and swearing, the man's heart finally gave way," she said as they reached the carriage. "And besides, that was months ago. If anything, the constant berating of his daughter would be enough to send the best of men to the grave."

Powell suppressed a chuckle as he opened the coach door.

"I'm not certain I've ever seen you so agitated," he said.

Janet had pushed the veil from her face, her eyes pensive. "While I may not agree with your decision to represent Mrs. Lloyd, I will not stand by and allow that hateful woman to disrespect my husband."

Moved by her fierce loyalty, he had no words.

"You are doing your job, Mr. Harrison," she declared. "And I shall do mine."

CHAPTER 20

TUESDAY, AUGUST 6, 1872

Powell held the telegram from Richmond in his hand. Drawing in a long breath, he stood from his desk and walked across the hall into Matt's office.

"Got a minute?"

Matt looked up over his spectacles. "By the look on your face, I can tell that whatever it is will take more than a minute. Did Kilgour find out that you are planning to take his job?"

"Not that I know of, although he'll find out soon enough when the announcements are made next week." Powell pulled a chair to the front of Matt's desk and sat. "I finally received the results from a theory I tested."

"What theory?"

"That the bismuth Randy Moore prescribed was responsible for the death of Maud Lloyd, and possibly Annie Lloyd."

Matt removed his glasses and sat back in his chair. "Are you about to tell me that Mrs. Lloyd may not be insane because you think that the girls died from bismuth?"

"Yes and no."

Matt scrunched his face the way he did when he knew he wasn't going to like what he was about to hear.

"When I interviewed Moore at his store," Powell explained, "I noticed that his clerk didn't clean the mortar well between mixing compounds for different customers. I became curious—perhaps the bismuth that Mrs. Lloyd administered to Maud was tainted *before* it came into her possession. So I enlisted Corrie and Mrs. Greene to assist in a little experiment."

"Mrs. Greene?"

"I was confident in her oath of secrecy."

Matt raised his brow. "What kind of experiment?"

"I instructed the women to enter Moore's store in succession. Mrs. Greene first, followed by Corrie a few minutes later so as to not arouse suspicion. Mrs. Greene requested thirty grains of pulverized arsenic. Corrie followed behind her with a prescription provided by my father-in-law for bismuth in the same amount. After the clerk weighed each order, packaged their purchases, and recorded the transaction, the women delivered the compounds here. I sealed both in separate containers and sent the bismuth to Richmond for analysis. I just received now the report from our cousin, the brilliant Dr. Graham Ellzey."

"Let me guess. The clerk didn't thoroughly clean the mortar, and Graham's analysis shows there is a trace of arsenic in the bismuth." Matt interlocked his fingers behind his head, leaning further back in the chair.

"More than a trace."

Matt brought his arms from his head to the desk and leaned forward. "How much?"

"About an eighth of a grain."

"Holy Jesus!" Matt said.

"Or something like that."

"How much bismuth did Moore prescribe for Maud Lloyd in the three days before she died?"

Powell shook his head. "I don't know, since Kilgour has Moore's notes. But I do have his file on Annie, the older daughter, whom Moore treated with bismuth the month before. I asked my father-in-law to look it over. From his interpretation of the shorthand and Moore's horrendous handwriting, the girl may have consumed nearly forty grains of bismuth salts throughout her illness and presented signs indicative of bismuth overdose in the postmortem."

"Forty grains?"

"If you factor that proportion mathematically, it's more than enough residual arsenic to kill a child."

"Yes, but it hardly adds up to fifteen grains. There would have to be a gross amount of residue left on the stone to account for that much poison in the bismuth. How can you explain fifteen grains of arsenic in the child's stomach to a jury?"

"Graham says that fifteen grains of arsenic would kill the child almost immediately. It would be impossible for her to linger for hours, let alone days, as she did."

"You're saying that there's an error in the analysis," Matt said.

Powell nodded. "Either an error in how the chemist calculated the weight of the precipitate in the specimen, or Freddie laid the stomach in a pile of arsenic at Moore's store."

Matt slid his chair up to the desk, leaning even further toward Powell. "To prove that the bismuth was contaminated, we'd need to compare Moore's arsenic sales to the days the bismuth prescriptions were filled," Matt said. "Assuming we could correlate the records, the chances of it happening once, fine. But multiple times?"

"I agree. And Moore does record every arsenic sale in a register, so we could do that analysis, assuming he doesn't destroy the records."

Matt pulled in his chin and a look of puzzlement engulfed his face.

"There was a page missing for sales in December 1868," Powell said, "the time when Charles Lloyd died."

"You cannot be serious."

"Moore had some excuse about an auditor from the state requesting it," Powell said. "I checked my sources there. They don't conduct audits in such a fashion."

"So why would Randy lie?"

"I have another theory on that." Powell shifted in his chair. "There may be something more to the relationship between Randy Moore and Emily Lloyd than doctor-patient."

Matt sat back staring at Powell blankly until he caught on. "He's fucking her?"

Powell tightened his mouth, uncomfortable with Matt's choice of words. "There's a strong indication that the two are in an intimate relationship, yes."

"Jesus, Powell! This would go to motive." Matt rubbed his hand over his mouth and chin. "Are you sure?"

"No, I'm not. It's based on rumors from two of the neighbors, only one of whom is a very credible witness, and he was unsure if Moore was visiting Emily or the woman next door."

"It won't matter which woman Randy's fucking. Kilgour will get wind of it. All it takes is a couple of witnesses pointing at Mrs. Lloyd, calling her an adulteress and a calculating killer. And there goes your insanity plea."

"Not if we don't plead insanity."

Matt sat back in his chair. "If I didn't know better, I'd think you were the one who is insane. She's charged with six counts of murder, Powell. How the hell do you present a winning defense for six murders without pleading insanity?"

"By trying only one."

Matt's face scrunched again.

Powell leaned forward in the chair, his eyes gleaming. "Kilgour has to *prove* her guilty of six murders. If I'm right about Moore and Mrs. Lloyd, Moore isn't going to testify that Charles Lloyd died of anything other than heart failure. Not if discovering that he's having an affair would point the finger at him as a suspect. As for the aunt and the other children, other than Billy Lloyd, who himself is suspect, I haven't interviewed a soul who can give any testimony that they died of anything other than natural causes. There's only one death in which Kilgour has any hard evidence against Mrs. Lloyd—the death of Maud. If I can corroborate that arsenic was purchased from Moore's store any time during the week that Maud became ill, I believe I can create enough doubt to convince at least one juror that Mrs. Lloyd is innocent. That is all I need to hang the jury."

"That's a big 'if.' What about Mrs. Lloyd's purchase of arsenic before Annie's death? And if her autopsy results show arsenic?"

"The purchase is circumstantial, at best. The woman did have rats. And the autopsy won't matter because the jury will never see those results."

"And how in God's name do you plan to keep postmortem analysis out of evidence at trial?"

"By pointing out to Judge Wallace at the indictment hearing that it was the deceased Bobby Bentley who delivered the specimens to Baltimore."

Matt looked over the desk at his brother for a long moment before a smile grew across his face. "It's a pretty smart move. One Kilgour won't see coming. And it might just work. But let's not forget that Wallace and Bentley were friends. You could lose the motion."

"And if I do, I'll have a second bite at the apple when the case is moved to the circuit court. Even if Annie's autopsy is admitted into evidence, we'll prove the results invalid."

Matt raised his brow with disbelief on his face.

"First they powdered the corpse with some sort of lime dust that we'll claim compromised the specimen," Powell said. "Then Doc Cross used the same knife on both Maud and Annie without cleaning it between procedures. Since Maud's autopsy was conducted first, should the results of the analysis not be in our favor, we can claim that arsenic was transferred from Maud's sample to Annie's."

Matt shook his head. "It's risky, you know that, right?"

Powell brought his gaze to his brother's.

"It's about finding the truth, Matt. And the truth is that I don't believe Mrs. Lloyd is insane or a murderer. Is she odd? Yes. Is the evidence against her incriminating? Yes. But is it enough to convince twelve men that she murdered her own children? I don't think so. Not with what I'm discovering under each rock I kick. Dr. Berkley believes her when she says she's innocent and he sees no signs of brain disease. Nor have we found evidence of insanity in her family. Dr. Stribling at Western State said that abuse can precipitate mental disease—and heavens knows we've seen that ourselves in Alice—but I just don't see the evidence in Mrs. Lloyd. Is she odd? Yes. And she's forgetful and plagued by insomnia and night terrors. But she doesn't present the symptoms of insanity. When you combine the loss of her children with how these men preyed upon her—her husband, Sam Orrison, Randy Moore . . . He's the sickest one of all, if you ask me—a married man sleeping with a grieving mother." Powell shuddered at the thought. "If anyone is the victim here, it's Emily Lloyd. And I intend to prove it."

CHAPTER 21

.

"All rise," the bailiff announced as Judge Wallace entered the court-room and the August session of county court was called to order. Powell rose from his chair, JW and Matthew standing with him. Mort Kilgour and Charles Lee were across the aisle at a table on the left. Emily, behind a dark veil, was sequestered in the dock on the opposite side of the room. After the judge took his seat, he called the court to order and instructed the bailiff to bring in the grand jury. Within moments, the men were settled in their chairs behind the paneled, waist-high wall of the jury box, watching the bailiff closely as the charges were read.

"On the first count of murder in the first degree," the bailiff read, "the Commonwealth of Virginia charges that on March 21, 1872, in the town of Leesburg, the defendant, Emily Elizabeth Lloyd, adminis-tered one and a half grains of white arsenic to her three-year-old child, Maud Lloyd, that thereby caused her death on March 24, 1872."

Powell looked at Matt. With a graphite pencil, he scratched a note to his brother on the paper pad in front of him. *1½ not 15?*

Powell tossed the pencil on the pad and sat back in his chair as the bailiff continued reading the charges.

When the bailiff finished, Judge Wallace turned his attention to Powell. "Counsellor, I assume you have advised your client on the particulars of this morning's proceeding?"

"I have, Your Honor," Powell said, standing.

"And she is aware that it will not be necessary for her to make her plea, assuming she is competent to do so, until after all evidence in the complaint has been presented to the grand jury, and they have issued their indictment?"

"The defendant is aware, Your Honor."

"Very well, then," Wallace said. "Mr. Kilgour, you may proceed in presenting the state's substantiation of the charges."

"Your Honor," Powell interrupted. "Before the prosecution gets underway, the defense moves to exclude certain evidence as inadmissible."

Kilgour turned to Powell in a huff. "What evidence and on what grounds?"

"Your Honor," Powell said. "The defense will be happy to present our argument as to the inadmissibility of certain evidence as soon as the grand jury is removed from the room."

He kept his eyes on the judge, watching Wallace's reaction. The judge held his gaze to Powell's for a moment before addressing the bailiff.

"Remove the jury from the courtroom until Mr. Harrison has made his motion," Wallace instructed.

Powell glanced at the prosecution table to gauge Kilgour's reaction. His flushed face told Powell all he needed to know. Once the jury left the room, Wallace turned to Powell again.

"All right, Mr. Harrison. The jury is out of earshot. Make your motion," Wallace said.

"May I approach, Your Honor?" Wallace nodded, and Powell stepped from behind the table with the pleading in his hand. As the bailiff had not yet returned, Powell walked to the front of the courtroom and handed the judge one set of his papers, and on his return to the defense table, he handed the other set to Kilgour. He assumed his position behind the table.

"Your Honor, if it so please the court, the defense contends that the portions of the digestive system collected on June 1, 1872, from the bodies of Maud Lloyd and Annie Lloyd are inadmissible. The defense contends that the state cannot validate that at all times the specimens were in its custody. Therefore, the analysis of those specimens is inadmissible and cannot be presented as evidence to the grand jury." Kilgour's eyes nearly popped out of his head.

Wallace straightened his shoulders and frowned. "Mr. Harrison, it is up to the grand jury to decide if the evidence is sufficient to support the charge. You'll have your opportunity to argue the validity of the results at trial."

"I am not arguing the validity of the results, Your Honor. I am arguing that the results are inadmissible because the specimens themselves are inadmissible. Unless, of course, the prosecution can provide testimony to corroborate what happened to those specimens once they left Union Cemetery."

Frowning more, Wallace looked down at the paper before looking back at Powell. "I'm not understanding your point, Counsellor."

"Your Honor, the custodian of the specimens, the individual the state appointed to transport the evidence to Baltimore, was Mayor Robert Bentley, who, at present, is deceased. Unless Mr. Kilgour can verify that the late Mr. Bentley had those specimens in his possession at all times until they were delivered to Professor Tonry in Baltimore the following day, by law, those specimens and any findings resulting from their analysis are inadmissible. The grand jury cannot be privy to the results of any analysis stemming from the graveside postmortem without creating bias in their judgment in deciding to indict my client on the state's charges. Unless Mr. Kilgour can produce a witness who accompanied Mr. Bentley to Baltimore or can otherwise assert through sworn testimony that the state maintained proper chain of custody, the postmortem samples taken from Maud Lloyd and Annie Lloyd on May 21 are inadmissible."

Powell kept his eyes on Wallace, watching for the telltale bite of his left lower lip.

Wallace looked down at the motion before bringing his gaze to the prosecution.

"Mr. Kilgour, is there any witness the prosecution can summon to validate the proper custody of the specimens?"

"Your Honor, I am outraged by the defense counsel's insinuation that Mayor Bentley would sabotage the evidence. Robert Bentley was a highly esteemed elected official, an honorable man. How dare counsel impugn his character and question his integrity in such a reckless and shameful manner!"

"Defense is not questioning Mayor Bentley's integrity or impugning his character. We are demanding that which is required by statute—that the prosecution validate that the chain of custody of crucial evidence was not compromised. If Mr. Kilgour can offer testimony to confirm the proper control of the specimens, then we have no objection to the presentation of the analysis results to the grand jury. If he cannot, then the law is quite clear. The evidence is inadmissible."

"Your Honor," Kilgour protested. "The postmortem analysis shows that Annie, too, suffered from arsenic poisoning. This evidence is crucial to the state's case."

"Mr. Kilgour," Wallace said, "can the prosecution offer testimony to assure the court that the samples were in the state's custody at all times?"

"The mayor was unaccompanied on his journey to Baltimore."

"Can the state validate the chain of custody?" the judge repeated, his patience thinning.

"Not unless Mayor Bentley can testify from the grave," Kilgour fired, shooting Powell a look of contempt.

Wallace gave Kilgour a cautionary glance before moving his gaze back to the motion in front of him. And there it was, a nibble at the far corner of the judge's mouth. Powell smiled to himself and left off rubbing the inside of his ring. Wallace looked back at Powell.

"I'll grant your motion, Mr. Harrison, but without prejudice. Should Mr. Kilgour produce witnesses that can validate the adherence to proper controls over the specimens, I will allow the evidence to be admitted at trial."

"Understood, Your Honor," Powell said. Without the analysis showing that arsenic was found in Annie's remains, Kilgour was going to have a difficult day. And if Powell convinced Wallace to grant his motion to move the trial to the circuit court, he was confident those results would never see the light of day.

◆ ◆ ◆

"I don't know how you did it, Powell," JW said as the three attorneys took a table at the back of the dining room of Pickett's Inn, "but you pulled it off!"

"And I don't think I've ever seen Kilgour that angry," Matt said. "At one point, I thought he might charge across the aisle and pummel you with his fists right there in open court."

"I'm certain he was angrier when he read the notice announcing my intentions to campaign for commonwealth's attorney," Powell said, pulling his napkin into his lap. A serving girl with a white apron around her waist and a mobcap on her head approached their table and took their order.

"Well, you certainly got the better of Mortimer today," Matt said as the server left and headed toward the kitchen.

"I had a lot of help," Powell said. "Your argument that speculation is not evidentiary was particularly effective." Powell raised his glass of ale to Matt.

"As I recall, that's one of your favorites to hit Kilgour with," Matt replied, bringing his glass to Powell's.

"He expects it from me. It caught him off guard coming from you." Powell laughed.

"What I cannot understand is why Kilgour would have exaggerated the charges so egregiously," Matt said.

"Are you referring to the amount of arsenic they supposedly found?" JW asked. Matt nodded.

"My bet is that it was a typeset error," Powell said. "The scientific annotation for one and a half is one point five. Whoever transcribed the report must have eliminated the decimal."

"But why not tell us that earlier, when they found the error?" Matt asked.

Powell raised one brow higher than the other. "Do you really have to ask?"

"A grain and a half only further validates our theory," JW offered.

"It certainly makes it more plausible, yes," Matt said.

"All in all, it was a good day," JW said with a lift of his tankard. "The grand jury's indictment on only Maud's murder and getting the trial moved to the circuit court. We couldn't ask for much more."

"I knew the minute Wallace figured out that we were

abandoning the insanity plea, he'd want the case out of his court," Powell said.

"Did you see the look on his face?" JW said.

Powell smiled. "I did."

"It was priceless," JW said. Clearing his throat, he pushed his chin to his neck to imitate the judge. "'Mr. Harrison. Is your client pleading not guilty of her own accord?' And Powell says 'Well, Your Honor, she is the one who stands accused.' I thought the vein might explode from Wallace's temple! For a moment I was concerned he might keep the trial in his court just to spite you."

"And that's why I argued the motion to change the venue to Staunton and let Matt argue for moving the case to the circuit," Powell said. "I knew he'd reject the move to Staunton, so I let him feel like he had one on me. And I also know that Judge Wallace doesn't like saying no to Matt, since Matt's the one who got him that appointment to the bench."

"It wasn't anything Wallace didn't earn on his own merit." Matt raised his mug. "To a good day, gentlemen."

"Hear, hear!" JW and Powell echoed as they lifted their beers and drank. After setting his glass on the table, Powell ran his index finger around the rim. While the victory was sweet, he knew that getting an acquittal would be an uphill battle. He lifted his gaze to the other two.

"It was a good day. We won our motions and managed not to give Kilgour any insight into our strategy. But we do have a problem."

"One and a half grains of arsenic is still a lot of arsenic to explain," Matt remarked.

"Exactly," Powell agreed. "We have several avenues to pursue. We need to shore up our evidence to prove these theories, and we need to do so without tipping our hand. But now this case has visibility. Did y'all notice the reporters outside the courthouse waiting for the indictment? One of the men that approached me was from the *New York Herald*, if you can believe it. It's going to become increasingly difficult to keep our theories quiet with all of this attention. So from here on out, we hold the particulars of the case among ourselves. No discussing anything with anyone, not even our wives or families."

"That means no pillow talk for you, JW," Matt teased.

"I'll have you know I do not talk to my pillow," JW replied.

"And no talking to whatever pretty head might be lying on it either." Matt chuckled before turning to Powell. "And speaking of wives and families, you and I are going to have hell to pay when ours get wind of the change in plea."

"I hadn't really thought about it," Powell said.

"Well, you had better," Matt said. "Word travels fast in this town, and chances are Janet will have heard about it by suppertime."

"I doubt I'll be home in time for supper tonight. I have a couple of folks I need to interview this evening after I see Mrs. Lloyd."

Matt raised his brows.

"Just a theory I need to either prove or let go," Powell assured.

"Better send a messenger letting your wife know—and to gauge the temperature, if you know what I mean." Matt laughed as the waitress brought plates of catfish and corn cakes to the table.

◆ ◆ ◆

"Mrs. Lloyd," Powell said, pulling the chair from the cell's small desk with one hand and holding a folder in the other. He seated himself, facing her. "I need to ask you a few questions about the results from Annie's postmortem."

Emily tilted her head, looking at him with curiosity. "But it doesn't matter now since I am only charged with causing Maud's death."

"But it will matter if I'm unable to keep Kilgour from mentioning it at trial. Should that happen, I need to convince the jury that the evidence is tainted. Do you understand?"

Emily nodded.

"I have Dr. Moore's notes on Annie. If you'll look here, you'll see that he prescribed bismuth salts for her quite often." Powell leaned toward where she sat on the bed, pointing to the writing on the paper.

"I see," she said with a nod. "He did."

"And did you give her all the medicine that he prescribed?"

"I gave it to her exactly as he said."

"After Annie died and Maud died, what did you do with the remaining medicine?"

"I threw it out."

"In the trash heap behind your house?"

Emily nodded again.

"Very well, then." Powell offered her a reassuring smile before launching into the purpose of his visit.

"Mrs. Lloyd—"

"Emily, please. Call me Emily."

"We have only a short time before trial. And as your attorney, not only must I prepare my arguments but also my response to the prosecution's accusations. Which means I need to know everything there is to know about you, your life, and your family's life. And I need to know what others might say—wrongly or rightly—about you. Because we cannot risk being caught off guard. And if I know one thing about Mr. Kilgour, it's that he likes to sling mud, hoping to soil you in front of the jury. I cannot do my job if I'm not aware of everything Mr. Kilgour might try to use against you, no matter how insignificant it might seem or how painful and upsetting it might be to discuss." Powell narrowed his focus, his eyes intense and sincere. "So I'm going to ask you a few questions. And it is important that you answer honestly, even if the answer is uncomfortable. As your attorney, I am duty bound to hold any information you share in the strictest confidence. Do you understand?"

"I understand," she said hesitantly.

"All right, then." He smiled again. "Mrs. Lloyd—Emily," Powell corrected himself and drew a long breath, "do you have any romantic interests at present, or have you had any since the death of your husband?"

Emily blinked several times as her eyes darted over Powell's face. "I'm not certain I understand what you are asking."

"Are you in a romantic relationship with a man?"

Emily blanched. "Heavens no!"

Powell offered another reassuring smile. "There is nothing immoral about having warm feelings for a gentleman in that way, Mrs. Lloyd. You are a handsome woman and unmarried. Certainly over the past three years there has been someone with whom you have shared affection."

"I have done no such thing. Until recently, all of my affection has been showered on my children."

Drawing a long, slow breath, Powell shifted his position in the hard, uncomfortable chair. "Which is certainly understandable. The trouble is, Mrs. Lloyd—the trouble is that there are rumors on your street to the contrary."

Emily, too, shifted her position, straightening her back and shoulders. "What rumors?"

Powell could see ire rising on her face and hear indignance in her tone. "That you and Dr. Moore share a special relationship."

Emily threw her head back with a loud laugh. "Of course we do!"

It was now Powell who was confused. "Are you saying that the rumors are true? That you and Randy Moore are engaged in amorous congress?"

Emily's eyes widened, her irises like pastel-green saucers on white serving plates. "No, no, no! That's not what I meant. Dr. Moore has been a godsend to me. And I think I have been a good friend to him. He's a lonely man, you know. A pious man in a house full of heathens. I feel sorry for him, really, and like to think that his visits are a welcome respite from his strife at home."

"Does he visit you frequently?"

"He used to stop by every so often for a slice of pie and coffee and to check on me and the children."

"I don't want to offend you, but I have to ask. Are you and Dr. Moore intimate?"

"Are you suggesting that I have shared my bed with Dr. Moore?"

"Not suggesting. Simply asking."

Emily glared at him. "Dr. Moore is a married man."

"Unhappily, I hear."

"Happy or unhappy, he is married, and adultery is a sin. Dr. Moore respects the word of God too much to let wanton passions of the flesh tempt him from his faith. Shame on you, Mr. Harrison, for suggesting such a thing!"

"I have a duty to you in preparing your defense to investigate and refute these rumors. Regardless of your belief in Dr. Moore's fidelity, I have to ask if you think it's possible that Dr. Moore would be engaged in amorous congress with one of your neighbors? Perhaps one of the women who live next to you?"

"Dr. Moore would never commit adultery." Emily shuddered as if something were crawling between her shoulders. "And certainly not with the trollop that lives next door."

Powell flipped through his notes. "I believe you said her name was Lilith."

• • •

"Kind of late for you to be stopping by," Maggie Greene said as she peered at Powell between the door and its frame. The sun had just set, but the streets had yet to darken.

"I've been with Mrs. Lloyd at the jail and then had to follow up with a few of the men on the inquest jury," Powell said. "May I come in?"

"Aren't you concerned about what the neighbors will think?" she said as she swung the door wide.

"What your neighbors might say about me is the least of my worries. It's what they might say to Mort Kilgour that concerns me." Powell hung his hat on the rack in the hall and followed her into the parlor.

"You're referring to the rumors about Emily and Dr. Moore?" She offered him a chair and took a seat on the settee across from him.

"Rumors that she denies. Did she confess anything more to you since we last spoke?"

"Nothing. Although I've been thinking about my conversations with her on the subject and have been meaning to drop by your office to speak with you about it, but you've been so busy, and, well, Matthew always seems to be there. And you know how he and your father judged me so."

Powell straightened in the chair and leaned forward. "What is it?"

"As I told you, she denied any truth to the rumors. So I tried to get her to open up by sharing my own experience in being widowed and the frustration of having affection for a man married to someone else." Maggie paused, her eyes meeting Powell's briefly. "It was then that she went on about how miserable Dr. Moore was at home. And how horribly his wife treats him. That the woman doesn't know how lucky she is to have a man like Randy. It was when she called him by his given name that my ears perked up. While I can't say that they have slept together, I will say that she cares for him deeply."

"So you think they may have had an affair?"

"I'm not certain either way."

Powell moved his gaze to the window, collecting his thoughts, before looking back at her. "I have a favor to ask."

"Another one? Where shall I send the bill for my fee?" she teased.

"You can deliver it to Matthew."

Maggie tossed him a look. Powell grinned as he removed a folded paper from his pocket. "This is another prescription from my father-in-law for bismuth compound, exactly as Moore keeps on his shelf. I need you to go to Moore's pharmacy again first thing tomorrow and have him fulfill the order. Once you have it, come straight to my office. Will you do this for me?"

Maggie furrowed her brows. "Corrie and I already got the samples for you. Were they no good?"

"They were perfectly fine. But I need a second sample after his servant cleans the store, which, according to my housekeeper, happens this evening. The clerk won't need to compound this order, but sometimes he uses the stone as he weighs and packages orders. I want the stone to be clean, just in case, so I need you to be there when he opens, before any other customer."

"Why, Powell? I thought the entire point of the experiment was to prove that the bismuth was contaminated by the arsenic residue on the stone."

"That was the purpose of the experiment last time. But now I'm testing another theory."

"And you aren't going to tell me what it is."

"Correct."

"I should have figured as much." Maggie shook her head with a sigh. "Fine. I'll do it, but on one condition."

"A fee?"

"A trade. A bit of your time in exchange for mine."

Powell raised his brow.

"Will you join me for a cup a coffee and a bit of ginger cake?"

Powell hesitated. He glanced at the clock on the mantel. He had already missed supper. "I suppose I can manage it."

• • •

"I've been waiting for you," Janet said as she rose from the parlor's settee, her arms folded over her chest.

Powell closed the front door behind him and laid his hat and satchel on the bench.

"I sent a messenger that I would be late." He walked to her. "I'm sorry, Jannie," he said, and wrapped his arms around her waist. He felt her body tense at his embrace. "I hate it when I miss supper with you and the girls."

"I heard about what happened in court," she said, her mouth tight.

"A big victory. The grand jury only indicted on—"

"You changed the plea, Powell," Janet interrupted, pushing away from him. "We agreed that you would represent her because she is insane. And now you're defending her with the intent that she gets away with murder!"

"I don't believe she committed murder."

Janet put her hands on her hips, her visage cross. "And what about those instincts of yours that are never wrong? Those instincts that told you her mind was diseased and that because of her illness she couldn't be held responsible for her acts. And that no one else could represent her like you would because of your understanding of insanity. Your understanding because of Alice. What about all of that? Thrown out the window because you suddenly believe her?"

"I had doubts, Janet. From early on, there were doubts creeping into my mind. And like always, I began to explore alternate theories of what might have happened. And nearly every theory I've tested has proven true."

"Like the theory that Corrie and Mrs. Greene assisted you with?" Powell looked at her in surprise. "Anne Marie told Hattie. Hattie told me."

"I'm sorry, Janet, but you know that I don't discuss the details of my investigation with anyone. I didn't think it would be an issue."

"I'm not asking you to compromise your client's confidence, nor the specifics of your inquiries. But I do expect my husband to tell me that he has asked the assistance of his former love interest so that I am not made to look like a fool when I hear about it from my sister-in-law."

"I'm sorry, Janet."

"Are you, Powell? Are you truly sorry? Because this is not the first time that you've kept your activities with Mrs. Greene from me."

From the look on her face, he knew there was no denying it. "How long have you known?"

"Does it matter?"

"She was my best friend's wife. And you know my promise to watch over her as he lay dying in my arms. That's all there is to it."

"I believe you. I do. But what I can't understand is why you keep your visits with her from me." Her face was drawn, and there was hurt in her eyes.

"Because I didn't want to upset you."

"And why would you think I would be upset if, as you say, there's nothing to it?"

Powell didn't have a ready answer. "I don't know," he said finally.

Janet turned her back to him and moved to the window, staring into the shadows that were falling over the street. Powell came behind her and placed his hands on her shoulders, bending to her ear.

"Jannie," he whispered, resting his cheek against the side of her head. "There is nothing between me and Maggie Greene. There hasn't been anything between us since long before the war. You know this."

"It is not your relationship with Mrs. Greene that I'm upset about," she said, turning to face him. "You had every opportunity to marry her after the war had you wanted to. Her husband was dead. Your father was dead. There was nothing stopping you from taking her as your wife. Yet you didn't. What upsets me is much more than your fanning some old flame—it's your lack of trust in me. Your unwillingness to confide in me. To be open and honest. That's what hurts most of all."

"I do trust you. And I have been honest. There's no flame to fan."

"Keeping secrets from me about your meetings with that woman is not being honest. Not telling me that you were changing Mrs. Lloyd's plea is being deceptive." She narrowed her focus and looked him in the eye. "I am not like your sisters, where everything you do is scrutinized and questioned. And I'm doing my best to learn to trust your judgment, even when I disagree with your decisions. Sometimes it's a struggle for me to put my own opinions aside and to follow your lead. But when you mislead me, it makes it even harder."

Powell drew a heavy sigh. "I was over there tonight."

Janet stiffened. "Instead of having supper with our family, you were with Mrs. Greene?"

"No. I was interviewing members of the inquest jury during the supper hour. Afterward, I went by Mrs. Lloyd's neighborhood in search of those two women who live next door. And then I stopped by Mrs. Greene's to ask her to assist in testing another theory in the Lloyd case."

Janet glared at him, her eyes angry and hurt. "I'm going upstairs to bed." She slipped from his grasp and hastened to the door, leaving him alone in the parlor.

He stared at the doorway after she left, not knowing if he should follow her or leave her be. He turned to the window and rested his palms on the sill. Looking out at the street beyond the wavy panes, he watched as the shadows darkened and continued their slow creep as night fell. *Why, Powell?* he asked himself. Why had he said yes to Maggie's invitation for coffee? He lowered his head. *Why?*

Maggie Newton. So vivacious and full of life twenty years ago when they met. And so very different from the debutantes who had been arranged for him. The way she laughed. The intensity in her eyes when she spoke. And the flash of fire in them when she was angry. No other woman had made him feel the way Maggie had. How in love he had been! And when he discovered the barbarity of her father—the welts on her body and the bruises on her face—the rage he'd felt. He'd told his own father that he wanted—no, needed—to marry her. *"No son of mine will marry the daughter of an overseer, let alone the spawn of John Newton!"* Powell closed his eyes. The venom in his father's voice still stung. The next day, Powell was sent back to Charlottesville to finish his last year of law school, forbidden to see Maggie Newton again, but vowing to himself that when he completed his studies, he would marry her despite his father's disapproval. A few weeks later, a letter from his brother William that Maggie Newton was engaged to be married cut him to the core. Another letter would come the following day from his lifelong friend Danny Greene. *Twice betrayed.*

Powell closed his eyes as the memory of Danny dying in his arms rushed forward.

"Make me a promise, Powell," Danny had said, his voice weak and breathy.

"Anything," Powell had said as the rain poured over them both.

"Don't let her live as a widow."

"Not an issue, because you're too ornery to die," Powell replied, knowing that he was lying.

"Marry her. It's you she loves anyway."

"You are wrong, my friend. It is you whom she holds in her heart."

Danny forced a smile as his strength waned. "Marry her, Powell. For me."

Powell remembered being overwhelmed in that moment. His oldest friend dying in his arms, and old heartbreak erupting from where he had buried it.

Powell had nodded, but that hadn't been enough for his friend.

"Say it."

Danny's eyes pleaded.

"I promise."

But it was a promise he wouldn't keep. The betrayal had been too much. The scar too deep.

After he informed Maggie of Danny's death, he asked his brother William to watch over her, vowing to never again return home. But he'd broken that vow to make another. *Janet.* When his sister Corrie had introduced them, Janet had beguiled him, so graceful with those violet-blue eyes, long ebony locks, and haughty looks. Janet, with her clever wit and kind heart. Janet, for whom he'd left his life in Staunton to start a new one in the town in which he thought he could never again find happiness. And now, here he was, married to the love of his life, a woman who had given him a family and a dowry greater than any his father could have arranged, and yet, if he was going to be honest with himself, he was still wrestling with his old feelings for Maggie and the guilt of a promise broken.

Opening his eyes, he lifted his head, disappointed in himself for not trusting Janet enough to confide in her. He drew a long breath, forming an apology in his head, and turned toward the stairs.

CHAPTER 22

Their law clerk was sweeping shards of broken glass when Powell arrived at their offices. The large windows fronting the street had been shattered. Powell stepped carefully around the pile of debris and walked into Matt's office.

"At least they didn't throw torches in with the rocks," Matt said from behind his desk, sweat glistening on his brow. His sleeves were rolled to his elbows, and his jacket was hanging on the coatrack behind him. The August heat was already stifling, and it was not yet nine o'clock. "I spoke with the glazier. He'll have the panes replaced by the end of the day."

"What happened?" Powell asked, removing his own coat and taking a chair.

"Seems that a Bentley loyalist didn't take too kindly to our challenging the chain of custody yesterday and decided to express his displeasure."

"Or maybe it was someone who feels threatened by our change of plea."

"Now don't jump too far ahead of yourself, Counsellor. There was a note attached." Matt picked up a crumpled piece of paper from his desk. "'Curtsy—*c-u-r-t-s-y*—of Mayor B.,'" he read before looking back at Powell. "Since I cannot imagine that our rock-throwing friend is suggesting that Mayor Bentley was bowing to us from his grave, I assume that he broke our windows as a *courtesy* on behalf of the late mayor."

Powell took the note from Matt. The words were printed in block letters like those of a child.

"Probably one of the commoners that live along the tracks," Matt continued. "They loved him down there."

"Because they subscribe to his bigoted views," Powell said, and tossed the paper on the desk.

"Thus the reason neither you nor I would ever be elected mayor of this town," Matt said as he twisted the corner of his mustache.

"Glad I wasn't counting on that vote for commonwealth's attorney."

"You don't want support from men like that." Matt threw Powell a half smile. "It doesn't come free."

Powell watched as the clerk scooped the glass with a coal shovel and into an ash can. "I think I'm going to send Janet and the girls to her parents' until the trial is over. Between this rock-throwing incident and Whiskers, I don't want to take any chances should things escalate."

"Can't say that I blame you, but you know that Janet won't go. Hell, I'd send Hattie to Morrisworth, but leaving her alone with Anne Marie and Bettie longer than a day? She's probably safer at home."

Powell chuckled along with his brother.

"And there's other bad news." Matt picked up another piece of paper from the desk. "John Orr sent us a note." Powell raised his brow as Matt handed him a correspondence. "Now that we've altered the plea, it seems John has had a change of heart."

Powell took the paper from his brother and quickly scanned the page: . . . *morality prevents me from consulting on the Lloyd matter any further . . . no interest in returning a murderess to the community such that she can kill again.* He tossed the letter back on the desk. "No great loss, although I was counting on access to that library of his."

"Perhaps he'll be amenable to allowing you to use it," Matt suggested. "That shouldn't compromise his moral principles."

"I didn't realize a staunch supporter of slavery and secession had such high moral standards."

"Those days are long gone, my friend," Matt said. "Best to leave the past in the past."

While Powell agreed, he often found it difficult when the attitudes of men like Orr, Kilgour, and the late mayor had not changed from those they carried from before the war. He shifted in his chair.

"Mr. Matthew," the law clerk called from the doorway of Matt's office. "Mr. Hackney is here to repair the windows and needs to discuss his fee."

Matt pushed back from the desk and stood.

"I'm heading over to Moore's pharmacy this morning," Powell said as Matt walked past him and into the hallway. "Mrs. Lloyd finally signed a statement granting permission for Moore to release her file. And he promised me that he would make his notes on Maud and the rest of the Lloyd family available. Without Maud's records, I cannot correlate that arsenic purchase recorded on his register to Maud's prescriptions. Plus, I want to see if arsenic was sold prior to Annie's prescriptions being filled. Want to tag along?"

◆　◆　◆

"What do you mean we're not permitted to view the poison register?" Powell exclaimed, a mixture of disbelief and indignance in his voice. Randy Moore stood behind the counter, his reading glasses low on his nose.

"Just what I said," Moore said, brows arching as he looked at Powell over his wire rims. "I have been advised by the prosecutor that I am not to share any documents or information with you."

"Including your files on the Lloyds that you promised to show me?"

"The commonwealth's attorney took those records into his possession last evening. He informed me that my notes on Mrs. Lloyd and members of her family are considered evidence of the state and are protected as such."

"The commonwealth's attorney is afforded no such protection," Powell said, a blush erupting on his cheeks.

Moore shrugged a shoulder. "Take it up with Kilgour."

"My brother's correct. As a former prosecutor, I can assure you that the state is entitled to no such privilege," Matt said. "And as Mrs.

Lloyd's counsel, we have a right to examine any and all information that might aid in her defense. Surely, as her physician, you would want to do everything in your power to provide such assistance."

Moore tightened his mouth, narrowing his eyes as he leaned over the counter toward them. "Look, fellas. I've reviewed the log and my notes numerous times—there is nothing that incriminates her. I'd like to help, but I simply cannot risk getting further involved."

"'Further involved'?" Powell said, his frustration mounting. "You're involved up to your chin. You were the Lloyds' physician and treated all of the family members who died. You conducted the initial autopsy on Maud. Your store sold Mrs. Lloyd medical compounds." He bit his lip before he said any more. "Just let us have a look at the log. If, as you say, there's nothing in the book that incriminates Mrs. Lloyd, what's the harm? All we're looking for is evidence that might exonerate her. Isn't that in our mutual interest?"

"As I recall, Counsellor, at the grave site, you claimed that my interests were in conflict with the defense. And frankly, given a choice, I'd rather remain in conflict with you than be at odds with Mort Kilgour."

Powell felt the hair rise on the back of his neck.

Matt placed a hand on his brother's forearm. "No reason for any of us to be at odds with the other. We'll take the matter up with Mr. Kilgour, as you suggested. Come, Powell. Let's take leave of the good doctor."

Powell held Moore's gaze before tipping his head and turning for the door.

"Kilgour cannot withhold evidence like this," Powell said, the little bell jingling behind them as they stepped onto King Street.

"I agree," Matt said. "We can file a motion to compel when the court meets. But that's the first day of the trial. Not ideal, but it's the best we can do."

Powell released a quick, frustrated breath as the pair started toward their office. Matt raised a brow and looked over at him as they walked. "I'm not certain that I've ever seen you this riled up. It's not like you."

"I know. I shouldn't let him get to me." Powell blew out a long stream of air through his mouth. "How can he stand by and not do everything in his power to help her, considering—"

"Considering the compassion he should have as her doctor? Or the sensitivities he should carry in his heart since he's"—Powell shot Matt a cautionary look—"er, since he's *involved* with her."

"Both, actually." Moving his gaze to a distant point up the street, Powell shook his head. "I can't stomach that man. How compromised he is! And a Quaker to boot. Don't they believe that only good deeds lead to salvation? How does he justify such sordid behavior?"

"I think Randy Moore was disowned by the Society of Friends the day he married Virginia Bentley. And certainly serving as an officer in the Confederacy didn't earn him any sympathies among his family in Waterford."

The thought of Randy Moore taking advantage of someone as vulnerable as Emily made Powell nauseous. A patient should be able to trust a physician. He drew a long breath to quell his rising anger and restore his calm. As they crossed the street to their offices, he forced his mind to focus on how to get his hands on Moore's records. How might he convince Kilgour to grant them access?

"Why don't you approach him?" Powell said as they reached the office entrance, where the glazier was on a ladder, taking measurements of the window. "You and he were chummy during the war and have remained friendly."

Matt pulled in his chin. "I barely saw Randy during the war, and while my relationship with him is congenial, it's hardly friendly."

"No, I mean Kilgour," Powell said as they walked inside. "He would never acquiesce to me, especially now that my candidacy has been announced. Perhaps an appeal from you might convince him of the inevitable ruling against him when we go to trial."

"I'm happy to make the effort, but you know Mort as well as I do. Unless there's something in it for him—"

"We'll get nothing." Powell pressed his lips together. "The crux of our defense rests on correlating arsenic purchases recorded in Moore's logbook to the medicines compounded for the child the weekend she died."

"When you reviewed the register earlier, wasn't there an arsenic purchase that weekend?"

"Yes, but I don't remember the specific date. And I was hoping to find a similar purchase around the time of Annie's illness." He shook his head, scolding himself for being overly concerned about tipping his hand to Kilgour and not retrieving the records sooner.

"You still have the argument that Freddie contaminated the specimen from Maud when he laid it on the counter at the store," Matt said. "And we can always point the finger at the brother-in-law or the lecherous Dr. Moore, if need be."

"You know how I feel about insinuating unfounded claims in the courtroom."

"I do. But you and I know that it's all about creating doubt in the jurors' minds. We must be prepared to let fly every arrow in our quiver if we cannot otherwise prove that Moore's bismuth was tainted before it came into Mrs. Lloyd's possession."

"I understand that. But I'd prefer to cast that doubt based on the truth."

CHAPTER 23

"JW, you're not hearing me," Powell said. "There is no possible way a circuit court judge will grant a motion to quash an indictment simply because Kilgour didn't sign it."

"Judge Keith is new on the bench. I think it's worth a shot," JW said. Matt, Powell, and JW had been behind closed doors in the Harrisons' conference room all morning, arguing their trial strategy. With only a few weeks before the start of the October court, they were running out of time.

"He may be new, but from what I hear, he is anything but naïve," Powell replied.

"My friends in Fredericksburg say that he's barely out of nappies and that his appointment was a favor to his father. He wouldn't want to disappoint his old man by making any mistakes. My bet is that he will at least consider it. And who knows, we might get lucky."

"And should we get lucky and he grant the motion, the only effect will be a delay of the trial to spring," Powell said. "Explain to me what that buys us?"

"It would provide us the opportunity to petition the court for Moore's records and give us a chance to adjust our strategy, if need be. You said yourself that without correlating Maud's records to the poison register, we're walking into court blind on your theory that Moore's gross negligence is responsible for the death of the child."

"While I agree with you on the importance of getting our hands on those files, nothing short of a continuance will buy us a delay," Powell reasoned.

"The court will never grant a continuance," said Matt, who was sitting at the head of the conference table.

"Agreed," Powell said. "But if you want to move the court to quash, Jay, then by all means, be my guest."

"Mr. Harrison," the law clerk said, interrupting the exchange. "The letter that you've been waiting for just arrived."

"Is it from the cousin in Canada or from Richmond?" Powell asked.

"From Richmond, sir."

Matt and JW raised their brows in tandem as the clerk handed the envelope to Powell.

"And what have you been waiting for from Richmond?" Matt asked. "Another theory that you've neglected to tell us about?"

"You know I don't like to share my inklings until I have some evidence to validate them," Powell said.

"Well, the cat is out of the bag now. What's in the envelope?"

"It's the analysis on the bismuth salts from Moore's pharmacy that I asked our cousin Graham to examine," Powell said, running a finger under the seal.

"I thought you already had that tested once," JW said.

"I did. But I wanted to test a sample that was directly from Moore's shelf," Powell said.

Tilting his head to the left, JW furrowed his brows. "I'm not following."

"Those blue lines on both Maud's and Annie's gums have been bothering me. According to both my father-in-law and Dr. Ellzey, that marking is indicative of bismuth poisoning. And Graham says that if consumed in its raw form, it's just as toxic as arsenic. So I did a little research. Bismuth is a metal, and although its weight is heavier than lead, it's actually very brittle and easily pulverized. It's a pinkish color with a silver tinge. When used as a medicine, bismuth is usually combined with citrate, nitrate, or another salt, giving the compound's tint that shimmery blush. Sometimes the physician will add other substances to the bismuth salt, like salicylic acid, but those substances are not pink. When I asked Mrs. Lloyd about the bismuth she gave to Annie and Maud, she made an offhand comment that Maud liked taking the medicine because it was such a pretty pink when she mixed it with water. Not a pale blush color, but a bright pink. So I asked myself, what if Moore's bismuth salts had a higher than normal concentration of bismuth?"

"You're suggesting that the girls may have been poisoned from an overconcentration of the pure metal in Moore's bismuth salts?" JW asked.

Powell nodded. "That's the premise of my theory."

JW shifted in his chair. "How do you account for the arsenic in the autopsy results?"

"Bismuth and arsenic have similar natural properties," Powell explained. "In fact, they're in the same grouping on Mendeleev's chart of elements. Graham says that when conducting the Marsh test, a high concentration of bismuth in a sample will produce a similar residue on a porcelain plate as arsenic produces. And that it could be difficult for an inexperienced eye to discern the difference."

"Like the youthful eyes of Professor Tonry?" Matt said.

"That's exactly what we will point out on cross-examination," Powell said.

"I'm impressed, brother," Matt said. "You're beginning to sound more like a chemist than an attorney."

"We're all going to need to understand a lot more about chemistry by trial," Powell said.

"I'm not convinced that we can sell this to a jury," JW said, shaking his head. "Are there other cases we can point the jury to where someone died of bismuth poisoning?"

"Not that I have found. But with my electioneering, I haven't had time to really delve into the case law from other jurisdictions yet. That's what I had planned for Orr to help us with, before he withdrew from the case."

"And what about the fact that Maud didn't have the black tongue that Dr. Fauntleroy said is a certain indication of bismuth overdose?" JW asked. "Kilgour will surely use that to debunk your theory on rebuttal."

"He might. But he'd have to produce an expert to testify that the blackening of the tongue persists postmortem. And I think that will be a problem for him."

"If your theory is correct and Moore's salts are, indeed, toxic," Matt said, "the question in every juror's mind will be: Why haven't Moore's other patients been poisoned by this bismuth?"

"Who's to say they haven't?" Powell quipped. "According to my father-in-law, it would take years before an adult succumbed to the effects of bismuth poisoning. And their deaths would be attributed to other causes, such as disease of the kidneys or the stomach, the very thing that bismuth was prescribed to treat. Because Annie and Maud were so young, their fragile bodies were more sensitive and couldn't easily process the metal, thus their rapid demise."

"If you're right and his bismuth is toxic, what do we do?" JW asked. "Shouldn't we alert Moore so that he doesn't poison another child?"

"I've wrestled with this dilemma," Powell said. "And I keep coming back to our oaths. As defense attorneys, our first obligation is to our client. If we inform Kilgour, what's the probability that Moore's concentrated bismuth will quietly disappear and the bismuth replacing it will have no abnormalities when tested independently by the state?"

"You distrust Kilgour that much?" JW asked.

"I trust no one on the other side of the aisle. Especially Mortimer Kilgour and especially since I'm his challenger in the race for commonwealth's attorney. For Emily Lloyd's sake, it's a risk I'm not willing to take."

"And what if another child dies?" JW asked.

"Trust me, I've considered it and discussed it with my father-in-law, who tends most of the children in town," Powell said. "According to Jack, the Lloyd girls were the last of Moore's pediatric patients. Let's hope Jack's right."

"I agree with Powell," Matt said. "We can't disclose any part of our defense to Kilgour. While I don't believe he would tamper with evidence, I do believe he would tear our theory apart in court. He'd have entirely too much time to prepare his rebuttal argument. Our obligation is to Mrs. Lloyd."

"Before we get ahead of ourselves, let's first find out if Moore's bismuth is overconcentrated or not." Powell scanned their faces before looking down at the envelope he held in his hand. JW was right to be skeptical. There were a number of hurdles to overcome for a jury to buy this theory. Powell's heartbeat was thumping on his eardrums, and a mix of anticipation, hope, and fear was swelling in his chest as he removed the correspondence from the envelope. Laying the envelope aside, he unfolded the papers and scanned the first page, a letter from his cousin. After he finished reading the second paragraph, he glanced across the table at JW.

"What is it?" JW asked.

Powell stared at the letter before lowering his eyes and reading the paragraph again. He hastily flipped to the second page containing the details of the results. His breath hitched.

"Powell, what is it?" JW repeated.

Powell dropped his hand that held the correspondence to the table, the color draining from his face. He shook his head, bile rising and sickness churning in his stomach.

"For the love of Mother Mary," Matt said. "What does it say?"

Powell handed Matt the papers and closed his eyes. *As attorneys, our first obligation is to our client,* he reiterated in his mind.

"Holy Christ!" He heard Matt exclaim and opened his eyes. Matt was staring at the letter, a stunned look on his face. He looked up at Powell. "What in God's name, Powell, do we do now?"

AUTUMN 1872

From the commencement of the investigation down to the present hour, she has been calm, cool and collected—asserting all the time in the most insinuating manner her entire innocence—but if guilty, her stoicism is unaccountable and stamps her the most heartless of criminals.
—*Loudoun Mirror*, October 1872

CHAPTER 24

MONDAY, OCTOBER 21, 1872

So intense was the beating rain against the windows that Powell could barely hear the clerk announce the case in the October court. Despite the inclement weather, the courtroom was packed, men and women standing in the doorway and out in the halls. Newspapermen from as far away as New York City had crowded onto the benches for firsthand reporting of the trial. Had the weather been more cooperative, Powell suspected the bailiff might have opened the windows so that those not finding seats inside could witness the day's event from the courtyard.

Dressed in his usual crisp black suit, his burnished watch chain extending from a button on his waistcoat to a pocket on his breast, Mort Kilgour stood from the prosecution's table. Charles Lee, in a suit that seemed to have been made by the same tailor, sat to Kilgour's left, his hands folded in front of him. Powell wondered if Kilgour would allow Lee to present any of the state's case or, like always, be the lone, booming voice of the people.

"J. Mortimer Kilgour as the attorney for the commonwealth, Your Honor." He puffed his chest and looked over his nose at the judge. "The people are ready for trial."

Judge James Keith, new to the bench and new on the circuit court, was young. By the looks of him, Powell guessed he had yet to celebrate his thirtieth birthday. He was a small-framed man with sandy hair and an overly pale complexion. Set against the stark black robe, his visage appeared ghostlike. Rumors in the legal community were that Keith's frail looks had deceived more than one attorney since he had taken his seat on the bench, and Powell had been warned that underneath the judge's pallid façade was a man as tough as nails.

"Bailiff, bring in the defendant," Judge Keith said.

JW, who was sitting on Powell's right, stood from the defense table. JW, too, was in a dark, tailored suit, while Powell wore his usual gray. Matt sat at the far end of the table in brown tweed.

"Your Honor," JW said, "if it please the court, before we move to trial, the defense would like to call the court's attention to a defect in the bill of indictment. You will note that the document does not include the signature of the commonwealth's attorney. As such, the defense hereby moves the court to quash the indictment against the defendant, as the state's attorney has not authorized it."

"Your Honor, this is preposterous," Kilgour bellowed from the opposite table. "This is simply a delay tactic by the def—"

"Aack!" Judge Keith snapped. He held up his hand, palm forward. Kilgour flinched and pressed his lips together. Keith moved his gaze to the papers in front of him. He turned over a few pages before looking back at Kilgour. "The defense is correct. Your signature is not on the indictment. Does the state take issue with the grand jury's findings?"

"No, Your Honor. The state had hoped to amend the evidence presented to the grand jury with the intent to reconvene the panel. Unfortunately, that evidence was not available in a timely fashion."

"And the state is prepared to argue the charges in this indictment?" Keith asked, holding up the papers.

"We are, Your Honor," Kilgour said.

"Your Honor," JW began. "The preparedness of the commonwealth is irrelevant. Without the prosecutor's signature prior to today's court, the bill of indictment is defective and therefore invalid."

"Not so fast, Counsellor," Keith said, turning his attention to JW. "Whereas the Federal code requires the signature of the prosecuting attorney on felony indictments, it is not necessary under Virginia code any longer. Eighteen months ago I would have been compelled to consider your motion. But now, as Virginia has reentered the Union and is no longer under martial law, the Federal statutes no longer take precedence. And if I'm not mistaken, according to section A of statute three under the new Virginia Code, the signature of a grand jury foreman is sufficient to validate the bill of indictment." Keith looked down at the paper on his desk and then lifted his gaze to Kilgour. "Mr. Kilgour, was a Mr. Braden Fox the grand jury foreman?"

"He was, Your Honor."

"And this is his signature?" The judge held up the bill of indictment and pointed to a line of hand script with his index finger.

"Yes, it is."

"Very well, then." Keith looked back at JW. "Mr. Foster, your motion to quash is denied." Keith brought his gaze to the bailiff. "Deputy, would you please bring in the defendant?"

Powell could read the discouragement on JW's face as he returned to his seat.

"At least you tried," Powell whispered to JW under his breath as the door at the rear of the courtroom opened. "I've heard he has an indelible memory, so we'll need to make certain that there are no inaccuracies in our citations of the code or in the case law when we present our motions." JW nodded, appreciative of Powell's reassurance and his advice.

Emily Lloyd appeared in the doorway. Heavily veiled and wearing a black dress, she was poised and her gait firm as she walked alongside Sheriff Atwell to the dock. Taking her place behind the rail, she stood stoically as the clerk of the court read the indictment.

"Mrs. Lloyd," the clerk continued. "Having heard the state's charges against you, what is your plea?"

Emily lifted her chin, holding her head high. "Not guilty," she said loudly, her words echoing in the courtroom. Powell held his eyes on her and tipped his head, affirming his approval. She nodded back and took her seat. *Good girl, Emily. Just like we practiced.* Powell straightened the notes in front of him, which contained over one hundred names of potential jurors, as the bailiff brought the first group into the courtroom to the jury box, and jury selection began.

"Your name, sir?" Kilgour asked the man seated in the first chair.

"Henry Nelson," said the balding man in a rumpled jacket.

"Are you a resident of this county?"

"I am."

"Do you know the defendant, Mrs. Emily Lloyd?"

"Yes, I've read about her plenty in the papers."

"Is there any reason, morally or otherwise, you could not convict a mother of knowingly and deliberately murdering her three-year-old daughter?"

"No reason whatsoever."

Kilgour turned his attention to Judge Keith. "Your Honor, the state finds this juror acceptable."

"Mr. Harrison," Judge Keith said. "Do you have any questions for this juror?"

"Yes, Your Honor," Powell said, buttoning his jacket as he stood. He approached the jury box and offered the veniremen a warm smile before turning his attention to the man in the first chair. "Mr. Nelson, you stated that you knew the defendant from what was published in the newspapers. Is it your testimony that you have not met Mrs. Lloyd before?"

"That's correct." Mr. Nelson folded his arms across his chest. "Never met her."

"And what might it be that you think you know about the defendant?" Powell asked, placing an elbow on the rail.

"That she poisoned all those little children. Ain't right what she done, and she ought to hang by the neck for it," Nelson said with an affirmative nod of his head.

"Thank you, Mr. Nelson," Powell said with a polite smile. He straightened his shoulders and walked back to the defense table, making a note on the list before turning toward the bench. "Your Honor, defense moves to strike this juror."

"Motion granted," the judge said. "Mr. Nelson, the court thanks you for your service. You are free to go."

Flustered, Nelson fiddled with the hat in his lap before standing from his seat in the box. The bailiff opened the rail and escorted him to the side entrance.

And so it went. Of the first twenty-eight jurors interviewed before the midday break, all but two were dismissed. If Kilgour or Powell didn't object, the men called had a variety of excuses—their wife was ill, their business failing, they held prejudice against the defendant—to avoid serving on the jury. As the hour neared five o'clock, over one hundred potential jurors had been interviewed and only ten men had been selected to serve on the jury. As the next group filed into the courtroom, Powell noticed a familiarity about the man who took the first chair but couldn't place him. There were only five men in this group, not the normal twelve that had been in the previous assemblies brought in by the bailiff. As the clerk swore them in, Powell leaned forward and caught JW's attention.

"Is this the last of the jury pool?" he asked in a whisper.

JW riffled through the papers. "It must be. But there are dozens of others on the list that haven't appeared."

"It's the rain," Matt said. "Always makes for a bad turnout."

Powell shook his head and leaned back in his seat. Judge Keith wouldn't allow the trial to be delayed to summon more potential jurors. The last two jurors would be selected from this lot, whether Powell concurred or not.

Kilgour had stopped bothering to approach the jurors hours ago, questioning from his seat. From the table, he called to the man closest to him in the jury box, "State your name, please."

"Robert Bentley Junior."

Powell shot from the chair. "Your Honor, the defense objects to this juror."

Keith furrowed his brow and frowned. "You object to the man's name?"

"Mr. Bentley is the son of the late mayor of this town. Considering the close involvement of his father in this case, the defense believes that Mr. Bentley's opinions are biased against the defendant."

Judge Keith turned to the juror. "Mr. Bentley, do you harbor any bias, any resentment, any negative feelings, toward the defendant, Mrs. Lloyd?"

"No, Your Honor."

"Mr. Kilgour, any objections to this juror?" Judge Keith asked.

"No objections from the state," Kilgour said, a nearly imperceptible smile curling the corner of his mouth.

"Mr. Harrison?"

"Defense restates its objection," Powell said.

"Objection overruled," Judge Keith said. "Mr. Bentley, please follow the bailiff back to the jury room until you're called with the other jurors."

Powell sat down and scanned the faces of the remaining four men in the box. He knew none of them.

Kilgour interviewed the next three men and objected to each of them. One told the court that he could never be convinced that a mother would harm her child, and the other two did not believe in the death penalty. Judge Keith sustained Kilgour's objections despite Powell's protest, leaving one remaining candidate to fill the last spot on the jury. With the way the interviews of the last four candidates had gone, Powell had little confidence that this juror would be as liberal in his thinking as the three the judge had just dismissed.

Without looking up from his notes, Kilgour bellowed from his chair, "State your name."

"Jason William Nichols."

"Do you know the defendant, Mrs. Emily Lloyd?"

"I do."

Raising his head, Kilgour narrowed his eyes and looked at the juror. "And how might you know Mrs. Lloyd?"

Glancing at Emily, a broad smile broke over the man's face. "Why, she and I used to be sweethearts."

"Sweethearts? When exactly was this?"

"You mean, when were we, uh, together?" From Nichols's accent, he was likely a farmer from the more liberal, western part of the county. Powell's pulse quickened.

"That's exactly what I mean." Kilgour was losing his patience, knowing what was about to happen.

"Before the war."

"Was your relationship with Mrs. Lloyd intimate?"

Nichols lost the smile on his face and shifted uncomfortably in his chair. "Why, that's none of your business."

Kilgour looked at the judge. "Your Honor, the state objects to this juror."

"Noted," Keith said and looked at Powell. "Mr. Harrison? Questions?"

"No, Your Honor. The defense finds this juror acceptable."

"Good," Keith said. "Mr. Nichols, please stay seated. Bailiff, please bring in the rest of the jury to the courtroom."

"Your Honor," Kilgour said, jumping to his feet. "The state vehemently objects to this juror based on his prior relationship with the defendant in what most certainly amounts to bias and sympathy for the defense."

The judge turned to the lone man in the jury box. "Mr. Nichols, is there any reason you could not convict the defendant should the evidence prove her guilt beyond a reasonable doubt?"

"No, sir," Nichols said firmly.

"Very well, then," Keith said.

"Your Honor!" Kilgour protested.

"Overruled, Counsellor," Keith declared. Kilgour started to complain again, and the judge held up his palm. "We've been at it all day, Mr. Kilgour. I have sustained all of your objections but this one. Likewise, I have sustained every objection of the defense sans one. Call it even. Call it unfair. Call it whatever you'd like, but I am calling it a day. Once the jury is instructed of its duties, I'm going back to my room at the inn next door, getting a hot supper and a good night's rest. I advise you to do the same. It's going to be a long week."

Kilgour huffed before throwing himself into his chair. Powell checked his watch. It was coming up on six o'clock. Judge Keith was right. It had been a tiresome day, and the week wouldn't be any different.

• • •

Powell returned home from the courthouse, weary and wet from the rain, just as supper was ready to be served in the Harrison dining room. Shedding his coat and hat, he didn't bother to wash up and joined Janet and his daughters at the table. After the meal, Janet left for the kitchen with Rebecca, and the girls moved to the hall to play with their dolls. Powell retired to his study, preparing for his cross-examination of Dr. William Cross, whom Powell assumed would be the prosecution's first witness.

What was Cross's experience in poisoning cases? he wrote on his notepad. *How many? Arsenic? Involving children?* He tapped the pencil on the desk, thinking. *Had Cross ever witnessed a patient suffering from too much bismuth?* No, he thought, and scratched through the writing. He would save any questions regarding bismuth poisoning for the defense's case. Powell's concentration was interrupted by a squeal as Lalla ran down the hall past the study's doorway. Nannie was chasing behind her.

"You're it!" Nannie screamed. "Now you're supposed to tag me!"

Powell lifted his head from his notes. "Nannie, I need for you and Lalla to settle down. Papa needs it quiet so he can work."

"But she won't play fair," Nannie protested.

"Please, Nannie. Why don't you play quietly with your dolls?"

"We want to play tag."

"Not inside."

"But, Papa!"

"Dolls. And quietly," Powell insisted.

Nannie pouted for a second before taking off down the hall after her sister.

Powell returned his attention to his cross-examination. *Symptoms of stomach congestion,* he wrote. *Cholera?*

A sudden shriek from the hallway caused him to startle in his chair. Lalla fell in front of the doorway with Nannie tumbling on top of her. Lalla was crying and Nannie was screaming.

"You aren't playing *fair!*"

"Dammit, Nannie!" Powell shouted, his patience gone. "I told you to settle down!"

Nannie stood, her lower lip protruding and eyes welling with tears.

"Powell Harrison!" scolded Janet, emerging from the back. She scooped Lalla from the floor.

"How am I supposed to work with all this noise!" Powell shouted.

"Not by yelling at the children," Janet countered sternly.

"Why isn't Connie watching them?"

"Because I gave her the evening off," Janet said as she consoled their youngest daughter.

Powell looked from Janet to Nannie, who was staring at him, trying desperately not to cry. Powell's anger was instantly replaced with guilt. He stood from his chair behind the desk and went to his daughter.

"I'm sorry, Nannie," he said, and he picked her up. "Papa didn't mean to be cross with you."

Nannie sniffled and nodded her head before laying it on his shoulder.

Janet threw one of her disapproving looks in Powell's direction.

"I'm to blame," Powell said. "I shouldn't take my pressures out on you or the girls." He smiled apologetically. "Let me help get them to bed."

With a frustrated sigh, Janet turned toward the stairs.

"Can we have a bedtime story, Papa?" Nannie asked, her head perked.

"I don't see why not," Powell said with a grin. "How about the one where the brave attorney wins a big case in court against the big, bad prosecutor?"

"Well, that would be one way to ensure they fall asleep quickly," Janet said with a half roll of her eyes.

Powell laughed and followed behind with Nannie in his arms.

CHAPTER 25

"Wake up, Emily."

Emily's eyelids flew open at the sound of the familiar voice. She sat up on the bed, afraid to look beyond the bars into the corridor. "How did you get in?" she whispered.

"Mr. Goldilocks, who is supposedly guarding this place, is asleep and the door to the block was open," Lilith said. "So I let myself in."

"You aren't supposed to be here." Moving against the wall, Emily brought her knees up to her chest and pulled the bed linens tightly under her chin. "Lara said y'all had left."

"You don't think Lara would abandon her precious Emily for long, now, do you?"

"I hadn't thought about it."

"That's your problem. You wouldn't be in this mess had you taken a moment to actually think!"

Emily remained silent.

"It's of no matter. Lara will most certainly do all your thinking for you now that she's back."

"Where is she? Mr. Harrison wants to speak to her. And why isn't she here instead of you?"

"I'm here because she's too much of a prude to tell you herself. The two of you with your black, your Bible, and your veils." Lilith spat in disgust. "I'm here to tell you that you cannot be wearing that nun's habit and expect those men on the jury to feel sorry for you. No, sir, your job is to get them thinking about how to get you out of jail so they might get a bit of that crumpet, if you know what I mean."

Emily's eyes widened. "You're despicable!" she said, louder than she had intended. She brought her hand to her mouth.

"Be that as it may, I'm trying to save your ungrateful hide." Lilith's voice was low and dark. "For once, you need to listen. You've got to stir the desires of those jurors. Especially that little worm that used to come calling on you. Make him yearn for you. Make certain that farmer boy understands that if he gets you out of jail, you'll be more than happy to let him grind *your* corn any time he likes."

"I'll do no such thing!" Emily said, thumping her fist into the mattress.

"You'll do exactly such a thing if it means keeping your neck out of a noose!" Lilith hissed.

"I will not!"

"Do you have any idea what it's like to hang?" Lilith leaned forward, her stare intense and menacing. "If you're lucky, the force of the drop will be *just* enough to ensure that your neck snaps cleanly and you die instantly. But luck has never been on your side, now, has it?"

Emily looked away from her.

"No. With your luck, I can't imagine it will go easy at all. Too much of a drop, and just like that"—Lilith clicked her finger against her thumb, and Emily jumped—"your head snaps off, rolling like a ball into the crowd. Not enough drop, and you'll thrash about while your throat is slowly crushed. Minutes go by as you swing on the end of the rope, eyes popping from their sockets, pissing and soiling yourself before you slip into the abyss and meet the cold arms of death."

Emily put her hands over her ears. "Stop it!"

"Now, you listen to me, you prissy little bitch! I promised Lara I'd help you, so you better listen up and listen good. You need to play the part. Look in the bottom of your trunk. I slipped in one of my dresses as you were packing for jail. Figured you might have a need for it at some point. It's not too loud in color, but the bodice is tight and the neckline low enough for our purpose. In the pocket, I left you a little tin of rouge. In the morning, you're going to put on that dress and tighten those laces so that those men on the jury can see the tops of your tits. And lose that goddamned veil and wear your hair down. I want to see a rise in the crotch of those jurors' britches when you walk into that courtroom."

Emily pressed her forehead to her knees, her hands still over her ears. "I cannot listen to this."

"Oh, you're going to listen. And you're going to do what I say."

"I won't do it."

"We'll see about that. We'll see."

CHAPTER 26

TUESDAY, OCTOBER 22, 1872

The foul weather had carried over from the previous day, with rain pouring from the skies and the autumn air damp and cold. A fire burned in a stove next to the jury box. Powell glanced around the courtroom. There were fewer spectators in the gallery today than yesterday. Kilgour was in his usual spot, but Powell noticed that he was sitting alone.

Powell leaned to Matt, nodding in Kilgour's direction. "Looks like Charles Lee is running late."

Matt glanced over at the prosecution's table. "Maybe he grew weary of being Mort's secretary."

Powell chuckled and turned to JW, who was sitting at the other end of the defense table. "Are you ready?"

"Ready as always!" JW said with a confident smile.

"What the hell!" Matt exclaimed, looking toward the dock.

Powell followed Matt's gaze and stared in horror. The side door had opened, and Sheriff Atwell was escorting Emily Lloyd into the courtroom, dressed in a tight-fitting gown. Her bosom looked as if it would explode from the bodice at any moment. Her hair was flowing across her shoulders, and her lips were painted with the same red worn by the women who worked in the brothels down by the tracks.

"What does she think she's doing?" Matt asked.

Powell watched her take her seat. "I do not know, but I'll put an end to it at the midday break."

The bailiff called the court to order. Draped in his black robes, Judge Keith entered the courtroom and took his chair at the bench. As the gallery resumed their seats, a man in a dark suit slid in on the opposite side of Kilgour at the prosecution table. He was too tall and too thin to be Charles Lee. Powell leaned forward. His heart jumped into his throat when he saw the man's face.

Powell turned to Matt. "John Orr just sat down at the table next to Kilgour."

"He what?" Matt asked, pulling his reading glasses down lower on his nose as he looked over at the prosecution. "What does John think he's doing?"

"I don't know, but just let him open his mouth for the other side," Powell said, the vein in his temple pulsing.

The bailiff brought in the jury, and the clerk stood to read the charges.

"The Commonwealth of Virginia charges that on March 24, 1872, in the town of Leesburg, the defendant, Emily Elizabeth Lloyd, committed murder in the first degree against her child, Maud Emily Lloyd. Count one. On March 21, 1872, Mrs. Lloyd administered white arsenic by mouth to Maud Lloyd, thereby causing her death. Count two. On March 21, 1872, Mrs. Lloyd administered white arsenic to Maud Lloyd by injection. Count three. On March 21, 1872, Mrs. Lloyd administered the poison in solution with water or some other substance, thereby causing her death."

"Mr. Kilgour, is the state ready for trial?" Judge Keith asked.

"We are, Your Honor."

"Very well, then, please proceed with your opening statement."

Kilgour stood from his chair and approached the jury. "As jurymen, the duty before each of you is high and important. Under any circumstance, the charge of murder against any human being is terrible—thrilling every nerve and shrinking the stoutest of hearts. But murder by a woman, that sex toward whom, in our chivalric devotion, we are ever ready to render homage, and whose very weakness appeals to all high-minded men for protection?" Kilgour raised his brow at his question and, with sadness in his eyes, slowly shook his head. "And what makes this case doubly appalling is that the accused is not only a woman, but a mother—the murderess of her own child, the offspring of her own bosom."

Kilgour paused as if overcome with emotion.

"The sweetest three words in the English language: mother, home, and heaven. *Mother* first, because at its very utterance, all the tenderest sympathies of our nature gush forth. At the mention of *home*, our memories turn to the days of childhood and bending at the maternal knee, the holiest altar known to man. It was at that holy altar where we first lisped 'Our Father who art in *heaven*,' when we first learned of that promised paradise. With her daughter's hand hypocritically clasped in her own and all her maternal affections dried up, Mrs. Lloyd, a most unnatural mother, dragged her young child from this altar, not to dash out her brains in the hurry of heat and passion but to rob the child of life by the insidious means of poison. Mrs. Lloyd deliberately and willfully murdered her three-year-old daughter." Kilgour leaned toward them, looking each juror in the eye as he spoke. "When we remember that the child suffered more than three days before succumbing, we realize the far-reaching gravity of our duty—the duty that is upon each one of *you*.

"In trying this case, you are not to know Mrs. Lloyd as woman, mother, friend, or neighbor. You are to be without passion or preconceived notions, but instead remain unbiased and impassive. Whether the verdict consigns Mrs. Lloyd to the gallows tree or remands her back to the desolated hearthstone that will never again be cheered by the innocent prattle of her children, so be it. As jurors, you are merely ministers of the law, duty bound to execute its mandates. And those mandates are to find justice regardless of the sex of the defendant or any sympathies you may have for her. This, gentlemen, is your solemn duty."

Kilgour extended his stare across each of the jurors' faces before turning and walking away.

With a bemused look on his face, JW rose as Kilgour took his seat. JW shook his head, chuckling under his breath as he approached the jury box.

"Listening to all that, you might think Mr. Kilgour actually gives two hoots about seeking justice. But then, we all know better." JW glanced over at Kilgour and shook his head again before turning back to the jury. "Gentlemen, I am James William Foster, and I, along with the Harrison brothers, represent Mrs. Emily Lloyd, a most *natural* mother. A doting mother who cared for and loved her children. And let me tell you what—Mr. Kilgour and his representatives have been anything but impassive and unbiased in how they have treated Mrs. Lloyd and how they have conducted themselves in this matter. In fact, they have allowed their preconceived notions to encumber every aspect of their investigation into the death of little Maud Lloyd, and any shred of evidence that might shine the light of truth on this case, they have deliberately and willfully withheld from the defense. No, my friends, do not allow Mr. Kilgour's eloquence of speech to beguile you. Because the suspicions of guilt that he casts are like the gathering clouds that Elijah witnessed from his perch on Mount Carmel. And like that little cloud over the sea of Galilee, at first smaller than the smallest hand, this scandal has gathered on the horizon and has transformed the skies over our town into a dark tapestry of hateful gossip and intrigue. And like Ahab, the prosecution has believed every word."

Matt leaned to Powell's ear. "If I didn't know any different, I'd believe JW was a churchgoing man."

"Sunday-evening service was part of the deal he made with me when I agreed to let him open," Powell whispered back with a grin.

"Unlike Elijah," JW continued, now in his stride, "Mrs. Lloyd has not fled from the threats of Jezebel but instead has taken comfort in her faith, leaning on Psalms 31:20 in her darkest hours. 'In the shelter of Your presence You hide them from the intrigues of men, in Your dwelling You keep them safe from accusing tongues.' Mrs. Lloyd has no ravens, no Cherith, no Zarephath—no human to offer sympathy, and some days, she must feel as if the very presence of God has left her. Yet still she cleaves to her faith. Faith in Our Lord above. Faith in me and my colleagues to defend her and speak on her behalf. Faith in each of you to weigh the evidence carefully as Mr. Kilgour suggests, without bias or the influence of accusing tongues. Faith in this court to serve justice by finding the truth. And the truth, gentleman, is that Mrs. Emily Lloyd is not guilty of any of the crimes of which she is accused."

JW tipped his head and bowed before turning toward the table where Powell and Matt sat.

"Kings and Psalms?" Powell whispered as JW walked past him.

"I thought you'd be impressed." JW winked and took his seat on Matt's right.

"Mr. Kilgour, you may call your first witness," Judge Keith said. A burst of lightning illuminated the courtroom in an ethereal flash, and thunder rumbled overhead.

Kilgour stood from his chair. "The state calls Mary Delphina Lozenburg."

Powell glanced at his brother. The choice of Kilgour's first witness was a surprise.

In an olive-green dress with an ivory lace collar, Delphi walked to the front of the courtroom and stepped into the witness box. Her eyes darted nervously over the faces in the gallery as the bailiff swore her in.

"Your Honor," Kilgour said, "if it please the court, the state has retained Mr. John Orr as assistant prosecutor. Mr. Orr will be interviewing Miss Lozenburg on behalf of the people."

Powell sprung to his feet. "Objection, Your Honor. Mr. Orr was consulting for the defense prior to the indictment hearing, and his working for the prosecution is therefore a conflict."

Judge Keith narrowed his eyes. "Is this true, Mr. Kilgour?"

"It is, Your Honor, and the state, having thoroughly reviewed the matter, finds no conflict exists," Kilgour said.

"Your Honor—" Powell started before Judge Keith held up his hand and beckoned the two attorneys.

"Approach, Counsellors," Keith directed.

"I do not like this, Mr. Kilgour," Judge Keith said in a low whisper as Powell and Kilgour reached the bench.

"The prosecution is shorthanded, Your Honor," Kilgour explained. "A trial this lengthy, I will need assistance."

"What about Charles Lee?" Powell asked. "He was in court yesterday as your assistant counsel."

"Mr. Lee has taken ill," Kilgour answered before pleading to the judge. "Mr. Orr's assistance is required in examining witnesses. When I questioned him about his earlier engagement with the defense, Mr.

Orr assured me that his involvement was limited. He never interviewed the defendant and only provided defense counsel cursory advice pertaining to case law relevant to insanity pleas. When Messrs. Harrison abandoned that defense, Mr. Orr took leave of the case. The state is confident that Mr. Orr's prior engagement has no bearing on the defense's strategy in the matter at present."

"That is a complete exaggeration by the prosecution, Your Honor. Mr. Orr was a participant in numerous strategy discussions on behalf of the defense. He was present during the autopsy conducted at Union Cemetery—"

"You're referring to the autopsy that the district court excluded from evidence in this trial?" Kilgour interjected.

"Yes," Powell confirmed, looking at Kilgour, "where the defense discussed our counterarguments to the state's analysis of all the forensic evidence in this case." He turned his attention to the judge. "Your Honor, any involvement by an attorney of the defendant for the prosecution is a betrayal of the defendant's right of confidence and a blatant violation of the attorney-client privilege."

Judge Keith held his gaze to Powell's for a long moment before looking over at the prosecution table. "Mr. Orr, please approach, will you?"

Orr stood and joined them at the front of the courtroom.

"Mr. Orr," Keith said. "Did Mrs. Lloyd retain you to assist in her defense?"

"No, she did not. My only involvement was that I was asked by her defense counsel, Matthew Harrison, to provide advice in regard to a possible insanity plea," Orr answered. "When experts from Western State Lunatic Asylum determined that Mrs. Lloyd was of a sound mind, my services were no longer needed."

"Do you have a retainer agreement with Mr. Harrison that you can provide the court?"

"I do not, Your Honor. Mr. Harrison asked me to consult as a favor. We've known each other for a long time, and neither of us felt the need for such formalities."

"Did you sign a representation letter with Mrs. Lloyd?"

"I did not," Orr said.

"Very well, then," Keith said, and shooed them away with a flit of his hand.

Powell knew the judge's ruling before he announced it. Matt was old-school, and this time it was going to cost them.

"Mr. Harrison, your objection is overruled. Mr. Orr, you may proceed to question the first witness."

Orr nodded at the judge and turned to Powell. "My intent was not to cause any hard feelings, Powell. I honestly didn't think this would be a problem. Let Matt know, will you?"

"You can tell him yourself," Powell said, giving Orr a hard look before returning to the defense table.

Orr waited as Powell took his seat. Straightening his shoulders, Orr drew a long breath and focused his attention on the witness box, where Delphi waited.

"Miss Lozenburg," he said as he walked toward her, "how do you know the defendant, Mrs. Lloyd?"

"She is my employer," Delphi said.

"And what is it that you do for her?"

"I help her with housework, cleaning, cooking, and caring for the children."

"And in the past two years, all four of Mrs. Lloyd's children died rather abruptly, didn't they?"

"Objection," Powell said. "The state is leading the witness."

"Sustained," the judge ruled.

"What were the names of Mrs. Lloyd's children?" Orr asked, seemingly ignoring the judge's ruling.

"George, Henry, Annie, and Maud," Delphi answered before Powell could object.

"Your Honor!" Powell complained.

"I'll allow it," Judge Keith said with a nod at Orr. "Continue, Mr. Orr."

"And you tended them at Mrs. Lloyd's home on Loudoun Street?"

Delphi brought her gaze to Orr. "I did."

"Were you tending Maud when she took ill last March?"

"Yes, I was."

"Can you tell us what happened the week Maud died?"

"On that Thursday, I had been out at the shops gathering things that Miss Emily told me she needed. When I returned, Maudie had a fever and was throwing up something awful. Miss Emily sent me to fetch Dr. Moore, like she always does. He came over and told us it might be the cholera. That's what took little Annie, and it had us both real worried that Maudie might have it, too. He said he'd send some powders over and told us to give her milk and lime water. Friday, she was worse. But Sunday morning, she seemed a lot better. She was up and playing with her doll. I fed her a little cake, and she seemed to take it with no problem. But that afternoon she got sick again, and by Sunday night it was awful. She started shaking in her bed and then she wouldn't look at us or talk or nothing. That's when Miss Emily sent me to find Dr. Moore. He came over with another doctor, and they told us Maud was going to die."

Delphi bit her lip, tears in her eyes. "They gave her some powders and then she died right after. Just like that, poor little Maudie was gone."

Orr proceeded to ask Delphi a battery of questions about what Maud ate, what she drank, who was with her at various times, and who came to visit. After nearly an hour and a half of questioning, his focus shifted to what Powell assumed was the true intent of his interrogation.

"At any time, did you administer any of Dr. Moore's powders to Maud?"

"No, sir, only Miss Emily and Dr. Moore gave her medicines."

"Did Mrs. Lloyd ever purchase arsenic and bring it to the house?"

"Not that I know of, but she should have. We had heaps of mice in that house and some rats, too."

Orr nodded his head and paused, his mind clearly at work. He glanced at Kilgour, who rose to his feet.

"Your Honor," Kilgour said. "It's beyond the noon hour. Might I suggest a recess for dinner?"

Judge Keith glanced at the large wall clock that hung at the back of the courtroom. "It's a quarter after now. We'll reconvene the court at half past one."

"Want to grab a bite at Pickett's next door?" Matt asked after the judge left the courtroom.

"You two go on. I'll catch up." Powell watched Freddie lead Emily from the courtroom. "Mrs. Lloyd and I need to have a word."

◆ ◆ ◆

"That didn't take long," JW said as Powell approached the table where Matt and JW were sitting at the rear of the dining hall at Pickett's Inn.

"Mrs. Lloyd and I quickly came to an agreement," Powell said, smoothing the rain from his hair before pulling a chair to join them.

"We took the liberty of ordering for you." JW pushed a plate covered with a pewter lid toward him. "So what did she have to say for herself?"

"Seems one of those sisters that live next door paid Mrs. Lloyd a visit last night," Powell said as he removed the lid from the stewed meat and vegetables steaming on the plate. "Apparently the woman named Lilith convinced Emily that she needed to arouse the passions of the jurors to invoke their sympathy."

"Arouse passions?" Matt scoffed. "So she decides it's a good idea to dress like a harlot?"

"I suggested she put the veil back on and cover her bosom. And from here on out, she will dress like she's going to church. I assured her that the only way to gain a juror's sympathy is to look like a grieving mother." Powell pulled the napkin to his lap and picked up a fork. He hadn't realized how hungry he was.

"The sisters are back in town?" JW asked.

"Apparently," Powell said, digging into the food.

"We need to speak to them," JW said. "I'll head over there tonight and pay them a visit."

"Make certain they haven't spoken to Kilgour and that any testimony from them won't impact our case," Powell said.

"Er, about our case." Matt drew a deep breath. "I owe you gentlemen an apology. I thought I could trust John as a man of his word."

Powell looked up from his plate. "No need for an apology, Matt. It's right to have confidence in a man's word. But I trust words a lot more when they are put to paper."

Matt nodded and shifted in his chair. They ate in silence while the clinking of silver against china and conversations of other guests swarmed around them.

"Is anyone besides me surprised that they brought Delphi as their first witness?" JW asked as he pushed his plate away.

"I'd have thought they would bring Dr. Cross," Matt said in

between chews. "If I were the prosecutor, I would have first established the child was murdered."

"I agree," Powell said, with a swallow of sweet tea to wash down his last bite of stew. "Kilgour is up to something, I'm certain of it. I just don't know what yet."

•   •   •

"Miss Lozenburg," Orr said, "before the break, you testified that you were unaware of any purchases of arsenic by Mrs. Lloyd. Would there be any reason for Mrs. Lloyd to purchase arsenic?"

"Objection," Powell said from his seat. "Calls for speculation." He glanced over at the dock. Although still in the same dress, Emily sat poised in the chair with the veil back over her face and a scarf wrapped loosely around her neck, covering her bosom.

"Sustained," Keith agreed.

"Were you troubled with rodents at Mrs. Lloyd's home?" Orr continued.

"I didn't like the mice," Delphi replied, looking at her hands in her lap.

"Mice?"

"Yes, sir, lots of mice," she answered without looking at Orr.

"What about rats?" Orr asked.

Delphi shrugged her shoulders, her eyes downcast.

"Miss Lozenburg, have you ever seen rats at Mrs. Lloyd's house?"

Delphi shook her head without looking up. "I ain't never seen any rats."

JW moved forward in his chair and glanced down the table at Matt and Powell. Powell remained perfectly still, careful not to give the jury any indication that this new testimony from Delphi was of any concern.

"You stated before the break that there were rats. Is it now your testimony that there were no rats at Mrs. Lloyd's?"

"I said there were mice. But I didn't see no rats. I ain't never saw no rats at Mrs. Lloyd's."

"So if there were no rats in her home, why would Mrs. Lloyd need to purchase arsenic?"

"Same objection, Your Honor," Powell said.

"Mr. Orr," the judge said. "Let's not ask the witness to speculate."

Orr nodded. "Did Mrs. Lloyd ask you to purchase arsenic on her behalf?"

"No, sir."

"You mentioned that Mrs. Lloyd asked you to fetch Dr. Moore like she always does. How often does Mrs. Lloyd send for Dr. Moore?"

For the first time in her testimony since court resumed, Delphi looked up from her lap. Orr offered an encouraging smile. "Lots, I guess."

"How many times? Once a month? Once a week?"

She shrugged her shoulders again. "A couple of times a week, I reckon."

"Thank you, Miss Lozenburg," Orr said with another smile. "Your Honor, the state reserves the right to recall this witness later in the proceedings."

Judge Keith nodded and looked at the defense team. "Mr. Harrison?"

Powell stood. "Defense defers our cross-examination of the witness until the whole of her testimony has been taken."

"Very well," Keith said. "It's your turn again, Mr. Kilgour. Next witness?"

"The commonwealth calls Dr. Randolph Moore."

• • •

"And you are certain, Doctor?" Orr asked, leaning closer to the witness box than he should. Orr had spent nearly an hour asking Moore about every ailment that Maud Lloyd had suffered, including every detail of his treatment of her illness the weekend that she died. Powell looked over at the men on the jury. In the back row, two jurors had their eyes closed, another softly snored, his head listing toward his left shoulder. Orr was losing them.

"I stand by my statement that nothing I observed then or now leads me to believe that Maud Lloyd died from anything other than congestion of the stomach," Moore said. Although it was chilly in the courtroom, Powell noticed beads of perspiration on Moore's brow. Powell straightened in his chair.

"Even though the autopsy results indicate that there was arsenic present in her stomach?" Orr asked.

"Objection, Your Honor," Powell interjected. "He's badgering the witness."

"Overruled," Keith said with a pointed look at Powell. "I'll decide when the prosecution crosses boundaries, Mr. Harrison."

"Yes, Your Honor," Powell said with a glance at the jury.

Orr eyed Moore, waiting for his answer.

"I cannot explain the autopsy analysis," Moore said. "The results are inconsistent with my observations of the child."

Orr fixed his gaze on Moore for a long, awkward moment before Kilgour stood from the prosecution's table and walked toward the witness box. Orr released his stare and returned to the table and took his seat.

"Dr. Moore," Kilgour said. "Would you restate for the jury the powders you prescribed for Maud while she lay ill the weekend of March 21?"

"I gave her calomel and opium to set upon the liver and to quiet the action in the bowels. When it appeared that was not working, I switched her powders to bismuth with opium. And then, with Dr. Cross's concurrence, we gave her Huxham's tincture and cerium."

"And the specific elements of the last prescription?"

"One grain oxalate of cerium, one-sixteenth grain of morphine every two hours with a tablespoon of Huxham's tincture of bark," Moore repeated from his earlier testimony. Powell made a note.

"Who conducted the postmortem on Maud Lloyd?"

"I did. Dr. Cross and Sheriff Atwell were present, as were Deputy Fred Roberts and Mayor Bentley."

"Would you explain in layman's terms the procedure you conducted?"

Moore turned and looked at the jury. "I cut into the child's abdomen with a blade and located the stomach. I tied the upper and lower orifice so that the contents remained with the stomach when I removed it from the body. I also took the duodenum, the outlet next to the stomach. I placed both organs in a clean jar and put the glass stopper on top. I then wrapped the vessel in a white muslin cloth and handed it to Deputy Roberts, who walked it over to my store. I finished closing the child's abdomen, and Dr. Cross and I left the Lloyd house. When we arrived at my pharmacy, I cleaned the exterior of the jar, as some blood had found its way on the cloth that the deputy had used to carry it from the house. I proceeded to seal the jar with wax and gave the jar with its contents to Deputy Roberts to deliver to Professor Tonry in Baltimore."

Powell studied Moore's face as he lied under oath, looking for a tell.

Orr handed Kilgour a brown glass jar. "Do you recognize this?" Kilgour asked Moore, who nodded.

"Yes, it's the jar I used for the stomach specimen."

"Were any chemicals or poisons ever stored in this container?"

"No, sir," Moore said. "And I washed the vessel thoroughly at the hydrant in my store before I took it to Mrs. Lloyd's."

"Did you attend Maud Lloyd's funeral or the internment at Union Cemetery?"

"No, unfortunately they had already left the house by the time I arrived. But I was present at the cemetery when the sexton had Maud's body and the other Lloyd children exhumed for further examination."

Powell was on his feet. "Move to strike, Your Honor. Any testimony on this subject is inadmissible, and Mr. Kilgour knows it."

"Dr. Moore was simply answering my question in his own words, Your Honor," Kilgour said. "The defense is overreacting."

"I concur with the defense on this one, Counsellor. Your objection is sustained, Mr. Harrison." Keith turned to the jury. "Gentlemen of the jury, you are instructed to disregard the last statement of the witness."

"Your Honor, that is all the prosecution has for this witness at this time. We reserve the right to recall him later." Kilgour took his seat.

"Your witness, Mr. Harrison."

Buttoning the top button on his jacket, Powell stood and walked toward the witness box.

"How long have you known the defendant, Mrs. Lloyd?" he asked.

"About twenty years, if I had to guess," Moore replied.

"And how long have you been her family physician?"

"Since about 1865, thereabouts."

"As a physician, did you find that Mrs. Lloyd took good care of her children?"

"Objection! Foundation?" Kilgour questioned.

"Your Honor, I am asking Dr. Moore's professional opinion as to whether or not Mrs. Lloyd provided appropriate care for her children. That is well within his expertise as a physician to the children to answer."

Keith nodded his head. "Objection overruled." He looked at Moore. "You may answer."

"Yes, Emily was a good mother to her children. She was attentive to them. Taught them to read and write. Made certain they were well clothed, well fed, and bathed. At the slightest cough or sniffle, she would send for me. She doted on those children. Especially the youngest one, little Maud."

"Was the father alive when Maud was born?"

"I don't believe so."

"And you were with Mrs. Lloyd when Maud was born?"

"I delivered the child, yes."

"So it's fair to say that you have been the physician to Maud all her life and, as such, would know the most about the condition of her health?"

"Yes, that's a fair assessment."

"How would you describe Maud's health?"

"She was colicky as an infant and suffered numerous gastrointestinal ailments."

Powell walked back to the defense table and picked up his notebook, lowering his eyes to the paper in his hand. "In your statement to Mr. Kilgour, you mentioned that Delphi had called for you on Thursday, March 21, and that you first examined Maud around three o'clock that afternoon." He looked back at Moore.

"That's correct."

"And did you examine her on each of your visits that weekend?"

"Yes, of course."

"Did you examine her gums?"

Moore was slow to answer. Kilgour sat up in his chair, a puzzled look on his face.

"I probably did, yes," Moore said at last.

"Did they appear normal in all aspects?"

Moore looked at Powell as if he hadn't understood the question.

"Were they abnormal in some manner?" Powell offered. "Or were they healthy and pink around the gumline?"

"I'm not certain I recall."

"What about the tongue? Was it coated? Or was it normal like a tongue should look?"

"Normal, I suppose."

"Are you certain?"

"Yes."

Powell laid the notebook on the table and walked across the room toward the jury. "You testified earlier that you prescribed bismuth with opium for Maud. Can you be more specific about when you changed Maud's powders from calomel, what compounds were specifically prescribed, in what quantities, and how often?"

Crossing his arms, Powell leaned against the corner of the jury box awaiting Moore's answer.

"On my second visit that Friday, I gave the child two grains subnitrate of bismuth compounded with one-fourth grain of opium. I told the mother to administer the powders every four hours in lime water."

"And the child received this medication as prescribed until Sunday when she died?"

"From all indications, yes."

"So if my arithmetic is correct, from Friday evening until the time she died was approximately thirty-six hours. I'll assume Mrs. Lloyd followed your instructions precisely and administered two grains of bismuth every four hours. Take thirty-six and divide it by four, you get nine. Nine doses of two grains . . ."

Powell's voice trailed as he rolled his eyes up, calculating in his head and giving time for the jury to do the same. "That would mean that Maud consumed eighteen grains of bismuth subnitrate over the course of three days."

"Sounds about right."

"Is that a lot for a child?"

"If it were a long-term treatment, yes, it would be overly aggressive, but considering the child's condition at the time, I deemed it an appropriate remedy."

"Is this the only time you prescribed subnitrate of bismuth to Maud?"

"No, I had given it to her in the past."

"How often?"

"I couldn't say without my notes."

"And do you have these notes with you such that you could refer to them and answer my question?"

"No, sir, they are in the possession of the commonwealth's attorney."

Powell looked over at JW, and he stood from the table. "Your Honor, the defense motions the court to compel the state to produce Dr. Moore's notes." JW handed a paper to the bailiff to deliver it to the judge. Taking the paper, Judge Keith reviewed the motion and handed it back to the bailiff, who gave it to Kilgour.

"Mr. Kilgour, do you have the doctor's files?"

"I do, Your Honor, but they are at my offices at the present time."

"At the end of today's proceeding, you will deliver those notes to the defense," Keith ordered. "Motion granted."

Powell turned back to Moore.

"Where did you purchase your bismuth salts?"

"From my supplier in Baltimore, Thomson and Block."

"And do you remember the last time you purchased bismuth from them?"

"I'd have to check the exact date, but it would have been late last year. I inventory my compounds upon return from summer holiday and place my order by September so that I have an adequate supply before the beginning of the winter season."

Powell walked toward the witness stand. "In your testimony earlier this afternoon, you told Mr. Orr that there was nothing that led you to believe that Maud Lloyd had died from anything other than natural causes."

"My opinion is that the child had not been poisoned, if that is what you are asking."

Kilgour shifted noisily in his chair.

"Thank you, Dr. Moore. My brother has just a few questions for you." Powell offered a cordial nod to the doctor before walking back to the defense table.

Matt rose, a broad smile on his face. "Dr. Moore," Matt said, not bothering to fasten the button on his coat as he approached the witness stand. "About the postmortem you conducted on Maud Lloyd at Mrs. Lloyd's home." Matt walked Dr. Moore through every detail of the autopsy again: Where was Dr. Cross at the time? Standing where in the room? When was the cloth wrapped around the specimen? Oh, you said around the jar?

As Matt asked questions, Powell compared Moore's responses to the notes Powell had taken during Moore's testimony with Kilgour. To Powell's consternation, Moore was well rehearsed. Not once did he contradict himself. Powell was certain that John Orr had a hand in Moore's preparedness.

When Matt exhausted his questions, he turned his back to the witness stand and walked toward the defense table, seemingly finished with his interrogation. But before reaching his seat, he turned to Dr. Moore again.

"One last question. Did your store sell arsenic to Mrs. Lloyd?"

"Not that I have a record of, no."

Matt addressed the judge. "If it please the court, the defense reserves the right to recall this witness, but we have finished our cross-examination for today."

◆ ◆ ◆

At his desk in the Harrison law offices, Powell was in the midst of deciphering Moore's handwriting when he heard the door that faced the street open. He looked at the clock on the wall. It was well after nine. Matt was long in bed, and the clerk had no reason to return. Powell moved his hand to the drawer where he kept a revolver, opened it, and reached inside. In the glow of the streetlamps, the shadows of bare branches danced over the walls and floor. The rain seemed to have stopped, and the wind had picked up. *Perhaps a gust caught the door.* The wooden floor of the hallway creaked with the sound of footsteps. A silhouette of a hooded figure rose along the hall's wall.

"Matthew?" He felt the cold grip of the gun in his palm as he drew it from the desk. "Is that you?"

The floor creaked again. Powell held his breath and stood from the desk. He pulled the gun's hammer back.

"It's me, Powell," said a woman's voice.

"Janet?"

He eased the hammer down and returned the pistol to the drawer.

With the cowl of her cloak covering her head, Janet stood in the doorway.

"What are you doing here, darling?" Powell asked as he walked around the desk. In a gray coat and a red scarf, Delphi Lozenburg was in the hall behind her.

"Come in," he said, with a glance at his wife and a puzzled look on his face. "Please, have a seat."

Delphi removed the scarf from her head and took a chair. Janet remained at the door.

"Delphi told her sister, Connie, what happened at court today," Janet explained, pushing back her hood. "Delphi was reluctant to tell you, but Connie assured her that she could trust you. When Connie came to the house this evening to help me with the girls, Delphi was with her and told me the details." Janet narrowed her eyes. "I didn't think it should wait until morning, so I brought her to you here."

Powell nodded and took the seat next to Delphi.

"Your sister is correct," he assured her. "You can trust me to keep your confidence."

"Connie told me that you aren't afraid of Mr. Kilgour. Is that right?" Delphi locked her gaze on Powell's, her brown eyes skeptical and suffused with fear.

"There are many things in this world that I am afraid of. I'm afraid of justice that ignores truth. I'm afraid of laws that are unfair. But I am not afraid of men like Mortimer Kilgour." Powell offered an encouraging smile. "So tell me, Delphi, why are you afraid of Mr. Kilgour?"

CHAPTER 27

WEDNESDAY, OCTOBER 23, 1872

Emily was in the dock, heavily veiled and wearing the black of mourning. The weather was even more disagreeable than the day before, with heavy clouds, high winds, and thunder rattling the windows when it clashed.

"Your Honor, at this time, the defense wishes to cross-examine Miss Delphina Lozenburg on her testimony from yesterday," Powell said.

Kilgour pushed back, but the judge granted Powell's request.

Delphi approached the stand, seemingly more nervous this morning than the day before, her voice shaking while she affirmed her oath to tell the truth. Powell approached her with a warm smile.

"Yesterday morning, you told the court that Mrs. Lloyd's house had mice and rats. Is that correct?"

"Yes, sir," she said with her eyes fixed on Powell.

"But yesterday afternoon you stated that you have never seen rats at Mrs. Lloyd's home."

"Yes, sir."

"Why did you change your testimony?" Powell asked, turning his focus from Delphi to the jury.

"Because on the break yesterday, Mr. Kilgour told me that if I didn't, they were going to lock me up in jail."

A clamor erupted among the people in the gallery as Kilgour exploded from his chair. "Objection!"

The judge pounded his gavel to quiet the courtroom. He motioned to the attorneys with his fingers. "Approach. Now."

Judge Keith leaned forward as Kilgour joined Powell at the bench. "I will not tolerate theatrics in my courtroom, Mr. Harrison."

"Miss Lozenburg's testimony is not for show, Your Honor. The defense was informed that Mr. Kilgour and Mr. Orr, with the assistance of the sheriff, sequestered the witness during yesterday's dinner break and intimidated her to change her testimony."

"That is not at all what happened!" Kilgour said. "No one instructed her to change her testimony."

The judge stared at Kilgour. "You spoke to the witness outside of the courtroom in the midst of her examination?"

"My only objective in doing so was to prevent her perjuring herself."

"By telling her to swear that she never saw rats when, indeed, she had?" Powell asked, his voice rising above a whisper.

Keith shot him a cautionary glance.

"She never actually *saw* them," Kilgour said. "Go ahead and ask her while you've got her on cross."

For the first time in a long while, Powell had to restrain himself from throwing a punch. Drawing a sharp breath, he unclenched his fists.

"I want to hear what this witness has to say," Judge Keith said, clearly irritated, "and then I want to hear from Mr. Orr and the sheriff exactly what was said in this meeting with Miss Lozenburg." He straightened his posture in the chair and called the bailiff. "Please remove Mr. Orr from the courtroom."

The bailiff escorted Orr from the room. Men and women in the gallery gawked in confusion, and Powell caught a look of disbelief on his brother's face. Powell approached Delphi in the witness box, her face ashen with fear. He offered her a reassuring grin, and a wink.

She pressed her lips together, fighting a smile.

"Miss Lozenburg, you just told the court that Mr. Kilgour

instructed that if you didn't change your testimony, they were going to put you in jail. Who were 'they'?"

"Mr. Kilgour. That other lawyer, Mr. Orr. And they had the sheriff there ready to do it, too, if I didn't say it like they wanted it."

"Can you please tell us how they approached you?"

"I was leaving the courthouse to go home to get something to eat, and the sheriff grabbed my arm and told me that Mr. Kilgour needed to talk to me. He led me through the alley behind the courthouse and then out on the street to an office over by the jail."

"Mr. Kilgour's offices?"

"I think. And the other lawyer was there, too."

"Mr. John Orr, the assistant prosecutor," Powell clarified.

Delphi nodded. "Mr. Kilgour said that I wasn't telling the truth in the court and that I needed to tell the truth, no matter if it hurt Miss Emily or not. He told me that if I didn't see a rat in the plain light of day, then I had to say that I never saw no rats. I told him that I had heard them plenty. And sometimes I would see something move in the hallway, but he told me that unless I saw it in the light, then I was lying to the judge, and the sheriff would put me in jail. And he said if I told you or the judge about our meeting, I could get locked up for betrayin' the state."

Kilgour was on his feet. "Objection, Your Honor. This is preposterous."

"Aack!" the judge said. "You'll have your turn. Overruled."

"I can assure you, Miss Lozenburg, that no one is going to put you in jail for disclosing your meeting with Mr. Kilgour to me or to the court," Powell said. "Just to clarify, did you believe there were rats in Mrs. Lloyd's house?"

"Yes."

Powell turned to the judge. "No further questions at this time, Your Honor."

"Thank you, Miss Lozenburg. You are dismissed."

"The state is entitled to question this witness on rebuttal," Kilgour said.

"I want to hear from Mr. Orr first," Judge Keith said. "Bailiff, bring the assistant prosecutor to the stand."

It took a moment for Orr to return to the courtroom and take his oath. The judge permitted Kilgour to question Orr first.

"Mr. Orr, would you please tell the court what occurred in your office between myself, Sheriff Atwell, and Miss Lozenburg?" Kilgour asked after Orr was sworn in.

"I instructed the sheriff to bring Delphi to your office so that we could meet with her. When she arrived, you directed her to tell the truth no matter who it hurt. You emphasized that she must be truthful in her statements. I cross-examined her because I wanted to know what her evidence was going to be. And again, you were very clear that she was to tell the truth about what she saw or didn't see. That was the extent of our conversation with her."

"Thank you, Mr. Orr." Kilgour returned to the prosecution's table.

Powell stood from his chair. "Mr. Orr, did Mr. Kilgour tell Miss Lozenburg that if she did not change her testimony, she would be charged and put in jail?"

"That is not at all what Mr. Kilgour said."

"Did either you or Mr. Kilgour threaten Miss Lozenburg with jail?"

"No threats were made. He simply informed her that lying under oath is considered perjury, which is a crime punishable by incarceration. And I encouraged her to testify to exactly what she saw."

"And not to testify to what she heard?"

"We cautioned her to be certain in her testimony. If she wasn't certain . . . if she hadn't seen an event with her own eyes, then she could not be assured that her statement was truthful."

Powell looked at Orr and smiled. "No further questions."

He had shown the jury enough. In Powell's opinion, whether or not there were rats in Mrs. Lloyd's house was inconsequential, and why Kilgour needed to coerce Delphi to change her testimony was beyond him. But the revelation of the prosecution's actions was Kilgour's first misstep.

"The people call Dr. William Cross," Kilgour announced after Judge Keith had brutally admonished him and Orr at sidebar.

For over an hour, Kilgour interrogated Cross about his visit to the Lloyd house with Dr. Moore the night that Maud died and about the autopsy performed the next day. Powell watched as two of the jurymen dozed again during the testimony. Even Matt was having difficulty staying awake. Cross's testimony was largely repetitive of Moore's version of events except for Cross's insistence that the cause of death was poisoning. It wasn't until Kilgour asked Cross his impression of how the poison affected the child that both Matt and the jury reengaged.

"The specific symptoms of arsenical poisoning are no different from any other poisoning. There would be burning in the esophagus, heat in the stomach, and purging, of course. A small dose may kill a life very quickly, but a full stomach would impair its action. Only one-twenty-fifth to one-thirtieth of a grain can be taken safely. Two grains will destroy an adult, whereas only a half grain would cause death in a three-year-old child."

◆ ◆ ◆

Court resumed after the midday break. After asking Dr. Thomas Edwards to confirm Emily's purchase of arsenic, Kilgour summoned his next witness.

"The people call Mrs. Margaret Greene."

Surprised, Powell turned toward the gallery and caught Maggie's eye as she rose from the pew. From the look on her face, she was surprised, too.

"Mrs. Greene, how are you acquainted with the defendant?" Kilgour asked after she had taken her oath.

"I live a few doors from her."

"And you're friends?"

"We enjoy friendly relations, yes."

"Were you present at any time during Maud's illness?"

"I had heard the child was not feeling well and brought over some ginger cakes on that Friday."

"At any time during the child's illness did you notice an improvement in her condition?"

"Yes, on Sunday morning when I arrived, she seemed better and was playing on her bed."

"Yet, the child died that night," Kilgour said, looking at the jury. He turned back to Maggie. "Did you ever see rats in her house?"

"I heard them when I was there once."

"But you never actually saw a rat."

"No, I did not."

"Did you ever give Mrs. Lloyd arsenic?"

"I did not."

"Did Mrs. Lloyd ever ask you to buy arsenic for her supposed rat problem?"

"No."

Kilgour turned to the judge. "No further questions at this moment, but the prosecution reserves the right to recall Mrs. Greene."

Judge Keith nodded and looked at Powell with arched brows.

"Defense will cross-examine after all testimony from this witness is taken," Powell said.

Maggie left the witness stand, and Kilgour summoned his next witness. "The people call Miss Mollie Ryan."

The three defense attorneys exchanged uneasy glances as Mollie Ryan walked past their table and took the stand. As she swore her oath, Powell drew a long breath to ready himself for whatever was to come.

"Miss Ryan, how do you know the defendant?" Kilgour asked.

"Mrs. Lloyd lives on the same square as me and my mother."

"Do you and your mother socialize with Mrs. Lloyd?"

"Not so much anymore. My widowed mother is in poor health, so she doesn't leave the house these days. And since the summer the Lloyd boys died, I rarely stop by Mrs. Lloyd's house."

Kilgour turned to face the jury as he asked his next question. "And why is that, Miss Ryan?"

Mollie's eyes darted from Kilgour to the jury box. "Because Mrs. Lloyd frightens me."

Kilgour spun on his heels back toward Mollie. "Frightens you? Why would you be frightened of a gentle widow like Mrs. Lloyd?"

"Because she might get it in her head to poison me like she poisoned Henry and George."

Powell leapt from his chair. "Objection, Your Honor. This testimony is irrelevant. The prosecution has presented no evidence that Mrs. Lloyd poisoned anyone, let alone her two sons, who died from natural causes. Any fears that Miss Ryan may have are based on nothing more than innuendo and gossip and do not constitute legitimate testimony."

"If it please the court," Kilgour interjected, "Miss Ryan's testimony will provide adequate justification for her fears and is directly relevant to establishing that Mrs. Lloyd had the means to commit the crime of which she is accused in this case."

Judge Keith hesitated, sizing up the situation, before nodding. "I'll allow it for the moment."

"Thank you, Your Honor." Kilgour shifted his focus back to Mollie Ryan. "Miss Ryan, what did you witness that made you fearful that Mrs. Lloyd might poison you?"

"It was July the summer before last. Mrs. Lloyd had stopped by our house to drop off a pie for my mother. As she was leaving, Mrs. Lloyd mentioned that she had rats and asked me if we had any arsenic. I told her that we didn't have a problem with rodents and didn't have any poisons. Then she asked me if I would buy some poison for her. I told her that if she wanted arsenic, I saw no reason why she couldn't buy it herself. At that point, Mrs. Lloyd became angry. She called me an ugly name and told me that if I wouldn't purchase the arsenic for her, then she would have Mrs. Greene buy it for her. She stormed off the porch and stomped up the street toward Mrs. Greene's house. And then the following week, both her little boys died."

"Thank you, Miss Ryan." Kilgour turned and walked toward the prosecution table. "Your witness," he said to Powell on his way to his seat.

Glancing at Matt, Powell rose from the table and approached the witness box. "Miss Ryan. Did you witness Mrs. Lloyd administer arsenic to her son George Lloyd?"

"Of course not!" Mollie Ryan sat up straight and sounded indignant.

"Did Mrs. Lloyd, while in your presence, administer poison to Henry Lloyd?"

"Not that I know of."

"What about Annie Lloyd? Did you witness Mrs. Lloyd administering poison to Annie?"

Mollie shifted uncomfortably in her chair. "No."

"And Maud? At any time did you witness Mrs. Lloyd administer an injection to Maud?"

"Of course not!"

"What about arsenic? At any time, did you see her give arsenic or any poison to Maud or anyone else?"

"Not that I saw directly, no," Mollie said with a defeated huff.

Powell headed toward the defense table, then paused and turned to face her again. "The weekend of March 22 of this last year, did you drop off something for Maud Lloyd during her illness?"

Kilgour looked up over the rims of his reading glasses.

"I brought her some penny candy that she was fond of," Mollie said hesitantly.

"What does this penny candy look like?" Powell asked.

Mollie tilted her head questioningly. "It's just sugar crystal."

"Any particular shape or color of this sugar crystal?"

"They are shaped like little flowers—green, pink, and yellow, I think."

"Flowers like roses?"

"Yes. The candy resembled little rosettes. I think that is why poor Maudie liked them."

"Thank you for your testimony, Miss Ryan." Powell looked at the judge. "No further questions."

Kilgour rose to his feet. "The state recalls Mrs. Margaret Greene."

Maggie took her seat on the witness stand, and the bailiff reminded her that she was still subject to the oath she had sworn.

"Mrs. Greene, during your examination, you testified that Mrs. Lloyd did not ask you to purchase arsenic for her. Yet just now, we hear from Miss Ryan that when she declined Mrs. Lloyd's request to purchase arsenic on her behalf, Mrs. Lloyd stated she would ask you to purchase the arsenic. I will remind you that you are under oath, and the penalty for perjury severe. Now again, did Mrs. Lloyd ask you to purchase arsenic on her behalf?"

Maggie moved her eyes nervously toward the defense table and looked at Powell. He stared back without emotion or acknowledgment.

"Mrs. Greene!" said Kilgour. "Don't look to the defense for your answer. Did you purchase arsenic for Mrs. Lloyd?"

"No, I did not."

"But she did ask you to purchase arsenic for her, didn't she?"

"I had forgotten about it until Mollie's testimony reminded me." Maggie bit her lip, her eyes glancing at her hands in her lap before looking back at Kilgour. "Yes. Mrs. Lloyd asked me to purchase arsenic. I don't really remember when it was. If Mollie says it was the summer before last, then I take her at her word."

"And did you," Kilgour asked, hands on the rail of the witness box, leaning, his manner intimidating, "purchase the arsenic for her?"

"I already told you that I did not. When she asked me, she said that she had purchased ten cents' worth the day before but had managed to lose it on the way home and was afraid to admit her carelessness to the clerk. She thought she might get into trouble for misplacing it. I told her that she was being silly. There was no such rule, and who cared what the clerk at Moore's store thought. And that was the end of the conversation. I hadn't given it another thought until now."

Moore's store? Powell had checked Moore's logbook around the time of the boys' death and remembered no record of Emily purchasing arsenic.

"You didn't think her request suspicious when her two boys died of poisoning the following week?"

"No, because they didn't die from arsenic poisoning. They accidentally ate pokeweed berries when they were blackberry picking. Why would I assume they died from any cause other than what the doctor and coroner determined?"

"You are certain you did not give Mrs. Lloyd any arsenic?"

"I did not."

"And why should we believe you now after you lied in your earlier testimony?"

"Objection," Powell interjected.

"Overruled," Keith said, with a dismissive wave of his hand. "Mrs. Greene did, indeed, mislead the court. She needs to answer for herself." He turned his attention to her. "Mrs. Greene?"

"As I stated, I hadn't given it any mind. Her request was more out of worry than urgency, and she displayed no emotional reaction when I declined. It all seemed so insignificant and was so long ago that, frankly, it had slipped my mind."

Kilgour scowled at Maggie. "I'm finished with this witness."

Judge Keith looked over at Powell. "Mr. Harrison?"

"No questions at this time," Powell said. Maggie had explained herself well enough, and any answers to his questions might hurt their case further.

"Very well," Judge Keith said. "Next witness, Mr. Kilgour."

"The state calls Julian Hutchinson."

As the name was called, Powell caught his brother's reaction. Powell leaned close and whispered, "Who is Julian Hutchinson?"

"Owns a mercantile out in Goresville."

The weight that had been pressing in Powell's stomach sank lower. Powell glanced over at JW. His stony expression confirmed what Powell had already surmised. While JW had interviewed every apothecary in the county, he hadn't considered that some of the general stores sold arsenic. Neither had Powell.

Kilgour approached the witness box. "Mr. Hutchinson, do you know anything about the purchase of arsenic by the defendant, Mrs. Lloyd?"

"I do indeed," Mr. Hutchinson said through what looked to Powell like a mouthful of crooked teeth. "Yes, sir. She got it from me twice. A whole ounce on the sixth of July 1871, and a half ounce on the eighteenth of March of this year. She did not tell me what it was for."

"And where is your store?"

"'Bout ten miles north of town, just outside of Goresville."

Kilgour smiled and nodded his head at the witness. "No further questions."

"Mr. Harrison," Judge Keith called.

Powell leaned to Matt. "You want to take his testimony since you know him?"

With a nod of his head, Matt stood and walked to the front of the courtroom.

"Good morning, Mr. Hutchinson. You testified that the defendant purchased arsenic from your mercantile on two separate occasions. Did you make a memorandum of the transactions on a register?"

"I did."

Matt turned to the judge. "Your Honor, the defense wishes to review this register to affirm its authenticity before questioning this witness any further. I assume the prosecution has it in their possession?"

Keith nodded his head. "Mr. Kilgour, can you produce the register for examination by the defense?"

"I have it right here, Your Honor," Kilgour said, holding a cloth-bound book in an extended arm. The bailiff took the book and handed it to Matt.

Matthew pulled his reading glasses from his breast pocket and placed them on his nose. After a moment of thumbing through the pages, he raised his eyes over the rims of the spectacles. "It looks as if you record poison sales in your own hand. Is that correct?"

"I do."

"So you don't require the purchaser to sign for the chemicals?"

"Nope. I make the memorandum myself."

Matt riffled through the pages before turning the book toward the witness and placing it on the ledge of the witness box. He moved his finger down the page to the entry in question. "So here on July 6 in '71, I see your notation. 'Mrs. E. Lloyd 1 oz. white arsenic.' And this is in your hand?"

Hutchinson narrowed his focus to the writing on the page. "Yes, sir."

Matt pursed his lips and nodded. Turning the book toward himself, he thumbed through a few pages and presented the book to the witness again. "Now here we have the entry on March 18, 1872." He pointed to the entry and tapped his finger on the paper. "This notation appears to be from a different hand. Am I correct in my observation?"

Hutchinson bent close to the book, squinting. "Yes, sir. That's my wife's handwriting."

Matt took the book and looked at the page again before bringing his eyes back to the witness. "So you personally didn't sell arsenic to Mrs. Lloyd on March 18 of this year."

"No, sir, but my wife did."

"Were you witness to this transaction?"

"No, sir."

"So you have no idea whether this notation by your wife's hand of 'E. Lloyd' is 'Elizabeth Lloyd' or 'Ellen Lloyd' or 'Edmonia Lloyd' or 'Edward Lloyd,' for that matter."

"My wife said that a woman made the purchase."

"But you, Mr. Hutchinson, have no idea who purchased arsenic on March 18, 1872, because you were not present at your store on that day, isn't that correct?"

Hutchinson glanced at the floor. "That's correct," he said in a low voice.

"No further questions, Your Honor."

When Matt returned to the table, Powell scribbled a note on the paper. *Nice job.* Matt nodded.

"Prosecution wishes to rebut," Kilgour said, and Keith nodded. "Your Honor, the state asks the court to order Mrs. Lloyd to remove her veil."

"Objection," Powell fired. "No foundation."

"Overruled," Keith said.

"Then the defense objects on grounds of relevance," Powell pushed. "Mr. Hutchinson testified that he was only witness to the purchase in 1871, not 1872. Any identification of Mrs. Lloyd as the purchaser in 1871 is irrelevant to this proceeding."

"Still overruled, Counsellor," Keith said.

Certain that the judge's ruling was wrong, Powell picked up his pencil and made a note, in case the worst happened and they needed to appeal the jury's verdict.

The judge turned to Emily. "Mrs. Lloyd, please lift the veil and face the witness."

Muffled whispers whirred throughout the courtroom as all heads turned toward Emily. With both hands, hesitantly she lifted the veil above her head, holding it steady as she looked across the courtroom toward the witness stand.

"Mr. Hutchinson," Kilgour said. "Do you recognize the defendant as the 'Mrs. E. Lloyd' who bought white arsenic from your mercantile?"

Hutchinson squinted at Emily before nodding. "She's thinner now and her hair is up, but I sure remember those eyes. It's the same woman."

"Thank you, Mr. Hutchinson. No further questions."

CHAPTER 28

Powell flung his satchel on the bench of the hall rack and tossed his hat beside it. As he was removing his coat, Janet emerged from the back to greet him.

"By the look on your face, I'd say the afternoon did not go well," she said as she took his coat from him.

"I'm not certain it could have gone any worse."

"I thought you were wonderful this morning, the way you handled the situation with Delphi," she said as they walked into the parlor together. Powell gave her a questioning look. "I was there for this morning's testimony but left once Dr. Cross took the stand. I could hardly keep my eyes open, so I thought it best for the jurors not to see the wife of the lead defense attorney sleeping in the gallery."

"That would be assuming that they were awake and alert enough to notice." Powell attempted a smile. "Thank you for coming. And I'm sorry I didn't notice."

"You were busy." Janet took her chair to the left of the fireplace while Powell poured himself a whiskey. "So what happened that has you imbibing before supper?"

Powell blew out a heavy sigh. "What didn't happen?" He replaced the crystal stopper on the decanter and joined her by the fire. "After Mort finished with Doc Cross, he called Tom Edwards to testify that Mrs. Lloyd bought arsenic at his store in February."

"Which we already knew," Janet interjected.

"Yes," Powell said, taking a drink from the glass, "but then Mort called Mrs. Greene."

"Maggie Greene?"

Powell nodded. "Who testified that a week before the two boys died last summer, Mrs. Lloyd had asked her to purchase arsenic for her after she supposedly lost arsenic that she bought from Dr. Moore earlier the same day."

"Dear God!"

"And it gets worse from there. A merchant from out in Goresville had evidence that Mrs. Lloyd made purchases of arsenic just days before Maud's death."

Her eyes narrowed. "How on earth did Mr. Foster miss all of this?"

"I can't blame JW for not canvassing every general store in the county. Although I am puzzled by Mrs. Greene's selective memory."

"I shall refrain from offering my opinion of Mrs. Greene. You already know how I feel about her." She smiled at him. "Don't worry, darling, I'm not judging, nor am I looking for a row."

"I thank you for that." He smiled back. "And I fear you may be right. My guess is that Maggie assumed that I would not have taken the case had she been up front about the incident. In fact, I would have. But had I known all of this, I may not have abandoned the insanity plea."

"What does Mrs. Lloyd have to say?"

Powell rolled his eyes. "She denies it. All of it. She says she didn't purchase arsenic. Or if she did, she doesn't remember."

"How can she not remember traveling to Goresville?"

"Oh, she remembers that. Says she has a friend out there that she visits and that she was in that neighborhood the week before Maud became ill. But she doesn't recall any purchase at Hutchinson's Mercantile. And for some godforsaken reason, I believe her when she says she doesn't recall."

"You believe her to be insane?"

"I don't know what to believe. She is so convincing in her pleas that she didn't make those purchases. So adamant about her lack of memory of certain events and conversations."

"Sounds like a memory of convenience, if you ask me," Janet said, picking at a thread on her skirt.

"I don't think she's playing me. But then again . . ." Powell shook his head and took another drink from his glass.

"Could it be some sort of intermittent amnesia?" Janet suggested. "Like the old-timers develop after they live too long?"

Powell laughed under his breath. "I have no idea. Perhaps your father could provide some insight."

"I can ask him to join us for supper so you can speak with him." Janet looked at her feet, lost for a moment in thought. "But, Powell." She looked up at him. "You cannot let Mrs. Lloyd's state of mind distract you. At this point in the trial, it doesn't matter if she's insane. Unless you can change her plea."

"You know the law doesn't allow that."

Janet nodded. "Then you have to focus on doing the right thing."

Powell looked at her. "Which is what?"

"Honoring your oath." Her eyes locked onto his.

"What about the truth, Jan? What if she is insane? What if she did, indeed, murder those children?"

"As difficult as it may be, you cannot think about that right now." Janet narrowed her eyes. "When you made the decision to take her case and decided her plea, you promised to defend *her*. You made no promise to defend the truth. It's not up to you to prove if she is responsible for the deaths of her children or not. Not now. No matter how horrible it is to think about." She closed her eyes momentarily, shuttering the thought.

"And what about doing what's right?"

"Honoring your oath *is* doing what's right. You must defend Mrs. Lloyd to the best of your ability." Looking at him again, she forced an encouraging smile. "You must have faith in the Lord, darling, and trust Him to take care of the rest."

CHAPTER 29

"The state calls Professor William P. Tonry," Orr said, rising from his seat. In a vintage suit styled from before the war, his hair greased to one side, Orr looked even more scholarly today than usual. Powell had anticipated it would be Orr soliciting testimony from the scientific men. He was more experienced in forensics than Kilgour. And, in Powell's opinion, smarter.

Powell studied the professor as he took the stand. Not much more than an inch or two taller than five feet, the man was slight with hazel eyes and a mass of black hair. Like the judge, Tonry seemed younger than his age.

"Professor Tonry, would you state your qualifications for the court, if you please," Orr asked as he approached the witness stand.

"I teach chemistry at the Maryland Institute," Tonry answered.

Powell was struck by the thick Irish brogue and the low register of Tonry's voice.

"Would you tell the court how you became involved in this matter?"

"I received a telegram from Mr. Kilgour on the twenty-fifth of March of this year requesting me to analyze a specimen for poison and informing me that I would receive the sample from his agent. That evening, Deputy Fred Roberts arrived at my office with a jar containing a stomach, its contents, and a duodenum portion of intestine. The jar was wrapped in paper, sealed, tied with string across the top. The name *Maud* was written on the paper and scratched in the wax of the seal. I placed the jar in the closet of my office that I reserve for poison specimens."

"And who all has access to your office and this closet, Professor?"

"No one can enter my office when I am not there without a key, and I hold the only one. Not even the janitor has access to the room."

Orr nodded. "Please tell the court about your analysis of the contents of the jar."

Tonry turned to face the jury. "When I was ready for the chemical analysis, I proceeded to prepare the child's organs first. I removed the stomach from the jar and drained its contents into a beaker, which I had washed from the hydrant in my office. After setting the beaker aside, the stomach and duodenum were placed on a clean plate and cut up very finely with a clean shoemaker's knife. I transferred all of the cut-up pieces and the stomach contents to a porcelain evaporating dish. I diluted muriatic acid with distilled water and poured it over the liquid and solid specimens. The dish was placed over a boiling bath, and I added chlorate of potash, a few grains at a time, to the mixture. The contents of this mixture were digested over this water bath for the greater part of two days, taking ten hours in all. As soon as the tissues began to break up, the water became clear. At this point, I filtered the solution with filter paper and muslin to keep the paper from breaking up. The yield was about seven ounces, of which this was a part." Tonry held up a small vial of clear fluid to show the jury. Powell, watching them closely, noticed the color drain from the face of a juror in the second row.

"After removing the contents of this vial, I tested half of the solution for mineral poison by heating copper turnings with sulfuric acid. You see, if arsenic is present in the specimen, passing sulfurous acid through the solution will create arsenic acid. The resulting solution was passed through a stream of sulphurated hydrogen and gently heated for an hour and a half. I let it stand for eight hours before filtering it again to separate the precipitate from the liquid. The filter and its contents were then spread out in a dish and ammonia was added."

"Ammonia?" Orr asked in a clear attempt to keep the jury's attention. "Are you talking about the same ammonia that my wife uses to clean our kitchen?"

"Aye," Tonry said, readjusting his position in the chair and addressing Orr directly. "It be pretty much the same as your wife uses. Interestingly, arsenic is soluble in ammonia. The object of treating the precipitate with ammonia is to dissolve any sulfide of arsenic from the solution. If arsenic is present, it will be in the form of a sulfide, and the ammonia will take up the arsenic sulfide, leaving any other metal that might give a canary-yellow or bright-orange color to the precipitate."

"And what is the purpose of eliminating arsenic sulfate from the sample?" Orr asked.

"To confirm that no other metals are responsible for generating the yellow precipitate in the remaining sample," Tonry repeated.

"I see," Orr said. "And did the remaining precipitate produce any color?"

"It was brown in color, meaning no other toxic metal was present in the sample," Tonry said. "Next, I halved the remaining solution to repeat the test I had just completed, but without adding the ammonia. I reserved the other half of the solution for a test using the Marsh apparatus.

"I prepared one half of the solution exactly as I did before, passing it through sulfurous acid, reducing it to near dryness, hydrogenating it with sulphurate to create arsenic sulfide should any arsenic be present. When I passed the solution through the filter this time, the yellow color of arsenic was clearly visible."

"And you are certain it was arsenic?" Orr asked.

"The ammonia from the first test eliminated any arsenic that might be present in the first sample. Had any other toxic mineral been present, the color would have shown on the filter. The only possible reason the filter would turn yellow in the second test is because of the presence of arsenic.

"Next, I wanted to put the solution through the Marsh apparatus to see if it created spots on porcelain. As always, I ensured the integrity of the apparatus by burning the jet rings to see if they generated spots. As you can see, they did not." The professor handed a porcelain plate to Orr, who showed it to the jury. The plate contained no markings.

"I combined the sample fluid with hydrogen sulfide in the presence of hydrochloric acid," Tonry continued, "which, when arsenic is present, produces a lustrous precipitate. As you can see, the solution gave spots on the porcelain, of which these are some." Tonry handed Orr another porcelain dish with five shimmery black spots. "If you look here, you'll see the sheen on the spots. That sheen indicates the presence of arsenic sulfate."

"So both tests confirm the presence of arsenic in the stomach of Maud Lloyd at the time of her death," Orr stated, parading before the jury, his arm outstretched with the dish for each man to examine the tiny, damning spots. Concluding his demonstration, Orr handed the porcelain back to Professor Tonry. "From these tests, can you determine how much arsenic was in little Maud's stomach at the time of her death?"

"I most certainly can. Using French Zero, it weighed .35, meaning that the weight of the precipitate was thirty-five milligrams for half of the substance. Doubling the quantity, and calculating the sulphurate in the arsenic acid, and then converting French grams to English grains, that result is eighty-six-one-hundredths of a grain of arsenic in half of the specimen. When I double that to compensate for using half of the solution in my first analysis, I calculate that there were approximately eight-fifths, or a little more than one and a half grains, of arsenic in the stomach and duodenum of Maud Lloyd."

Tonry handed a small vial to Orr and continued. "Now here is a sample of the precipitate that is mixed with distilled water. The specimen's yellow color is a clear indication of the presence—"

"Judge," the juror in the second row raised his hand and called, interrupting the testimony. "I think I'm gonna be sick."

The bailiff rushed to the stove and grabbed the coal bucket and brought it to the juror.

"Let's recess," Judge Keith said as the man lost his stomach contents into the pail. "We'll reconvene at two o'clock."

Powell turned to his cousin Dr. Graham Ellzey and his colleague Dr. William Taylor, seated in the pew immediately behind. "Let's meet over at our offices."

• • •

"Without seeing the details of Tonry's analysis," Dr. Graham Ellzey said, "I cannot validate his calculations."

"Kilgour has refused to let us examine the report," Powell said. "But I plan to raise the issue with the judge on cross."

"The report will be helpful, but I still have concerns," Ellzey said. "As I told Matt last evening at supper, my analysis does not account for the amount of arsenic that the state's chemist produced. Unless I understand his testing methods, it will be difficult to dispute the integrity of his process."

"Based on this morning's proceedings, there's no need to dispute the integrity of Tonry's testing methods," Powell said. "Just the result."

"Without knowing every chemical element Tonry considered in his assumptions when he conducted his analysis, it's still a risk," Matt remarked.

"Tonry testified that Kilgour's telegram requested an analysis for poisons. And if my instincts are accurate, Tonry only tested for arsenic and antimony," Powell said. "He won't have considered bismuth."

"You need to pin him down on the specific shade of the precipitate in his first analysis," Ellzey advised. "And find out whether he used nitric acid at any point in the process."

"Don't worry, I know what I need to do," Powell said. "And you know what you need to do."

"Not to worry," Ellzey said. "I made the purchase this morning and have it right here." He patted the side of the satchel on the table. "We'll be ready."

• • •

"Before the recess," Orr said, resuming his examination of Professor Tonry, "you were telling the court about the sample in the vial."

"Aye," Tonry said. "The solution from which that sample was taken was heated and reduced to crystalline form, and when viewed under the microscope, it is clearly arsenic. I diluted a few crystals in distilled water to illustrate the canary color of the arsenious acid."

"And what is arsenious acid?" Orr asked, his thumbs tucked under his suspenders.

"White arsenic is its popular name."

"Are there any other tests you performed using the apparatus?"

"Aye. In addition to Marsh, I performed the Reinsch test, a Scheele's Green analysis using copper sulphate, and two tests using silver. I have included the plates from those tests in this box." Tonry handed a pasteboard shoebox to Orr. "In all instances, white arsenic presented in the sample."

Orr offered a satisfied smile to the witness before turning toward the judge. "No further questions," he said and took his seat.

Powell stood, talking as he walked toward the front of the courtroom and offering the professor a friendly grin. "From the accent you carry, I'd say you are not originally from this area."

The jurymen, along with the spectators in the courtroom, laughed.

"I was born in Sligo, Ireland, and emigrated to Massachusetts with my parents when I was ten."

"Interesting heritage," Powell commented. "Would you mind elaborating a bit more on your credentials in the field of chemistry?"

"I have been practicing as an analytic chemist since 1866 and am currently engaged as a professor at the Maryland Institute. Before accepting the position there, I had a private laboratory in the city of Baltimore. For five years, I was an assistant chemist in the US surgeon general's office in Washington, DC. I also taught chemistry as an adjunct professor at Georgetown University, where I began my course of study."

"Have you ever testified in a poisoning case before?"

"This is my first case analyzing a human body for arsenic."

"But you have analyzed a human body for poisons other than arsenic, like antimony, for example," Powell said, placing his hand on the rail of the witness box. "Perhaps at the Wharton trial earlier this year?"

Tonry shifted in his chair. "Aye. I was called to testify on behalf of the state at that trial."

"As I recall in that case, the accused was acquitted because of inaccuracies in your chemical analysis of the postmortem specimen, is that not correct?"

Kilgour jumped to his feet. "Move to strike, Your Honor. His question is both leading and irrelevant, and the jury should be instructed as such."

"Your Honor, I am simply validating the credibility of the witness."

"Sustained," Keith said.

"Your Honor," Powell protested.

"Jurors shall disregard Mr. Harrison's question, and should Mr. Harrison wish to validate the witness's credentials, he will rephrase his question so as not to mislead the jury."

"Yes, Your Honor," Powell said. He turned his attention back to the professor. "You stated that you were called as an expert for the prosecution in the Wharton trial last December. Can you tell the jury why Mrs. Wharton was accused of murder in that case?"

"The victim, General Ketchum, had visited Mrs. Wharton in her Baltimore home in an attempt to collect a debt. When he suddenly died after drinking lemonade prepared by the accused, a postmortem was conducted. Professor William Aiken of the Maryland Institute analyzed the contents of the victim's stomach and found that it contained twenty grains of tartar emetic, a toxic compound containing antimony. After the defense had called into question the initial autopsy analysis, I was consulted to verify the state's results."

"And?"

"There was sufficient poison in the stomach of the victim to cause his death."

"If that was indeed the case, can you give us your professional opinion as to why Mrs. Wharton was acquitted?"

"Objection," Kilgour shouted. "Calls for speculation."

"Defense is asking for the witness's opinion in his capacity as a chemist, Your Honor," Powell argued.

"Overruled," the judge said.

"Your Honor!" Kilgour protested.

Judge Keith raised a brow at Kilgour before turning to Tonry. "You may answer."

With a loud huff, Kilgour took his seat.

Tonry moved his attention from the judge to Powell. "Mrs. Wharton's attorneys argued that the local doctors who had attended the general before his death and conducted the postmortem, as well as Professor Aiken, who performed the chemical analysis, were all University of Maryland Medical School colleagues and thus were covering for each other's mistakes," Tonry said. "The chief prosecutor had the general's remains exhumed and asked me to analyze his liver and kidneys. At the time I represented no bias, as I was employed by the surgeon general's office in Washington, DC. Despite finding evidence of antimony poisoning in Ketchum's organs, my evidence was too little, too late. The jurymen had already bought into the defense's alternate theory that the general died of cerebrospinal meningitis and, as such, returned a verdict of not guilty."

"So the jury had no confidence in the state's chemical analysis and decided that the general had, indeed, died from natural causes," Powell stated.

"One could make that interpretation, I suppose, but I can assure you the chemical analysis indicated otherwise."

"So you say." Powell walked to the defense table and consulted his notes. "Earlier this morning, you testified that you estimated that there were one and a half grains of arsenic in Maud's stomach and contents, but the original indictment of the accused states that there were fifteen grains of arsenic in the specimen. Was there an error in your report?"

"My analysis states one point five grains. I never reported fifteen."

"Your Honor," Kilgour said, rising from his seat. "The telegram the state initially received from the professor indicated fifteen grains of white arsenic were in the child's remains. We subsequently discovered the error and corrected the figure when we forwarded the matter to the grand jury."

"You never informed the defense there was an error," Powell exclaimed. "And we have yet to be provided any documentation regarding the state's postmortem analysis."

"Hmm," Kilgour said. "I thought we had at the indictment hearing. But the specific amount of arsenic used to kill the victim is not part of the bill of indictment issued by the grand jury, so it has no effect on the matter at hand."

"The defense is still entitled to review the postmortem analysis report," Powell argued.

"You have your opportunity to review the analysis now on cross," Kilgour replied.

The judge looked at Powell with indifference. "Mr. Kilgour is correct. The bill of indictment is not specific on the amount of poison. And your experts are in the gallery to validate or dispute the state's expert testimony. There is no reason to compel Mr. Kilgour to share his expert analysis with the defense." He waved his hand at Powell. "Carry on, Mr. Harrison."

Powell glared at Kilgour. Kilgour was getting away with it. Powell drew a long, silent breath to compose himself before turning his attention back to Tonry.

"You indicated that in your first analysis you added ammonia to the solution from Maud Lloyd's stomach contents and organs. Is that correct?"

"Aye. I did. In order to eliminate any arsenic from the specimen so as to not obfuscate the results of the analysis."

Powell looked across the room at the jury. "To avoid a false positive?"

"Exactly."

"And you testified that the filter did not turn yellow or orange, but brown. Is that correct?"

"Aye."

"What shade of brown was it?"

Tonry furrowed his brows. "I'm not quite certain I understand your meaning."

Powell turned his gaze back to the professor. "I'm interested in your recollection of the exact color of the precipitate."

Powell pulled a number of thin wooden shingles from his pocket and placed them out on the rail of the witness box. "I brought paint samples to assist you in remembering the color."

"Objection," Kilgour cried. "Mr. Harrison's paint chips are not evidence."

"I did not indicate they were evidence," Powell argued. "They serve simply as a tool to help the witness recall the specific color."

"I'll allow it," Keith said with a dismissive wave.

"Thank you, Your Honor," Powell said and looked back at Tonry. "Now tell me, Professor, which color is closest to the shade of the brown precipitate in your first experiment?"

Tonry leaned forward in the chair, his eyes scanning the five painted shingles in front of him. "I'd say this one." He pointed to the second sample from the right.

Powell lifted the shingle and held it for the jury to see. "A bit of a reddish undertone, wouldn't you say?" He flipped the shingle and read the color aloud. "Burnt sienna. And you are certain there was no yellow in the precipitate."

"That is correct."

"What might produce a yellow color?"

"Antimony for certain would produce a bright-orange color," Tonry said.

Powell nodded. "What about medications like yellow jasmine?"

"Contrary to its name, yellow jasmine produces a crimson precipitate."

"And bismuth?"

Tonry hesitated before answering. "Depending on its concentrate, a deep orange or reddish brown," he said slowly.

Powell extended his arm and looked at the paint sample in his hand. "Like burnt sienna?" He flipped the shingle and held it up so the color on the wood faced Tonry.

"Possibly," Tonry said.

Powell showed the jury the sample again before pushing the shingle into his pocket with the others. "Now, the next test that you performed used the Marsh apparatus."

Tonry uncrossed his legs and shifted his position on the chair. "That's correct."

"And when you prepared for that test, did you infuse nitric acid into the solution to eliminate any bismuth that might be present prior to conducting the test?"

Orr's face reddened as if suddenly heated. He turned around in his chair, whispering to his other two chemistry experts sitting behind him.

"At that point in my analysis, I had not."

"And would bismuth also create the lustrous spots on the porcelain?"

Tonry hesitated before answering. "Aye."

The courtroom erupted in loud murmurs.

"You also stated that you performed the Reinsch test on copper plates and got the same black spots, yes?"

Tonry nodded. "I did."

"And do you have with you the plate from that test?"

"It was in the box that I handed to Mr. Orr."

Powell turned to the bench. "Your Honor, the defense requests that the state make available the evidence that Professor Tonry provided here today and, again, requests the notes from his analysis so that our experts may examine them."

Keith eyed Powell for a moment. "The defense may have the evidence that was presented in court as part of Professor Tonry's testimony. But as I ruled earlier, any analysis or documentation outside of the professor's courtroom testimony belongs to the prosecution. Mr. Kilgour may share it at his discretion."

"Your Honor, Mr. Harrison is welcome to examine the plates the professor presented, but the state refuses the defense access to the state's work product." Kilgour shoved the box of plates across the table. The bailiff stood and retrieved the box and brought it to Powell.

Pasting on a smile, Powell took the box from the bailiff and walked it to the witness stand. "Professor, can you identify the copper plate used during the Reinsch test?"

Tonry opened the lid and removed the plates. Sorting through them, he pulled one out and handed it to Powell.

"As you can see, these are the black spots to which I was referring," he said, pointing with an index finger to a number of discolorations on the metal.

Powell bent close to examine the spots. "Is that the same luster you were referring to in your testimony regarding the results of the Marsh test?"

"Aye. You can clearly see the black marks indicative of arsenic acid," Tonry replied.

"I'm confused, Professor," Powell said. "You told us earlier that you did not add nitric acid to the solution before you tested it. Without the addition of the nitric acid, bismuth could also be in the solution, correct?"

"Possibly."

"And while bismuth and arsenic both create lustrous black spots on porcelain in a Marsh test, there is a difference in the illumination of the spots on copper in the Reinsch test, isn't that correct?"

"Aye, there is."

"And what is that difference?" Powell asked.

"On copper, the black spot created by arsenous acid is a dull matte black, whereas the spot created by bismuth has a sheen to it," Tonry said while Powell walked to the jury box, plate in hand, pointing to the shimmering black spots on the copper.

"Like this," Powell said to the jury.

"Aye, but—" Tonry stopped.

"But what, Professor?" Powell asked, his back to the witness stand, ensuring each juror could see the shiny black spots.

"But in my test using the last quarter of the specimen, I indeed did pass nitric acid through the solution on the pretext that the child might have been treated with bismuth subsalicylate. The nitric acid would have eliminated the bismuth, leaving no possibility that the crystalline I used to calculate the amount of arsenic present was compromised. The crystalline in the precipitate was bright yellow, clearly that of arsenic," Tonry insisted.

"And on that point, the defense does not disagree," Powell said.

A gasp sounded from the gallery and across the courtroom.

Powell spun back to the professor. "My question, Professor Tonry, is whether you analyzed the amount of *bismuth* that might be present in the specimen?"

"I was instructed to analyze only for toxic metals."

"In your professional opinion, is bismuth a toxic metal?"

Tonry blanched. "Bismuth salts are commonly used medicinally without toxic effects." ·

"What about in its pure form?"

"In large enough quantities, it could be."

"But you didn't analyze specifically for the amount of bismuth?"

"No, I did not."

Powell smiled at Tonry. "Your Honor, Mr. Foster will take over examination of the witness."

Keith nodded as JW approached, and Powell took his place back at the defense table.

"I only have a few questions, sir," JW said with a notepad in his hand. "When you were reducing the solution from the stomach and its contents, you testified that the process 'took nearly two days,' but then you said that the process took ten hours to complete. Can you clarify your meaning?"

"Of course. I started the initial process in the afternoon, and after about three hours, I turned the heat off and covered the solution for the night. The next morning, I resumed the process for another seven hours or so."

JW lifted his chin. "Ah, I see. So the process took ten hours and was completed over two days because you went home for the night."

"Aye. And I made certain that no contamination occurred and that my room was locked."

"So can I assume that you typically work during the day?"

"I prefer to work when there is daylight, as I find it very difficult to conduct chemical analysis by lamplight."

"I can understand completely," JW said. "Exactly where is your office in Baltimore?"

"I'm at Second Street in the Maryland Institute building on the second floor."

"I'm familiar with the area. During the war, I spent some time in Baltimore at that prisoner camp that was on Forrest Street, a few squares from the Centre Market."

"My office overlooks the market, actually," Tonry replied.

"Lots of wagons and heavy vehicles on that street, if I recall. And the rail lines, aren't they just one square over on Pratt?"

"They are," Tonry replied. "It's quite a busy area."

Powell watched Kilgour pull his watch from his vest to check the time.

"Just a few more questions, I assure you," JW said, fighting a grin as he, too, noticed Kilgour's impatience. "You know, I was never very good at mathematics, or even arithmetic, for that matter. Guess that's why I ended up in law school." He chuckled and checked his notes. "You said that you calculated the amount of arsenic in milligrams." JW looked back up at Tonry. "Exactly how much is a milligram?"

"A milligram is one-thousandth of a French gram. And a French gram equates to about fifteen and a half English grains."

JW chuckled again. "As I said, Professor, my arithmetic skills are not very good, and if I had to guess, many of the gentlemen on the jury are just as confused as I am about grams and grains."

A number of the jurors nodded their heads.

"So maybe you would make it a little simpler for us. About how many grams are there in a teaspoon of sugar?"

Tonry considered for a moment. "I would estimate that a teaspoon of sugar weighs about a quarter gram."

JW nodded. "Now, during your testimony, you said that you weighed thirty-five milligrams of arsenic crystals in the precipitate from the autopsy sample. If the arsenic crystals were sugar granulate, how much would that be?"

"It would depend on how finely the sugar was milled."

"Assume that it's milled like the sugar us Southerners spoon into our four-o'clock tea." A number of men on the jury smiled at the reference.

"I would estimate that about five granulates of sugar would weigh thirty-five milligrams, thereabout," Tonry said.

"Five granulates!" JW exclaimed while looking at the jury. "How do you weigh something that small?"

"I have very specialized scales."

"You must!" JW said. "How are they impacted if you touch the table when you are weighing something as small as five granulates of sugar?"

"I have nailed my table to the floor for this very reason," Tonry replied. "The slightest movement can cause the measurement to be inaccurate."

JW nodded. "Thank you, Professor. No further questions, Your Honor."

◆ ◆ ◆

"Do you have a moment?" Maggie asked as she rapped a knuckle of her gloved hand on the doorframe of Powell's office.

Powell looked up from Dr. Moore's notes, which had finally been delivered to the defense. After court recessed for the day, Powell had taken supper at the inn and returned to the office for a long night.

"I didn't hear you come in," he said.

"I suppose you were too absorbed in those papers there to take notice when your clerk greeted me," she said as she stepped into the room.

Powell closed the file and stood. "How can I assist you, Mrs. Greene?"

"I wanted to apologize to you about my testimony yesterday. I completely forgot that Emily had approached me about the arsenic. Honest. It was so . . . arbitrary. I thought nothing of it at the time, and it never crossed my mind until Mollie's testimony." She lowered her head. "I am sorry, Powell."

"Had I known—"

"You might not have taken her case, I know," Maggie interrupted. "And I can assure you that I would have told you, had I remembered."

"That's not what I was going to say," Powell said. "Had I known, I would have not changed our strategy from an insanity defense. I would have taken her case regardless. The mentally diseased are entitled to the same protections under the law as any accused man or woman— guilty, innocent, or insane."

Maggie narrowed her brow. "So you think that Emily is insane?"

"It doesn't matter what I believe. My only aim is to keep her from the gallows."

"Powell—"

"Really, now, Mrs. Greene," he said, cutting her off. "I must get back to my work."

"Maggie." She arched her back and firmly held her stance. "It's Maggie, Powell."

He shifted his shoulders uncomfortably. "Maggie."

An awkward silence fell between them as they stood facing each other.

"Will you ever forgive me?" she asked at last.

"Nothing to forgive, if it is as you say."

"I'm not talking about the situation with Mrs. Lloyd," she said, tightening her lips over her teeth. "I'm talking about my marriage to Danny."

Powell looked down at his desk, scanning the papers as if searching for the answer among them. After a long moment, he brought his eyes to hers.

"I forgave you both the day he died."

She held his gaze. "It was you who I loved."

"Yet you married someone else." The words tasted bitter as he said them.

"You left, Powell," she said. "What choice did I have?"

"You could have waited for me." He felt a conflict of emotion—hurt, betrayal, regret—rise within him. "I would have married you had you waited."

Maggie knitted her brows and stared at him. "If you had only said that then."

Powell stared back at her in silence, not knowing what to feel or what to say. After a long moment, she gave him a hard last look before turning and walking out the door.

CHAPTER 30

"It was a dreadful day, Lara!" Emily pulled her shawl taut around her shoulders as she sat on the cot, staring into the corridor through the bars. "To be forced to listen to what that horrible man did to poor Maudie! He cut her into bitty pieces and cooked her like she was meat for stew!" Unable to hold back the tears any longer, she gave in and began weeping.

"There, there, my dear," Lara soothed. "Poor Maudie is with the Lord Christ and knew nothing of it. You must remember this—your dear child possesses a heavenly body now and is long gone from her earthly one."

A wind gust outside caused the flame of the hall lantern to flicker. Emily shivered between sobs and pulled the quilt draped over her shoulders tighter. "I don't think I can bear another day of this."

"The worst is over," Lara said reassuringly. "Now it's up to the experts to show that this vile little man from Baltimore hasn't a clue as to what he is doing."

Emily lifted her head. "Do you truly think they can do that?"

"Of course, I do. Mr. Harrison certainly has confidence in them. And he has clearly hired enough of them! No need to worry. Mr. Harrison has everything in hand, I can assure you."

"Have you met with him yet?" Emily asked.

"No, dear. There is nothing that I have to say that has any bearing on these proceedings."

"He wants to speak with Lilith also."

"Do you really want him to speak with Lilith?" Lara asked.

"He thinks she may know something that might help," Emily said.

"I'm not certain I would trust any testimony from Lilith."

Lamplight streamed into the corridor as the door to the guard's desk opened.

"Miss Emily," Freddie called from the doorway. "You have a gentleman caller. Do you want me to bring him back?"

"Who could that be?" Emily whispered to Lara.

"I wager it's that newspaperman," Lara said. "Didn't you tell me that he asked to stop by after supper to interview you?" Emily nodded with a sniffle. "You need to pull yourself together. You don't want to give him the impression that you're concerned in the least about today's testimony."

"Mr. Harrison told me not to meet with reporters."

"Apparently, Mr. Harrison hasn't been reading the papers. No, I think it is important to tell your side of the story. As it stands now, the public is only hearing the horrible lies of the prosecution."

"So you think that I should talk to him?"

"It can only help."

"All right, then," Emily said, wiping her eyes with the back of her hand and straightening her shoulders.

"Good girl," Lara said. "Well, I'll run along. We don't need some nosy reporter inquiring about my business."

"Miss Emily," Freddie shouted again. "Shall I bring him back or not?"

"Yes, Deputy Roberts," Emily replied. Smoothing her hair with her hand, she stood from the chair. "I will receive him."

She looked through the bars and into the shadows of the hallway. The lamps were turned down low, making it difficult to see. The backlight of the outer room caught Freddie's golden hair as he moved into the corridor. A man walked behind him, carrying a large box under his arm. He was taller than Freddie, and his hair was dark. Emily squinted, confused.

"Well, hello, little lady," said the man from the shadows. "I heard that I might find you here."

She stared as lamplight from the wall lantern fell over his face. Her eyes widened before she squeezed them shut.

CHAPTER 31

"Powell," said JW, his hair wet and windblown as he knelt between the two Harrisons sitting at the defense table. "I was just talking to the reporter from the *New York Herald*."

"I thought we agreed to refrain from speaking to the press," Powell said with a scowl.

"Did Mrs. Lloyd make that same agreement?" JW said. "She's the one who spoke with him."

"She did what?" Matt's unruly eyebrows raised in tangled knots.

"She informed him that after all this is over, she's leaving Leesburg with her beau. That he's asked her to marry him and that once she's acquitted, the two of them will be on the train to Chicago to take their nuptials."

"A beau? She's gone mad!" Matt exclaimed. He looked around before leaning closer to whisper. "Did the damned doctors get this wrong? The arsenic purchases and now this?"

"We've always known that she's eccentric," Powell said calmly. "There's nothing new in that fact. And don't forget the evidence that we have. Let's not let Mrs. Lloyd's oddities distract us from what we know."

Matt shook his head resignedly and sat back.

"Trust me, Matthew," Powell said as JW stood from where he knelt, and took his seat.

The townspeople in the gallery quieted when Emily, dressed in a gray traveling suit that hugged her waist tightly, entered the court-room on the arm of the sheriff.

"Sweet Jesus," Matt said under his breath as Emily approached the dock. He pointed his index finger first at Powell and then JW at the table's end. "I don't care how you do it, but you two need to get that loon under control."

"I'll talk to her," Powell said, watching her take her seat in the close-fitting, floor-length dress.

"The commonwealth recalls Dr. Randolph Moore," Kilgour an-nounced after the judge arrived and the court was called to order.

"Why recall Moore at this stage of his case?" JW whispered, glanc-ing at the six men sitting on the bench behind Kilgour. "Why not put the rest of his experts on the stand to finish corroborating yesterday's testimony?"

Powell pursed his lips as the sick feeling returned and sank into the pit of his stomach. "He's saving them to rebut our chemists."

With a quick glance at Powell, Matt leaned forward and looked at JW. "They spent the last three days establishing method and means. Mort's moving on to motive."

JW threw his shoulders back in the chair. Powell stiffened his pos-ture, bracing himself for what was to come.

After Moore took the stand, Kilgour stood from the prosecution's table. "Dr. Moore, you testified earlier that your store keeps a register of every transaction involving a sale of a poison. Is that correct?"

"Yes, I do."

"On Wednesday, Mrs. Greene told the court that Mrs. Lloyd bought arsenic from your store in July 1871, but had lost it before she returned home. Oddly, upon review of your poison register, I could find no such transaction. Can you explain?"

Moore assumed a bewildered expression and shrugged his shoul-ders. "I can only speculate that she was confused. Mrs. Lloyd does suf-fer from occasional memory lapses. Perhaps that is the explanation. But I can assure you that she never purchased arsenic from my store."

"How can you be so certain?"

"My practices are rigorous in regard to the handling of poisons and the documentation of their sale. Either myself or one of my clerks would have recorded the transaction in the log."

Kilgour picked up a clothbound book from the table and walked with it to the witness stand. "Do you recognize this?"

"Yes," Moore said. "It is the poison register from my store."

Kilgour opened the book and thumbed to a page. "Can you tell me why there is a page missing for the period between November 1868 and March 1869?"

"From my recollection, one of my clerks removed it to satisfy an audit by the state."

"A state audit," Kilgour said to the jury. "Dr. Moore, were you the physician attending Charles Lloyd at his death?"

"Objection," Powell said. "Relevance."

"Overruled," Keith said.

Kilgour turned to Moore. "Doctor?"

"I was his physician," Moore affirmed.

"When did he die?"

"Mr. Lloyd died in December 1868, I believe."

"How do you explain the overlap of that date with the dates of your register's missing page?"

Moore shrugged his shoulders again. "An inconvenient coincidence."

"Or perhaps Charles Lloyd was the inconvenience," Kilgour said.

"Objection!" Powell shouted.

Kilgour opened his hands and raised them in a gesture of surrender. "Withdrawn, Your Honor." Placing his hands on the rail, he leaned toward Moore. "Could it be that Mrs. Lloyd removed the page?"

"No. As I told you, my clerk removed it."

"The name of the clerk?" Kilgour asked, eyes narrowed.

"I don't recall who was working for me at the time."

Kilgour frowned with an exaggerated nod of his head. "Another inconvenience?"

"Excuse me?" Moore said, shifting in his chair as Powell objected.

"Withdrawn, Your Honor," Kilgour said before the judge admonished him. He lifted his frame from the rail. "Isn't it true that

Emily Lloyd wanted her husband dead because he was abusive toward her?"

"Objection," Powell interjected. "Calls for speculation. And the prosecution has absolutely no foundation."

"I'll rephrase," Kilgour offered. "Do you have knowledge of any abusive conduct toward Mrs. Lloyd by her husband?"

"I never witnessed Mr. Lloyd abuse his wife and certainly know Emily well enough to know that she would never wish death on anyone, let alone her husband."

"Doctor, I didn't ask if you *witnessed* any abuse, rather whether you were *aware* of any abuse. As her physician, did you ever treat Mrs. Lloyd for injuries consistent with abuse?"

"Not that I recall."

Kilgour shifted his position and leaned an elbow against the rail, facing the jury. "As her physician, would you say that Mrs. Lloyd was in good health or in poor health?"

"Overall, she's in good health."

"Then why so many house calls?"

Powell felt his mouth go dry.

"Pardon?" Moore said, looking confused.

"If Mrs. Lloyd is in good health overall, then why is it that you are seen visiting her house on a regular basis?"

"Her children were sickly, and I was called frequently by the housekeeper to attend to them."

"And were you also attending Mrs. Lloyd on these calls?" Kilgour asked, still facing the jury.

"Sometimes. She suffers anxiety from time to time and has difficulty sleeping."

"What about social calls?"

Moore looked confused again. "Pardon?"

"Did you see Mrs. Lloyd socially when you made these house calls to attend her children?"

"Occasionally I would have tea with her."

"Is that all you had?"

"Pardon?"

At the defense table, JW leaned forward in his chair and whispered, "Where is Kilgour going with this?"

"Nowhere good," Powell whispered back with a cutting glance at Matt.

Kilgour turned to face Moore. "Do you have feelings for Mrs. Lloyd, Dr. Moore?"

"Of course I do, as any physician would have for the well-being of his patients."

"What about romantic feelings?"

The color drained from Moore's face. "I'm a married man."

"So you are saying that you have never shared Mrs. Lloyd's bed?"

"Your Honor!" Powell protested, jumping to his feet. "Foundation?"

"I deny it absolutely," Moore declared before the judge ruled.

"I'll withdraw," Kilgour said. "For the moment." He gave Moore a long, scrutinizing look before he turned and walked over to the prosecution table. Orr handed him a document.

As Powell sat down, Matt leaned to him. "I don't like this."

"Me either," Powell whispered through clenched teeth.

Taking his reading glasses from his pocket, Kilgour put them on and examined the papers in his hand. After a tense moment, he looked over the rims at Moore. "Charles Lloyd died December 28, 1868. Is that correct?"

"I believe so," Moore said.

"And the victim in this case, Maud Lloyd, was born in March the following year, correct?"

"As I recall, yes."

"So when Charles Lloyd died, Mrs. Lloyd was with child?"

"Yes, she was in her third trimester at the time."

"And that child was Maud?"

"Yes, as you just said."

"But Charles Lloyd wasn't the father, was he?"

Moore's brow etched with confusion. "I don't know what you mean."

"Wasn't the child fathered by you?"

The courtroom exploded.

"Objection!" Powell jumped to his feet again. "What evidence does the prosecution have to support such a preposterous claim? And how is any of this testimony relevant?"

"Your Honor," Kilgour said, "the state asks for a bit of leeway as my question goes to motive."

"I'll allow it, but take care, Mr. Kilgour," the judge cautioned.

Kilgour turned to Moore. "Isn't that why you cut the page from the poison register? To protect your lover? To protect the mother of your daughter?" Kilgour pressed.

"Objection!" Powell said again. "Is Mr. Kilgour testifying or the witness? And is he planning to provide any proof of these wild statements?"

"Mr. Kilgour?" the judge said, his eyebrows raised in question.

"Yes, we can support our argument, but first I'd like to provide the doctor the opportunity to set the record straight."

"Get to it in short order, Mr. Kilgour," the judge warned.

Kilgour turned his attention back to Moore. "Dr. Moore, were you the father of Maud Lloyd?"

"This is preposterous!" Moore said, clearly rattled. Kilgour stared at him, waiting. "No."

"Have you engaged in amorous congress with Emily Lloyd?"

"As I told you before, no!"

Kilgour held his stare. "I have five witnesses waiting outside this courtroom who will testify to your numerous evening visits to the Lloyd home, your overnight stays, and other incriminating observations over the last several years." Kilgour, lowering his voice, leaned on the rail again, his eyes sympathetic as Moore dropped his gaze to his lap. "The last thing I wish to do is embarrass you and your family, Dr. Moore. I know this is difficult, as it would be for any man to admit his transgressions in public, but this is a murder trial, and you are under oath. If you admit to the allegations, I will have no need to call the witnesses. However, I must advise you that, should you deny the affair, you leave me no choice." He lifted his chin and raised his voice. "Dr. Moore, at any time in the past five years, have you had intimate relations with Mrs. Emily Lloyd?"

Except for the patter of rain on the windows and the fire crackling in the stove, the courtroom was silent, waiting for Moore's answer. Moore cradled his head in the fingertips of both hands, and his eyes remained downcast. Drawing a long sigh, he closed his eyes. After a moment, he moved his hands to his lap and brought his gaze back to Kilgour.

"I will not disgrace my family." Moore shook his head and turned to the judge. "I cannot be compelled to bear witness against myself. I will not answer."

"Your Honor, if it please the court," Powell said, rising to his feet. "As this is a criminal proceeding, answering such a question could very well implicate the doctor. Under Amendment Five of the constitution, Dr. Moore is well within his rights to refuse to answer Mr. Kilgour."

"The prosecution withdraws the question, Your Honor," Kilgour said. "I think the jury heard the doctor's answer loud and clear." He looked at Moore with pity in his eyes. "Nothing further."

"Mr. Harrison, do you wish to examine the witness?" Keith asked.

"We will hold any further questions for Dr. Moore until we present our defense," Powell answered.

All eyes in the court watched in silence as Moore left the witness box and took his seat in the second row behind the prosecution. Kilgour announced his next witness.

"The state calls Mr. Pendleton Slack."

One after another, Kilgour called Emily's neighbors: Mr. Slack; his wife, Catherine; Mollie Ryan; and Colonel Nixon. Each recounted the numerous occasions on which they witnessed Dr. Moore or his carriage at the Lloyd house. Pendleton Slack's testimony went further, not only detailing Dr. Moore's visits to the Lloyd house but also recounting the mysterious death of his chickens on Palm Sunday—the Sunday that Maud Lloyd died. The gallery exploded at the testimony, the women aghast and the men shaking their heads. Through it all, Randy Moore sat stone-faced in the second row. Emily, on the other hand, seemed to be paying little attention today to the goings-on in court. In her traveling dress, she reclined in the chair, nonchalant and reading from a newspaper. She turned the pages noisily, and the distracting sound resonated throughout the courtroom. With each turn of the paper, Powell tightened his mouth and shot her a look of disapproval. And each time, Emily paid no mind. Until the testimony of the fifth witness.

"State your name and residence for the court," Kilgour asked.

"My name is Georgia Jones, and I live on the east end of Church

Street." Emily abruptly lifted her head from the paper and turned to the witness. Narrowing her focus, she glared at the woman in the witness box.

"And how do you know the defendant?"

"I was Mrs. Lloyd's midwife for the birth of her daughters."

"Can you tell the court about the day Maud was born?"

"Mrs. Lloyd had sent her girl for me that morning. When I arrived, Mrs. Lloyd's labor was rather advanced, and she was in much discomfort. She told her girl—Delphi, I believe was her name—to fetch Dr. Moore. I told her that would be unnecessary, that the baby would arrive in short order. But Mrs. Lloyd was insistent."

"And how long did it take for Dr. Moore to arrive?"

"Not long at all," Mrs. Jones replied. "He was very worried about her condition. He asked me a few questions and pushed me aside. Said my services were no longer needed, but I stayed anyway. It was Dr. Moore who delivered the child. After the baby came, I swaddled it and handed the child to the mother. Dr. Moore joined Mrs. Lloyd on the bed, admiring the baby. At first, I found his doting odd, but I had heard that Dr. Moore was a caring man, so I dismissed it. A few minutes later, when I prepared myself to leave, Mrs. Lloyd said something that gave me pause."

"And what did Mrs. Lloyd say?" Kilgour asked and turned to face the jury.

A feeling of dread rushed over Powell as a satisfied look washed over the face of Mrs. Jones.

"Mrs. Lloyd said, 'I do believe she has your eyes.'" Loud whispers flooded the gallery of the court. Emily turned her attention back to her reading, opening the newspaper with a loud jerk.

"Do you recall the color of the child's eyes?" Kilgour asked.

Mrs. Jones looked across the courtroom to where Moore was sitting. "Her eyes were the same sky-blue color as Dr. Moore's."

Kilgour turned to Powell, a smug grin on his face. "Your witness, Counsellor."

Powell returned Kilgour's smirk with a wry smile before looking at JW. "Do you have our notes on Charles Lloyd?" he whispered. JW nodded and riffled through a few documents before handing Powell a number of pages. Powell scanned the papers and stood.

"Mrs. Jones," he said as he approached the witness. "You said that you attended Mrs. Lloyd at the birth of both of her daughters. Do you happen to remember the color of Annie Lloyd's eyes?"

"I believe they were blue."

"And what about the color of her sons' eyes?"

Mrs. Jones thought for a moment. "I don't recall the older boy's, but the younger one's were the same eerie color as his mother's."

"And what about Mr. Lloyd? Do you recall his eye color?"

"I do not," she said.

"Let me see if this might refresh your memory." Powell handed her a paper from his notes. "Would you read for the jury the notation from Mr. Lloyd's militia service record?"

Mrs. Jones lifted her chin and, looking over her nose, brought her gaze to the paper that Powell was holding. He pointed to the specific passage.

"Height five foot eight. Complexion dark. Hair brown. Eyes blue," she read aloud.

Powell took the paper away and thanked her. "Now, at any time, did Mrs. Lloyd tell you that Dr. Moore was the father of her child?"

"No."

"Did Dr. Moore tell you that the child was his daughter?"

"No, he didn't."

"Do you have definitive proof that anyone but Charles Lloyd was the father of Maud Lloyd, other than an offhand comment from Mrs. Lloyd after hours of arduous labor?"

"I do not."

"No further questions."

◆ ◆ ◆

"You continue to lie to us, Mrs. Lloyd," Powell said as he and JW entered the room at the back of the courthouse where Emily was eating dinner.

"Lie about what?" she said matter-of-factly, looking up from her bowl.

"You told me specifically that your relationship with Randy Moore was one of friendship and nothing more. Yet in court today, Randy Moore all but admitted that you and he were having an affair."

"I never had any such conversation with you. And Dr. Moore never admitted a thing," she said flippantly and took a spoonful of soup into her mouth.

"His refusal to answer the question is tantamount to an admission," Powell said, taken aback by her smugness. "Now, did you or did you not have an intimate relationship with Dr. Moore?"

"My relationship with Randy Moore is none of your damned business, Mr. Harrison." Powell was stunned.

JW, by the look on his face, was flabbergasted, too. "So it's true?" he sputtered. "You and Dr. Moore?"

"I've got the same thing to say to you that Randy had to say to that other lawyer. Not a goddamned thing."

"What about Mrs. Jones?" JW continued, his eyes bulging. "And your neighbors? They seemed to have a lot to say."

"Meddling busybodies," she sneered. "They haven't a clue as to what they think they have seen or what they think they heard."

"Do you understand that this goes to motive, Emily?" Powell said, confounded by her dismissiveness. "Mr. Kilgour is going to suggest to the jury that you and Dr. Moore conspired to kill your husband. And while you are not yet on trial for your husband's murder, Kilgour will suggest to the jury that if you killed once, you are certainly capable of killing again."

"Mr. Kilgour can suggest all he likes. He can't prove what isn't true."

"Which part, Emily?" Powell asked. "That you didn't have an affair with Dr. Moore? Or that the two of you didn't conspire to kill your family? Because the latter is what we are trying to defend you against."

"I'm through with answering your questions. Freddie!" she shouted. "Please show these gentlemen out. I want to enjoy my soup in peace."

◆ ◆ ◆

With his chest puffed like a peacock's, Kilgour announced his next witness. "The state calls Mr. Samuel Orrison."

Orrison rose from the gallery, took his seat on the witness stand, and swore his oath. Powell glanced at JW, who acknowledged him with a nod.

"You are the executor of the estate of Charles Lloyd and were the guardian of his children, including Maud. Correct?" Kilgour asked.

"I am," Orrison confirmed.

"Would you tell the court how much money Mrs. Lloyd stood to gain from the death of her daughter Maud?"

"Of the initial nine hundred dollars Maud inherited from her father's estate, eight hundred and sixty dollars remained, and that went to Mrs. Lloyd at the child's death."

"And how much did Mrs. Lloyd inherit at Charles Lloyd's death?"

"Charlie's estate was valued at over six thousand dollars," Orrison explained. "Each child received nine hundred dollars, and Mrs. Lloyd, the balance. All told, after the death of her last child, Mrs. Lloyd received in excess of four thousand dollars."

Muted whispers whirred through the crowd.

"Did Charles Lloyd's estate include the house where Mrs. Lloyd resides?" Kilgour asked.

"It did not," Orrison replied with a shake of his head. "That house was owned by Mrs. Elizabeth Hammerly. When she died, she left the house to her niece, Mrs. Emily Lloyd."

"I'm confused," Kilgour said, his brow furrowed. "Any property that a wife inherits belongs to her husband. Why wasn't the house part of Charles Lloyd's estate as well?"

"Because Charles Lloyd died before Mrs. Hammerly. Mrs. Lloyd got the entire house all for herself."

"So, had Mrs. Hammerly died first, and the house had become part of Mr. Lloyd's estate, how would that have been handled at his death?"

"Mrs. Lloyd would have had to share the value of the house equally with her children. Instead of inheriting one hundred percent of the house, she would have only inherited a fifth of it. Of course, she would have ended up with it all anyway since she killed the children."

"Objection!" Powell screamed as Kilgour said, "Nothing further," and retired to his seat.

"The jury shall ignore the last statement made by the witness," the judge instructed.

Powell sat in his chair, firing a knowing glance at JW. JW rose to his feet.

"Mr. Orrison, you testified that Mrs. Lloyd inherited the *entire* house. I believe those were your words," JW said in his slow Southern drawl. "Now, you do realize that the house is a twin, is it not?"

"Yeah. So?" Orrison replied, a smug look on his face.

"So your testimony isn't entirely accurate, is it? Mrs. Lloyd inherited only half of the house."

"Objection, Your Honor," Kilgour shouted. "Argumentative! Mr. Foster is splitting hairs."

"I'm simply making certain the jurors understand what Mrs. Lloyd inherited and what she did not."

"Overruled," Keith said.

JW turned back to Orrison. "Isn't it true that Mrs. Hammerly left Mrs. Lloyd one side of the only house that Mrs. Lloyd has ever known?"

"That ain't exactly right either, Counsellor," Orrison said. "Mrs. Lloyd knew that house over in Clark that she burned her father up in."

A rumble of loud whispers resounded over the courtroom. Judge Keith pounded the gavel. "Let's settle down, folks."

As the crowd quieted, JW responded, "Mrs. Lloyd was not yet four years of age and a victim herself of a horrific event that left her an orphan." He turned to the jury, incredulous. "I'd say it's a little more than unfair to accuse her of perpetrating a tragedy that happened when she herself was just a child." He turned back to Orrison. "Let's get back to your testimony from earlier, shall we? You stated that Charles Lloyd's estate was valued at six thousand dollars. How much of that value included Mr. Lloyd's tavern?"

"Twenty-one hundred dollars."

"That's the amount you paid for the tavern after Mr. Lloyd's death, correct?"

"That's correct."

"But that's not what you initially paid, is it?"

"Don't know what you're talking about," Orrison replied with a scowl.

JW smiled. "Isn't it true that you initially paid Mr. Lloyd's estate eleven hundred dollars for the tavern, and when Mrs. Lloyd questioned the transaction and threatened to sue you, you agreed to increase that amount to twenty-one hundred?"

"We negotiated and agreed to a price," Orrison said matter-of-factly.

"Were you angry at Mrs. Lloyd at the time?" JW asked.

"I wasn't real happy, but we settled the matter."

"How so?" JW asked, leaning on the rail.

"She got what she wanted, and I got what I wanted."

"So you paid the estate twenty-one hundred dollars, the estate that you still manage, is that correct?"

"Yes."

"Seems you still got yourself quite a deal," JW said, casting another look at the jury.

"As I said, I paid a fair price," Orrison replied.

"A fair price for you, Mr. Orrison, but not such a fair price for Mr. Lloyd's heirs," JW said, walking over to the defense table. He picked up a sheet of paper and carried it to the witness stand. "I have here an accounting of the tax paid on the property located on Royal Street. Have you ever shared this assessment with Mrs. Lloyd?"

"Why would I?" Orrison said with a smirk. "I'm the executor. The woman has no right to that information any more than you do."

JW smiled again before looking at the paper in his hand. "According to the records, that property is taxed at an assessed value of three thousand four hundred dollars." JW showed the document to Orrison and pointed to the figure.

"So?" Orrison said.

"So it seems that Mrs. Lloyd was not the only individual who benefitted from Charles Lloyd's death, wouldn't you say? Could one say, Mr. Orrison, that Charles Lloyd's death improved your situation?"

Orrison offered JW a contemptuous look. "You may say what you want, Counsellor, but it ain't the truth. The only person that benefitted from Charlie's death was Mrs. Lloyd."

JW smiled at Orrison one last time before turning to the jury. "Nothing further."

Glaring at JW, Sam Orrison rose from his seat. As he walked by the defense table, he threw a threatening look at Powell, who responded with a chilly smile.

Kilgour rose to his feet. "The state calls Mr. Patrick Gill."

Emily dropped her hands and the newspaper in them to her lap and straightened her posture. Powell caught her glance before she looked away. She seemed rattled. He followed her gaze. A man in an ill-fitting suit walked past him and took the witness stand.

Turning to his brother and JW, Powell silently mouthed the question "Who is he?" Matt shrugged. JW shook his head.

Powell sat back in the chair and looked at the man swearing his oath. Tall and wiry, with dark hair parted in the center and greased to a shine. His face, long and gaunt. A thin dark mustache ran across his upper lip.

"Mr. Gill, where is your place of residence?" Kilgour asked, walking to the front of the courtroom.

"My name is Paddy. Paddy Gill. And I lives in the great city of Chicago, Illinois," he said, flashing a yellow-toothed smile.

"And what is your occupation, Mr. Gill?"

"I'm a huckster with the Great Northwest Company. As I said, sir, the name's Paddy."

Powell glanced at JW.

"And how do you know the defendant?" Kilgour continued.

"Met her at Orrison's tavern, where I rent a room when I visit your lovely town. First time I saw her, she was chatting up a fella at the counter, and, well, I just couldn't take my eyes off her. I bought her a drink, I did, and we went to my room, where she and I could become better acquainted."

Emily abruptly stood from her chair, catching the attention of the men on the jury and everyone else in the courtroom. Her face was flushed and her bottom lip quivered. She placed both hands on the rail, steadying her stance.

"Am I to assume that you and Mrs. Lloyd have an intimate relationship?" Kilgour asked with a quick glance in Emily's direction.

"I don't know no Mrs. Lloyd, but if you're referring to the lovely Miss Samson in the chair over there, then you can assume what you'd like. Paddy Gill is not the fellow to kiss and tell."

"I am not Miss Samson, and this man is a liar!" Emily shouted from the dock.

Judge Keith pounded his gavel on the bench. "Mrs. Lloyd, you need to sit down and remain silent, or I will have the sheriff remove you from this courtroom!"

Collecting herself, Emily sat back down in her chair. Powell looked at the jurymen to assess their reaction. *Your outburst may have helped us,* he thought, reading empathy on their faces.

"When is the last time you met with Mrs. Lloyd?" Kilgour asked as the townspeople quieted.

"Like I said, I don't know her as Mrs. Lloyd. Never knew she were married, let alone that she had youngsters until youse fellas told me. But then again, I never asked, and she never mentioned—"

"Mr. Gill," Kilgour interrupted. "When did you see her last?"

"You mean before last evening?"

"You saw her last night?"

"I did indeed. You and the sheriff told me yesterday that she was in jail, and, well, I just had to see her. So I went to the jail to give her a gift that I had been carrying around since summer. I thought it would be nice for her to have something new, you know. I must say, it sure is nice to see her wearing it today." He moved his gaze to Emily, smiling lustily. A look of horror and disgust consumed her face.

Blotchy red spots erupted over Kilgour's face. "Your visit with her last night is not relevant to my question." He was losing control of the interrogation and his temper. "Before last evening, when did you last see the defendant?"

"Last time I saw her was in February," Gill said, bringing his gaze back to Kilgour.

"Would you tell the jury what the two of you were planning?"

"She was coming to Chicago with me. She told me that she had a cousin who had lived there, and she'd seen picture cards of the city and thought it looked real nice and all. I told her that I'd be glad to have her accompany me there if she wanted. She said she couldn't go right away, that she needed a little time to get her affairs in order, but she'd be ready to join me on my return."

"I see," Kilgour said. "And when would that have been?"

"I told her I'd be back for her in July. But when I came to call, she was nowhere to be found. Now I know why."

"Thank you, Mr. Gill," Kilgour said, relief on his face as he walked back to the prosecution's table.

"Your witness, Mr. Harrison," Judge Keith said.

Matt put his hand on Powell's sleeve.

"Just a moment, Your Honor," Matt said. He turned to Powell and whispered, "The man's a loose cannon. Without knowing what will come out of his mouth, we are taking great risk cross-examining him."

"Messrs. Harrison?" Judge Keith called, his voice booming throughout the room. "Any day now."

"Don't, Powell," Matt implored. "It will only make matters worse."

The voice in Powell's head was blaring: *Is there no truth from this woman? I need the truth!* As if hearing Powell's thoughts, Matt shook his head, his eyes warning.

Powell sat back in his seat. *Who's the truth for, Poe? Mrs. Lloyd or you?* He straightened his shoulders. "No questions at this time, Your Honor."

The judge blanched. "Are you certain, Mr. Harrison?"

"No questions," Powell repeated.

"Very well," Keith said. "Mr. Gill, you are free to go." Gill stood from the witness box. On his way from the courtroom and in plain view of the jury, Gill threw Emily another admiring smile. The look of disgust on a number of jurors' faces caused Powell's stomach to lurch.

Kilgour stood from the table. "Your Honor, the state rests."

CHAPTER 32

"Jesus Christ, Powell!" Matt said as Powell joined him and JW at their offices. "How could Kilgour know about a lover, and we didn't?"

"Sam Orrison has been holding out on us," JW said from the chair that fronted Matt's desk. "And Mrs. Lloyd has been playing us for fools."

"Something's not right," Powell said, his brow furrowed.

"That's an understatement," Matt retorted.

JW scoffed. "What's not right is Mrs. Lloyd."

"While I believe Mrs. Lloyd misled us about Moore, something's amiss in her reaction to the huckster's testimony. I'm not convinced he was telling the truth."

"If he's lying, how do you explain the dress she's wearing?" JW asked. "And what she told the *Herald* reporter?"

"I don't know," Powell said, tenacity in his voice, "but I'm about to find out."

• • •

When Freddie opened the cell door, Emily was heaped in a chair, crying. She looked up at Powell, her eyes glassy and wet with tears. "Why would a stranger say such horrible things?"

"Who, Mrs. Lloyd?" Powell's patience was wearing thin.

"That man from Chicago with the awful teeth!" she cried, dabbing her eyes with a handkerchief.

"Are you saying that you have never met Mr. Gill?"

"I know of him, yes," she said between sniffles. "He's the one who calls on that woman next door. But I certainly haven't met with him at a tavern or in his room!" Her eyes clouded with a mix of tears and anger.

Powell studied her closely. The hateful attitude from earlier had been replaced by the vulnerability he had come to expect from her.

"Are you certain that Mr. Gill is the man who visits your neighbor?"

"Yes. I've see him, his cart and mule in front of my house."

"When he called on you."

She jerked her head, her eyes knifing. "When he called on Lilith!"

"And he called on you here last evening," Powell followed.

"He most certainly did not!"

"His name is on the visitors log, Emily. And I checked with the guard. Mr. Gill was here last evening, visiting with you."

Emily searched Powell's face, her brow stitched in confusion. After a moment, she dropped her gaze to the floor, her eyes darting. "That can't be. I don't remember any other visitor last evening."

"He brought you the dress. The one you are wearing."

Emily held her gaze to the floor, her eyes searching for answers.

"Mrs. Lloyd, I am trying to help you, but you have to start telling me the truth."

She stood from the chair and glared at him. "I am telling you the truth!" Turning away, she wrapped her arms around herself and began to pace. "I don't understand why this happens," she said, wild eyes scanning the floor and walls as she walked. "Why can't I remember?"

"You've had these spells before? Of not being able to remember?"

She nodded, pacing and tightening her embrace on her midriff.

"And you told Dr. Berkley about them, yes?"

She nodded again.

"Tell me, what do you remember about last night and today?"

She clenched her hands into fists, talking more to herself than Powell. "After supper last evening, a neighbor stopped by for a quick visit when Freddie came into the corridor and told me that someone else was here for me, a gentleman, he said. She and I said our goodbyes, and Freddie escorted the caller into the block. I looked through the bars, over Freddie's shoulder and down the dark hallway. I saw a figure in the shadows and it was a gentleman, but when he came under the lamplight—well, I don't remember. I couldn't see his face, and then—I don't know what happened. Then this morning, when I awoke, I was changed into my nightgown. And the traveling dress was lying on the chest. I thought you and Mr. Foster had it delivered to me." She glanced at Powell before moving her eyes to the floor again, staring as she spoke. "When I was dressing this morning, I wondered where I might be going today since my attorneys brought me traveling clothes. Then Freddie came to the corridor to take me to court. And I remember him saying something . . . What was it he said? A reporter?" Her voice faded as she narrowed her eyes, struggling to recall the memory. Her eyes moved back to Powell. "Then I was in the courtroom, listening to that awful man saying horrible things about me, implying that I had been alone in his room with him." Tears welled in her eyes once more. "I couldn't listen to his lies. I couldn't sit there and say nothing!"

"So you spoke to the reporter this morning?" he asked.

She shook her head. "You told me not to."

Powell blew out an exasperated breath. "What about Dr. Moore's testimony this morning?" he asked, watching her face. "And your neighbors? Like Mr. Gill, were they lying, too?"

She looked at him blankly. "What are you talking about? What neighbors?"

"Mr. and Mrs. Slack. Colonel Nixon. Mrs. Jones. Your neighbors who refuted Dr. Moore's testimony."

"Dr. Moore wasn't in court this morning."

"Mrs. Lloyd," Powell said, anger giving way to pity. "Dr. Moore testified most of the morning. Don't you remember what he said?"

"I—" She brought her fingertips to her lips. "I wasn't in court until this afternoon."

He spoke gently. "If you weren't in court this morning, Mrs. Lloyd, then where were you?"

"Here in this cell, I suppose. Although I can't say that I know that for certain either."

"Do you remember speaking to me and Mr. Foster during the midday dinner hour?"

She shook her head. "Why does this happen to me? Why can I not lift this veil that obscures my memory so?" Biting her bottom lip, she closed her eyes and brought her hands to her face.

Powell reached for her shoulder. "I wish I knew, Mrs. Lloyd." He lifted her chin so she would look at him. "I need the truth, Mrs. Lloyd. About the huckster. About Dr. Moore."

Emily raised her eyes to his. "I'll tell you whatever you wish to know."

•   •   •

Powell stepped onto the brick walkway from the jail's entrance, wind whipping the flaps of his overcoat, his thoughts whirling. In all his life, he had never encountered anyone like Mrs. Lloyd. A confounding mystery, she was. How could he trust her word when she herself had no recollection of her conversations or her whereabouts half the time? Let alone any awareness of what the truth might actually be. Yet somehow he believed her to be innocent. He looked up at the darkened angry sky, wanting to ask the Lord for guidance. Clouds of indigo and gray gathered and moved briskly with the wind as moonlight struggled to break through. After a moment, he shook his head and lowered his gaze to the street.

"No," he said aloud. "I won't." Shoving his fists in the pockets of his coat, he turned west on Market Street, and headed home.

CHAPTER 33

"And you believe her?" Janet asked as she poured tea for the three of them. Her father, Dr. Jack Fauntleroy, had been at court every day and had joined his daughter and son-in-law for supper earlier that evening.

"For some unbeknownst reason, I do," Powell said, watching as she set the pot on the table and took a seat next to her father.

"And she had no recollection of the morning or the evening prior?" Jack asked, spooning sugar into his cup.

Powell shook his head. "None."

"Surely she is playing on your sensitivities," Janet said. "I don't think you appreciate how manipulative women can be when it comes to getting a man to believe what we want."

"I disagree, darling," Powell said. "I've enough experience to see through those kinds of charades. There is something else going on with Mrs. Lloyd that perhaps Dr. Berkley missed."

"I thought we agreed that her state of mind should not be of concern at this point in the trial," Janet said.

"But I can't ignore the truth, Janet," Powell said. "Without it, I'm blind. How else can I defend her if I don't have the truth to guide me?"

"What you are describing could be attributed to a certain hysteria that induces an amnestic state," Jack said. "I've seen it in children who have witnessed a horrific event. And in young soldiers during the war."

"Dr. Berkley mentioned that as well," Powell said.

"Memory loss?" Janet asked.

"More like memory repression," her father replied.

"Would she be cognizant of the hysteria afterward?" Powell asked. "Would she at least know that she had been in an amnestic state?"

"Sometimes a person is aware when the hysteria comes on. And it doesn't always cause amnesia. It can put them in a state of agitation just as easily as it could bring on melancholy or amnesia. Other times, the person doesn't express any outward symptoms of hysteria and has no memory of the episode at all."

"I still believe it's a memory of convenience," Janet said, blowing on her cup's rim.

"Think of it as sleepwalking," Jack said. "Even in a dead sleep, we can have consciousness of self and can know who we are. But that consciousness of self can also vanish in sleep. We forget who we are, become someone else, then remember that we are sleeping and thus dreaming and wake back to our reality. This could be the explanation of what we witnessed today in the courtroom and aligns with what Mrs. Lloyd told you this evening."

"You're saying that she might have been sleepwalking?" Powell asked.

"In a crude sense, yes. And most certainly attributable to a latent hysteria that Dr. Berkley warned could be triggered by an event that would excite her mind. I suppose the stress of the court proceedings would qualify."

"Why now, Pa?" Janet asked. "Why wouldn't she have descended into such a trance earlier? Like when she was arrested or when Mr. Kilgour was interrogating her at the inquiry? Why wouldn't Dr. Berkley or Powell have spotted her daydreaming before now?"

"Self-preservation is a peculiar duty, I suppose. When a man is in a reverie, he has no circumspection, nor any manner of attention to his own interest. And yesterday it appears that whatever prior experience Mrs. Lloyd had with that huckster brought on her need to defend herself from it."

"Are you thinking this huckster may have defiled her in some manner?" Powell asked. Janet put the cup back on the saucer, wide-eyed.

"Possibly," Jack said. "But she won't tell you. Like a bad dream, she either can't remember or doesn't want to."

"If Dr. Berkley missed this," Janet said, looking at Powell, "then it is not your fault if she is, indeed, insane. You made the best decision about how to defend her based on what you knew at the time. You can't be faulted for what you didn't know."

"I don't think sleepwalking or daydreaming or whatever it was that we witnessed today constitutes the legal definition of insanity," Powell said.

"I agree," Jack said. "Mrs. Lloyd's ability to wake from these spells seems to support Dr. Berkley's assessment. Insanity occurs when the consciousness of oneself becomes completely lost to the dream—and the ability to understand right from wrong is lost with it."

♦ ♦ ♦

The clock in his chamber beat like the tedious click of a metronome. Facing the window, Powell shut his eyes tightly and tried to force the monotonous ticking from his ears and thoughts from his mind. *The darkest day of any trial is the day the prosecution closes,* he told himself. And while it was normal for him to be nervous on the eve of the defense's presentation, tonight's uneasiness was more than the usual jitters. Ordinarily, he relied on prayer and the truth to steady him. Having given up his talks with God, he was relying on the truth and his own wit to guide him. Tonight he had confidence in neither.

Frustrated, he opened his eyes and rolled onto his back, staring at the ceiling. Above his head, shadows of branches moved rhythmically in an erratic waltz to the clock's beat. *It was like sleepwalking,* he thought, recalling his father-in-law's explanation of Emily's gaps in memory. Powell could understand how she might forget parts of the trial. *Even Matt slept through some of it!* And he could understand her wanting to forget. *But she wasn't sleeping when Gill arrived at the jail.* She had told Powell that a neighbor was visiting at the time, yet when Powell checked the visitor log, the only two names on the register were Gill and the *Herald* reporter the next morning. *I'll have JW ask Freddie tomorrow if there was another visitor.* Powell heard the grandfather clock in the dining room chime twice. He drew air deep into his lungs and released it slowly. He needed sleep. And perhaps he needed to listen to his wife's sage counsel for once. Emily's state of mind wasn't relevant any longer, and he needed all his focus on her defense. Drawing another sigh, he pulled the sheet under his chin and rolled away from the window onto his side. He squeezed his eyes closed again, trying to catch a few hours of sleep before court tomorrow and the opening of his case for the defense.

CHAPTER 34

Nearly double in size from the previous day, the crowd packed into the gallery quieted as Powell rose. Sun streamed through the court's hazy windowpanes, illuminating particles of dust floating in the air. For the first time since the trial began, it wasn't raining. The day was bright.

With a lift of his chin, Powell announced his first witness. "The defense calls Dr. Graham Ellzey."

As his cousin took the stand, Powell looked over at Emily Lloyd. Once again, she was wearing the black mourning dress with a veil. *The veil*, he thought, recalling her words from the day before. *"The veil obscuring my memory."* He glanced down at his notes. *You have to rely on your own agency now and have no room for distraction. Focus.* Lifting his head, he approached the witness stand.

"Dr. Ellzey, would you please state your occupation and qualifications for the court," Powell said, positioning himself on the far corner of the witness stand so that Graham was in the jury's direct line of sight.

"I am a physician, and I specialize in the application of chemistry to my medical practice. I am a graduate of the Department of

Analytical Chemistry at the University of New York and received my medical training at the University of Virginia."

"You were present in the courtroom during the testimony of Professor Tonry, yes?"

"I was."

"In your professional opinion, how would you assess Professor Tonry's process for analyzing the stomach and contents of Maud Lloyd?"

"I would have to say that overall I found Professor Tonry's methods satisfactory," Ellzey stated. From the rumblings in the courtroom, Powell guessed that Ellzey's concurrence had come as a surprise to more than just the state's attorneys.

"That said," Ellzey continued, "I do not believe that his process was precisely accurate for separating arsenic from other compounds."

"How so?" Powell asked.

"As counsel pointed out during its cross-examination, in his initial test, Professor Tonry had not eliminated bismuth from the arsenical compounds. Further, I am not satisfied that the professor had adequately eliminated moisture from the crystalline. Moisture, of course, would impact the ability to accurately quantify the amount of arsenic present in the sample."

"I see," Powell said. "But am I understanding you correctly? You agree with the professor's conclusion that there was, indeed, arsenic in the stomach of Maud Lloyd?"

"I do."

"And why is that, Dr. Ellzey?"

"It is only logical that Professor Tonry would find arsenic in the stomach of the child because arsenic was in the bismuth she was prescribed."

Gasps rushed from nearly everyone in the courtroom.

"Objection!" Kilgour bellowed, nearly knocking over his chair as he jumped to his feet. "Does counsel have some proof of this outrageous claim?"

"If Your Honor would allow Dr. Ellzey to explain?" Powell asked the judge.

"I'll allow it," Keith said. "Overruled. For now," he followed up, his brow arched. Powell nodded and looked to Dr. Ellzey.

Ellzey turned toward the jury. "On two separate occasions prior to this hearing, Mr. Harrison provided me samples of bismuth obtained from Dr. Randolph Moore's store. Using the Marsh apparatus, I tested a small portion of each sample and achieved the dull dark spots that could only be attained if arsenic was present. Later I conducted a more thorough analysis to quantify the arsenic present in the bismuth powders Maud was prescribed. In each case, arsenic was present in the bismuth salts. Two days ago, I acquired forty grains of bismuth from Dr. Moore's pharmacy directly. Having brought the Marsh apparatus with me from Richmond, I conducted three separate tests on thirty grains of the bismuth sample. In every instance, I achieved the same results." Ellzey handed Powell three porcelain plates. "In each case, the matte spots appear, providing clear evidence of the presence of arsenic in the bismuth."

"And you are certain?" Powell asked.

"I am positive," Ellzey said as Powell showed the plates to the men empaneled on the jury. "There is no compound other than arsenic that makes spots on porcelain like those."

Powell walked over to the prosecution table and gave the plates to Orr. As he walked by the defense table, JW handed him a scrap of paper decorated with pink flowers, faded leaves, and a bright-green trellis.

"Dr. Ellzey, do you recognize this?" Powell asked as he held the paper so that both Ellzey and the jury could see it.

"Yes. It is a cutting of wallpaper that I removed from the bedroom where Maud Lloyd and her sister, Annie Lloyd, slept."

"Can you explain to the court the significance of this wallpaper taken from little Maud's room?" Powell asked as he showed the jury the paper.

"When I was first contacted by the defense to provide chemical analysis testimony in this case, I asked Mr. Harrison if there was any green wallpaper in the Lloyd house. You see, arsenic is used in dye to create the bright color we all know as Scheele's Green. While the arsenic in the dye typically remains stable and causes no harm, sometimes the dye can become unstable, and the arsenic released and breathed through the lungs."

"What can cause the dye to become unstable?"

"Moisture or dampness will cause the dye to deteriorate. The age of the paper is also a factor. As the wallpaper disintegrates, the arsenic will discharge into the air. When Mr. Harrison confirmed that, indeed, there was wallpaper in the child's room, I asked him to provide me a sample. I conducted the same analysis used by Professor Tonry and confirmed the presence of arsenic in the wallpaper. Upon my arrival to this town three days ago, I visited the defendant's home. The house was very damp and had a musty smell. I retrieved a second sample of paper from the child's bedroom. As you can see, the paper is brittle, indicating that it has been on the wall for a very long time. I cut a sample from the wall and took it to the Harrison Law office. Much like the analysis performed on Dr. Moore's bismuth, I used a soot flame to burn the paper and forced the gas through the Marsh apparatus. It produced arsenical spots on the porcelain." He held up a porcelain plate with the telltale distinctive black markings. Powell took the plate from him and showed the jury.

"In your professional opinion, could the child Maud Lloyd have experienced the effects of arsenic poisoning from the wallpaper in her room?"

"It definitely is a possibility. She most probably inhaled it, but considering the amount of delamination, she may also have consumed it, as a child might."

Powell handed the wallpaper and the plate to Orr and returned to the front of the courtroom.

"Dr. Ellzey, you were present in the court when Dr. Moore testified that he had prescribed eighteen grains of bismuth to Maud Lloyd. As a chemical expert as well as a physician, can you give the court your experience using bismuth as a medicine?"

"Bismuth is used to treat various ailments of the digestive system. For example, I have used it to treat chronic diarrhea in adult patients. It is a metal with chemical properties similar to arsenic and antimony and produces a metallic taste in the mouth. In its purest form, bismuth is very toxic. This is why the concentration of bismuth in the salts must be carefully assessed before prescribing, as it is fairly easy to administer too much of the pure metal. This is why I test bismuth when I receive it from my distributor. As a matter of practice, I test every chemical compound that comes into my pharmacy for the presence of toxins like arsenic, antimony, and the like."

"That sounds like a lot of work," Powell added with a glance at the jury.

"Those of us in the practice of medicine swore an oath to do no harm. I believe it is our duty to ensure just that."

"I see. Do you often find contamination of the medicinal compounds you purchase?"

"Occasionally."

Powell shifted his stance. "You stated that you have used bismuth to treat patients. Have you treated patients that were poisoned by bismuth?"

"Indeed I have."

"And how would you describe symptoms in those patients?"

"A person suffering from bismuth toxicity will develop a bluing of the gumline. The tongue will blacken. Patients also can present with symptoms common to arsenic poisoning. As the effects of the metal sets on the heart and lungs, the pulse will accelerate and weaken. Breath will quicken and become shallow. Oftentimes, disorientation will seize the brain. I have witnessed overly concentrated bismuth destroy a person when administered over a period of time."

"Did you also conduct an analysis to quantify the concentration of bismuth in Dr. Moore's bismuth compound?"

"I did, and I found that the bismuth salts from Moore's bottle contained an overconcentration of the pure metal. In my estimation, his powders contained forty percent more bismuth than I would deem safe for medicinal use."

"Forty percent," Powell repeated. "And what effect might that have on a child?"

"I couldn't say definitively, but compounded with the presence of arsenic in the bismuth, the effects could very well be deadly."

"Thank you, Dr. Ellzey." Powell returned to the defense table as Kilgour stood and approached the witness.

"Dr. Ellzey," Kilgour said. "I have just one question before my colleague Mr. Orr conducts the state's cross-examination of your testimony. You say Mr. Harrison sent you samples prior to trial. How might you know Mr. Harrison?"

"I have provided analysis for him on numerous occasions while he was in practice at Staunton."

"Is that your only manner of acquaintance?" Kilgour's brow narrowed.

"I'm not certain I understand your question."

"If I am not mistaken, you and Mr. Harrison are blood relatives."

"Yes, he and I are cousins," Ellzey replied.

"And close cousins, I might add, as you attended his wedding a few years back."

"Yes, I did," Ellzey answered.

"Thank you, Dr. Ellzey," Kilgour said with a nod. "Mr. Orr?"

John Orr stood and spent over an hour of his cross-examination delving into the minutiae and every aspect of Ellzey's analysis and process. Based on their expressions, the men on the jury were patently bored. Their interest piqued, however, when Orr pressed Ellzey and the exchange became contentious.

"When you analyzed the bismuth, how much arsenic did the samples contain?" Orr asked.

"In the first analysis I conducted," Ellzey answered, "I found nearly one-eighth of a grain of arsenic per grain of bismuth in a ten-grain sample. In the second analysis conducted a few weeks ago, I found less, one-sixteenth of a grain of arsenic in each grain of bismuth from the sample."

"According to what you said earlier, the first two samples were provided by defense counsel."

"That's correct. I received the first sample in May of this year and the second sample in early September. I was told that they both were procured from Dr. Moore's store."

"Why were there differing quantities of arsenic in the samples?"

"I couldn't tell you."

Orr scoffed. "Couldn't or won't?"

"I certainly would tell you if I knew," Ellzey replied with a glibness that seemed to get under Orr's skin.

"Could it be because of errors in your analysis?" Orr asked with a facile smile. "That the chemicals you used were tainted?"

"There were no errors in my process. And I tested every chemical in my analysis. None contained arsenic or any other compromising compound."

"What about the bismuth you obtained directly from Dr. Moore's store? How much arsenic was present in that sample?"

"I do not pretend to know how much arsenic was in the sample that I got from Dr. Moore directly. The equipment that I brought with me is insufficient to make such an analysis. But I can unequivocally confirm that arsenic is present in the bismuth in the bottle at Dr. Moore's drugstore."

Murmurs rumbled throughout the courtroom.

"Let me present you a hypothetical question," Orr said, clearly frustrated. "If a child three years of age was suddenly taken ill by purging and vomiting and within several days died, and, upon postmortem, one and a half grains of arsenic were found, what, in your opinion, would be the cause of death?"

"I couldn't say."

"There you go again, Doctor. Can't say or won't say?"

"I would have to examine the child."

"Would it or would it not be from arsenic poisoning?" Orr insisted.

"I decline to say, sir," Ellzey insisted. "But what I will say is that if I were attending a child three years of age who was purging and vomiting, I would never, ever administer eighteen grains of bismuth. Not from my own pharmacy and certainly not from Dr. Moore's bottle."

Randy Moore, who was sitting in the second row behind the prosecution, abruptly stood. Powell noticed that the suit Moore wore was rumpled and his face unshaven.

"Nothing further at this time," Orr said as the gallery watched Moore, his head lowered, make his way down the aisle toward the exit.

As the rear doors slammed shut, Powell stood, cleared his throat, and called his next witness, Dr. P. B. Wilson, another prominent chemist.

"Dr. Wilson," Powell said, "please tell the jury your qualifications and involvement in the matter at hand."

"I hold a doctorate in chemistry and have devoted sixteen years of my life to the profession," Wilson answered. "My office is in Baltimore, and I was hired by the defense to perform an independent analysis on the bismuth procured from Dr. Moore's store."

"Can you tell us about the process used to conduct this analysis?"

"Of course," Wilson said. "Several days ago, I accompanied Dr. Ellzey to Moore's pharmacy to purchase forty grains of bismuth. Ten grains of bismuth were packaged separately with the intention for me to test the bismuth independently. Dr. William Taylor accompanied me to my hotel, where I conducted my analysis using my own equipment and testing chemicals that I brought with me from Baltimore. The results are here," he said, and handed Powell a porcelain plate. "You will see the markings are identical to those produced by Dr. Ellzey and indicate the presence of arsenic in the bismuth. In total, we conducted the test three times and achieved the same results."

"Did you measure the amount of arsenic in the sample?" Powell asked.

"I had no appliances to determine the specific amount," Wilson said.

"What impression do you have of Professor Tonry's analysis to quantify the amount of arsenic in the sample from Maud Lloyd's postmortem analysis?"

Wilson shook his head. "I have lived in Baltimore since 1867. No one can get an accurate weight on delicate scales in the city of Baltimore during the daytime. With all the wagons and heavy traffic on the streets, especially around the markets and the rail lines, there is entirely too much jarring. This is the reason that I do all my weighing of chemicals at night when there isn't all that rumbling."

On cross-examination, Orr attempted to discredit Dr. Wilson's testimony by questioning him in the same fashion as he had Dr. Ellzey. After twenty minutes of not getting what he wanted, Orr dismissed the witness.

Powell called his third and final expert. Dr. William Taylor was a professor at the University of Virginia and a forensic scientist for the commonwealth, specializing in poisoning cases. Taylor testified that he had seen eight cases of arsenical poisoning and had analyzed countless stomachs of people who had succumbed to the substance. He explained to the jurymen that symptoms were so varied that it would be difficult to determine whether a person was suffering from arsenic poisoning, poisoned by another substance, or ill from a natural cause, such as stomach congestion or cholera. He corroborated both Dr. Ellzey's and Dr. Wilson's methods for determining the presence of arsenic in the bismuth and agreed that Tonry's system for quantifying the amount of arsenic present in the postmortem was flawed. His testimony was crushing for the prosecution.

When pressed by Orr on cross-examination, Dr. Taylor stated that although he was fairly confident that Maud Lloyd died from arsenic poisoning, in a court of law, where a mother's life lies in the balance, he felt the need to be more certain before making such a conclusion. With that statement, Powell watched the seeds of doubt that had been planted all morning sprout in the jurors' minds, and their skepticism showed in their expressions as the court recessed at two thirty for dinner.

◆ ◆ ◆

"We'll start with Corrie and Maggie first when we reconvene this afternoon," Powell said as he selected a roll stuffed with ham from the tray of sandwiches that Janet had sent over to their offices. "JW, are you ready to take their testimony?"

"Worked on it last night. And I will cut off all avenues for Kilgour to attack the chain of custody of the samples."

"Based on her earlier testimony, Mort will impugn Mrs. Greene's credibility," Matt said with a mouthful of bread and cheese. "Maybe we shouldn't call her."

"Graham already testified to testing a second sample," Powell said, spreading a dollop of mustard on the roll. "Better for Kilgour to attack Mrs. Greene's integrity than to leave the jurors wondering what became of it. Without her testimony, Kilgour will make it look like we have something to hide."

"Have we decided if we're recalling Moore?" JW asked, picking the crust from his sandwich, and making a mess of the crumbs.

"I don't think we need to," Powell said. "He already testified that he prescribed the bismuth and told the court when he purchased it and from whom. The prosecution may call him on rebuttal, but I see no need to cause him further embarrassment."

"So if Moore's out, we call your father-in-law, and I'll take his testimony on his observation of Maud's gums," Matt said.

"Correct. But do not let Dr. Fauntleroy expound on his examination of Annie at the grave site. We don't want to open that door for Kilgour."

"I didn't just fall off the turnip wagon, Powell. Give your old brother a little credit."

"And I'll close with Freddie telling the jurors that he carried the stomach in a cloth, not a jar, from the Lloyd house to Moore's store," Powell said, ignoring him. "That should send Mort through the ceiling. And then we rest."

"An unfortunate casualty of the deputy's testimony is that Randy Moore will be labeled a perjurer," Matt said.

"Trust me. Dr. Moore has more worries than giving perjured testimony."

"Speaking of Randy and Freddie," JW said, "during your examination of Dr. Wilson, I ran over to the jail like you asked. When I spoke with Freddie about Mrs. Lloyd's visitors, he said that other than Mr. Gill on Thursday evening and that reporter from New York the next morning, she had none."

A puzzled look fell over Powell's face. "Are you certain? Emily said that she was chatting with a neighbor who was visiting when Gill came to call on Thursday night."

"Freddie was adamant. He did say that Mr. Gill came 'round again last evening. Said she became hysterical and refused to see him. But she had another gentleman caller that she didn't refuse." Powell raised his brow.

"Let me guess," Matt said with a shake of his head.

JW grinned like a Cheshire cat. "None other than Dr. Randolph Moore."

"I'm not surprised," Powell said. "She finally confessed to me about her involvement with him."

"Really?" Matt said, leaning forward in his chair. "Do tell."

"That it was a long time ago. When her marriage was in a bad way, she suffered a 'moment of indiscretion,' as she coined it. Said it never happened again but that the two remain close."

"So Moore was the father of the child," JW said.

"I would assume," Powell replied.

"But were that fact," Matt said, "I could make the argument to exonerate both of them. Randy Moore certainly wouldn't protect Mrs. Lloyd if he knew she had harmed his daughter. Exposing that Maud was their love child doesn't help Mort's case in the least."

"You know Kilgour as well as I do," Powell said. "He figures if he throws enough mud, some of it is bound to stick."

"You can bet he'll argue in his closing that Dr. Moore and Mrs. Lloyd conspired to kill the husband," said JW.

"Well, I don't like it," Matt said. "All it does is further tarnish Moore's reputation. As it stands, I don't know how the man will be able to walk down the street in this town, let alone practice medicine."

"Don't feel so sorry for him, Matt," Powell said. "He made his choices. Like the rest of us, he'll have to learn to live with them."

◆ ◆ ◆

As Dr. Jack Fauntleroy left the stand and Matt returned to the defense table, Powell stood and announced their next witness.

"The defense calls Deputy Frederick Roberts."

The deputy approached the witness stand from the side door, where he had been waiting. The bailiff swore him in, and he took a seat in the box. Powell noticed that Freddie looked paler than usual. Despite the chill of the courtroom, perspiration beaded at his hairline and marked his shirt at his armpits. His eyes darted nervously to the prosecution table as Powell approached him.

"Deputy Roberts, you were at Mrs. Lloyd's home when Dr. Moore conducted the initial postmortem on Maud Lloyd, correct?" Powell asked.

"I was."

"And you witnessed the procedure?"

"That's right."

"After Dr. Moore completed the autopsy, would you explain to the jury how the specimen was transported from the Lloyd residence to Dr. Moore's pharmacy?"

"Sure. Dr. Moore removed the specimen from the body, placed it in a jar, and put a lid on the top. Then he wrapped a rag around it so that Mrs. Lloyd wouldn't see what was inside, then he handed it to me. I went downstairs with it and walked it over to his store, set the jar on the counter, and waited for him and Dr. Cross."

Powell felt the air leave the room. "You're telling me now that Dr. Moore placed the specimen in a jar *at the Lloyd house* and not at his store?"

Freddie glanced at the prosecution table again before nodding.

"It was at the widow's house," he said, wiping sweat from his brow with a knuckle.

Powell walked over to the table and picked up his notebook, turning pages.

"In April, you stated that Dr. Moore, and I quote, 'wrapped the stomach up in linen and tied the top. Said he forgot to bring a jar. Then he handed the bloody mess to me. Told me to take it to his store and wait for him. That he wouldn't be long.'" Powell looked up from his reading. "Isn't this the testimony you gave during my interview with you?"

Freddie shook his head. "I don't recall that conversation, Mr. Harrison. Back in April, I had a fever off and on for a couple of weeks. Could be that I was confused. But I'm pretty certain it happened like I just said: Dr. Moore put the stomach in a jar and wrapped it up."

"Pretty certain? But not one hundred percent certain."

"Since Gettysburg and the shelling my company took, ain't nothin' one hundred percent about my memory," Freddie said with a nervous chuckle.

"Mrs. Lloyd and Miss Lozenburg both recall that you carried the specimen out of the house in a blood-soaked rag. Could it be that the specimen was placed in linen and not inside a jar?"

"I suppose some of the blood from Dr. Moore's hands could have got on the cloth that was around the glass. That might be what the ladies saw." Freddie glanced again at the prosecution. Powell turned around and gave Orr a hard look.

"'I suppose' and 'pretty certain,'" Powell mocked, locking his eyes on Orr's. "Nothing further."

CHAPTER 35

Dr. Randy Moore stood a long time with his hand on the knob of his front door before he found the courage to turn it.

"Where have you been!" Virginia shouted from the parlor as he pushed the door open and entered the house.

"Court," Moore said, his gaze downcast with his coat still on.

"All of yesterday, last night, and half of today?" She stood from the settee where she had been embroidering. Setting her sewing on the side table, she followed him into the hall. "Did you sleep with that woman? Is what they're saying true?"

Moore said nothing and walked past her toward the back of the house.

"I deserve an answer. Were you the father of that child?" Her voiced cracked with emotion. "Answer me, Randy!"

Moore opened the door to the backyard.

"And where are you going?" she cried.

He turned around and brought his eyes to hers. An angry flush reddened her cheeks, and her eyes were puffy from a sleepless night of tears. Guilt seized him once again, reaffirming his self-loathing and shame.

"I am so sorry, Virginia." He turned away from her and walked onto the veranda, closing the door behind him.

The waning afternoon sunlight poured through the autumn foliage of the maples, dappling the grass that still held the green of summer. Moore stepped off the porch and made his way across the leaf-littered lawn to the stables at the rear of the lot. Pulling open the heavy oak door, he slid into the shadows. As the door shut, he stood quietly for a moment, waiting for his eyes to adjust to the dim light. He drew the earthen, damp air into his lungs, the scent of horse and hay, triggering memories of his boyhood, of his father's stern jaw, and of the simplicity of life on their Quaker farm. So much had changed since then. Everything, in fact.

In the tack room, Moore found what he had come for. He took the coil from the hook, feeling its heavy weight as he laid it on the bench. The task didn't take long. Satisfied with his handiwork, he carried it to the main part of the barn. Spotting a wooden crate leaning against a wall, he picked it up with his free hand. The horses eyed him curiously as he looked at the girders overhead. He set the crate on the ground before tossing one end of the rope over the center beam and tying the other end to a post. Placing the crate on the dirt floor beneath the swaying rope, he made an adjustment to its length. He checked the knot again, just to be certain, before climbing on the box. Pulling the noose over his head, he positioned it firmly under his chin and pulled it tight. He stood on the box for a long moment before emotion overtook him and all-consuming pain engulfed him once more.

"I am so sorry, Maudie," he sobbed. "So terribly sorry." Tears streamed down his face as he closed his eyes and kicked the box away.

CHAPTER 36

"Shouldn't you be headed home?" Matt said, standing in the doorway to Powell's office and donning his overcoat.

"Closing arguments are Monday, lest you forget," Powell said, an elbow propped on the desk, the side of his forehead leaning against his extended fingers. "And you know how my wife feels about me working on the Sabbath."

"I would have thought you'd written that weeks ago."

"I did, but one can never be too prepared for Kilgour's table pounding."

Matt chuckled. "You know what they teach you in law school. When you've got the facts, pound the facts. When you've got the law, pound the law. When you've got nothing—"

"I know, I know. Pound the table." Powell smiled. "Unfortunately, Kilgour's got a lot more than nothing. Freddie's false testimony about the specimen, for one. We have John Orr to thank for that."

"True. But calling Delphi back to clarify what she saw countered that damage. And we still have Dr. Moore's tainted bismuth and all that damning chemical analysis."

"While we may have poked holes in Kilgour's method theory, he still has means and motive."

"Well, my friend, Mortimer must first prove to the jury that there was, indeed, a murder. And your job is to cloud their minds with doubt that there wasn't."

Powell knew this, of course, but it wasn't what was eating at him.

"What do you believe, Matt? Do you believe that the child's death was all just an unfortunate sequence of errors?"

"Doesn't matter what I think," Matt said as he wrapped his scarf around his neck. "What matters is what the jury believes."

"The jury believes what we convince them to believe. What I'm asking is, what do *you* believe is the truth?"

"The truth?" Matt raised his brow. "Do you really want to know what I think?" A sudden seriousness engulfed his expression. "I think Emily Lloyd is stark raving mad. Crazier than a betsy bug, that woman. And underneath Mrs. Lloyd's helpless façade is a manipulative she-demon that has everyone fooled, including herself. Including you."

"What are you saying?" Powell asked, shifting in his chair.

"I'm saying you don't want to know the truth. And neither do I. Your task is to win her acquittal. To win. That's what we Harrisons do. We *win*, Powell. And leave the rest to the courts of heaven." Matt put his hat on his head and picked up his satchel. "I'm taking the carriage home tonight. Shall I send it back for you?"

"The weather is improved. I think I'll walk."

"Suit yourself. I'll see you at church on the morrow," Matt said as he headed out the door.

Powell watched through the window as his brother climbed into the coach. *"The courts of heaven"!* The only courts Powell knew were the courts of men. And while Matthew might not need the truth, he did. Wasn't that why he became an attorney in the first place? To search for truth, to find justice? *You need to focus, Poe.* He glanced down at the edits he'd made to the draft of his closing argument. *You need to prepare.* Something Matt had said triggered a memory from one of his early conversations with Emily. *Something about a demon.* He stared into the lamp's flame, trying to remember.

"'Who knows what demons are buried among the ashes,'" he said aloud as the gist of her words came to him. "Ashes," he repeated. He recalled Sam Orrison's testimony blaming Emily, a mere child, for the fire that had killed her father and stepmother. *The house fire.*

Powell pushed back from the desk and checked the clock on the wall. *Not yet eight o'clock. He should still be in.* He picked up papers from his desk, shoved them into his satchel, and blew out the lamp.

Grabbing his coat, he raced out the door to pay a visit to Ol' Pat M'Intyre at the *Loudoun Mirror.*

◆ ◆ ◆

"I remember when the child showed up," M'Intyre said. Ol' Pat, as he was called, had been a newspaperman in town since the second war with the British. He'd been a Federalist, a Democrat, a Nullifier, a Whig, a Constitutional Unionist, and now a Democrat again. Powell had no idea exactly how old he was and, chances were, neither did Ol' Pat.

"It was about the same time that William Henry Harrison was elected president, and we Whigs were robbed by that fool Tyler," M'Intyre continued. "Frank Hammerly had been one of the organizers for the Loudoun Whigs supporting Harrison's election. Frank was fit to be tied when Ol' Tipp died after being in office only a month and Tyler took over the presidency."

"You know we're related—Tipp Harrison and my father were cousins."

"Indeed I do. Good man, Burr Harrison. Always liked a good fight."

"Do you remember any of the circumstances around how Mrs. Lloyd became orphaned?" Powell asked, not wanting to talk about his father or distract Ol' Pat with the subject of politics any further.

"House fire on the other side of the Blue Ridge is all I recall. Being the child was Liza's niece, the Hammerlys took her in. Terrible tragedy, but from what Frank said, the child was better off with them. But now, seeing what happened to all her children, who knows. Sounds like it might have been better if she had perished in the fire, too."

"Let's not rush to judgment, Pat," Powell said. "Mrs. Lloyd has had more than her fair share of tragedy. Do you have copies of the papers from that time frame that I could see?"

"All depends," M'Intyre said with a cagey smile. "Depends if our paper gets an exclusive interview with the defendant and her lawyers."

"You know that I don't usually give interviews to the press."

"And I don't *usually* make my archives available to nosy attorneys."

Powell grinned. "You're suggesting a quid pro quo?"

"I don't know what that means, but if you want to make a trade, I'm happy to oblige."

"Fine. I will grant you an interview with me about the trial once the verdict comes in. But I cannot commit Mrs. Lloyd. You do understand, don't you? Especially should things not go in her favor."

"Fair enough." Pat smiled. "The papers are stored in cabinets down under the stairs. They are labeled by year. Like I said, I think it was 1840 or '41. Around Christmas or thereabouts."

M'Intyre directed Powell to a storeroom on the lower level of the old brick building. The cabinets, too, were old, the doors warped from moisture, and the papers brittle and specked with dots of black mildew. In the dim light of the lantern, Powell set to work. After forty or so minutes of scanning through volumes of old news, he found what he was looking for. On the third page of a paper dated January 8, 1841, marred by spots of mildew and blotches of mold, he read:

House Fire in Clark

In the early hours of Sunday morning a fire . . .
home of John Samson. Rescue attempts . . .
made more difficult by the inclement . . .
suspicious as the exterior doors appeared . . .
Samson and his wife, Matilda, lost their . . .
missing are two of three daughters, ages . . .
girl, age 4, escaped the flames and was . . .
wandering in the snow.

With a thumb, he wiped the obscuring mold from the right-hand side of the print. Moving the lantern closer, Powell squinted to make out the words beneath the light and read the article again. Powell lifted his eyes from the moldy paper and stared across the filthy storeroom floor, trying to make sense of it . . . *missing are two of three daughters*. He pictured the photograph in the silver frame on the dresser in the neighbors' bedroom. Bringing his gaze back to the paper, he read it again, rubbing his hand over his mouth and chin as the pieces fell together.

◆ ◆ ◆

His collar pulled tight and walking briskly, Powell turned the corner from Market Street onto his street and noticed Matt's carriage parked in front of his house. It was well past ten, and there would be no good reason for Matt to be calling. Powell braced himself for the worst.

"Matthew," he called as he opened his front door and stepped inside. His brother, JW, and Janet were waiting in the parlor.

"I went to the office, figuring you'd be there," Matt said. "When you weren't, I thought you had called it an early night after all."

"We've been worried sick, darling," said Janet as she rose to greet him, a shawl wrapped taut about her shoulders. "Where have you been?"

"I've been at the *Mirror* with Ol' Pat, doing a bit of research, that's all," he said, kissing his wife on the cheek as he removed his coat.

"Well, thank the Good Lord you're home," she said, taking his coat and hanging it in the hall.

"What's happened?" Powell said, moving into the parlor with the others.

JW was standing at the Parsons table, pouring whiskey. "Here," he said, extending his arm and handing Powell a glass. "You're gonna need this."

"Are one of you gentlemen going to tell me what is going on?" Powell said, looking at JW and his brother.

Matt pushed his fingers through his thinning hair. "Remember during Mortimer's rebuttal this afternoon when he recalled Randy Moore to the stand, and he was nowhere to be found?"

"Yes." Powell's eyes were questioning.

"They found him," Matt said. "His wife did."

"At the end of a rope," JW said, throwing back a glass of whiskey and pouring another.

"What?" Powell was suddenly winded and hoarse as if the air had been knocked from his lungs.

"According to Sheriff Atwell, Dr. Moore hanged himself in his stable," Matt explained. "His wife said he had come home around three. She told the sheriff that they had argued, and he went out to the backyard. Said that he liked to groom the horses and clean tack when he was upset, so she let him be. She thought he'd come in when it got dark. When he didn't, she went to check on him and found him deader than a doornail, hanging from the rafters. Ol' Doc Cross said he had been there for a couple of hours."

"My God!" Powell sunk into a chair.

"Poor Dr. Moore, blaming himself for something that wasn't his fault," Janet said. "And while I am not exactly fond of Virginia, I wouldn't wish such horror on my worst enemy."

She stood behind the chair where Powell was seated and put her hand on his shoulder. He reached for her and interlocked his fingers with hers, pressing the back of her hand to his cheek. At the touch of her skin, he closed his eyes, remembering the day he was called to the asylum. The day he saw his sister's limp body hanging from the gas lamp and bed linen that she had used to end her life. When she had attempted to jump from the window weeks before, Dr. Stribling had moved her to a room on the first floor. But no one had thought to remove the lighting overhead.

The images of his recurring nightmare roared through his mind. Her contorted face. The unnatural twist of her neck. The heinous laughing and screaming and rantings of lunatics outside the door melding into a whirling pool of monstrous noise as Alice hung above it all at the end of a white sheet in a white room, wearing a white dress. Matthew was saying something. Yes, it was Matthew talking now. *Open your eyes, Poe.*

"—that there was no reason to delay, as they were fine without the rebuttal testimony," Matthew was saying.

"I'm sorry," Powell said, struggling to refocus. "What were you saying?"

"Kilgour doesn't want a continuance," Matt said. "He told me that Randy's testimony was not crucial to their rebuttal, so he's fine to make his closing argument first thing Monday morning if we're in agreement."

Powell jerked his head, shaking away the nightmare of his sister's death. "Did either one of you inform Mrs. Lloyd?" he asked.

"I did," JW said. "Not knowing where you were, I thought she should hear from one of us before the news made its way to the jailhouse." He poured himself another drink. "And she did not take it well."

"How so?" Powell asked.

"Let's just say that I am lucky that I wasn't in the cell with her when she received the news."

"Really?" Powell said, letting go of Janet's hand, leaning forward.

"At first, she just stood there with a blank stare, like she was struck or something. I thought she might faint, so I told Freddie to open the door. He was fumbling about with the keys when the commotion started. Those cat eyes of hers got all big and bulgy. I thought they might pop from their sockets. And that's when she started hollering. She came flying at me through the bars, nails clawing like a mountain lion in a cage, hissing and spitting. Told me I was lying, and when Freddie assured her that it was true, she called me every name in the book and then some. Says that it's all of our falsehoods against him that are to blame. I'm telling you, Powell, I barely recognized her. She was hysterical. I stopped by Doc Edwards's on the way here and told him to go over to the jail and give her something to calm her down."

"I'm not certain we want her in court for the remainder of the trial," Matt said. "The last thing the jury needs to see is another outburst."

Should I tell them? Powell asked himself and then shook his head. There was no reason to mention the article, he reasoned. Matt had all but told him he didn't want to know. And JW would overreact. It was irrelevant at this point in the trial anyway. Monday he'd be delivering his closing argument, and he didn't need the distraction.

"If she doesn't appear on the dock during closing, it will be worse," Powell said, dismissing the thought. "The jury will assume grief for her lover as the reason for her absence. And Kilgour will surely drive home that point in his closing argument. We'll sedate her if need be, but she is going to be there if I have to carry her into the courtroom and tie her to the chair."

CHAPTER 37

"This is all your fault," Lara said. "Had you not continued your seduction of him after he ended the affair, none of this would have happened!"

"Me?" Lilith fired back. "You're blaming me? My Randy is dead! *Dead!* And you have the audacity to accuse me?"

"Had you not poisoned the girls to lure him to your bed, we wouldn't be in this mess."

"I told you I only gave them a little bit," Lilith said. "It hadn't hurt them before."

"After Annie, you promised no more!"

"What choice did I have? I missed him dreadfully. And he wouldn't come over anymore unless it was to attend to Maud."

"It was wrong, Lilith," Lara scolded. "Wrong! And you know it."

"Oh, don't you lecture me about right and wrong, Miss Goody Two-shoes! You and Emily started this entire mess when the two of you cooked up the idea to off Charlie!"

"That wasn't my idea at all! It was your lover who suggested it. He told Emily how the poison worked, how difficult it was to detect. It was *his* idea. His and Emily's. I merely assisted in its execution."

"You're lying. Randy wouldn't have had anything to do with such a scheme."

"Oh, he did! And you want to know why? Because he was in love with her. He loved her long before you entrapped him with your debauchery."

"You lying bitch!" Lilith seethed. "How could he love a woman who never let him touch her?"

"Come on, Lilith. Surely you don't think Emily was strong enough to deny him. Couldn't you see him in Maud's countenance?"

"I ought to slap you."

"You have no reason to lash out at me. You were fornicating with her husband at the time."

Lilith lifted her nose in the air. "'You were fornicating with her husband at the time,'" Lilith parroted, her expression pinched as she mocked her sister. "Why can't you just say it outright? That I was fucking her husband at the time. And why was I fucking Charlie, Lara? Hmm? Did you ever bother to ask why? I'll tell you why. Because she wouldn't. And when she refused him, what did he do? He beat her. And he raped her. He would make those boys watch as he slapped her around and boasted, 'This is how it's done, boys.' So do you know what I did? I let him take his twisted perversions out on me to relieve Emily of the burden. You have no idea of my sacrifice, Lara. None. So don't sit here on your high horse and assume that you know everything. Because you don't."

"I've seen your game, Lilith. I've watched you with men. Men like that huckster. You enjoy it when they hurt you."

"Oh, I enjoy it all right," Lilith sneered. "Charlie Lloyd taught me how to like it. Just as Father did."

"Don't speak of him in my presence."

"I'm sorry, I forgot," Lilith said with a sarcastic roll of her eyes. "We aren't allowed to speak of the fire and your *first* elimination."

"It wasn't any of *my* eliminations that started this mess," Lara said.

"Last I checked, Emily was charged with four that belong to you," Lilith retorted.

"She's only on trial for yours."

"How was I to know that the medicine contained arsenic?"

"And if she is found guilty, you can explain that to the judge."

"You most certainly aren't going to sell me out?"

"I most certainly will," Lara affirmed.

Lilith leaned back and crossed her arms. "Go right ahead, sister.

And I'll tell the judge about Charlie and Aunt Liza and the boys. And while you may be successful in pinning Charlie on Randy, and perhaps you'll even convince them that you eliminated Aunt Liza out of love and to end her suffering, you'll have a tough time explaining Henry and George."

"You know I had no choice. George was already developing a mouth. They would have become monsters like their father. And they would control every aspect of their mother's life when they came of age. I couldn't let it happen. I wouldn't let it happen."

Lilith scoffed. "And you judge me."

"I'm tired of arguing with you," Lara said. "I understand you hate me and are upset about the death of your lover, but we've got bigger troubles."

"You don't understand at all. Randy Moore was the only man who was ever kind to me. He was decent and he was gentle. What we shared was—I don't know how to describe it. It was special."

"I don't rightly care how special he made you feel. Right now, I need to think." Lara brought her hand to her forehead and rubbed her brow. "I need to think how to get Emily out of this if she is convicted."

"Emily, Emily, Emily. It's always Emily with you! Well, what about Lilith? What about what Lilith needs?"

Lara lifted her head and looked at Lilith, a seriousness in her eyes. "You still don't get it, do you? We're sisters, Lilith. And what have I always told you? All we have is each other."

CHAPTER 38

SUNDAY, OCTOBER 27, 1872

Pacing back and forth with the draft of his closing argument in one hand and a mug of coffee in the other, Powell had difficulty concentrating on his speech as his discovery in Ol' Pat's files and Dr. Moore's suicide preoccupied his mind. It was his fourth coffee that evening. Not that he needed the caffeine to stay awake. His anxiety was doing a fine job of that.

As he rehearsed his oratory, Janet's comment from the night before rang in his ears from seemingly nowhere: *"Dr. Moore blaming himself for something that wasn't his fault."* He stopped midpace. *That's the question, isn't it, Poe? Who's to blame?* Setting his mug down, he took the papers in both hands, rereading the summation he had spent weeks preparing.

"It's not right," he said aloud, tossing the papers on his desk. *The jury needs someone to blame.* Without the truth to guide him, he was lost. He interlocked his fingers on top of his head and began pacing again, searching for the words to convince at least one juror that Mrs. Lloyd was innocent. As he walked back and forth over the floor, his fatigued mind returned to his imagined vision of Moore at the end of a rope. Of Alice's contorted face hanging from the lamp. And the crumbling skeleton of the Lloyd boy. The sunken eyes of little Maud on her deathbed. Bo's blond hair floating in the springhouse pool. His chubby hands folded over his chest as he lay in his coffin. Powell could not stop the reel playing in his head, unable to free himself from guilt and doubt.

"Dear God, why?" he asked. He closed his eyes, silent tears welling and rolling down the hollows of his cheeks.

"Why?" he sobbed and fell to his knees, overwhelmed by exhaustion and the burden he had carried for so long. Minutes passed as he knelt on the rug, head down, weeping.

Emily's words of faith came to him: *"We may not understand the Lord's ways, but we must trust His worth."*

". . . trust His worth," he repeated, lifting his chin, his hurt softening.

"We must have faith, Mr. Harrison," she had said.

Faith . . .

Powell clasped his hands together and brought them to his chest.

"Our Father, who art in heaven," he began hesitantly, interlocking his fingers and bowing his head. "Hallowed be Thy name . . ." At the close of the Lord's Prayer, Powell shut his eyes tight. "Father in heaven, if You cannot give me truth, then please, Lord, grant me the wisdom to do Your Will."

When he finished praying, he opened his eyes and pulled a handkerchief from his pocket to wipe his tears, and stood from the floor. He looked over at his desk, where his closing argument was strewn over the surface, his notes and papers in disarray. The coffee mug sat at the desk's edge next to the sugar bowl and pot of coffee Janet had left for him. He noticed spilled sugar from when he spooned it into his last cup. Walking closer, he paused, looking at the white granulate scattered over the polished wood. He ran his index finger through it, lost in thought.

Where to assign the blame? he pondered as he studied the crystals that had stuck to his fingertip. Glancing up, his eyes caught the framed cabinet card of his daughters on a shelf behind the desk.

"Blame," he said aloud.

He held his gaze on the photograph for a moment before looking back at the sugar on his finger and on the desk. He closed his eyes and raised his face to the heavens as the answer came and a new strategy formed in his mind.

CHAPTER 39

MONDAY, OCTOBER 28, 1872

The skies had grayed again, and a bitter wind rattled the weights in the sashes of the courthouse windows. In his customary dark suit, his watch chain glimmering over his breast, J. Mortimer Kilgour rose to his feet and approached the box where the jury was assembled.

"May it please the court and you, gentlemen of the jury," Kilgour said, his voice booming. "While you are called upon today to deliver on your oath and solemn duty—solemn as the grave and as momentous as life itself—to extend the shield of law to prevent wrong to the prisoner, you are also called to extend that same shield of law to protect the people of the Commonwealth of Virginia.

"On March 21 of this year, the prisoner, Mrs. Emily Lloyd, was living in this city with the victim, Maud, who was three years of age. The child was taken ill and within seventy-two hours was dead. The child's guardian, Mr. Sam Orrison, suggested that the prisoner agree to a postmortem examination to relieve any suspicion. Mrs. Lloyd refused. Upon further insistence the next day, she at last agreed, and a postmortem examination and coroner's inquest was conducted. The results of the postmortem analysis show one and one half grains of white arsenic present in the stomach of Maud Lloyd at the time of her death. The jury of the county found an indictment against her for murder. The charge was that Mrs. Lloyd administered arsenic to her little daughter Maud, thereby poisoning her. These are the unfortunate circumstances that have brought us here today."

Kilgour paused, scanning the faces of the jurors.

"For you to find Mrs. Lloyd guilty of the charge of murder, you must first decide if Maud Lloyd died from arsenical poisoning and, second, was it Mrs. Lloyd who administered that deadly drug. Dr. Cross addressed the symptoms of arsenical poisoning. Dr. Moore testified to the history of the child's sickness and her symptoms. The similarity is undeniable. Dr. Moore also testified that he did not suspect poisoning and thought her death had resulted from congestion of the stomach. But when the stomach was taken out and held to the light, Dr. Cross and Dr. Moore both informed you that the stomach presented no trace of that disease. And while nothing pains me more than to slander the reputation of a gentleman, especially in light of this weekend's sad circumstances, I am compelled to remind you of that which is relevant. During these proceedings, we learned of Dr. Moore's romantic involvement with the prisoner, thus offering a possible explanation for why he was so adamant in his declaration that little Maud's cause of death was stomach congestion. A most chivalrous act to protect the woman for whom he had such tender feelings."

The entire town, including the men on the jury, knew of Dr. Moore's suicide. Kilgour conveniently cleared his throat as if fighting his own emotion. Powell watched the jurors' reaction to Kilgour's theatrics; they were clearly buying in.

"Professor Tonry, an expert chemist from the city of Baltimore, explained to you in great detail his process for analyzing the stomach and its contents that were taken from Maud Lloyd during the postmortem examination. One and a half grains of white arsenic were found. Even experts of the defense concurred with the conclusion that white arsenic was present in Maud Lloyd's stomach. Further, defense expert Dr. Taylor indicated that he was nearly certain that arsenic was, indeed, the cause of death.

"Dr. Cross explained that arsenic would have only been in the stomach for a few hours before passing to the liver and spleen, where it would have been absorbed. Through an unfortunate circumstance, the county court ruled the analysis of those organs inadmissible in this proceeding. The fact that so much arsenic was present in the stomach indicates that Maud was administered the deadly substance just hours before her demise.

"The defense has tried to convince you that the arsenic in Maud's stomach might have come from Dr. Moore's bismuth or from the counter at his pharmacy or even from the wallpaper in the child's room. But the defense was unable to quantify the arsenic from Dr. Moore's bismuth jar. And while they did quantify the arsenic in samples obtained by defense counsel's sister and by Mrs. Greene, how are we to trust that those samples were not altered? Are we to believe Mrs. Greene, a friend of the defendant, who in this very court proved herself to be a liar? How far might Miss Harrison go to protect her family's good name and her late father's law firm's reputation? How much trust should we put in the words of women, especially women with such conflicting interests?"

Anger rose in Powell's chest as he listened to Kilgour malign his sister's character. He glanced over at Matt, whose face was all but blistering. Powell was certain that Kilgour's insults would destroy whatever friendship remained between the two.

"And let's not forget that Dr. Ellzey and the Harrison brothers are first cousins." Kilgour paused and raised a brow before continuing. "What is most peculiar is that if we are to believe that these bismuth samples contained arsenic, the defense's own calculations do not account for the quantity of arsenic found in the contents of Maud's stomach. Are we to believe that one-sixteenth of a grain of arsenic per grain of bismuth equates to one and a half grains of arsenic in her stomach? Their arithmetic and their logic, gentlemen, does not compute.

"The defense also suggested that the wallpaper in Maud's room contained arsenic and that somehow a little green trellis was the culprit that took Maud Lloyd's life. But did the defense present evidence that proved how that wallpaper ended up in Maud Lloyd's stomach? Of course not!"

Kilgour was on a roll, his eyes wide, his expression animated. "And let's not forget their bismuth theory. The bismuth is responsible! Again, what proof did they provide that Maud Lloyd died from an overdose of bismuth other than a little blue line purportedly witnessed on the gum of a corpse? The answer, gentlemen, is that the defense proved no other cause of death. Because the only cause of death was one and a half grains of arsenic in the stomach of little Maud Lloyd.

"Now that we have proven to you that Maud Lloyd was poisoned by white arsenic, the question becomes, who is responsible? Who had the means and the motive? And, gentlemen, all fingers point in one direction."

Kilgour lifted an arm with his index finger extended and pointed at Emily. "It is she, gentlemen. The person a child trusts most to protect her from the world. Her mother." He stared at Emily for a moment before dropping his arm and turning his attention back to the jury.

"Not more than a week before the death of each of her children, Mrs. Lloyd purchased arsenic. She said the arsenic was for rats in her home, yet not one witness could attest to seeing any rats. And how odd is it that these supposed rats only needed to be poisoned within days of the poisoning of her children? And then there is the missing page from Dr. Moore's register. Coincidence, or the work of chivalry again?

"Mrs. Lloyd had access to the child and, more importantly, access to the murder weapon. In a town suspicious of foul play in the deaths of her other children, she simply traveled to Goresville for her weapon of choice. But why, you ask? Why would a mother kill her child? The answer, gentleman, is as old as the ages. Money. And a man.

"Mrs. Lloyd gained nearly one thousand dollars from the death of her daughter. Mr. Gill told us the prisoner intended to run off to Chicago once she settled her affairs. Mr. Gill didn't know that she had two beautiful daughters because Mrs. Lloyd had no intention of traveling to Chicago with her children. Mrs. Lloyd wanted to be free of her duty. And she found the perfect method to relieve her of the burden: white arsenic.

"Gentlemen of the jury, over the past week, you have heard testimony that proves without a doubt that the defendant, Emily Lloyd, willfully and intentionally poisoned her daughter Maud to escape her God-given responsibility as a mother so that she might selfishly pursue a new life with a new man in a new city, wearing a new dress with a pocketbook full of blood money. And the defense has offered no proof to definitively counter these truths. It is your solemn duty to deliver a verdict of guilty to protect the people of the commonwealth, and it is your *moral* duty to avenge the murder of little Maud, whose spirit cannot rest until her killer is punished and justice is served." Kilgour bowed to the jurymen and took his seat.

The courtroom was silent. The windows rattled in another gust of wind, and the draft in the stovepipe caused coals to crack. All eyes were now fixed on Powell, who, oblivious to their stares, sat with closed eyes.

Powell drew a long stream of air deep into his lungs. With his exhale, he released all doubt and freed himself from any misgivings. His body was merely a vessel to deliver a performance. As always, he would orchestrate the final act from a place outside himself, critiquing his every word, his every gesture, and making the necessary adjustments based on his read of the jurors' reactions and emotions. Opening his eyes, he rose from his chair and fastened the top button on his jacket. He was ready.

"Gentlemen of the jury," Powell began as he stood facing them in the middle of the courtroom. "Some of you I know. And many of you I had never met before this proceeding. While I grew up in this county, I removed myself to Staunton after my studies and remained in that great city until only a few short years ago, when I returned home to start a family. I have two daughters, and the oldest, Nannie, is now about the same age as little Maud was when she died. And I had a son who was three years old when my wife and I lost him two summers ago, the same summer Mrs. Lloyd lost her boys. Since I took this case, I have thought often about the tragic accident that claimed my son's life. What if I had lost all of my children? My entire family? This case has made me realize just how fortunate I am. To still have my little girls after losing my son. To still have a family.

"Family," he said as he slowly approached the jury box. "Mrs. Emily Lloyd, too, had a family. A family that she cared for, that she fawned over, doted on, and loved. Yet she will never go home to them like I do. Like you do. One by one, the fates took them, first her husband from heart failure, then her two boys from mistakenly eating poison berries, then Annie by cholera, and then, finally, poor little Maud. Can you imagine her grief? Can you imagine if you lost all of your children? Or all of your brothers and sisters? Everyone you loved suddenly stripped from you?" Powell looked over at Emily, her head bowed, shoulders slumped, softly weeping. "My heart breaks thinking about the pain Emily Lloyd holds in her breast." He looked back at the jurors. "Because Mrs. Lloyd, too, is a victim."

Powell looked each man in the eye as he spoke. "Mr. Kilgour just told you that the defense failed to meet its burden in proving Maud Lloyd's cause of death." Clenching a fist, he leaned forward, his eyes piercing and filled with indignance. "The defense has no such burden! It is the duty of the prosecution and the prosecution alone to determine cause of death and prove beyond any reasonable doubt that a murder occurred. It is my job to defend Mrs. Lloyd's innocence. And Mr. Kilgour's job to prove otherwise. Gentlemen, Mr. Kilgour and Mr. Orr have proved *nothing*!

"Mr. Kilgour and Mr. Orr would have you believe that one and a half grains of arsenic was found in little Maud's stomach. And were that a fact, then I would be before you making a much different argument. But one and a half grains was computed by proportional analysis and is based entirely on Professor Tonry's ability to accurately determine the weight equivalent to a few granulates of sugar."

Powell pulled a small envelope from his pocket and opened it. Carefully, he emptied the contents. Several tiny grains of white granulate spilled onto the railing of the jury box.

"Steady there," he said, speaking to the sugar before looking at the jurymen. "According to the prosecution's expert, these granulates together weigh thirty-five milligrams." Powell jumped into the air, and as he landed, he stomped both feet on the floor. The men on the jury startled, as did everyone else in the courtroom. The granulate moved about on the railing. "That was a rumble, gentlemen." He stomped his foot and the granulate moved again. "Imagine the continuous jar of wagons." He stomped again. "And heavy vehicles." Another stomp. "And trains." Powell stomped a final time. The granulate had moved around so much that one had fallen from the railing onto the floor. "This is the basis upon which the prosecution determined that there were one and a half grains of arsenic in the stomach of Maud Lloyd. On the weight of five minuscule pieces of moving granulate."

With a hand, he wiped the rail, knocking the remaining sugar to the floor.

"Did Maud Lloyd die from poisoning?" he pondered, pacing in

front of them, the fingertips of each hand pressed together as he spoke. "Most probably. Was it from arsenic? Possibly. Was it from the arsenic in the bismuth? Maybe. Could little Maud have eaten the crumbling poisoned wallpaper because the flowers and green leaves looked like penny candy?"

Powell pulled from his pocket two pieces of rose-shaped sugar crystal, one pink and one green, and held one in each hand between his thumbs and forefingers. "I purchased these this morning from the mercantile across the street. The candies come in all sorts of colors, but as I understand it, Maud was particularly fond of the pink and green ones, as they reminded her of the roses on her walls." The men in the rear row leaned forward to look. Powell held them up so that each man could see before returning the candy to his pocket.

"Was the overconcentration of the bismuth responsible? Dr. Fauntleroy told you that Maud had the telltale blue gumline that Dr. Ellzey said was a sure indication of bismuth poisoning. Or did arsenic make its way onto the stomach when Deputy Roberts, despite memory issues that he readily admits, laid it on the counter at Dr. Moore's apothecary? Because Professor Tonry included the organ and its contents when he prepared his sample, we don't know if arsenic was inside the stomach or on the outside." Powell stopped pacing and looked at the jury.

"So who is to blame?" Powell stood silently, watching the faces of the jurymen. After a moment, he shrugged a shoulder and slowly shook his head, his brow furrowed in question.

"I must tell you, gentlemen, that I have studied this case for over six months and I still don't know for certain how little Maud died or the source of the arsenic found in the postmortem specimen. Neither does the prosecution. And, gentlemen"—Powell paused, looking at each of them again before turning and pointing at Kilgour and Orr— "that was *their* responsibility, and not mine, to prove. And they have failed miserably."

Powell turned back to the jurymen.

"If there is any doubt at all in your minds as to how Maud Lloyd died, then it cannot be murder. And if there is no murder, then there can be no murderer. No one to blame and no option other than to find Mrs. Lloyd not guilty. Because Mrs. Lloyd is not guilty. She is innocent of what she has been accused. And yet she has remained stoic as best she could through some of the most horrendous testimony that no grieving parent should endure.

"If you will humor me for just a moment, I'd like you to try to imagine Mrs. Lloyd's pain. She had just buried her five-year-old daughter six weeks before little Maud fell ill with similar symptoms. For three days, the child suffered until she finally succumbed. Little Maud was still warm, her soul had yet to leave her body, when Sheriff Atwell and Sam Orrison barged into Mrs. Lloyd's home and insisted that she allow them to cut Maud up. Not surprisingly, she refused. A few hours later, they returned and insisted again. This time she bowed to the pressure. She watched as her child's body was desecrated before her very eyes. And then little Maud's innards were hauled out of the front door in a blood-soaked rag and carted down the street with dogs and pigs following behind and lapping up her blood as it dripped on the walkway. The child's innards were hurled onto a druggist's dirty counter into God knows what, tossed into a jar, and shipped off to a distant city, where it was left on a laboratory shelf for days as trains and wagons rumbled on the dusty streets below. For hours last week, Mrs. Lloyd sat there on that dock, forced to listen to Professor Tonry explain how he sliced parts of her daughter's body into little pieces and cooked her up as if he were preparing a man's dinner. Imagine if it were your daughter. Or your sister. Imagine if this were your wife—your widow—sitting there in the dock, alone and without your protection to shield her from Mr. Kilgour's zeal. Imagine if your widow had to endure what Mrs. Lloyd has endured. If every friend abandoned her. And every neighbor turned every physician's visit to tend to your sick children into something nefarious. Imagine if a traveling salesman forced his way into your home and defiled your grieving widow, threatening your child's life should she report him to the authorities. And imagine her reaction when some months later that same huckster, after learning the value of her estate, claims to be her fiancé in order to enrich himself. Imagine how your widow would feel. Imagine her outrage and indignity and pain. Imagine how *you* would feel. The anger. The rage!"

Powell studied the face of each man on the jury. He could see water welling in a few pairs of eyes. And all he needed was one. He drew a pronounced breath and stepped away from them, squaring his shoulders.

"Gentlemen of the jury, Mrs. Lloyd cannot be guilty of murder because there was no murder. Mr. Kilgour and Mr. Orr are unable to prove whether Maud Lloyd was poisoned by arsenic or bismuth because they haven't a clue what caused her death. They haven't proven the source of the arsenic in the postmortem. They haven't proven a thing. The only thing Mr. Kilgour and Mr. Orr have done is persecuted a childless mother. A grieving widow. An innocent woman."

Powell nodded to the jurymen and returned to the defense table. As he took his seat, he held his gaze forward, staring at the judge's bench. Matt knew not to speak to him until the judge gave the jury his instructions and Powell had come back into himself. Powell's ability—like their father's—to pull at the emotions of the men on the jury from somewhere beyond himself had not been gifted to Matt.

As the jury left the courtroom, charged with their duty, Powell rolled his head from shoulder to shoulder. He looked at Matt and JW.

"It's just about five o'clock," Powell said with a glance at the clock on the wall. "I say we wait here until six. If they aren't back by then, we're in big trouble."

"Your summation was brilliant," JW said. "Not a dry eye in the house. They'll acquit, and it won't take them long."

Matt looked over at the prosecution table. Kilgour and Orr were packing their satchels. "Looks like Kilgour is confident. He's calling it a night now."

"Kilgour won't have had time to remove his hat before he's called to return," JW said.

Powell nodded his head in the direction of the dock. Freddie was assisting Emily from her chair. "Shall we wait with our client in the back?"

"Be my guest," Matt said. "I'll stay here and guard the table."

"I'll keep Matthew company," JW said.

◆ ◆ ◆

"What happens now?" Emily Lloyd asked.

"We wait," Powell said.

"How long?"

"I have no idea. It could be within the hour. Or it could take hours. We just need to be patient."

Emily Lloyd looked out the window, staring into the darkening shadows.

"Mrs. Lloyd," Powell said. She didn't acknowledge him. "Emily."

Emily turned her head and brought her gaze to his.

"I know about your sisters."

She stared at him, her expression blank, saying nothing.

"Your two sisters. What are their names?" Powell asked. She held her stare, her brow furrowing as if she were having difficulty understanding his words. "Lara and Lilith, right?"

"I'm not sure of your meaning," she said finally.

"The women who live next door in the other half of your house. They're your sisters, aren't they?"

Emily opened her mouth to speak when the door opened.

"Mr. Harrison," Freddie said. "The jury. They're back."

Powell stood. "Already?"

"Yessir. They have a verdict."

◆ ◆ ◆

"Have you completed your deliberations?" Judge Keith asked as the jurymen settled into the chairs and the court was called to order. Powell looked at the clock on the wall. *Five thirty.*

"We have, Your Honor," said the foreman, and he handed a folded paper to the bailiff to give to the judge. Keith took the note from the bailiff and opened it. His face remained expressionless as he read.

"And you are unanimous in your decision?" he asked, lifting his eyes from the paper.

The foreman stood. "We are, Your Honor."

Keith drew a long breath and looked at Powell before directing his attention to Emily. "Would the prisoner please rise?"

Emily had difficulty getting to her feet. Freddie offered her an arm to assist her out of her chair. Powell, Matt, and JW also stood.

"Gentlemen of the jury, what say you?" Keith commanded.

"On all counts of murder in the first degree, we, the jury, find the defendant, Emily Elizabeth Lloyd, not guilty."

Emily's legs gave way, and she nearly fell to the floor. The crowd in the courtroom gasped. Judge Keith rapped his gavel on the bench.

"Order. I'll have order!"

The crowd quieted.

"Gentlemen of the jury, the state appreciates your service, and I do believe you made the correct decision in your deliberations." He turned to Emily. "Mrs. Lloyd, you are free to go." He pounded the gavel on the bench again. "We are adjourned."

CHAPTER 40

MONDAY, NOVEMBER 4, 1872

Lara lifted the silver frame from her dresser to pack in her trunk. With a thumb, she rubbed dust from the glass that had been covering the faces. Three frowning girls in their Sunday frocks. She tossed the picture into the trunk. That was the last of it. The last of what she wanted to take with her. The rest would remain behind. Lara left the room and went downstairs. Lilith's trunk was open, empty of contents, and Lilith was sulking.

"You haven't started to pack yet?" Lara asked and checked the clock on the mantel. It was nearly noon. Their hired coach was arriving at half past one to take them to Harpers Ferry, where they would catch the last train to Baltimore. The next morning, they would leave for Jersey City, the terminus of the B&O Railroad. Lilith was under the impression that they'd be traveling west to Chicago, but Lara had no intention of settling anywhere near that huckster or in any city in the States. Lara's plan was to leave the country altogether. And fast. From Jersey City, they would catch the first passenger train on the Lackawanna Railroad heading to Syracuse and on to the port city of Oswego, New York. There, steamers sailed daily across Lake Ontario to Toronto. Once safely in Canada, they could stay with their cousin

Mary, she reasoned, who lived not far with her husband in the mining community of Allan's Mills, until they found a place of their own.

"I don't want to go," Lilith said.

"We cannot stay here, Lilith. You know this."

"I want to stay close to Randy."

"Have you lost your mind? The man is dead. And he isn't coming back from the grave, so it's best to move on. I'm sure there are plenty of men in Chicago who will be happy to entertain you."

"It won't be the same."

"Oh, for heaven's sake!" Shaking her head, Lara reminded herself that she had resolved to be more understanding toward Lilith even though she didn't understand her at all. Lara had to do whatever was necessary to protect Emily. After all, Emily's well-being was critical for their survival. It would be better if the three of them could learn to get along.

"Come on, Lil," she said gently. "There will be other men who will love you. But not in this town. Not anymore. Now, please. Help me finish packing. The coach will be here in an hour or so. We haven't much time."

There was a knock at the door.

"Who in blazes could be calling?" Lara said, arching her back. She glanced at Lilith with a raised brow. "You didn't invite some fella over, did you?"

"Of course not. As you said, with Randy gone, there's no one here for me anymore."

Lara bit her tongue and walked to the window. She peered through the curtain and froze.

"Who is it?" Lilith asked.

"What purpose could Mr. Harrison have to call?" Lara said under her breath.

"Mr. Harrison?" Lilith asked, moving behind her.

"Miss Samson?" Powell hollered through the door and knocked again. "Miss Lara? Or is it Miss Lilith? I know you are there. I can see you through the curtain."

"Go on, Lara. Let Mr. Harrison in."

"Shhh," Lara whispered. "There can be no good reason for him to be here."

"Miss Samson, please," Powell said. "I would just like a few words and then I'll be on my way." He knocked again, this time more insistently.

"Wouldn't you like to thank him for all he's done for Emily? For us?" Lilith said.

Lara turned and looked into her sister's pleading eyes.

"What harm could come from it?" Lilith asked. "We're leaving anyway. He was always so kind to Emily. And you like him."

Lara drew a reluctant sigh. "Fine. As long as you are packed and ready when the coach arrives."

Lilith nodded, her eyes igniting happily, stepping closer.

Lara turned and placed her hand on the knob. With a twist, she pulled the door toward her. Powell Harrison was standing on the stoop in a long dark overcoat with a tall black hat on his head. As he removed the hat to greet her, Lara squeezed her eyes shut. The rumble of a passing cart and sounds of the street whirred to white noise, like water rushing around her, until it faded to silence. She felt light, floating over mute, warm waves, disappearing as she drifted into still darkness. The quiet was interrupted by a voice. A man was calling from somewhere far away.

"Mrs. Lloyd?"

◆ ◆ ◆

"Mrs. Lloyd?" Powell said.

Staggering awkwardly, Emily put a hand on the doorframe.

"Are you all right?" Powell asked, taking her elbow.

"I—I don't quite know," she said. "I just need a minute to gather myself."

"Ma'am?"

She glanced about again before bringing her gaze to his. "Is there something I can do for you, Mr. Harrison?"

"Mrs. Greene mentioned that you were leaving town, and I wanted to wish you well. There was no answer at your door, but when I heard voices, I . . ." Powell's eyes narrowed as he looked over her shoulder into the empty hall. "Might you introduce me to your sisters?"

"As I've told you, I have no family here."

"Your neighbors, then, Miss Lilith and Miss Lara. I'd like to meet them," Powell said as he stepped past her into the house. He had finally caught the recluses at home and would not be deterred. "I heard them speaking just a moment ago."

Powell walked into the parlor. An opened trunk sat near the settee. Other than the sparse furnishings he remembered from when he and JW had broken into the house, the room was empty. He turned to Emily, who was now behind him.

"Where are they?" he asked.

"They aren't here at present."

Powell glanced down the hall. "If they aren't here, why are you in their home?"

Emily furrowed her brow in confusion. "I don't know."

"Surely they let you in." Powell called down the hallway. "Miss Lara? Miss Lilith? It's Powell Harrison here." He started toward the kitchen at the back of the house.

When he entered the kitchen, he noticed a thick blanket of dust covering the shelves and table. The stove, too, was dusty and cold. He turned to Emily, who had followed him.

"Where did they go?" As she shook her head, he pushed past her and headed for the stairs. At the top of the stairway, he turned left and made his way to the bedroom that faced the street. The door was open, and he could see another trunk in the room's center.

"Miss Lara?" He rapped on the door and poked his head through the doorway before entering. Again, he noticed the dust crawling over the edge of the nightstand and dresser's top.

"You can't be in here," Emily exclaimed, out of breath as she made her way down the hall toward him.

Powell glanced in the trunk. Clothing, a pair of boots, the silver framed photograph of three little girls and their father. Powell noticed that the door to the closet was partially open, and daylight emanated from inside. *How can that be?* he thought. *Unless . . .* As he walked toward the closet, Emily rushed into the room.

"You can't be in here," she repeated and reached for his arm.

Powell shrugged from her grasp and pushed the door open. The small door at the rear of the closet was ajar, as was the door to Emily's closet on the other side. Looking through the opening to Emily's bedroom, he spotted a third trunk with its lid raised.

"I thought you said you didn't have a key," he said, turning to Emily, who was standing in the closet's doorway, her eyes closed, and swaying. "Mrs. Lloyd?" As he reached to steady her, he noticed the dress she wore, made from worsted wool that had been ravished by moths. Its sleeves were too long for her arms and the bodice much too large for her small frame. He looked at the dresses still hanging on the rod and then back at Emily.

"Think of it as sleepwalking . . . We forget who we are and become someone else . . ." His father-in-law's words boomed in his head. Powell's mouth went dry. *Could it be?*

"Miss Lara?" Powell asked, his voice cracking.

Emily's eyes fluttered and opened.

"Mr. Harrison," she said, her voice low and steady. A wry smile slowly broke over her face. "At long last, we meet."

WINTER 1872

And here the curtain falls—God grant that we may never be called upon to record its like again.
—*Loudoun Mirror*, November 1872

EPILOGUE

"I just received a message from Mortimer," Matt said, walking into Powell's office. "The state has decided not to pursue any further charges against Mrs. Lloyd."

"Since he's won reelection," Powell said, "I suppose he figures he doesn't need to bow to public opinion these days."

"The ten-thousand-dollar cost of the last trial was more likely the reason for his decision."

"I guess there's something more important to Kilgour than his ego after all."

"You're sounding a bit salty, my friend," Matt said. "It was a close contest."

"It's for the best to let the matter go," Powell said. "The election and Mrs. Lloyd."

"Where did she move?" Matt asked. "Don't tell me that she went to Chicago with that huckster."

"Mrs. Greene said she left for Canada to live with her cousin. You know, the one we could never find."

"Figures," Matt said and headed back to his office. "As you said, it's best to let the matter rest."

Powell's gaze drifted to the alley beyond the frost-etched window. He shook his head. *Emily Lloyd.* Following the law and finding truth hadn't failed him before. Opening the drawer, he reached underneath his gun and removed a brown envelope. He unfastened the flap and pulled out the article he had torn from Ol' Pat's archived newspaper. For what must have been the hundredth time, Powell read the words:

House Fire in Clark

In the early hours of Sunday morning a fire broke out at the home of John Samson. Rescue attempts for the family were made more difficult by the inclement weather. Officials remain suspicious, as the exterior doors appeared locked from the outside. Samson and his wife, Matilda, lost their lives in the blaze. Still missing are two of three daughters, ages 12 and 8. The youngest girl, age 4, escaped the flames and was found by neighbors wandering in the snow.

After finding Emily alone at the neighboring house, Powell had traveled to Clark to confirm the fates of the older girls and his suspicions. He'd found answers to his questions in the Clark County death registry. The deaths of John and Matilda Samson were recorded on January 9, 1841. Three days later, the deaths of Lara, 12, and Lilith, 8, were added. Powell asked around the courthouse and learned that the only survivor was a little girl, who had just turned four. Neighbors had found her wandering barefoot in the snowy woods, ash on her face and soot on her nightdress and in her hair. Emily Samson. According to an older gentleman at the local pub, John Samson was intemperate and ill-tempered and "had no business raisin' girls." Powell understood his meaning, and it sickened him.

Powell considered Dr. Berkley's words about the effects of trauma on a child's mind.

Could that explain it?

He glanced out the window again, recalling his father-in-law's words about amnesia: *". . . only when the person becomes lost to the dream."* Was it all an innocent fantasy, like his daughter talking and playing with her imaginary friends? Or by living in a make-believe world where her sisters were alive and residing next door, was Emily Lloyd lost to the dream? If, in her mind, she became one of them, then yes, she was lost and, by definition, insane. But that didn't necessarily make her a killer. *And there were other explanations for Maud's death,* Powell assured himself. There was the arsenic in Moore's bismuth. Arsenic in the wallpaper. There was the bismuth itself.

Powell glanced toward Matt's office. "You don't want to know the truth," Matt had said to him the night he'd learned that Dr. Moore had ended his life.

"Thanks for the words of wisdom, brother," Powell said under his breath.

Maybe Matt was right. Powell didn't want to know. Maybe Powell didn't need to know either. *Isaiah 55:9,* he reminded himself. *"For as the heavens are higher than the earth, so are my ways higher than your ways."* Powell had done his job. He'd upheld his oath and honored his duty. And he trusted that God would do the rest.

AUTHOR'S NOTE

Dissociative identity disorder (DID), or multiple personality disorder, was largely misunderstood, if acknowledged at all, as a mental disorder in the early 1870s. It was first described in the United States as "episodic amnesia," and by the late nineteenth century, scholars had termed it "double consciousness" and frequently described it as a state of sleepwalking. And while there was a general acceptance in the medical community that emotionally traumatic experiences could cause long-term psychological disorders that might display a variety of symptoms, the concept of multiple personalities residing within the same person was not commonly understood until the 1898 study of Clara Norton Fowler and the 1906 publication of *The Dissociation of a Personality*. It wasn't until the 1978 trial of an Ohio man that DID was used successfully in an insanity plea within the legal community.

Whether Emily Lloyd suffered from DID is unknown, but there is evidence from her behavior in the courtroom and testimony given at both the inquest and indictment hearings that would support the theory. During the trial, it was reported in newspapers covering the proceedings that Mrs. Lloyd would arrive in the courtroom wearing various outfits that raised eyebrows. While most days, she wore a heavy veil and the black of mourning, on one occasion it was noted that she arrived dressed "most inappropriately" for a grieving mother. On another day, she arrived wearing a traveling suit and told the reporter from the *New York Herald* that after the trial she was headed to Chicago to marry her beau. Some days, she was attentive during the proceedings. Other days, she sat on the dock reading a newspaper as if she hadn't a care in the world. She claimed amnesia of certain events during the pretrial hearings and was described by witnesses as suffering from insomnia and forgetfulness. The deciding factor for me was when I read an article in the *Alexandria Gazette* that mentioned that her father and stepmother, not wishing to care any longer for the toddler, turned Emily out of their home into the snow. The two-year-old had wandered in the woods until she was found by neighbors and taken to an aunt and uncle, who raised her. It was reported that teenage Emily would leave her home on foot without telling her aunt where she was going, disappearing for several days with no recollection of where she had been. When found, Emily was described as sleepwalking and suffering from amnesia.

After careful study of the disorder, I put my theory to the test. I "presented" Emily Lloyd to a psychologist familiar with DID. She agreed with my conclusion, and together, we built a profile of Emily Lloyd that resulted in my creation of the alters Lilith and Lara. And while there would most certainly be more alters than just these, I decided to limit them to two for the purpose of simplifying the story.

In addition to accurately portraying the varying behaviors associated with DID, I was challenged by the limitations my 1872 characters would have understanding such a disorder, the primitiveness of forensic science of the time, the lack of settled case law used to support insanity defenses, and the inconsistency in the application of the law itself, which was much different than it is today. For example, there were no discovery rules in Virginia at that time. The prosecution had no requirement to share their analysis or expert reports. Witnesses were called, recalled, and called again, and were in the courtroom listening to the testimony of others before they themselves testified. In the Lloyd case, it is true that Delphi was threatened by the prosecution to change her testimony about the rats without consequence (or sanctions imposed) by the court. While on the witness stand, the deputy who first testified that he had carried Maud's autopsy specimens from the Lloyd house in a rag was later coerced by the prosecution to change his recollection of his actions that day. John Orr did, in fact, consult with the defense before the Harrisons changed the plea, and was allowed to assume the role of assistant prosecutor during the trial. Most astonishing was the juror who claimed to be a former sweetheart of Emily Lloyd. He was permitted to remain on the jury after their relationship was disclosed to the judge.

Another difference between the nineteenth-century justice system and Virginia courts today is the reimbursement of trial costs. In 1872, if a defendant was acquitted, the state would pay the defense attorney fees. I can only assume that when the Harrison brothers discovered that the bismuth prescribed for Maud contained arsenic, they felt more confident they could win an acquittal and had a strong financial reason to change their strategy.

Like all my novels, this story of Emily Lloyd and Powell Harrison's defense of her are based on true events. That said, I have added narrative to fill gaps and changed details to fit my character's arcs and the storyline, improve pacing, and intensify drama. For example, Dr. Randy Moore is a fictional character based on the doctor who attended Emily and her family, Dr. Armistead Randolph Mott. I changed his name because I veered significantly from Mott's actions in real life. There is no direct evidence of an affair between him and Lilith/Emily, although at one point in the trial, court testimony teased that Dr. Mott was called to the Lloyd residence frequently, implying that there might be something more between the two. In real life, Mott did not commit suicide (and neither did Powell's sister Alice, although she did die unexpectedly in 1870). Dr. Mott (Moore in my novel) did prescribe more bismuth than recommended by the defense's experts, and his bismuth was, in fact, tainted by a small amount of arsenic. Whether it was enough to kill Maud remains disputed, but it did create enough doubt in the jurors' minds to acquit Emily Lloyd.

Another composite character was Maggie Greene, who was created from the testimony of several witnesses at the trial, as well as from research about Powell Harrison's life before the war and from his time in Staunton. Characters such as Pendleton Slack, Colonel Nixon, Freddie Roberts, Mollie Ryan, Georgia Jones, Paddy Gill, Julian Hutchinson, and Sam Orrison, all of whom had some involvement in the Emily Lloyd case, were created completely from my imagination.

My purpose as an author is to write page-turning stories that keep my readers on the edge of their seats. My task in doing so is to find a blend of fact and fiction that entertains while at the same time stays true to the essence of the story. There is more truth in *Veil of Doubt* than fiction. Yet it is a work of fiction. I believe that my portrayal of both Powell Harrison and Emily Lloyd reflects the actuality of their lives in 1872 and the essence of the emotions during the trial that October. My hope is that their story touched you as it did me. And that you, too, find peace in leaving it to God to do what's right when truth is veiled and justice eludes.

ACKNOWLEDGMENTS

Authoring a novel may be a one-player sport, but it takes an entire team to bring a book to market. Publishing the story of Powell Harrison and the trial of Emily Lloyd would have been impossible without the support of so many talented people. I owe a debt of gratitude to each and every one of you on my team.

To my literary coach, and now agent, Jennifer Schober, for her encouragement to write this manuscript and for her hard work in getting it published. To my publicist, Sandi Mendelson, for her unwavering belief in both the story and my writing. You have stood by me through thick and thin, and I am forever grateful. To Debra Gitterman, my development editor, who worked with me throughout the writing process. Her input (and wordsmithing!) has proven invaluable. To Peter Behrens, the best "book doctor" on the planet, for his critique of the structure and the critical plot points of the story. To Lindsay Starck, whose honest feedback was instrumental in improving the book's pacing. To Kendra Harpster, whose reading helped me finalize the manuscript before sending it out to the world. To Carol Fitzgerald, on advising me in all things digital. And to Kristin Mehus-Roe, Sara Addicott, Georgie Hockett, Bethany Fred, and the awesome group of women at Girl Friday Books, thank you for all the enthusiasm and creativity you brought to this project and your love of this story. I couldn't have a better publisher!

In addition to the folks in the publishing world, I'd like to thank my friends and colleagues who provided valuable input into the development of the story. To Julie Fender, my literary psychologist (is there such a thing?!), for her analysis of Emily's "real life" background and behavior at the trial, and for the dissociative identity disorder diagnosis that led to the creation of Lilith and Lara. I also want to thank Julie for the many "sessions" where together we explored the personalities of Emily, her alters, and their behaviors. To Dr. Ed Puccio of Inova Loudoun Hospital for his assistance in describing the symptoms of poison victims. To my attorney friends John Whitbeck, Brandon Elledge, and Sonny Cameron, for their input into my legal arguments and objections, and their assistance in interpreting the Virginia Code in the nineteenth century and courtroom procedure in 1872 (and please forgive me if I got some of it wrong!). To Gary Clemons, the Loudoun County Clerk of the Court, and his staff, for first introducing me to the story of Emily Lloyd. To Dr. Joe Rizzo, former director of the Loudoun Museum, for his patience in answering my many questions about Lee's retreat from Gettysburg, the impact of the Civil War on Virginia communities, and the political climate in Leesburg in the early 1870s. To Pastor Gary Hamrick of Cornerstone Chapel, for his many lessons on scripture that I incorporated into the story and for his sermons that helped me find Powell's faith. To my early readers Jason Richards, Avery Miller, James Mason, Rita Seymour, Therese Bitanga, Jeanne Dagna, Donald Decker, and Michelle Freeman, a huge thank you for taking the time to read the manuscript when it was still very rough, and for being so open in providing your feedback. And to members of the Harrison family, specifically Robert Patton and Nicholas White, for sharing their memories of, and memorabilia from, Powell Harrison's children Burr Powell Harrison, Nannie Harrison Lynn, and Lalla Harrison White, and step-granddaughter "Miss Elizabeth" White that enabled me to bring Powell, Janet, and the rest of the Harrison clan to life.

I would also like to acknowledge the many sources of my research. In addition to Google and online subscription services including Ancestry.com and Newspapers.com, I consulted the Loudoun County Courthouse archives, the Library of Virginia, and the Thomas Balch Library in my search for records, articles, and information about the events and people depicted in the novel. Additionally, I relied on information from a number of nonfiction sources. For insight into the Harrison family dynamic, I found chapter two of *Life in Black and White: Family and Community in the Slave South* by Brenda E. Stevenson most helpful. To gain a sense of Powell's war experience, I consulted *18th Virginia Cavalry* by Roger U. Delauter, and *Brigadier General John D. Imboden, Confederate Commander in the Shenandoah* by Spencer C. Tucker. Numerous memoirs allowed me to acquire a better understanding of the economic and political climate of Loudoun following the Civil War. *Autobiography of Eppa Hunton* by Eppa Hunton, *The Comanches, A History of White's Battalion, Virginia Cavalry* by Frank M. Myers, and *History of the Independent Loudoun Virginia Rangers, U.S. Vol. Cav. (Scouts) 1862–65* by Briscoe Goodhart were terrific sources. I also found *Between Reb and Yank: A Civil War History of Northern Loudoun County, Virginia* by Taylor M. Chamberlin and John M. Souders to be a great trove of information. For understanding the Confederate retreat from Gettysburg, I consulted *One Continuous Fight: The Retreat from Gettysburg and the Pursuit of Lee's Army of Northern Virginia, July 4–14, 1863* by Michael F. Nugent.

To develop a full picture of the Emily Lloyd trial, I found chapter three, "Chaff before a Whirlwind—Arsenic and Old Lace in Leesburg," in Michael Lee Pope's book, *Wicked Northern Virginia*, combined with published reports during the trial by the *Alexandria Gazette* and the Loudoun newspaper *The Mirror* most helpful. To understand the progress of forensic science, medicine, and psychology in the 1870s, I relied on sources including *Dr. Francis T. Stribling and Moral Medicine: Curing the Insane at Virginia's Western State Hospital 1836–1874* by Alice Davis Wood, *Toxicology: The Basic Science of Poisons* by Lois J. Casarett and John Doull, and *The Trial of Mrs. Elizabeth G. Wharton on the Charge of Poisoning General W. S. Ketchum: Tried at Annapolis, MD., December 1871–January 1872* as well as articles published by the *Baltimore Gazette*.

Finally, I want to thank the people who matter most in the success of my books. My fans and followers on social media who bought and read my first book and continue to clamor for more. My friends and family for their constant encouragement and support. My sons James,

Luke, Zach, and Nick, and stepdaughter Avery, who are forever curious and excited about my writing. My ten-year-old grandson, Charlie, who authors and illustrates his own books while Nana is working on hers. And my husband, Scott, who has walked with me on every step of this journey. Without his patience and reassurance, I'm not certain I would have had the fortitude to keep writing. For that, I am most grateful.

ABOUT THE AUTHOR

 Sharon Virts is a successful entrepreneur and visionary who, after more than twenty-five years in business, followed her passion for storytelling into the world of historical fiction. She has received numerous awards for her work in historic preservation and has been recognized nationally for her business achievements and philanthropic contributions. She was recently included in *Washington Life Magazine*'s Philanthropic 50 for her work with education, health, and cultural preservation.

Sharon's passion truly lies in the creative. She is an accomplished visual artist and uses her gift for artistic expression along with her extraordinary storytelling to build complex characters and craft vivid images and sets that capture the heart and imagination. She is mother to four sons—James, Lucas, Zachary, and Nicholas—stepmom to Ben and Avery, and "Nana" to ten-year-old Charlie and toddler Bodhi. She lives in Virginia with her husband, Scott Miller, at the historic Selma Mansion with their three Labrador retrievers Polly, Cassie, and Leda.